WAR WHOOPS
FILLED THE CHILLY AIR

Seven or eight mounted Sioux galloped straight for Garth's position while he was alone and without cover. He scrambled to the side, and fell as shots scattered and men ran to their wagons for protection. Armed with only one revolver, Garth was caught in the crossfire—there was no escape. Finally able to get to his knees, he fired four shots before the first onrushing pony bowled him over.

All Garth could think of was Bird and what might be happening to her . . . when a sudden explosion rocked his head and blackness swept over him. . . .

CROW FEATHER

"Hawkins has blazed a long and sure trail in historical fiction. Written for a reader who demands the very best an author can give."
—Terry C. Johnston,
author of *The Plainsman Series*

CROW FEATHER

by

Paul A. Hawkins

A SIGNET BOOK

SIGNET
Published by the Penguin Group
Penguin Books USA Inc., 375 Hudson Street,
New York, New York 10014, U.S.A.
Penguin Books Ltd, 27 Wrights Lane,
London W8 5TZ, England
Penguin Books Australia Ltd, Ringwood,
Victoria, Australia
Penguin Books Canada Ltd, 10 Alcorn Avenue,
Toronto, Ontario, Canada M4V 3B2
Penguin Books (N.Z.) Ltd, 182–190 Wairau Road,
Auckland 10, New Zealand

Penguin Books Ltd, Registered Offices:
Harmondsworth, Middlesex, England

First published by Signet, an imprint of Dutton Signet,
a division of Penguin Books USA Inc.

First Printing, June, 1995
10 9 8 7 6 5 4 3 2 1

Cover art by Hiram Richardson

Ⓟ REGISTERED TRADEMARK—MARCA REGISTRADA

Printed in the United States of America

Book One

Tyson Bell Garth

Prologue

During the great Civil War of the United States, a Union post on the Mississippi River named Fort Pillow was captured by soldiers of the Confederate Army, including cavalrymen from General Bedford Forrest's famed marauders. In the aftermath, several Union Negro soldiers were hanged at the fort by irate Confederates. The officer generally held responsible for these atrocities was Colonel Henry Sturges. Upon learning that he was to be dishonorably dismissed from the Confederate Army, he deserted his post and offered his services to Union forces. Denied a commission, he was appointed to serve as an agent in the field at comparable pay. Three weeks later, a troop of General Forrest's Confederate calvary led by Captain Tyson Bell Garth, who also had been present at Fort Pillow, was ambushed at Jack's Fork Crossing in Tennessee. Sixteen men were killed and wounded by Federal soldiers, and six of the cavalry, including Captain Garth, were taken prisoner. These men were later imprisoned for the duration of the war at Jefferson Barracks in St. Louis. However, prior to their transfer, they had seen their former cavalry colleague, Colonel Sturges, conferring at the battle scene with Union officers, and since the Jack's Fork site had been considered a "safe place" known only to Confederates, the men realized that Sturges was solely responsible for the bloody ambush. While imprisoned, the six Confederate cavalrymen vowed vengeance. They drew straws to see which two would pursue the informer and kill him after the end of the war. Captain Garth and Sergeant Brevard Stanton drew the shortest straws.

In August of 1866, Garth and Stanton met in Jackson, Mississippi near the captain's home. After several weeks of searching, they encountered Colonel Sturges in Chattanooga. Sturges fled. Later that month, they caught up with him again in St. Joseph, but the colonel proved himself to be dangerous as well as elusive. Trapped in an alley, he shot Stanton in the thigh, putting the sergeant out of commission. Garth continued by himself. The trail was due west. He lost track of Sturges in the Dakota Territory. The weather had turned cold.

Chapter One

Dakota Territory, October 1866

Adjusting his spectacles, Elbert Craig, a Fort Laramie store clerk, stared curiously across the counter at the bedraggled newcomer. Craig had seen this particular man before. He was one of the arrivals of the previous day, and these hapless, wandering ex-soldiers usually were fundless, always men of small necessity, questionable reputation and purpose. This one was hard to miss. He wore a soiled Confederate cavalry hat.

But Tyson Bell Garth quickly enlightened the clerk's curiosity—he wasn't interested in trading for trinkets or sundry items, but instead needed some heavy stock: buffalo boots, mittens, woolen clothing, and warm underwear. He was riding north the next day, and from what he had heard around the post, the mountain weather was no better than the cold prairie weather at Fort Laramie. Furthermore, he had enough money to pay for his necessities, barely.

Somewhat perplexed, Elbert Craig nodded. "But if you're going with the troopers, I thought perhaps the quartermaster . . ."

"No, no," Garth protested testily. "I'm not one of their recruits, by jingo, no. I'm just going along for the ride, hired on as a scout, a damned messenger boy, if you will. Some slick Yankee down in Cheyenne City talked me into this infernal affair. Hostiles, he said, but it now appears that this wicked climate is going to be my worst enemy. He never said anything about how cold it is up here. Had a bad case of the chills when I woke this morning."

Craig said he fully understood and motioned Garth to the back of the store, where he pulled out several drawers filled with woolens. There were racks of heavy coats, shelves lined with boots and mittens of every sort, and buckskin jackets and pants, all with a rugged frontier look to them. Craig, handing various pieces to Garth, commented that the Indians had made many of them. The clerk finally introduced himself to Garth. He was the son of the owner, James Craig, and then after Garth returned the introduction, the younger Craig, handing him a box of mittens, said, "May I say, Mr. Garth, there *are* men with your convictions up here, your beliefs, men who were in the gray armies, southerners. Some are even troopers now."

"A travesty," Garth returned with a sour look. "A damned shame, nothing better to do than chase Indians. Why aren't they out there chasing gold with the rest of the pilgrims?"

Craig, sensing that this was going to be more indoctrination than conversation, smiled. "It takes a grub-stake to do that, and most of the men who come through here are down on their luck, without adequate funds, that is. A horse, a rifle, and the clothes on their back, little else. The fortunes of war, I suppose."

"Misfortunes." Garth sniffed. "On the other hand, maybe they're lucky. Most of my friends are buried."

Craig paused, watching Garth try on a pair of mittens. The clerk wondered. There was the mark of a gentleman on this Confederate, a touch of southern sophistication. Despite the obvious wear in his clothing, he was well groomed from the collar-length cut of his black hair to the delicate lip line below his full mustache. Lithe and slender, he appeared about six feet tall in his cavalry boots. Craig had seen only the touch of a smile on his face, and that was cynically thin. Yet there was a peculiar intensity, a spark of excitement in his features, especially in the deep, brown depth of his eyes. Craig asked, "And whatever brought you out here in the first place, all the way to Cheyenne from . . . from where?"

"Mississippi," Garth replied. He winked at Craig. "I'll tell you this, Mistuh Craig, I surely didn't ride a thousand miles to fight hostiles, no, suh. I've been trailing a no-good rascal for three months. He's probably up in one of those mining camps by now. I fell into this Fort Kearny business by accident, not purpose. I needed a job, and a place to winter. And I'll tell you this, when the weather warms up next spring, I'll be out of here . . . if old Jack Frost doesn't get my hide first."

"I didn't mean to be intruding on your business," Craig apologized, putting the mittens aside. "So, it's Fort Kearny where you're heading. I thought it might be Fort Caspar, up the river."

"Caspar? Just a stop along the way, I hear," returned Garth.

"I have dear friends at Kearny."

Garth nodded and put two pair of long johns alongside the mittens, trousers, and buckskin jacket. "Well, what about this Colonel Carrington? Do you know him?"

"I know him. He stopped here for a few days. He's a gentleman of the first order. He designed Fort Kearny. Everyone admires him, but unfortunately, he's leaving soon. The word around here is that he's asked for a transfer. He's not infantry, you know. He's an engineer, supply, maybe, one or the other." Craig began working with his quill, jotting down figures. "Understand, Mr. Garth, he was sent out there to build forts, not defend them, and the Lakota and Cheyenne have given him more trouble than anyone back in Omaha ever expected. Hardly anyone dares travel the Bozeman Trail. It's not safe, and it's a constant worry for us who have friends up there. If you want my opin-

ion, I don't think the officers at Fort Atkinson understand how serious the situation has become. They un-
derestimated the strength and resolve of the Indians."

"Nothing unusual about that," commented Garth, reflecting on past command decisions that had gone
awry. "Those scallywags at the top never do know
what's going on in the field."

Arranging Garth's supplies in a neat pile, Craig said,
"I don't suppose you know Mr. Bridger. He's the chief
scout up at Kearny. At least, he's one who knows what
the situation is. He's lived among those people most of
his life."

Garth said that he had never had the pleasure of
meeting the man but that he had heard many stories
about him, some rather incredible. Craig opined that
there was no better scout on the frontier, and he had
first met Gabe Bridger when only a lad, that even now
at his older age Bridger seemed as spry as a boy, and
could sit a horse with the best of riders. Craig said
there was an exception, a young woman called Bird
Rutledge, who just happened to be Craig's fiancée. No
one rode a horse any better than Bird. She was also up
at Fort Kearny with her mother and father. Jack
Rutledge had been hired as a sawyer or lead man for
the wood trains, the cutters and haulers of the fort's
wood and building supplies.

"It will be my pleasure to meet your friends, especially Mistuh Bridger," Garth said. "Perhaps the old man
will share the secret of his survival in this peculiar
country, enlighten me on whether it's attitude or manner of dress. That's where I've been having my biggest
problems." Pointing to his purchases, he added, "I
rather think this should prepare me for the worst, don't
you?"

Craig's eyes wandered back to Garth's faded cavalry
hat, and he offered reluctantly, "A winter headpiece?"

Garth simply plunked the brim of the hat with this
thumb. "Dammit, Elbert, I can't part with this. Don't

you understand, it's about the only thing I have left to remind me of my heritage. Why, once I get into the rest of this garb, I won't even be able to recognize myself."

"Your vanity may cost you your ears, Mr. Garth. Pride goeth before a fall, that sort of thing. Let's be realistic, not nostalgic."

Garth's brown eyes stared across the counter at the clerk. "Is my hat that bad?"

Craig looked pathetically away, then turning back, he said tactfully, "Well, it could be a topic of conversation. That's one way of looking at it."

T. B. Garth laughed outright. "Ah, is that a fact!"

"Honestly, Mr. Garth, besides the obvious it's not adequate for winter. Like I said, your ears . . . the hat . . . impossible. Certainly, you know nothing of frostbite."

"And you know nothing of me," retorted Garth. "No, I'm afraid the hat stays. I just can't part with it. There's a great deal of sentiment attached to this hat. Fact is, I had a scrap with two drunken scoundrels down at the saloon in Chugwater on the way up here. Why, one of them pulled a revolver! Damn fools weren't going to let me drink my coffee unless I removed this hat."

"My goodness! That's crazy, Mr. Garth. Whatever did you do?"

"Shot a hole in the table where they were sitting," Garth replied with a slow grin. "They backed off like crawdads. I threw their pistols down the latrine. Charlie. Charlie and Will, as sorry a pair as I've ever seen."

Elbert Craig cocked his head. "Charlie . . . Charlie Mullen?"

"That was one of them."

"Drifters. Charlie has crumpled ears."

"Well, I didn't have time to notice that," Garth said. "Place only had two lanterns in it. Bad light."

"Charlie lost the tops of his ears," Craig said. "Lost

them to frostbite." He grinned at T. B. Garth. "You say you have a lot of sentiment tied up in that hat, eh?"

Garth smiled back and nodded. "All right, Elbert, I'll concede to a compromise. I'll have one of your muffs to tie under it. A wool muff, bright red to better mark my presence in the field. By jingo, I don't want anyone to mistake me up there for one of those savages."

Shaking his head, Craig said, "I'm sure they won't mistake you, Mr. Garth, no, not at all." He found a red scarf and packed it with the rest of the purchases. After Garth had inspected and paid his bill, the clerk leaned across the counter and spoke quietly. He wanted Garth to deliver a package and letter to his fiancée, Bird Rutledge, at Fort Kearny. He doubted he would be able to see her until after Christmas, and since Garth seemed like a gentleman, would he do the honor? Garth, allowing that indeed he was a gentleman, agreed and told Craig he could bring the package over that same evening to his quarters on the post, an odious structure with a meeting hall and a few rooms.

"Bedlam?" asked Craig.

Garth nodded curtly. "Yes, I think that's what they've chosen to call it. Yankee levity. I recall reading once of a distant place near London, I think, an asylum for the insane. Same name, Bedlam." He tilted his head with an affected flourish, and swept up his packages. "Having known a few bluebellies in my day, I'll allow there is a similarity, a good reason to call the quarters Bedlam."

"But you were an officer, too, weren't you? Does it really matter now?"

"Wrong side, Elbert, wrong side. That's what matters." He walked toward the door, the clerk by his side. "Oh yes, they've extended me that one courtesy, a bed among my former peers. Yes, I was a cadet. I was an officer, too, a captain in the Confederacy. When it all started I was up at West Point, one year from my com-

mission. Ah, but being loyal to the cause, I went back
home and enlisted. After the war, the Federals disal-
lowed my return to the Point, a matter of principle.
Understandable. No forgiveness on that score. Not that
I would have actively sought the commission, anyhow,
because after four years of fighting and a stint in the
stockade, I picked up a few principles of my own, and
fondness for the Federals wasn't one of them. And
there's this other matter, offensive in nature, searching
for a traitor to the cause. I'm still trying to resolve it."
His smile was thin. "Feel like a traitor myself taking
on this scouting job for the winter."

"Well," Craig rationalized, "it's better than freezing
off your backside . . . your ears?"

"Touché, Elbert." Garth stood at the mercantile door
and stared out into the gray October sky, searching the
western horizon. If he were stalled on the great frontier, so was Sturges, somewhere out there, probably
denning up for the winter like an old bear. "Ah,"
mused Garth, "but enough of this prattle. I'll get along
now."

"I'm sorry for your troubles, Mr. Garth. "I hope you
find a solution, a profitable one. We were so removed
from the big war way out here, it's hard to understand
at times, the misery and horror. I suppose the consequences of the war go much deeper than we realize."

Sniffing the cold air, Garth said, "Well, Elbert, I've
been granted this one small victory, haven't I? Yes, a
bed among my former colleagues from the Point."
Garth threw back his head and laughed. "That's Lincoln's new republic for you. Yessuh, charity for all,
malice toward none, something such as that. Ah, that
President Abe could have lived to see it."

After stowing his new clothes into a duffel, Garth
picked up a few dried apples and headed for the corrals
below the parade ground to groom Jefferson, a chore
he had been neglecting too long. A blooded racer be-

fore the war, the horse had been his Pegasus during the long campaign of civil strife. In Garth's present financial state, Jefferson was the most valuable piece of property that he owned outside of the Garth House lands in Mississippi. As he approached the crowded stable area, he noticed preparations for the Kearny trip were well under way. Near one shed, soldiers were loading freight into wagons, and from the corrals, a half-dozen more troopers were leading mounts back and forth between the enclosure and the smithy's barn. The cloudy afternoon air was permeated with the odor of manure, forge smoke, and a steamy fragrance of hot iron, cavalry scents long familiar to him. The animals, traditional army bays and blacks, were already taking on their winter coats. Within a few days, most of them would be laboring through the disputed land along the Bozeman Trail toward Fort Phil Kearny, some two hundred miles away on the misty banks of the Big Piney River.

Garth moved to the side, observing, catching a casual nod from several troopers before he finally stepped through the poles and whistled up his eight-year-old gelding. While he was busy with a curry comb, Garth noticed several enlisted men leaning over the top rail, inquisitively staring at him. Instinctively, he politely touched his hat in greeting, then went back to work. One of the men finally spoke up in a familiar, southern drawl. "Hey, we were wondering who owned the black," the soldier called out. "That's a nice hoss, mistuh, a little too special to be way out here. Looks like he's meant for better things than troopin', I'd say." The Dixie ring in the man's voice brought Garth to a smiling standstill. "Yes, he's special," he replied. "I've had him since he was a colt, a present you might say."

"That's some kind of a present. Right pretty devil. What you calling him?"

"Jefferson."

One of the men, a corporal, hooted and scratched his

long sideburns. "If that don't beat all! You hear that, boys? Jefferson, you say! Now, would that be Thomas or ol' Jeff Davis?"

After they shared a laugh, another asked, "What's your name?"

"Tyson Garth."

"Cavalry?"

"Yes, I've ridden."

"What outfit?"

"General Nathan Bedford Forrest."

"Yahoo!" shouted the southerner gleefully. "By damn, he was the best of the lot of 'em, for sure!"

But it was the corporal who came forward and extended his hand through the fence. "Name's Daley, Boston Irish. This is Jim Cutter and Pete Boley." He grinned and pointed. "You might know, Boley's one of yours, a regular Georgia peach, galvanized, but he gets on. Grits, we call him. You two should have a lot in common. Grits rumped with Colonel Mosby until the Feds caught him stealing hogs. He ain't seen hide nor hair of a hostile yet, only the loafers around the fort. Cutter, here, he's a new bluebird just waiting to get his feathers." Cutter said hello. Boley, or Grits, grinned from ear to ear and firmly grasped Garth's hand. He had heard of Garth's arrival, and he knew a Confederate officer when he saw one, even without the hat trim, those old beechnut-colored trousers, the discolored shirt sans the epaulets. But Clarence Daley, the loquacious Irishman, went on, his boot firmly planted on the bottom rail of the corral fence. "For myself, Second Pennsy cavalry. Not much sweat there, but it wasn't the same when I got home, a no-good consorting wife, so I pitched over to the campaign out here, headquartered at Omaha for three months before coming here. Nothing like a damned woman to change your outlook on life."

"Or a war," mused Garth aloud.

"For a fact," answered Daley. He shook his head,

tutted, and looked back and forth, from Boley to Garth.
"Mosby and Forrest, huh!" He grunted, then spat a
stream of tobacco juice against the rail. "Now, that
makes a pair to draw to, damned if it don't. Big cards,
all right. Neither one the mettle of Sheridan, I calcu-
late, but they made do and real high on the hog while
she lasted."

"I wouldn't know that," answered Garth, sliding
through the poles. "We never had the pleasure of
meeting up with Little Phil, too busy spanking Grant's
bottom, and anyone else who chanced to get in our
way."

Daley guffawed, and Boley grinned proudly, saying,
"For certain, you must be the one signing on with
Gabe Bridger's outfit. We'll be riding along with you
all apiece, maybe the limit. Seems like there's no
shortage of Injuns up here like there is white folks."
He blew on his hands for warmth. "Injuns don't mind
the cold, you know. Born to it, I reckon, just like dark-
ies are born to the heat." He gave Garth an inquisitive
look. "What in tarnation ever possessed you to hitch
on up here, Cap? This ain't no place for the likes of us.
Shoot fire, last couple of nights, I had to sleep with my
socks on, and that's a fact. My pecker crawled back
into my belly this morning it was so cold."

"Yeah," Jim Cutter agreed. "When you start seeing
a skim of ice on the chamber pot you know it's getting
cold."

Garth smiled at them, reached over and gave his
horse a pat on the rump. "The truth is," he said, turning back, "I didn't allow I'd be spending the winter out
here. There's this fellow I've been planning to meet up
with again, a little unfinished business. I had the notion
he'd be out of the way, done and forgotten by now, but
he slipped me a couple of times. One thing and another
and I ended up down in Cheyenne. Oh, but he's out
here somewhere, probably no better off than I am. It's
just a matter of time, waiting."

The three troopers, their curiosity piqued, exchanged surprised glances. Cutter finally spoke up again. "You mean you've come all the way out here looking for some fellow, in this godforsaken place? You're on his tracks, is that it?"

Garth nodded. "That's right. I figure he's a week or two ahead of me. A couple of men in Cheyenne saw him. That was the last of it. He's going to have to hole up somewhere for the winter. I thought maybe next spring I'd have a look around, take one last crack at it before heading home."

Cutter clucked his tongue once, then said, "They say men have lost themselves out here in this country, Cap. Never heard of again, not even their bones have turned up, just plain disappeared."

Grits Boley said lowly, "Well, Lord a'livin', what's this ol' boy done to put such a bee in your bonnet?"

"A long story, that part of it," Garth said, "but the short of it is that he's a turncoat spy, got a passel of my troop shot up in Tennessee and the rest of it thrown in a Yankee stockade, including me."

Corporal Daley whistled through his teeth and looked at Garth in disbelief. "Jesus, the war's been over for over a year! And up here, why, it's like chasing a wild goose. Hell, if he don't get himself killed he might be getting himself all the way up the mining camps, and those places are regular anthills, people swarming like crazy all over."

Garth, forever on the outlook for new information, took out a small, leather folder from his back pocket and carefully unfolded it. In between the worn flaps was a picture. Showing it to the men, he asked, "Recognize him? His name is Henry Sturges. He was a colonel, relieved down at Fort Pillow, sacked, and he went over to the Federals after that."

Scrutinizing the picture, Grits Boley said curiously, "Fort Pillow?" Then, in afterthought, he exclaimed, "Why, that's where they strung up those Union dark-ies. Made a big stink about that, they did. I remember. But this fellow ..."

Tapping the photograph, Garth said, "He was responsible for that, did nothing to stop it."

Jim Cutter stared at the small picture intently. "Never saw the likes of this one," he finally said. And then Corporal Daley snatched the picture away, saying, "Here, let me look at that thing. I've been riding patrol off and on for two months. Almost nobody I haven't seen between here and Fort Caspar." But, he, too, gave a negative nod. "I can't recollect seeing him, Cap, and I'm good at faces, 'specially white ones. No, this jasper is a strange one." Watching Garth tuck the picture back into its leather binding, he added with a shake of his head, "Man, you've gone and bit off a big wad, I'd say, real sticky in this place, like running through a nettle patch with your boots off."

Garth grinned and replied, "I'll remember to keep my boots on, Corporal."

Then, sensing the approach of someone behind them, Daley cautiously glanced over his shoulder. Spitting between the rails again, he said lowly, "Seems like it's time for us to move out, Sergeant Tatum's coming. Yessir, and we got the duty." He spoke softly aside to Garth. "Now, don't be looking too hard, see. It's Sergeant Tatum, the old lard bucket. Gives all the orders in our troop. Just keep your wits out for him. He's not too keen on associating, if you know what I mean."

Boley, ex-Confederate, hastily explained, "What he's saying is that Tatum, doesn't take much to the likes of us southern boys. It's like he's still cavortin' with Jim Wilson and old man Sheridan's boys. Shoot fire, that's all he ever brags about, whompin' rebs. He's a regular asshole, he is."

The three idled off behind a friendly, parting wave from Garth. Meantime, Garth, feeling the cool breeze at his back, leaned over the fence and started rubbing Jefferson's long muzzle. Directly, Tatum was beside him, placing a boot upon the rail and resting his arms over the top pole. Neither man looked at the other, but Tatum, his eyes admiringly on Jefferson, finally commented, "That is one fine-looking horse, Reb, mighty fine." Garth politely thanked him. "My name is Tatum, Sergeant Tatum, but I suppose you know that already, seeing how you and the boys were passing the time of day."

"No, frankly, I didn't know that," Garth casually lied. "I do recognize the assumption you're making, though."

"Assumption?" Ward Tatum, inquired. "What's that supposed to mean?"

Garth, still scratching at the horse's nose, said, "Well, it seems that most sergeants have an instinctive notion that any group beyond their earshot has to be talking about them. Strange, isn't it? What do you make of that peculiarity?"

Ward Tatum grunted and rolled his chew once. "I make nonsense out of it."

Garth smiled ahead. "You mean you never get the least bit suspicious? You never wonder whether they're cursing you or commending you?"

"I don't make out the orders, I just relay them," Tatum, replied. "You should know that, Reb. I take all the shit. Nothing peculiar about that, is there?" He halfway turned and nodded at the departing troopers. "Those greenhorns been telling you all about what's going on around here . . . hostiles, all the ruckus up the valleys?"

"Greenhorns?" Garth asked with surprise. "Why, damnation, I took those boys for tried and true cavalrymen, veterans of the field! Now, don't tell me they're recruits."

"Humph!" Tatum, snorted scornfully. "They're greenhorns out here, and you know it, so don't bull me. This is a different war. Hostiles don't go by the book like we did. Oh, you'll find that out, just like the

boys, there. Can't tell about redskins, 'specially these
Sioux, Red Cloud's Oglalas mostly. Never know when
they're going to make a fight of it. They come in
screaming and carrying on something fierce, trying to
scare the hell out of you. Give 'em a chase sometimes,
and hell, they can disappear like smoke in the wind.
Yeah, forget 'em and they can sneak up and split your
skull and you never know it. These boys don't know
too much about that yet. It's my job seeing that they
learn."

"I'm sure you'll be a good teacher, Sergeant," Garth
smiled.

Tatum's words had come in a rush. He was breathing
heavily, his face red. But his complexion was always
this way, ruddy, florid, in continual blush like a lob-
ster. He, too, rubbed Jefferson's nose, adding sourly,
" 'Course, I can see you don't plan on fighting much.
Scout, eh? Quite a comedown for one of General
Forrest's officers."

"News travels fast."

"Oh, I read all of my paperwork, Mr. Garth. Tyson
Garth, ain't it? I know all the people connected with
this company's military operation. Part of my job."

"Ah, right you are, Sergeant," agreed Garth. "And I
suppose you know I was employed because of what I
do best, ride and reconnoiter as directed." With a sidelong glance, Garth added, "Brawling with savages isn't
my main concern. I'll allow that's another part of your
job, though."

Tatum, spat contemptuously to the side, the thrust of
Garth's barbs pricking his thick skin, his army pride.
"Well, you better know that I did some riding in my
time, myself. General Wilson, General Sheridan. Fact
is, I was with 'em when we put the run on old Jubal
Early, and I reckon everyone knows about that." Grinning triumphantly, he paused to hitch his suspenders.
He eyed Garth suspiciously for a moment, awaiting a
rejoinder which failed to come. Finally: "Can't figure

out what brings a fine, upstanding West Pointer like you out here, anyway, hiring on as a scout 'n all. Just seems to me you'd have something better to do than consort with the army."

"Everyone asks me that," answered Garth, momentarily reflecting. Tatum, was right—he did have better things to do, and he always felt a twinge of guilt when he dwelled on those matters that he had left behind for others to accomplish, such as the planting, the rebuilding of Garth House, badly fire-damaged by General Grant's Union forces on their march to Vicksburg. Garth had left brother Hugh to tend to the farming and the care of their heartbroken mother. Their father, Judson, had a stroke attempting to put out the fire. He died in Biloxi two weeks after the Union raid. But this search for Sturges, a pact sealed by the blood of Jack's Fork, had all but obliterated those obligations, duties that he, perhaps unfairly, had turned over to Hugh. He finally said, "Well, I'll tell you, Sergeant, I kept hearing about how the future was out here, how there was a big, open land filled with great mountains and wide, blue rivers, gold hiding in the rocks, so, by jingo, I thought I'd just ride out and have a look. Had some bad luck. Weather caught up with me down in Cheyenne, so one of your army friends there talked me into this. That rascal told me this place called Kearny would be a good place to spend the winter, a nice, warm fort, congenial company, good food, no wicked women to steal my wages, that sort of thing. That's what he told me."

"Humph!" grunted the sergeant, elevating his red nose, his eyes squinting up disdainfully at Garth's faded cavalry hat. "Didn't tell you about getting a decent piece of warm headgear, did he? You know, like getting rid of that thing."

"My hat?" Garth asked in affected innocence.

"Your *rebel* hat."

Garth's dark eyes twinkled, but he said seriously, "Oh, I can't do that. No, suh. It's my marker."

"Marker?"

"That's right, my marker," Garth said. "You see, I look at it this way. Now supposing a passel of those hostiles come down on us at full gallop, shouting and making all those fierce noises you were telling me about? Law, law, I don't want anyone confusing me with the troopers. I don't have any quarrel with these people. This is my marker. Sets me apart. Easier for you to see, Sergeant. Yessuh, you can just look for this old hat of mine and see it running over the nearest hill."

Tatum, aware that he had met his match for this day, sucked in his breath. He pulled his big frame to attention. Yes, the brief parry and thrust was over. He turned away, saying, "Like I told you, this is a damn fine horse you got here, probably smart as a whip, too. You take good care of him, 'cause you're gonna need all the help you can get."

T. B. Garth agreed, but he didn't say it. He returned to his quarters in Bedlam, where he wrote a long explanatory letter to his mother and brother Hugh. He had been detained on the great frontier. Any correspondence would reach him through Fort Laramie. He would return home as soon as pending matters were resolved.

Chapter Two

The brisk October wind unexpectedly subsided, and with it, the biting chill, and for the first two days Garth rode easily, comfortably, enjoying one of nature's peculiar whims on the frontier: contrary weather, the beginning of Indian summer. Two detachments numbering eighty men made a steady pace of it, slowed occasionally by the heavy-laden supply wagons that were being pulled by teams of black mules. One day on the distant horizon far to Garth's left, great mountains began to disrupt the landscape, hazily reaching up like giant sentinels. These were the timbered crests of the Big Horns guarding the Indians' sanctuary in the river valleys to the north, the Tongue, the Rosebud, and the Big Horn River itself. Even at such a far distance their immensity caused Garth to marvel. The old Blue Ridges of Tennessee seemed puny by comparison, and for the first time, he saw new beauty in the vast land unfolding before his anxious eyes. Clumps of trees were now hugging the hillsides, evergreens, the ubiquitous cottonwood, family groups of aspen, all etching golden and dark green accents against the browning wild grasses. Riding far to the front of the detachment, Garth had the sensation he was pioneering the way, the first to cross a wild, new, and untamed country, but his companion scout John Dominguez, the dark Spaniard known to the troopers as Domino, often pointed out subtle signs along the trail that shattered Garth's reverie of the primeval journey into the great unknown. On another day, Dominguez nodded ahead to signs decidedly less subtle, the first evidence of human violence, eight graves on a nearby hill. Below the neatly spaced rows of rocks were the blackened sideboards and charred wheels of six wagons, part of an unescorted freight expedition that had never made it. This, explained Dominguez, was the land of *Mahpiua Luta* or Red Cloud, chief of the Bad Face band of Oglala Lakota, the scourge of the Bozeman Trail, and a warrior who Dominguez had known for many years. It was told in his village that Red Cloud got his name from a meteor that turned the sky scarlet at the time of his birth. He was a powerful warrior who had counted many coup, a natural leader who eventually had become the spokesman for his people through his own force of character. Dominguez told Garth that Red Cloud possessed powerful medicine, and had been the major influence in bringing in other Sioux and Cheyenne tribes to fight the fort builders and valley interlopers. The veteran scout, with a dark look on his leathery face, said anyone underestimating the cunning of Red Cloud was making a horrible assessment of the Oglala chief. That miscalculation, he added, had already happened. It was his opinion that the very head of the western campaign in Omaha, Brigadier General George Crook, had not given adequate response and support to his officers in the field, thereby compromising the safety of the Bozeman Trail and the new forts as well. The hostiles, he estimated, now outnumbered the soldiers by twenty to one, and their support from other tribes was beginning to show. Bridger's scouts had reported that new Cheyenne and Arapaho bands were now camping along the Tongue, and there were Miniconjou, Hunkpapa, and Brule Sioux on the Powder.

In the grizzled personage of John Dominguez, Garth had not only found a new friend but also a seemingly endless source of information about the army and Indians, as well. A good friend of Blanket Chief, Jim Bridger, Dominguez, likewise, had at various times in his long career in the wilderness, lived with the Indians. He spoke some Sioux and Cheyenne, knew sign, and was thoroughly indoctrinated to frontier life, and had been part of the spring expedition when Colonel Carrington and seven hundred men, guided by Bridger, first rode into the headwaters of the Powder to build Fort Kearny. Through summer, the Spaniard scouted the trail ninety miles down the Big Horn where the smaller fort, C. F. Smith, was built under the supervision of Carrington's men. The great tribes of the Lakota or Sioux nation, were no mystery to Dominguez. He had smoked with many chiefs in his time. More significant to Garth was how the Indians fought, and he soon realized that the Spaniard's assessment of their military prowess was a sickening contradiction to some of the officers' arrogant opinions. The construction of Fort Kearny itself was a horrible contradiction, built at the staggering price of more than one hundred men killed, twenty wounded, and the loss of seven hundred head of stock. Garth, riding beside Dominguez and listening intently to both fact and opinion, became more appalled each mile they covered. At one point, Dominguez hunched forward in his saddle and pointed to more trailside debris, broken wagons, and tattered canvas, shreds of cloth clinging to the tumbleweed and sage, grim reminders of failed missions. "My friend," he said, "don't let anyone tell you these Indians don't know how to fight. They do very well with what they have, eh? Mostly bows, yes, but now a few new Spencers and Henrys, too, some captured from our *soldados,* some from the traders who come down from the north, muzzle loaders, even a few old fusils. Ah, but the ammunition, you see, is sometimes hard to get. What they can't buy or trade for they have to capture and steal." Dominguez gave his horse a slight nudge and looked across at Garth. "I tell you this, my friend, if these Indians had what we do, plenty of good rifles and ammunition, they would rub us out, swoosh, swoosh, just like that, like what you say ... shooting turkeys off a limb, eh?" Dominguez, clucking at his pony, turned off to the side toward a small hill, and Garth dutifully followed, frequently asking questions, and most often getting long Spanish-accented but intelligent replies.

Garth learned that Red Cloud and his allies were too smart to make an outright assault on Fort Kearny. It was well fortified, a solid bastion of defense set in such a strategic position that any ordinary assault upon it would be suicidal. Instead, the Indians planned their attacks to coincide with the routine activities of the fort, the wood gathering, cutting of hay in the nearby meadows, or movement of supply wagons, a few often captured and their valuable contents triumphantly carried off to the tribal compounds. These attacks were always methodically swift, brief encounters intermingled with terrible outcries and sporadic gunfire, and then the Indians would disappear. "I tell you this," Dominguez went on, "no one can bring a load of hay or wood into the fort without escort. On Piney Island, these woodcutters, eh, they can't saw the wood unless we have lookouts on Sullivant and Pilot." He emitted a chuckle. "Sometimes, I go up to those hills to watch, eh? I can see far off. *Qué bueno,* I say to myself, and you know what I see? *Los Indios, sí,* they are watching me, too. Yes, every day they peck a little here, a little there, along the trail, making life miserable for everyone. Peck, peck, peck, eh?" He smiled and winked at Garth, saying, "You understand what I mean? You see what they do?"

Garth grinned and nodded knowingly, the time-worn practice of provocation, the baiting tactic, lure the enemy out to terrain less advantageous. "Yessuh, I think I understand. One day, the boys at the fort will ride out there and try to cut their peckers off. Is that it?"

"*Más o menos.*" Dominguez shrugged. "*Sí,* either they have to come out and drive the Indians away, or they have to give up and go home." He stared pensively across the small valley below, where a few alarmed antelope were winnowing away like a school of minnows, darting back and forth until they disappeared over a distant hill. "Once, a long time ago," he said reflectively, "when I was up by a place called Henry's Fork, I heard much noise, maybe like a fight, eh? I came down through the trees to see what this is all about. I stop and get off my horse and sneak up, and I see a bear trying to eat on a carcass, maybe a calf moose, I think. But he's not having a good time, eh? *Los lobos,* the wolves, they are there, too, four of them, and everytime Señor bear takes a bite, a wolf comes up and tries to take a bite of him. So, after a while, our friend the bear, he can't take any more of this pecking, pecking, eh? So, he gets one big bite and runs off into the trees, and *los lobos* eat their supper." Tapping the side of his temple, he said, "So, you see, my friend, maybe the soldiers don't go chasing peckers like the Indians want. Maybe they just get tired and go away, back home to Omaha. Too many *Indios.*"

Smiling at his wizened companion, Garth answered, "I like your analogy, Dominguez, by damned if I don't, but it sounds a little too simplistic. Even if they did pack up, it wouldn't solve the mess. The trail is still here, isn't it? The fact that it's unsecured wouldn't make one whit of difference to some of these fools. Why, they'd go trekking up here anyway, probably end up like some of those people we just passed, under a pile of rocks. Nosuh, no one's going to walk away from this, and you know it. It's already gone too far for that. I'll allow this matter won't be settled until one side or the other gets a damned good thrashing. I just hope the good Lord I'm out of here when it happens. I sure didn't come all the way out here to get one of those permanent haircuts I keep hearing about."

"Ah, yes." Dominguez nodded. "I remember, my friend, you want to kill a white man, not a redskin, that Sturges *hombre*."

"Yes, suh," said Garth emphatically, "that sets me apart from the rest of these fellows, doesn't it? I have no quarrel with the savages ... the natives, the redskins, as you call them, but I sure as hell will kill Mr. Sturges if I ever catch up with him. Just dragging me all the way out here is reason enough, now."

Dominguez silently crossed himself, then after a pause, looked sorrowfully over at Garth. "This is too bad that you have to kill someone, even one so bad. As for me, I have no quarrel to settle with anyone. It's best this way, I think. You see, out here I have only three to trust. *Sí,* myself, my horse, and God. That's why I'm still alive." He jerked his thumb back at the long file of the troopers. "It isn't my place to criticize too much, only a little. I just ride and take orders, do what I can. Like you, I hope to stay alive, keep my gray hair. Ah, but I tell you, *'mano,* up here times are changing, and I don't like all that I see."

"Why do you stay on?"

Dominguez replied with a shrug. "Because I love this land, even with its many troubles. My father came with the land, far below here, and he taught me to ride. My mother was Mexican, eh? She taught me to pray. This is my life. What else can a man do at my age. eh?"

Garth pondered thoughtfully for a moment. Dominguez had told him about the small cabin he owned down below the big Rockies in Colorado country, a place he often went to spend the winter months, another land of grass and water. He finally offered, "Get yourself a few cows and a good bull, maybe raise some cattle down home. There's always a market for beef."

"Gabe Bridger tried that, farming, I heard," he replied. "He couldn't put up with it, couldn't stay away from the mountains, all of this up here. Maybe he got lonely, too, eh? Every year, almost thirty, now I come back. This, my friend, is the way it is. I can't explain it."

"Oh, I think I understand, Dominguez. I'll allow that's heart and soul speaking, and it doesn't need any explaining."

Another two days on the trail passed without incident, no confrontation with hostiles, and there was very little sign to indicate their presence. But the two companies of galvanized Yankees manning Fort Reno, where an overnight stop was made, assured everyone the trail was still dangerous. Though most of the Sioux had moved north, there were still a few cantankerous warriors in the Powder River bottom. The soldiers were disinclined to venture from behind the log walls. With snipers about, getting wood was a hazardous chore. And before departure the next morning, T. B. Garth had the impression that the Fort Reno garrison had no stomach left to fight hostiles. This lot of soldiers was one of the most miserable he had ever seen. Ranks were depleted by desertion; rations were in short supply, and the men were without adequate medical facilities. John Dominguez said one of the Fort Reno doctors, a captain named James Tolliver, had treated a captured hostile and aided his escape by stealing the commandant's horse. Captain Tolliver had been sent to Fort Laramie for a court martial, only to have escaped. The other doctor had been transferred to Fort Caspar, so the fort was left with only two enlisted medical aides. Dominguez laughed. Captain Tolliver, he said, was now reported to be living with a band of Oglala somewhere in the Black Hills, and every fort Indian at Laramie thought it was a big joke.

Garth was happy to leave Fort Reno behind. Settling into the routine of his work, he was now riding alone part of the time without benefit of Dominguez's guidance and conversation. Even the talk among the troop-

ers, usually laced with army humor and tall stories, had
become more brief and crisp, confined mostly to orders
and the business at hand. Things were a little too calm,
opined some of the veterans. Some sensed that an attack was imminent, that they had come too far too easily, and that this was contrary to usual Indian behavior.
Sergeant Ward Tatum, often trading barbs with Garth,
was everywhere, constantly passing along orders, be-
rating slackers, demanding the very best from his men.
While Garth and Tatum had come to respect each other's ability, neither could find any common ground for
a warm friendship. It was Garth's contention, so expressed to Dominguez, that the sergeant was always
going out of his way to embarrass him in front of the
troopers.

On this morning, just before the troop was under
way, it was the "hat" again. It was a cold day, the sun
barely up, and Garth thought it best to tie on his red
muffler to keep his ears warm. Tatum arrived on the
scene just as Garth was about to mount up and presented him with a crow feather that he had found in
the trail. He sarcastically suggested that Garth tie the
feather onto his hat to complete his appearance as the
troop's "fort squaw." To Tatum's chagrin, Garth cheer-
fully accepted it. And so as not to diminish his roguish
reputation, Garth fastened the plumage to his cavalry
hat and rode jauntily away, singing a verse from the
Rogue's March: "Poor old soldier, poor old soldier,
tarred and feathered, and then drummed out because he
wouldn't soldier . . ." Some of the troopers guffawed.
Tatum did not.

The troop was only several days south of Fort
Kearny, but the strange absence of the Sioux and
Cheyenne disturbed Captain William Fetterman, one of
the leaders of the small contingent. After conferring
with Dominguez several times, he concluded that most
of the Indians were busy grouping farther north around
Kearny and Fort C. F. Smith, at least within a day or

two ride of their villages near the valley rivers. Despite the lack of fresh pony tracks in their immediate area, Fetterman elected to double the scouting assignments at Crazy Woman Creek, a small stream where they halted to rest and water the stock. Captain Fetterman had done his paperwork, for this was a place some of the men remembered. Several troopers had been killed by a small band of Sioux on Crazy Woman Creek in July.

Fetterman sent Tatum and Corporal Clarence Daley ahead with Dominguez and Garth. At a point about a mile above the troop train, they stopped to take a bearing and select areas to reconnoiter, and it was at this precise moment that Dominguez's pocked nose tilted into the slight breeze wafting down the creek. He whiffed suspiciously several times, then grunted and pointed.

Tatum squinted curiously ahead. He asked, "Domino, you smell something?"

"Smoke?" queried Dominguez, trading looks with the others. "Smells like smoke, eh?"

Daley gave the Spaniard a questioning stare and a hapless shrug. "Hell, I can't smell nothing but these critters."

Dominguez turned to Garth, who sat impassively to the side, his cavalry hat pulled snugly down over his red scarf. The crow feather dangled near the front, hanging perilously close to his long nose. Garth blew sharply, sending the feather bouncing to the side. Then, staring up ahead into the creek's misty air, he said, "No sign of smoke up there, least not from here, Mistuh Dominguez." Turning to Tatum, he added, "I'll defer to Mistuh Dominguez, Sergeant, the accuracy of his proboscis."

"His what?" asked Tatum testily.

Garth placed a finger against his nose and tapped lightly. "His nose, Sergeant, his nose. Dominguez has the proboscis of a red bone hound. Trust him."

Dominguez grinned and addressed the sergeant. "What you think, eh, which way?"

With an annoyed look at Garth, Tatum turned away, vainly sniffed the air himself, detected nothing unusual. "I'll be damned if I know," he finally replied. "Reckon we better take a good look, anyways."

"Yessuh," Garth grinned, "who *knows*?"

Daley snickered once, Tatum did not. Ignoring Garth's pun, he pointed toward the brushy knolls to the left of the creek bottom and addressed Dominguez. "You and Daley take that side. Me'n the Reb will stay along here a'piece. Ten minutes and circle back to rendezvous in the bottom. No more, understand?" Tatum turned then and stared expectantly at Garth.

The scout made a gracious sweep with his glove. "Lead on, Mistuh Tatum, after you, suh."

"Huh-unh," Tatum retorted, with a negative shake. "You're the scout, ain't you? You get on up yonder above the trail to the right, 'case you run into some of them hostiles. That way, you can double-time it back down here real easy, see? I'll just mosey on up the crick a ways to the brow of that little hill." He grinned crookedly. "Now, you take care, hear? Don't get yourself all rattled and go catching an arrow in that smart-assed bottom of yours."

Garth, relishing these verbal duels, drawled back, "Oh, law, don't fret on it, Sergeant. I'll allow that with you along, there's not much chance of that, not with that big target you're sitting on." Smartly touching his hat to Tatum, he walked Jefferson slowly ahead. He chose a meandering course through the scrub and sage to either side of the trail. Moments later, he was riding alone.

A patch of streaky sunlight was beginning to filter down through the cold bottom where the bunchgrass bent over in solemn defeat under a heavy accumulation of hoarfrost. The frozen ground crackled fearfully in the stillness, and despite the cold, Garth suddenly felt thin pebbles of sweat forming under the band of his old hat. He kept his eyes on the brow of the long bluff ahead, near the rim, where any moment he fully expected to see the feathered heads of savages. Once, he stopped to survey the frosty creek bottom below where Tatum had disappeared in the tangle of willows, and saw only stiff-tailed magpies dipping and darting among the brush. Near the base of the hill, close to the point where the old wagon ruts took off for a gradual climb to the right, he suddenly stopped. There was no mistake about it—he also smelled smoke! Garth quickly led Jefferson to the side, tied him to a clump of tall juniper, and checking his rifle, he climbed carefully to the brow of the hill. A few minutes later, peering down through a tumble of sage, he saw a group of Indians far below, twenty or more, all bundled in robes. Huddled in several groups around small fires, they appeared to be eating breakfast, and at least forty horses and some captured army mules were grazing nearby. The sight sent Garth backing away like a startled crawdad, and once clear, he fell into a crouch and hurried down the hill.

Garth never made it to the bottom. A series of frantic shouts and high-pitched shrieks turned him in the direction of the creek. He took off running and finally came to the bend near where Tatum had left him. Garth's eyes bulged. The sergeant's horse was bounding away directly into the teeth of the Indian camp, two women on it, madly kicking its flanks. Garth stopped in his tracks, his jaw slack. Law, law, two women were actually stealing Tatum's pony! By now, the shouts from the creek were building to a crescendo, and without his own horse, Garth suddenly felt naked. Facing about, he went bolting the rest of the way down the hill to retrieve Jefferson, and once mounted, he galloped back up the bottom toward the outcries. When he finally reached the bend, he saw Sergeant Tatum stumbling out of the willows, wildly flapping

his arms like a wounded crow. Three women were
swarming all over him, one flailing him with a soggy
piece of wash, another beating him with driftwood, and
the third, clinging to his heavy leg, her teeth clamped
into his thigh. Swinging alongside, Garth attempted to
dislodge the yelling women by kicking out with his
boot, but to little avail. They were swarming all over
Tatum like hound dogs on a coon. Garth finally had to
bring the barrel of his rifle into play. He caught one of
the screaming women in the middle of the back, and
Tatum, at last, managed to tear away from the old
woman who had fastened onto his leg. The third
woman, hit broadside by Jefferson's rump as he turned
around, fell backward into the cold water of the creek.

"Jump on, Sergeant, jump on," Garth shouted
down, backing Jefferson into the sprawled women
again. "Let's get the hell out of here!"

Tatum, after two attempts, finally heaved himself up
behind Garth. His face was a mass of sweat, dirt, and
scratches, and his hat was missing. So was his horse.
He had seen two women riding it down the creek bottom. "My horse, goddammit, my horse!" he cried out.
"Get after 'em, Garth, they're stealing my horse!"

But Garth kicked away in the opposite direction.
"To hell with your horse," he yelled. "There's a whole
camp of Indians around that bend and I don't think
they're very friendly." Two shots, fired almost simultaneously, verified it. The screams of the distraught Indian women had brought several warriors running. The
bullets buzzed by Tatum and Garth, whining like angry
hornets. Both men hunkered, and Garth spurred Jefferson to full speed. Down below, he saw Dominguez and
Daley also cutting back to the frosty trail, they, too,
riding hard for the troop train. Garth's crow feather
was spinning like a berserk windmill, while Tatum's
vicelike arms, wrapped tightly around Garth's middle,
were near to crushing his ribs. "Hold on there, Ser-

geant," puffed Garth. "Hold on, old boy, and I'll get you home."

Tatum cursed again, yelling, "You let 'em get my horse, goddammit!"

"By jingo, is this the thanks I get? Don't go blaming me for those damned women. Better the horse than you." Garth let out a whoop as Jefferson stretched into full stride across the hardpan.

The more amusing aspects of the near-tragic incident at Crazy Woman Creek never fully surfaced in the brief report.

"Sergeant Tatum, scouting creek area, met five enemy." (He had stumbled, quite clumsily, upon five women washing winter underclothing.)

"He was attacked forthwith, and lost his mount in the engagement." (Two women had slipped behind him and had stolen his horse, the remaining three had assailed him with wet wash and sticks while calling for assistance.)

"Sergeant Tatum fought a retreat and remounted with Scout T. B. Garth." (Garth, hearing the shouts of the women, luckily rescued Tatum before hostile braves appeared on the scene.)

"The scouting party was fired upon but was unable to return fire. Company prepared for engagement with enemy but no contact made." (Garth and Sergeant Tatum were too busy making tracks even to think about firing upon the hostiles.)

Prior to the creek bottom fracas, Dominguez and Daley, on the opposite hill, also had sighted the hostile camp, approximately at the same time Garth was scouting it from his sagebrush ridge. Dominguez, in his report, identified the Indians as Cheyenne, probably en route to join the hostiles of Dull Knife, the name the Cheyenne chief, Morning Star, was called by the Sioux. And the report accurately concluded that more than twenty Cheyenne braves were in the group, in ad-

dition to a large herd of horses. Somehow, any notation
about the accompanying women had been completely
omitted from the brief log summary, which coinciden-
tally had been filed and signed by Sergeant Ward
Tatum. But Garth shared the secret of the Cheyenne
women. He figured that he now had Tatum by his short
hairs.

That afternoon, twelve Indians suddenly appeared on
the skyline above the creek trail. Motionless, almost
like silhouettes on the hazy horizon, they remained
fully in sight for ten minutes, silently observing before
melting away behind the ridge. The troopers put away
their rifles again and prepared to ride. Standing behind
one of the wagons, Dominguez was thoughtfully
munching on a piece of jerky as he watched the Cheyenne disappear. *"Hasta mañana,"* he said quietly, waving at the empty hill. Garth stared up at the barren
ridge with him, silent for a moment, his eyes searching
the perimeters. He finally asked, "What was that all
about?"

"Smart Indians, my friend," Dominguez said. His
jaw pumped several times, pulverizing the stringy, dry
meat. *"Sí,* just sizing us up. They have many ways to
make the white man worry, maybe to put some fear in
him, to make him wonder. Sometimes, they peck a little, sometimes a yell or two, and sometimes they just
sit and watch. Ah, but one way or another, they always
let you know they are there, not too far away." He
made a sweeping gesture around him. "Too many guns
here today." Nodding down the line toward Sergeant
Tatum, he laughed. "Ho, ho, but one less horse, eh?"
Between the chewing, he managed a wink and a toothy
yellowed grin.

A shout came from someone near the lead wagons
and the unit began to move ahead. Then, an order came
down for Dominguez and Garth to ride back up the hill
to make a thorough check on the departing hostiles. At
the same time, Tatum, red face glowing, galloped up

on his new mount and met Garth. Blocking the way, Tatum said lamely, "Listen, Reb, I reckon I'm obliged to you for what you did up the trail there. I owe you for that, but don't be making a big ruckus about those squaws. Bad enough losing my horse that way."

Garth, with some nonchalance, delicately flicked away the dangling feather fronting his vision. He realized Tatum's pride had been pricked because of the creek bottom fiasco, but unexplicably he felt no desire to push the thorn in any deeper. It seemed as though the bulky sergeant sitting the horse across from him had shrunk a full three feet. No use gaffing him anymore. Touching his hat, Garth said, "Let bygones be bygones, Mistuh Tatum."

But then to his surprise, Tatum suddenly swelled like a stump toad exposed to the sun. "Oh, no," he sputtered. "No, no, no. I wouldn't go so far as to say that. I'm just saying I'm obliged, that's all. Nothing more, nothing less. I'll have my day with you, Reb. Sooner or later, I'll have it."

One could only guess why the Cheyenne on Crazy Woman Creek failed to reappear along the trail somewhere, either to harass or pick off a few riders in ambush. Garth watched and wondered, expectantly, his hand always close to his new Henry rifle, but the Indians, as capricious as the autumn wind, mysteriously floated away with it. Not so unusual, opined John Dominguez. Probing the Indian's mind, he said, one so dictated by the whim or caprice of the given moment, the making of medicine, consulting the omens, or appealing to the holiness of nature, Mother Earth, why, that could be an outright exercise in futility. Who but the Indian really knew the Indian? Whatever, on the third day out of Crazy Woman Creek, the troopers, to the accompaniment of the Fort Kearny regimental band, proudly rode into the safety of the timbered

walls, unscathed and without the loss of a man, only
one horse.

After the last hurrahs, Garth shook himself from the
saddle and quietly assessed his new home. A sense of
well-being swept through him. He was safe at last in
the long knives' sanctuary. And the great fort was all
he had heard it to be, a tremendous rectangle six hundred by eight hundred feet. The stockade, built of pine
logs eight feet high, carried a loophole in every fourth
timber, and diagonal blockhouses sported cannon
ports. Formidable in every way, the interior community
was complete with barracks, officers' and family quarters a few spare rooms, and a warehouse. Another
stockade outside, always posted with sentries, contained wagons, stock, and hay. In such primitive surroundings, the fort was magnificent. Garth, with some
recollection of fortification study at the Academy, considered Kearny another excellent example of army ingenuity as well as its determination to protect the trail
to the north.

Some of that ingenuity also extended to Garth's
small bunking quarters, a converted clerk's office at
the rear of general headquarters, rustically furnished
with the bare necessities: a stove, bench, nightstand,
pitcher and bowl, and a homely, earthenware night pot,
or "thunder mug." Crudely hospitable, true, but a decided improvement over the cold soogans of the trail,
and more to his liking than the crowded coterie of the
barracks. He discovered that the wide-open space of
his new duty post would more than make up for his
tiny room. As Dominguez had predicted, Garth had
been assigned to Sullivant Hill, one of the two nearby
observation points overlooking the trails and small valleys surrounding the beleaguered fort. Sullivant's spa-
cious, sloping top stood out like the back of a
Mississippi terrapin. Located about two miles to the
northwest of the fort, its rounded cap commanded a
view of the wood road to Piney Island on the south,

and the rutted Virginia City or Bozeman Trail on the north. As Dominguez said, all a man needed was his field glasses and a swift pony. The grassy, sage-covered knob had almost no protection, nor did it need much. Hostiles were unable to mount Sullivant without being seen from a half mile or more in any direction, a strategic asset to the men who had to occupy the lookout and ride the perimeters.

It was dusk, one day later when Garth finally trudged across the grounds to deliver Elbert Craig's letter to Miss Bird Rutledge, and up until this point, it had been a very routine first twenty-four hours. Bundled in his shaggy coat and wearing his new boots, Garth looked almost like any other buffalo soldier at the fort. There was that one exception: he had yet to give up on his gray hat, his marker. While he did loathe his comic attire, particularly its military significance, the plain fact was that his first stint on Sullivant would have been unbearable without it. It had been a cold October day, and the wind over Kearny had the edge of a razor. He had shared the blustery ridge with John Phillips, a scout known as Portugee Phil by the troopers. The two scouts talked most of the day about Indians without so much as seeing one. It was a rare occasion when hostiles failed to make an appearance, but, Portugee, a veteran somewhat akin to Bridger and Dominguez, assured Garth that they were always near, that they came with regularity, if not today, certainly tomorrow.

Therefore, Indians in general had become a part of Garth's conscience and he found himself momentarily nonplussed that evening when a rather darkish, prim woman in a flowing dress and shawl greeted him at the Rutledge quarters. She spoke English, and to his consternation, he discovered that her name was Meena Rutledge, wife of Jack Rutledge, the sawyer boss. She was a full-blooded Cree, and of course, there was that awkward moment, his inner cry of alarm, "Lord a'mighty, this man has taken himself a savage for a wife!" And then, that swift reflection of his chats with the mild-mannered Elbert, the young clerk's sudden testiness when Garth had made several innocuous references to savages. Now, in a state of polite shock, he saw the word "savage" hurtling out the window like a riled tomcat. Hiding his discomfort, he listened as Meena told him that Bird was not at home, that she was delivering fresh wash to Mrs. Grummond, a chore that Mrs. Rutledge contracted weekly as a courtesy since the lieutenant's wife was expecting a child.

Anxious to be away, Garth immediately offered up the letter and package. However, instead of departing, he found himself confronted by Jack Rutledge, who insisted that he sit down and take a cup of coffee. The sawyer, Garth discovered, was not the most articulate man, but he was one of honest labor, ruggedly handsome with a reddish beard, and after those first few awkward moments, Rutledge made it bluntly clear he was also a man of honest opinion. First, he belabored the Sioux who had been picking off some of his woodcutters. He also had a word or two for the army's ineptitude in protecting his men. "Things are getting worse instead of better," Rutledge complained. "It ain't what the army promised. Come spring, we're heading back. No more of this, not even at double pay." He plopped his cup on the table planking and asked directly, "Say, are you a good shot, shoot a rifle good?"

Garth shrugged modestly. He was an excellent marksman. "Yes," he answered, "I shoot well enough, both rifle and pistol."

Rutledge quickly warned him, saying, "Well, better keep it to yourself, son. Don't go letting these busters know about it. Keep it mum, hear? Oh, we needs a few sharpshooters, sure enough, but that Sullivant area is a safer place. Find out you can shoot, and they'll put you to scouting below, just to back up some of those recruits they been sending in here. Likely to get your ass shot off riding with those fool boys. No use making a turkey outta yourself."

Garth, sipping his coffee, hearing yet another man's opinion of the fort strife, listened as Rutledge continued with further comments on conditions, the continuing building, the hardships of getting timber and firewood through the gates, the persistence of the Sioux and their Cheyenne friends.

"Thank you, Mistuh Rutledge, for the information and advice," Garth said at length. "As with you, it's not my war, but I suppose I'll be serving where Colonel Carrington and Mistuh Bridger feel I'm best suited."

"Ha, right now that would be everywhere!" retorted Rutledge. With a pathetic shake of his head, he said, "Ain't no one man alive who can settle this mess. The army's got a big griz by the tail. Our boys do their best, but hell's fire, they ain't got the proper training and manpower to fight these hedgehoppers, and any fool who's been here awhile can see it." Ultimately, to Garth's relief, Rutledge pulled out a gold watch from his pocket and checked it once, then got up and slipped into his winter coat, a great shaggy brown garment with a sheepskin collar. He had work to do, he explained, some forging down at the smith's shed. Tutting once, he went for the door. "Good fort here, Mr. Garth. Warm, safe, too. Sweat and blood built it, you know. Poor excuse for a garrison, though, considering there's more'n a thousand hostiles running about out here. Don't make sense, none of it. Be all hell to pay if they all decided to come running this way at once."

"Yes, I've heard about their numbers," answered Garth. He reached for his hat, preparing to follow Rutledge out the door. But the sawyer waved him down. "No need to hurry on my account. Sit on, Mr. Garth, finish your coffee and talk to the missus." Pulling his collar high, he waved once and disappeared into the darkness.

Directly, Meena was back at Garth's side with the big coffeepot. Once again, politely declining, he stood ready to excuse himself, when suddenly another woman came through the door right on the heels of Rutledge's departure. Garth gawked a second time, totally unprepared for the amazing sight that greeted him. It could only be Bird, Elbert Craig's fiancée. She came into the yellow light of the lamp smiling inquisitively at him and, in turn, staring at her mother. Shock begets shock, Garth had barely recovered from the revelation of mother Meena, a full-blood, but daughter Bird, a breed, spun him off into oblivion like a startled pigeon. Boyish in buckskins and woolens, what Indian blood Bird had inherited from her mother merely touched her burnished features. Law, law, what a fetching woman! Her nose tilted like a button, and by lamplight, her eyes looked like two ebony gumdrops. Garth had no chance to speak, only nod, as Meena hastily explained his presence and handed her daughter the letter and tiny package. The girl clasped them close, and with a smile, thanked Garth. Near the door, he made a small bow, and said graciously, "My pleasure, ma'am. Mistuh Craig sends his very best regards."

"Dear Bert," she said precisely. "And how is he, matters at the store, and so forth? The same, I suppose. Must you leave so soon?"

Garth momentarily flinched at her lucidity, her perfect English, the broguelike quality of it, almost as if she had come from the great island itself. "Why, Elbert . . . Bert, as you say, was well when I left him," he said, trying to collect himself. Was his stare obvious? His eyeballs seemed to be locked, and he couldn't blink his lids. He limped on, saying, "Busy, yes. That store is a busy place, but we talked a spell one evening after his hours." His eyes went to the letter. "I'll allow his affections come in the letter, Miss Bird. I just dropped by to deliver it."

"And I'll bet he never told you about me," she said with continuing smile. "Did he?"

Garth awkwardly nodded at the letter again. "A small favor, he called it, to his, ah, fiancée. Understand, Miss Bird, our meeting was brief. I recall that I did most of the talking, conditions on the frontier, Indians . . . hostiles, I mean to say."

"He's shy about expressing himself," she said. Bird pressed a finger to the tip of her nose, depressing its pertness even more. "I think it's his father," she said pensively. "Mr. Craig is, oh, very protective, you might say." She fondly touched the letter, saying, "This will enlighten me, probably about everything that's happening on the post, Mr. Garth, and I thank you."

"I'm obliged, ma'am." He grasped the latch. "I enjoyed meeting the family, Miss Bird. Yes, and, ah, you, the way you express yourself. After that long ride up from Laramie, your words are refreshing, like spring water."

"Really?" she replied, her brow arched. "Are you surprised as well as delighted?" His hand dropped away from the door, her big, dark eyes hypnotically redirecting his intention of opening it. She pushed a hand to her hair and said affectedly, "Where did I learn to express myself? Schooling? Is that what you are wondering? Yes, believe it or not, I've been to school. I was an eager learner, Mr. Garth. Some of the officer's wives resent me for it, because in this respect, they can't compete with me." Then, in a rapid change, she rattled off a sentence or two in her native tongue. In the background, Meena Rutledge laughed shrilly. With a twinkle in her large eyes, Bird translated brokenly, mockingly. "In Cree, Mr. Garth, this means 'Injun learn plenty good when get chance. Make plenty good whiteface woman. Make white fort women jealous, too.' "

Nonplussed, Garth was hesitant as to whether he should laugh or apologize, yet the sudden thought struck him, what a bitterly sweet, vivacious young woman. His inner senses tingled. Certainly, he wanted to know her better. "I think you've made your point, Miss Bird," he finally managed. "Yes, you surely have."

"I'm sorry," she said. "I shouldn't be so sarcastic and resentful. Papa says I talk too much, that I sometimes say the wrong things. But I won't stand to be demeaned in any way." She laughed. "I think he means that I'm uninhibited, but it's probably his fault. He sent me to school in Independence, a Methodist school for girls. I always came home for the summers. So, now you know." Her finger touched her nose again and she asked, "Are you passing through, going on to Fort Smith?"

"No, ma'am, I've been assigned here, working with Mistuh Bridger's men. They recruited me to help with the scouting."

"Hmmm, interesting." Her dark eyes widened in understanding. "Ah, then you must be the one they call Reb. Yes, you were a Confederate cavalry officer."

"My reputation always seems to precede me," Garth returned with a smile.

Bird Rutledge hastened to explain. "Oh, no, not at all, I've heard nothing of you, personally, really. No, I saw your horse, the beautiful black, outside the gate this morning. One of the men said some rebel owned it, a captain, and so now it's a simple matter of putting two and two together, your manner of speaking, brogue, is it . . . ? Yes, you and the horse. Obvious, you see."

Garth nodded. "His name is Jefferson in case you want to have a few words with him, sometime. He's a perfect gentleman. Has an affinity for dried apples, carrots when they're available. Do you ride as well as Elbert says you do?"

"Ah," she said knowingly, "then Bert did say a little

about me?" Turning to her mother, she called; "Mama, he asks if I ride well? What do you think?"

Meena answered proudly, "She rides with the wind, Mr. Garth. This is why they call her The Bird. The Sioux know her, all of them. Do you know something special? She rode messages to Horseshoe Station for almost two summers, until the singing wires went up."

Garth's eyes widened in astonishment. He knew Horseshoe Station, had passed it on the way north. Lord a'mighty, it was almost a day's ride from Fort Laramie! Elbert had not mentioned that part of it. The Bird, indeed, an amazing young woman! Bird caught his admiring stare, quite different from the look of surprise she had detected when she first entered the room. Obviously, Bert had told Garth very little about her, especially the fact that she was half Indian. She had sensed that almost immediately, the stupefied look on his face, the brief stammer. She spoke up again, explaining, "Papa wanted me to quit the Horseshoe run. He was afraid when all the trouble started, hostiles." She laughed. "I had several races, and then one of the friendlies at the fort told Papa that one of the Sioux braves had made a vow to catch me, steal my medicine, that sort of thing. . . ."

"Steal your medicine?" Garth asked. "You mean your ability to ride?"

Bird Rutledge winked at him. "Yes, that among other things."

"Oh, oh, yes," stammered Garth.

She went on. "Then, the telegraph came in, and that finished it. Papa was happy. I was crushed, completely and totally crushed. I loved that job. It was fun."

"Well," Garth tried innocently, "that probably wasn't the best job in the world for a woman, your medicine and all. . . ."

"Oh, but Bert didn't like me riding all the time, either," she put in. Her little nose suddenly wrinkled.

"He thinks horses are dangerous. He worries. He is a dear."

"Not very cavalier, that Elbert ... Bert."

"No, not very." She smiled. And then, abruptly: "I would like to ride Jefferson one of these days, maybe try jumping him. Would you mind that?"

"We'll surely see about it, Miss Bird," he said. "I'll keep you posted." His hand found the latch again, and with the other, he positioned his contentious gray hat at a rakish angle. "Good evening, ma'am," he said. The sudden draft through the wedged door wafted the black crow feather down the bridge of his nose, splitting his vision. His usual quick puff bounced it to the side. He said sheepishly, "Yes, my hat, like Elbert said, it's surely a topic for discussion up here." With a sigh and sad smile, he said, "I tell you, no one seems to appreciate the damned thing no matter how I dress it up." And on that discordant note, he left.

Bird's dark eyes were dancing, and she cried out merrily after him, "Oh, but I love it, Mr. Garth, I love it."

Garth turned in the darkness and waved. Strangely warm inside, he trudged away, whistling up a few bars from the Rogue's March.

Chapter Three

By early November, T. B. Garth and his companions were sighting Indians daily, distant parties most often to the north toward Peno Creek where the Fort Smith–Virginia City road crossed. And, dutifully, he alternated with his fellow scouts in galloping back from their patrols to sound an alarm. Usually, it was nothing more than that. By the time a troop was readied for possible engagement, the Indians had invariably disappeared like phantoms over Lodge Trail Ridge. Sometimes the hostiles took other directions, but wherever, it was the same—they vanished. So, by the day, the alarms and diversions continued, and though the tempo quickened, there was seldom a close quarter encounter. Only a few shots were fired, most from long range or ambush. The troopers had their orders—Colonel Carrington was reluctant to have his men drawn too far into the bristling hills by the provocations. Without the reinforcements that he so badly needed, he could not afford the chance of losses that might jeopardize the fort's defense. The nearby sawmill, turning out lumber for another warehouse, was constantly posted with soldiers, and the woodcutters, still taking the brunt of the harassment, went back and forth only under escort. Shots from ambush in the woods were perilous, came unexpectedly, and sometimes were telling.

John Dominguez, who continually read signs, both mysterious and factual, was becoming more apprehensive as the cold November days shortened into winter dress. This was only the prelude, he warned Garth; something imminently more dangerous was in the air, just what he did not know, but ominous signs and the deteriorating weather were dictating it. And the weather had suddenly taken on a new and meaningful significance, for in another month, by the end of December, the entire Big Horn country would be cold white, the trails obliterated by drifting snow. Dominguez nodded toward the dying sun, the frozen horizon, the ice blue valley of naked trees. "You see, it blows cold," he said. "If the Indian makes his move against the *wasichus*, it will have to be soon, my friend. Yes, before the *kissineyooway'o* comes, the cold winter death."

They were walking slowly from the corrals toward the main gate. Garth, struck by a muse finally said thoughtfully, "Dominguez, it now appears the only way the army is ever going to break this stalemate is to carry the campaign, run the hostiles out of these valleys. That means only one thing to me—annihilate them, and you and I both know that's impossible." He kicked his heavy boot against a frozen clod, and surmised farther. "We're in damned holding action, stranded, Dominguez, trapped inside this valley like a passel of mudcats in a backwater slough. It's a miserable task trying to rub out men in their own land, especially when the land holds the blood of their forefathers, and when these same men love the land enough. I can attest to that. They sure as hell aren't going to run out of grub, reinforcements, and places to hide like we did."

"Only time will answer that, my friend," Dominguez said. "Too many Indians, now, not the time, eh? Our friend Red Cloud wants us to come out and visit him, maybe split the garrison. I tell you, he won't try to come in. Why should he, eh?"

Up ahead, the lights of the fort began to flicker, and

to Garth, the security inside was, indeed, warming. John Dominguez was right—why should Red Cloud attack the fort when he already controlled the valleys? And then, entertaining other thoughts less military, he finally dismissed the hostiles. With faint heart, he said, "Oh, hell, maybe they'll ride back to their wintering grounds. It's getting too cold for this nonsense."

"Ho, ho," Dominguez laughed, "these people are already home. No, *amigo,* they'll stay here close. Yes, and one day soon they'll show themselves in big strength, not to fight, but to let us know their land is closed to everyone. This is how they win, maybe shut off our supplies, too."

John Dominguez's portentous predictions were something more than his own personal opinion. It was based partly on observation and frontier intuition. True, no one ever knew the Indian mind, but much like Bridger, the Spaniard always seemed to have a small but significant piece of it. At least a part of that feeling was being shared at the top of the ladder in Colonel Carrington's headquarters. The colonel's observations of the hostiles' growing strength were the same, and he was presently in the throes of making a decision. Traffic down from C. F. Smith had come to a standstill, nothing moving in almost two weeks. Additionally, he had to assume that Red Cloud's Sioux and Dull Knife's Cheyenne had completely closed off the northern section of the route from Fort Smith to the Yellowstone River, the source of supplies upriver by steamers. Carrington's assignment had been to stabilize the area, to make the Bozeman Trail safe for travel, to diminish the threat of the Lakota and Cheyenne nations, yet, instead, his command post had fallen into a virtual state of siege, and the road, both north and south, was unstable. Despite the presence of his new forts, the colonel had gained nothing more than a precarious foothold in the contested land. For the present he was stymied, but some of his younger officers were pressing, pleading for the chance to make one decisive thrust north into the hostile stronghold to clear the trail once and for all. They badly wanted to attack, not defend.

In other Fort Kearny matters less grevious, Bird Rutledge made her beautiful presence known to T. B. Garth. First, she struck an immediate rapport with the big black Jefferson. When Garth was off duty and not riding, she made her appearance in the corral with a tidbit, scratched his ears, and sometimes groomed the horse. She also mounted Jefferson and trotted around the inside of the compound. Within several days, Jefferson had his ears pricked, his nostrils flared, and neighed happily at Bird's approach. This was a love affair.

Likewise, T. B. Garth struck a quick friendship with the Rutledge family. Jack admired the easygoing mannerisms, the conversations of the former Confederate captain. He was appalled at the destruction wrought by the Union soldiers upon Garth's family property, but not surprised. War was a crime in itself.

Meena Rutledge saw Garth through the eyes of a woman. This man was handsome and gracious, yes, but he was engaged in a dangerous quest. Anywhere on the frontier was dangerous. A killer lurked beneath Garth's calm demeanor, a man seeking to destroy another because of traitorous dishonor. Yes, the frontier was bad enough, but this was like seeking out a rattlesnake. It could be a risk to his own life. Meena was intuitive, too. Her daughter not only had acquired a fondness for the beautiful horse, Jefferson; Bird, an engaged young woman, had her eyes on Jefferson's handsome owner. Meena had no idea what would develop or what she could do about it. Watch and wait. She admired Mr. Garth. It would be impolite to discourage his visits.

On the stoop of the little porch dusk was setting in and Garth was visiting. Bird, bundled in her furry coat and winter moccasins, was inquisitive. What did Garth think about her, her Indian blood?

"Elbert never mentioned it," Garth said. "I just assumed . . ."

"I knew you were surprised," Bird said. "Bert's that way. He's nice, not ashamed of me." She smiled. "He's a cautious one, though. Shy. He never courted until I came along. Papa says I have to look for security."

Garth said, "From what I've seen there's very little of it out here. Of course, there wasn't much down in Jackson, either. And I don't see any reason why Elbert . . . Bert should be ashamed of you."

She laughed. "Not my looks, no, not that."

"Blood then?"

"Half-bloods, breeds," Bird said. "Oh, out here it doesn't make that much difference, red, white. This isn't Boston or Philadelphia. Civilization makes a difference, and I learned the difference between color at school. There were others like me. We tried to conform, breeds of a color. We pretended. We all had our eyes on taking some rich merchant or fort trader for a husband. Papa always told me there wasn't much hope otherwise. Bert? I consider myself lucky. I can't do anything more for myself, Papa, or Mama. Marriage is a cause, my cause."

Garth nodded. He understood. "We could all do with a cause, Miss Bird."

"Is that why you came up here? Is this a cause, that man Sturges, your search?"

"God forbid, Miss Bird, I have no cause, not around this fort, not in persecution, not these Indians."

"But you, you're searching."

"Existing. This is a poor world now."

"This man? This traitor, I think you called him. What did he do?"

"Let men die needlessly," Garth replied. "Caused some of my soldiers to lose their lives. It's a very long story."

Bird's eyes widened. "And you still have hopes of catching him, way out here? My gracious, you may get lost yourself!"

Garth smiled wanly. "Now *that* could be a lost cause."

"You gave up on everything else back home?"

"I had to. We made a vow, a bond."

"It sounds like a tragedy."

"Oh, it hasn't been all been bad," Garth said. "I've enjoyed the change, seeing only what I once read or heard about, meeting people like you. I've had my share of the bad times, four years. I'm for change, yes, pleasant change."

Bird Rutledge sighed. "Sometimes it's not so pleasant up here. You'll soon find out."

"I've heard as much, seen little."

"Well, one day you'll be back," Bird said with a determined nod. "You'll take the place of your father, a rich planter, live the good life. Maybe you'll marry someone called Missy, someone you left behind."

Garth chuckled. "Romantic nonsense, the stuff of storybooks."

"I love books, fairy tales," replied Bird. "This is the way the world should be. It should be lived in one's imagination."

"You're a romantic, Miss Bird."

"Oh, I know it can't be. For this much of it, I'm a realist." She gave him a saucy look. "Honestly, you have no secret loves? I don't believe it. Romance?"

Garth chuckled again. "Ages ago. As I told you, I've been on the run. A running man always trying to catch up with the sunset."

Bird wagged a finger at him. "That Sturges is already hiding somewhere in the night. You should stop this running, take some rest, forget your poor world and think about a new one."

"This *is* a new one," Garth replied. "But man alive, I didn't have any idea it was such a cold one."

Bird Rutledge laughed merrily. "I like you, Mr. Garth."

"Yes ma'am, and I like you, Miss Bird."

During mid-November, activity outside the fort mysteriously diminished. Most of the hostiles observed by the scouts were ranging north and east beyond the two main lookouts, Sullivant and Pilot. They rarely came down the main trail bordering Big Piney, limiting most of their harassment to the wood trains coming from the hills west of the fort. Inside the big stockade, builders worked on the new infirmary. Logs were brought in almost daily by the sawyers, their wagons now heavily guarded by troopers.

Garth continued to visit the Rutledge quarters, occasionally accepting an invitation to supper, and afterward playing cards under the flickering lantern suspended over the long plank table. He enjoyed the frugal but homey atmosphere, the blunt woodsman talk of Jack Rutledge, the engaging, intelligent, and frequently provocative conversation of Bird, and the Cree Indian stories of Meena. He preferred all of this to the constant talk of war (or lack of it) in Officer's Row. He seldom made a call there, but several times had chats with Colonel Carrington and his wife, Margaret. Garth sympathized with the colonel, the dilemma confronting him. Wisely, much to the disappointment of his junior officers, he continued to follow the counsel of Jim Bridger. Bridger knew the strength of Red Cloud's army. Carrington still considered his ranks too thin to enter into a campaign against the hostiles. Defending the fort itself was problem enough. He was fearful of getting his garrison decimated, and for this decision, his subordinates secretly called him Old Jelly Spine and Granny Pussy Foot. Garth deplored this, but rather than joust with the junior officers over strategy, he avoided them.

Seeing Bird Rutledge was not a problem. When he

failed to make a call on Jack's one-room cabin, Bird managed to show up at the corral always about the time he was returning from a patrol or duty on one of the lookouts. No one paid much attention to this. After all, Bird was somewhat of a fixture around the barn and stock corrals. Not only did she know more about horses than any trooper on the post, she could outride any one of them. And that she had taken such a liking to Jefferson was understandable. Jefferson was a handsome piece of horseflesh, almost as good as Colonel Carrington's Kentucky jumper. Almost? Better, so a few of the stable hands began to say.

Late one chilly afternoon when the sun was dying, T. B. Garth came riding down the north trail alongside Big Piney. A few Indians had been reported earlier in the day up toward Peno Creek. Several scouts went out to investigate, using the ridges for sighting and cover. Nothing came of it. Bridger sent Garth out later the same afternoon, and he saw nothing either. He was now anxious to get back to the fort for warmth, comfort, and hot coffee.

About a half mile from the fort, he saw a rider coming toward him in a gallop. He knew it wasn't a hostile. Hostiles never used the road near the fort; they always rode in the shadows of the trees and in the creekside brush. When the distance between them closed to thirty yards, the oncoming rider halted in the middle of the trail. A crooked arm came up in greeting, and Garth heard a melodious shout. "Ho there, soldier! What news do you bring?"

Ye Gods, Bird Rutledge! What was she doing riding the trail alone? Grumbling to himself, Garth kicked ahead. She waited, dancing her paint around in a half-circle. Moving up beside her, he admonished her. "Your father would be full of wrath and cabbage, woman, if he knew you were riding this trail alone. What's the meaning of this?"

"I'm not alone," Bird replied smartly. "I'm with the Reb, the great Indian scout from Mississippi. Mississippi! Ha, ha, ha. My gracious! How many Indians are left down there, mistuh?"

"You didn't answer my question," he growled. "There *are* Indians out here. One might grab you, haul you away by the back of your hair."

Bird swung her horse around. "I came out to meet you. Isn't it obvious? I can't think of any other reason. Are there Indians about, really? How many did you see?"

Garth gave her a shrug and confessed, "They're about, all right, but I didn't see them. I'll allow a few saw me." He flicked his crow feather back from his nose. "They never seem to bother me, though. It must be this feather. Either they think I'm one of them or they think I'm crazy. You've been out here most of your life. Did you ever see one of those bucks wearing a crow feather?"

Bird laughed. "No. Crows aren't birds of distinction among my people."

"They don't think much of them back home, either." Garth grinned. "That must be it then. These Sioux don't take me serious, probably think I'm some kind of a clown."

"That's not entirely true," Bird replied. "The Lakota people honor clowns, hold them in high esteem in some of their ceremonies."

"Ah, well, there's your answer. High esteem. Yessuh, that must be it."

Bird said, "I doubt that. But I'll tell you one thing. They have a liking for gray soldiers. They know all about the war. Anyone who fought the bluecoats can't be bad medicine. They consider the gray hats to have big *wochangi*. Brave men."

"*Wochangi?*"

"Medicine."

"My medicine brought you out on the trail?"

Bird laughed again. "I know nothing about your medicine, Mr. Garth. I came to thank you for the nice book you left. Wherever did you get it? I couldn't believe it, Browning! You never mentioned you enjoyed poetry."

"I don't," he answered. "That little book and a volume of Shakespeare have been in my duffel since the shooting back in Saint Joseph. My partner, Brevard Stanton, they were his. I tolerate the great Bard. Browning is beyond me. You're a romantic. I thought you'd enjoy Mistuh Robert. I'll stick to Sir William." He gave her a sidelong stare. "I think the thank you could have waited until I got back to the fort, don't you?"

"I get tired of riding circles in that compound," she said. "I told the men I was going to romp for a hundred yards or so. I just disappeared through the trees. I knew you'd be coming along shortly."

Peowh! A distant shot came from a knoll to their left. The whine of the bullet passed over their heads. "Lord a'mighty!" exclaimed Garth. Leaping clear of his horse, he grabbed Bird and threw her ahead of him in the trailside brush and rock. "Get down, dammit! That's a sniper, a one-shot rascal, but those buggers know how to reload in a hurry."

Bird peered through a clump of sage. "Where is he? Can you see any smoke?"

"Not a lick of smoke, Miss Bird. He must be in one of those gullies, sneaked in on foot, probably up the creek bottom, otherwise those boys on Sullivant could have spotted him."

"Where's your rifle?"

"Oh law, woman, up on Jefferson, where do you think?"

Bird Rutledge giggled.

"Look here, now," huffed Garth, "when someone starts sniping the first thing you do is duck for cover.

Besides, who knows? There might be another one up there with him."

"Well, you can't hit anything from here with your pistol."

T. B. Garth sighed. "I know that! But if someone comes across that creek I'll put a hole between his eyes."

"I think I bruised my bottom."

"Damn lucky, I'd say. If that scamp had been any sort of marksman at all, it could be worse." Garth glowered at her. "Now how in the hell could I explain something like that to your folks? 'She just came out to thank me for some poetry and one of those red devils shot her.' Law, law."

Bird's shoulders shook in laughter. She beat her hand on the ground. She mimicked, "Law, law, Mistuh Garth, you are a caution."

"I thought you said those bucks respected my gray hat, my *wochangi*."

Bird imeptuously leaned over and kissed him.

Taken aback, Garth exclaimed, "Damnation, now what was that for? Some fool out there is leveling down on us and you come up and give me a peck!"

"He's gone." With that she threw her arms around him and kissed him again.

Garth reciprocated, then groaned. "The world has gone mad, woman. There has to be a better place to romance than these sticks and rocks."

"There is," she whispered. "Let's go back and see if we can find it."

Chapter Four

In an attempt to alleviate the discontent among his officers, Colonel Henry Carrington made a decision. At a duty meeting, he asked for two volunteers from the scouts to make reconnaissance to determine the exact location of the hostile war camp. Not only did he want to know the distance of the village from Fort Kearny, he wanted to know how many warriors Red Cloud had assembled. There was one important reservation. Colonel Carrington would mount no attack unless he received his requested reinforcements from Fort Laramie. Another point. Only information on the location and size of the war camp would determine if a campaign were practical. His foremost concerns were still the safety of the garrison and protection of the fort.

Now, who among the scouts would undertake this hazardous mission? For a moment the request, expectedly, stimulated nothing more than a quiet shuffling of heavy boots and several grunts of apprehension. Infiltrating Indian villages in the winter was not an appealing thought to any of these men, most of them veterans who knew what the task entailed, moreover the consequences of getting caught.

Yet to John Dominguez it seemed no more dangerous than riding point ahead of a wood train. After all, from the hills, the fringes of evergreens and aspen, a man could always see his way, and if need be, safely ride in the cover of night. He knew the hills and the prairie. He had escaped conflict more than once using his mountain man knowledge. He volunteered.

Garth, happy in his own comfortable circumstances, including one newly found joy, was reluctant to put his boot forward. The security of the big fort had become very rewarding to him. There was comfort in his small room—comfort, pleasure, and safety. However, an unexpected circumstance of the moment suddenly dictated otherwise. Nearby, Sergeant Tatum's ruddy face, radiating its usual contempt, seemed to be cornering in Garth's eyes. Garth instinctively knew without so much as returning a stare, that he was under scrutiny and challenge again. Who were the real men here? Tatum, the rascal, was nudging a few of his friends and pointing his chin toward Garth. And there was Dominguez standing there, too, a sly wink, as if to say the mission was nothing more than a Sunday canter around the stockade perimeter.

Garth, bravado scratching his pride, stirred uneasily inside, then reluctantly moved. He muttered to himself, "Oh, law, what do I have to lose." With nonchalance, he stepped forward and said loudly, "I'll ride with Dominguez." Inside, his enthusiasm rattled and groaned down to the very base of his bowels.

The belly of the small stove glowed like a ripe cherry, and a fresh pail of water atop it had begun to throw off a few threads of steam. Nearby rested an empty tin tub draped with a wet towel, at its base were winter Sioux moccasins delicately beaded at the high tops. Imprints, the barest trace of toes, were fading from the pine flooring. From the small oval mirror where he stood shaving, Garth caught her look of concern. The Bird, her long legs crossed in the fashion of an Indian, was quietly observing his bare back from the bunk. She had tucked the corners of the woolen blanket up around her neck, holding them with one hand, the other cupped under her chin, a finger pressed to pursed lips. It wasn't her presence in his bed that worried her all that much; this was the third time she had been here; she had no inhibitions about this. It was his scouting mission with John Dominguez that had set her to fretting, and she frankly told her new lover that he had made a damn foolish choice.

Garth regretfully agreed. One more look at the small bundle of beauty completely convinced him. As he had surmised from the very beginning, she was too much of a woman for Elbert Craig. She was a lovely cinnamon savage, not even her white schooling belied that. No wonder the fort women envied her. So, for a moment, they visually traded fondness, too much alike to deny themselves, Bird, young, eager, was beset by anxieties and her desire to share love with this man of her own choosing, one that she had admired from the very first moment she had met him. For Garth, now lovestruck but unable to admit it, the desirous spark had been instantaneous, too, and the consequences passionately pleasing. Their only problem now was secrecy.

This night was a stroke of luck, the weekly social at the commissary, the card games, the regimental band, the fiddling, the dancing. Bird declined to attend, and once her parents left, she fled to Garth's room, only to find it vacant, cold. Such precious time wasted. She felt like crying. She rekindled the fire, heated water, bathed, and wrapped only in a blanket, surprised him when he returned. Excitedly, she announced they were going to have three wonderful hours together. Like the gallant he was, Garth first kissed her. They shared a tin cup of coffee and talked while he washed and shaved.

For T. B. Garth, admittedly his new affair was a loving windfall, and after the initial shock that romance had struck, his honor crumbled like stale corn bread. He was as skeptical about love as he was life, but, just as Bird Rutledge, he wanted to live and he wanted to race. Scruples became extinct. What misgivings he had about Elbert Craig were hopelessly left at the post. Their clandestine relationship breathed, was new, the present, now. They enjoyed each other, seldom dwelled on the future, only on the consequences of disclosure. Regrets? Almost none, except this night—his decision to go scouting with Dominguez. Garth, of course realized he had stubbed his toe. But Bird? She was upset.

Staring into his bare back, she said, "Do you realize you can get yourself lost out there, or even worse? You may not even come back. What kind of pride is that?"

Garth, making several finishing strokes with the razor, said, "Pride?" Sighing, he added dryly, "Pure foolishness, my bugaboo, that's what it is, but the way those Yankee rascals were staring and grinning like possums, testing my mettle, well . . ."

"It's that damned Tatum," she cursed. "You don't see him volunteering for anything. You didn't have to do it, not to spite that big jackass."

"It's not his job," Garth explained. "This isn't any routine patrol. Besides, I'll be back in three or four days. Don't fret. Why, I'll be on old John's tail like a hound dog." He came to the bed and looked down at her. "I declare, I think you're worried more about this trip than someone coming through that door and finding you naked as a jaybird."

Unconsciously, she glanced at the latch. Laughing, she threw her arms around him, and the blanket dropped away baring her bosom, the nubbins protruding like two golden sand dabs resplendent with rosy caps. "You know better," she said softly. "I'm over the fright, but I do worry about all of this." The fuzzy, dim lamplight, the hazy shadows, cast her face in a soft patina. "Have you thought what's to be done? You know, about us? If someone does find out?"

Yes, Garth had dwelled on it, the risk, and Lord a'mighty, the consequences he knew not. He was just as pleasantly and hopelessly confused about what was happening as she was. Enveloped by amorous sensations of the moment, neither had discussed eventualities, not even a word about Elbert, obviously her sole key to security, a good home, a dutiful husband. Garth held her affectionately and said lamely, "Damned if I know what we'll do. We can't keep carrying on this way."

Bird said, "I should feel guilty about it, but I don't. I can't deceive myself, no more than I can deceive you."

"Me . . . ? Deceive me?"

"The first time," she whispered. "You knew I wasn't a virgin. You knew it, didn't you?"

"That scamp Elbert?"

"Gracious, no! We've seldom had a minute together alone."

"It doesn't matter."

"Yes, it does," retorted Bird. "I don't want you to think I'm a beast. I have to tell you. I must."

"Ah, bugaboo, a confession of love."

"It wasn't love. It was . . . experimenting."

Garth chuckled. "I declare, I never heard it called experimenting."

"At school, the church school, if you can believe it. The head pastor's son. Yes, several times, of all places, in a feed bin."

"A pastor's son, a man of the cloth!"

"He felt so guilty he wanted to pay me. Can you imagine? That ended it. Anyhow, I headed back home shortly after that little episode. I suppose it didn't really matter, but during the last couple of years in that place, I learned a lot more than what was in the history and reading books."

"I suppose a school like that was a lonely place for most of you, Indian girls, breeds, as you say, away from home, the villages, whatever."

"I told you," she said, "some of us studied. We learned, too, among other things, it wasn't the best place to fetch a white man, someone interested in marriage." She sighed. "They taught us to be proper, particularly in the customs of the household. They thought we could be nothing better in life but domestics, servants. I hated that. When I left I could compose better than the English teacher. Most of the girls never wanted to be in that school in the first place."

"You express yourself very well," Garth said with a smile.

"Yes, but I must be crazy," she replied. "I wonder? All of the big dreams I've had. And now this. Is it really possible I love you, really love you, or is it this, the way you make me feel, stealing my medicine? It's all so dangerous, isn't it? Maybe this is it, dangerous but good."

"Second thoughts?" Garth asked, sighing inside yet not daring to admit that he, too, was laboring with a muddled, thoroughly confused mind. And stealing her medicine! Oh, law!

"I don't want to think about it. Mama says everything always turns out for the best. Mama is a practical woman."

"Lord, Lord, I hope that woman is right."

"She is."

"Is that so?"

"Yes, this already is the best, isn't it? I love it. No more talk, please."

"I wasn't talking."

"Shush!"

Chapter Five

Shortly after dawn's first golden streaks, John Dominguez and T. B. Garth headed out, rode down through the gaunt cottonwoods lining Big Piney, and casually turned southeast, away from the valley. Subterfuge, explained Dominguez, who distrusted the far-ranging eyes of the Sioux scouts, for they knew the horizon, too, and lived by it. Eventually, when Dominguez thought it safe, he and Garth would turn north and in due time cross over Clear Creek and make a wide circuit into the rolling foothills. Somewhere in that broad range of valleys and broken coulees, the Spaniard expected to find and survey the main war village of the Sioux and Cheyenne. If anyone were to find the red army, it would be Juan José Dominguez.

Garth listlessly followed, his old feathered cavalry hat close against the rising sun. For some time he had been trying to persuade himself that this really was an honorable mission, one of great responsibility and necessity, a commendable chore, that he should feel that old familiar tingle of excitement. He did not. He felt foolishly numb, and he silently cursed the vanity that had sent him riding away from the fort's loving comfort and security into the cold, inhospitable world of the Teton. Actually, his mind was fluctuating like the thermometer, up and down, dwelling on an Indian of another breed, the one he had recently left behind. Indians, in general, were making a muddle of his already mangled life. He vainly tried to concentrate on the business at hand, his present threat, hostiles, but became only more aware that a lovely, doe-eyed creature back at the fort posed a danger almost as fatal. Passion's fateful nibbling, discretion on the wing. That must be it. Yet, even to be involved (or was it in love) with an engaged woman, half savage, no less, truly bewildered him. True, it was a volatile situation, but he now detected something more than passion behind the misty camouflage of delight. And he knew that forbidden fruit always had its inherent dangers. He saw at least two dangers staring at him like twin bogeymen. Romance was killing discretion, for both him and Bird, and that meant that their veil of secrecy was wearing dangerously thin. The thought of getting caught in such an illicit game unsettled him. And the second danger was Bird herself. She had changed, and in turn, had changed him. Once, in a moment of pleasure, she had professed that he had no obligations, and that had sounded good enough for what had begun as an affair of the evening. Afternoon? Oh, law, for that matter, anytime. But for some strange reason, he did feel obligated. Rogue that he was, or pretended to be, she had thoroughly implanted herself into his thoughts. She was becoming a part of his fitful life. Her sudden talk of love left him in another quandary. Love? By jingo, he thought, to what avail? Or was love merely an integral word to be used in justifying the act in itself? He tried to brush it off. Only a discontented woman's desire, he rationalized, and a man in need of "love," his conscience hiding between his thighs. Oh, the marvel of it, though! How else resolved? Had not he heard somewhere, "what's good only deserves repeating?" This "good" had been a good beginning. But, no end? No, he reasoned, if this young woman, indeed, were in love with him, somehow he must face up to the situation more honorably. Her well-being must be paramount. And, he said to himself, if by some quirk I really do love this pretty creature, I should not love her. I have no business or right to love her. I must admit to infatuation, and somehow, be done with it, for her sake, of course. But where does infatuation end and love begin? Garth wondered, a puzzlement, and mumbled aloud, "Lord a'mighty, what have I got myself into?"

A somewhat startled John Dominguez turned in his saddle. "What is it? What?"

Garth, embarrassed at his outcry, stammered, "Why . . . why, nothing. I must have been thinking aloud."

"Talking to yourself, eh?" The Spaniard tutted and gave Garth an inquisitive stare. "You haven't been out here long enough to start talking to yourself, so I think it's something." He chuckled and went on. "Ah, but maybe I understand, *amigo*. This is a lonely country. Alone, a man thinks too much. It's not good to be alone too much. You say, no, Dominguez, you are a hard man, a man who has seen this great land many times. You've seen too much of life to get lonely. You are too hard to cry. Ah, but do you know that the soul of a man cries? Do you know that? And if a man does not talk to himself, sometimes he goes *loco*. You might think this is funny, eh, but when I get lonely, I talk to my horse, Tony, here. Maybe that's not so strange. He listens good, but sometimes it's bad. Ah, the questions a man asks himself. I say, '*¿Antonio, como te parece?*' Yes, and what do you think? Ah, the horse is like the man—he cannot answer the questions, either."

Garth, as usual, listened to the quaint philosophy of his friend, strangely a man who seemed to be free of personal problems, his only professed worry that sometime his pony might go lame out in the middle of the prairie. Garth managed a grin. "Well, I'll allow there's a reason that horse doesn't answer you. Maybe old Tony only speaks English. You ever consider that?"

Turning back with a sad smile, Dominguez answered, "For a troubled man, you make bad jokes."

So they rode on, and it was a lonely, barren land in

the winter, interspersed with a few high points from which they could reach out for a mile or so with their field glasses. Like most frontier scouts, Dominguez put his faith in the higher ridges where the trails always seemed to be the worst, and consequently, the safest. They kept to the high country, their horses moving in a steady walk. Several hours north, they spotted a movement and focused in on their first Indians, a sizeable party, probably thirty, riding at a trot in the direction of Fort Kearny. The group was more than a mile away, coming up a distant rise from the Clear Creek fork of the Powder. After Dominguez took a careful look, he identified them as Sioux. No surprise, there. However, when the two men had crawled back over the brow of the hill to their horses, he paused and rubbed his chin doubtfully.

Thoughtfully, Dominguez said, "This is not so good, my friend. I think we are too close." He pointed to the east. "We should be over there farther, eh? You see, those Indians are coming from in front of us. If we stay on this side too much, maybe we ride right into more scouts in the hills. Not so good, eh? If they see us first, two or three shots, swoosh, and we get it. What do you think?"

Garth cocked a wary eye at his friend. "By jingo, I think you should think of something more cheerful for a change, that's what I think. If those boys are coming this way, let's move out of here."

Dominguez shrugged fatefully. "But life, that's the way it is. Swoosh, swoosh! I think we only live for one supreme moment. Yes, that's the way it is."

Garth replied testily, "Look here, Dominguez, that's your opinion, not mine. If you think we should be riding on the other side, well, let's move our butts over across the Powder. Another ten minutes or so and those hostiles will be close enough to chat with. I didn't come up here for any of this 'swoosh, swoosh' business. Fact is, I'll be damned if I know why I ever agreed to this nonsense in the first place. I should have kept my mouth shut and stayed back at the fort."

"Ah, but you didn't," the Spaniard returned with a yellowed grin. "You only see yourself in the mirror."

"What's that supposed to mean?"

John Dominguez confidently thumped his chest once. "Sometimes, you must look inside, eh? Sometimes another man is there, not the reflection you see in the mirror. Hey, I think you only try to fool yourself." Motioning to the distant hills to the right, he said, "*Está bien,* we move out of the way, one hour's ride, maybe two, then we cut back for another look."

"I concur," Garth immediately said. "If it isn't safe up in this valley, let's clean country."

Grinning at Garth, Dominguez said, "But *hombre,* I can't say how it is over there, either. Maybe no different. This is all their land, you know, anywhere we look."

"Yes, I know," growled Garth, his patience thinning. "That's why I keep trying to convince myself that I have no business trespassing. I don't have a damned thing against these scoundrels, and sometimes I get the notion you don't have a care in the world. Here today, gone tomorrow, so what the hell does it matter, that sort of thing. By jingo, Dominguez, you amaze me. Sometimes, you scare the hell out me, too."

"That's good, *amigo,*" he returned. "You pay attention, eh, you learn. Yes, this is good." With a sweep of his hand, he kicked away, Garth right behind him, as he had promised Bird, on John Dominguez's tail like a blue-tick heeler. They galloped across the broken ground, eyes to four sides, and slowed only when they came to the cover of a draw. The slope was gentle, the climb easy to a bald summit. Once on top, Dominguez stopped to take another bearing before moving north by northwest. Darkness finally caught them in the grassy foothills and they had to halt for the night.

The makeshift camp was cold, fireless out of necessity, their supper, rations of biscuits, corned beef, and dried fruits. Tired from the long day, they bedded down in a protective shallow banked with rosebushes. Garth felt safe enough, but staring into the dark infinity of space, he could not help but reflect on the comfort and warm companionship of recent nights. Yes, The Bird was back again, like an elfin sprite, cavorting in the canyons of his troubled mind. John Dominguez had expressed it well, simply, too: this was a lonely land. Drifting, reaching for Bird, grasping at slumber, he heard wolves howling from a distant plateau. Strange, up here, such a big land, yet no place to run, no place to hide, not from reality. He wondered if his old enemy, Henry Sturges, was also finding it this way.

In the bitterness of a wintry, cold prairie daybreak, the western sun is only a delusory fraud. One does not loiter. There is no warmth under a stark, lowering moon and the cold cry of dawn. They had no fire, no coffee to cut their chill, no alternative but to move ahead, and they did so for comfort. Hours later, near the main Powder Valley, John Dominguez stopped beside a rocky defile and glanced curiously at Garth. They stared at each other, listening, their breath bristling spurts of vapor in the cool air. And then it came again, distant barking. Dogs. And that meant only one thing—a camp. The two scouts, without exchanging a word, dismounted and scrambled to the niche above to investigate. The scene far below them at the floor of the valley was staggering and totally unexpected. It so startled them that after one quick look, they hunched down breathlessly against the cold rocks as though they were exhausted. Beyond them, along the misty banks of the river almost a mile away, was a huge war camp, vibrant with late afternoon activity. Garth and Dominguez, in their roundabout circuit to the left had come in behind the Indians, forty miles north of Kearny. It was sheer accident. And the sight was breathtaking, an endless camp where smoke from a thousand tipis curled upward against the dusky blue horizon.

"Ay, Dios mío," whispered Dominguez, crossing himself. He fumbled for his binoculars. "This is it! We've ridden right into the middle of the whole Lakota nation. No one will believe this! Look at it, the size of that village! That, my friend is a main supply camp for war, the biggest I've ever seen. Now, my friend, how would you like to take a few hundred troopers into this place, eh?"

Garth cautiously peeked over the rim again, and even staring at the incredible sight, he thought surely his eyes must be playing tricks. He choked inside. The edge of the plain was blanketed with painted lodges and small wickiups in what appeared to be a series of gigantic semicircles covering an area almost a mile in length. To the north, he saw horses by the thousands, grazing all along the foothills, all the way down to the river. He slumped back down, feeling a huge knot in his stomach. "I don't believe it, either," he whispered hoarsely. "Lord a'mighty, if we'd cut over below here a few miles, why, we would have . . ." His voice trailed off, and he let out a wheeze.

"Sí, amigo," Dominguez said dourly, "we might be staked out in one of those lodges." He chuckled and gave Garth a nudge. "Gone today instead of tomorrow, eh?"

"I don't want to think about it," Garth hissed. "Tell me, what the hell do we do, now? You're the guiding light. How do we get out of this hornet's nest before some lookout spots us? Do we retreat, beat it to the rear a few miles? You realize, we only have a little daylight left."

Dominguez, apparently in no hurry to answer Garth's frantic deluge, was focusing in, talking under his field glasses. "I didn't realize we were this close. I see Cheyenne and Arapaho markings on some of the those lodges, too. More than Sioux, eh? Everyone is gathering here. This, I can't understand. This village must be for battle and winter, both. Probably good hunting north and to the west of this place, plenty of meat. These people are ready for a long campaign. Yes, this is only a stroke of luck that we find them camped here along the Powder. Ah, but you see, when the winds come, these little hills on the southwest side will still have plenty of grass, eh, the bottoms protected, too. Yes, this is a stroke of luck."

Garth's brow jumped in alarm. "A stroke of luck! Oh, law, that's a queer appraisal. Luck, indeed! Look here, man, if you find us a safe way out of here, why, when I get back I'll tell Mistuh Carrington this was a stroke of military genius, like you knew where these bucks were all the time. Yessuh, you tracked and smelled your way right into them. Now, which way do we go, north or east?"

Dominguez grinned widely and gave Garth a sly wink. He chuckled, and fished out a piece of jerky from his jacket pocket. After taking a big bite, he positioned the meat to the side of his mouth to soften it, then said, "I have a better idea. Yes, it would be my honor to tell such a story to make you a hero. It was you who discovered this war village, the great house of Red Cloud and Dull Knife. Think of it, my friend, just how pleased it will make the fat one, Tatum. This is why you came, no? You want to fry some more fat, make the big one melt into a tiny grease spot."

Uttering a forlorn wheeze, Garth replied, "If I could ride into that fort now, I declare, I'd kiss that big bucket of lard's ass. Let's go."

After another minute of observation, Dominguez collapsed against the back of the shelf. He looked triumphantly at his companion and held up two fingers. "I will say there are over two thousand warriors here." Abruptly, he stopped, motioning to Garth's coat. "You write some of this down, eh? Make some scratches.

Make a little map." Chewing for a moment, he waited until Garth grudgingly produced a small notepad and graphite. "Two thousand braves, eh? The creek coming in over there, it must be Brushy Creek. There is no doubt this is headquarters for Red Cloud, but he has many friends with him, more than the Oglala and Hunkpapa alone. You say this—you saw Cheyenne, Arapaho, Miniconjou markings, maybe a few Brule, too. Now, you sketch their positions, marking the river and the creek, and how everything is placed below the foothills. You see, *amigo,* these Indians are smart like I told you many times, eh? There is only one line of cover if you want to attack this place without being seen too good, the trees there across the river. Ah, but this is risky, too. To bring the *soldados* across the water, maybe that's not so good, either. You see, in the trees more Indios are camped. Ho, ho, impossible, too many here, too few of us." Dominguez stopped his appraisal to swallow. Then, he grinned again. "Yes, and don't forget to mention the dogs barking. Plenty of dogs down there, and women all around searching for squaw wood and chips."

Garth's mouth dropped below his frazzled moustache, and he gave Dominguez a puzzled stare. "Now, you know I don't know about all those marks on the tipis. Hell's bells, I can't tell one of those red rascals from another. You expect those fellows back at Kearny to believe this?"

John Dominguez casually brushed off his question and cased his binoculars. "Have I taught you nothing, my friend? Have our days together been a waste of time?"

"You're teaching me to lie, that's what," Garth answered indignantly. Then, thoughtfully: "Well, I suppose I could say I told you about the tipis, how they looked, the marks and colors . . ."

"Ah, you see, you learn fast." Sighing, he began to edge away, talking over his shoulder. "You know, you're right, Señor Garth. It is a good thing we didn't cross and follow the river down. We would have never gotten this far, swoosh! Ah, but that way back, up the river on the opposite bank, only a night's ride to the fort, a good shortcut, eh?"

Garth paused to plunk his crow feather to the side. "Yes, too damned bad we can't take the valley trail back."

Dominguez suddenly stopped and held up one finger knowingly. "Ah, ha!" he exclaimed. "But why not? No, it's not impossible that way, not at all."

"You're crazy. Not up that valley, not me. To hell with it. Let's go back the way we came, even if it takes two days. At least we'll stand a chance of getting there without getting shot or catching an arrow in the back."

Dominguez turned in the path, his eyes narrowing into two fine slits. He grasped Garth's arm and whispered anxiously, "But I have it! Don't you know? Look, my friend, who can stop us in the dark? What do you think? We go tonight, back up the river, stay in the trees. Only thirty or forty miles. Yes, we give the horses their heads, let them guide us, watch the moon, listen for the river. Tomorrow, we'll be back home."

Frowning, Garth asked, "And in the meantime, today?" He made a sweeping gesture. "Just where do you suggest we hide in this neighborhood? You think we can turn into a couple of groundhogs? And what about the horses? And by the way, where in the hell are the lookouts for this camp?"

"But it is nothing," Dominguez said. "No lookouts needed, my friend. Who would go down there, eh? No, we'll go back to the rocks, hide like wolves. What else? Who will see us. Come on, *vámanos ahora,* no time left." Without waiting for another protest from his companion, he took off in a running crouch for the horses. And true to what Garth had told Bird, for the second time he was on the Spaniard's tail like a hound dog. He had no other choice.

Using the broken gullies for cover, the two men re-treated another two miles to the east until they found refuge in a small cirque, where they hid in the boulders and took turns trying to sleep. It was a long, anxious evening of waiting, listening, and watching. About two hours after dusk, they retraced their original route back to the rocky lookout niche. At this point, Dominguez thought it best to lead the horses, at least until they safely cleared the upper end of the camp perimeter. Dismounting, the two men carefully threaded their way down to the valley floor, and making a wide half-circle, they finally came out about three miles south of the village. Under black skies with a half-moon, they started moving upriver, weaving in between the big trunks of the cottonwoods.

Dominguez was a man of frontier talent and not prone to mistakes. He knew the tragedy of error in hostile country, but he wasn't infallible. His only mistake this blustery night was in fording the Powder River to its right bank, the safest side, he reasoned, since the encampment was downriver on the opposite shore. He, no more than Garth, expected a nighttime confrontation in the brushy river bottom. Yet it happened with only the barest thread of a warning, the whinny of an approaching horse, and then, coming out of a small grove of trees into the moonlight, the two men rode directly into a returning party of hostiles. In the dark, neither Dominguez nor Garth was prepared for such an emergency. The meeting was so sudden that their rifles were still tucked in their scabbards. The Indians, equally taken by surprise, also were momentarily confused when the two yelling *wasichus* strangely took off in opposite directions, one pounding away madly through the covered bottoms, the other galloping back toward the river.

It was T. B. Garth, who in the confusion had made a dash for the river, and within seconds he realized that he was riding alone. Dominguez, his frontier salvation, was not with him. It was too late to change course, and two shots behind him dispelled any thought of it. Hugging the neck of Jefferson, he plunged into the river's icy water, luckily hit a shallow riffle and his big black made it to the other side in six great leaps. Only then did he hazard another glance backward, but one look was quite enough. He saw fearful black shadows of riders loping along the opposite bank, trying to pick up his tracks among the rocks and sand. One more look over his shoulder and he saw two ponies thrashing in the water; the Indians were onto him, and for a moment, he thought it was going to be a race to the foothills. But by the time Jefferson's tremendous strides were coursing the first knolls, the Indians were mere specks on the snowy flat below. It had been a poor race, luckily for T. B. Garth. He finally stopped deep in the hills to rest the horse. At this stage, leaving nothing to chance, he continued at a walk, moving over to the grassy south slopes that were free of snow. He felt somewhat better, for the few tracks he was now leaving behind would be almost impossible to find in the night if the hostiles decided to try it.

Of course, in the anxiety of flight, fear had been only a mere nibble; fear only sets its teeth after the reflective pause, that sort of fear which should be called caution, that sixth sense which motivates men of discretion, men with a desire to live. And it was only after he had eluded his pursuers, when he stopped to take an accounting, that fright really began to attack. Several things immediately struck home: first and foremost, he was lost in the hills; then, in succession, Indians were near, it was very dark, a frigid hint of snow was in the air behind the stiff breeze, and, John Dominguez was gone. Perhaps his friend was even dead, if those distant shots, indeed, had been the "supreme moment." Garth couldn't help but shudder, fearful of everything that now stood in the way of his own return. He only knew that he had to keep moving, and he had no choice but to trust his horse. He was absolutely without bearing. Flanking Jefferson gently, Garth said, "Home, boy, home." The horse moved out, his tail to the threatening wind.

Behind the wind, came the snow, and it started to blow in sheets, forcing Garth into the only cover he could find, a small shelf of rock, an ancient burrow of a badger, or perhaps a fox or coyote. Fighting the cold, he frantically gouged at the crusted dirt, pulled away rock, bones, and debris, enlarging the opening. The wind continued to whip at him as he jerked at the straps holding his hot roll, and his fingers became numb. Wedging himself under the outcropping, he managed to survive the night in a dreadful doze with the fear of freezing. When morning came, he rolled stiffly out into six inches of fresh snow. Flakes were still in the air but, fortunately, the wind had ebbed. Silently, he gave thanks. Lord a'mighty, he was alive, and there was good old Jefferson, coal black, standing nearby, munching the last blades of grass in his white perimeter. Then, Garth searched the heavens for the faint light of the sun. It was nonexistent, and so was an accurate measure of direction. He stared around at the singular identity of the broad land, every hill, every valley, all hopelessly the same, all white, some shrouded in the thin mists of the waning snow. Only the tracks of a few jackrabbits were visible in the nearby sage. Yes, he was lost.

Chewing dried rations, Garth gave Jefferson the lead again, hoping for the best, offering up another silent prayer that his horse would take him in the proper direction. He guessed that he was riding generally in a southerly direction, and he based that assumption on the northwesterly wind of the night storm, the same wind that was now barely alive, just an occasional touch at his backside. After topping three rises, at a high point Garth looked behind, taking measure of his trail in the snow; it was almost a straight set of tracks, and this gave him hope—his horse wasn't wandering aimlessly. Hours went by. Garth stopped once to rest and let Jefferson feed. Bringing his binoculars into play, he hopefully scanned the white country ahead, but visibility was poor, and he saw nothing he could identify. Still another rise, and once again he paused. It was then that his faint heart suddenly filled with joy, the familiar stand of timber, the peculiar way it curled along the bottomland. Law, law, Jefferson had led him to Clear Creek, a tributary of the Powder River!

Now, it was almost dusk. Garth was coming in the same way that he and Dominguez had left, up Big Piney Creek. Off in the distance, he heard the warning signal of a bugle from Pilot Knob, an army sound, but it brought a smile to his cracked lips. "Lord a'mighty," he whispered down into Jefferson's ear, "we've made, it old boy, we've made it." When he rode through the main gate, a yell went up from some of the men gathered there. He heard someone shout his name, someone calling "Reb," and it sounded good. And then Garth discovered that John Dominguez, after a chilling ride in the blizzard, had made it back earlier that day. The Spaniard was there, too, standing with Gabe Bridger by headquarters, and others were running forward to greet Garth.

Smiling, waving, Dominguez called out, "*Bueno,* my friend, I told them you were too smart for those Indians. I told them."

Garth sidled up next to his friend, grinning, trying to hide his joyous relief. Smart? Lord a'mighty, what could he say? How could he ever explain his ordeal, that he had made it back alive? That it was an accident, like most of his recent life? That most of it had been pure horse sense? Finally, with some affected bravado, he finally muttered, "Yessuh, had a few of those hostiles on my tail most of the way. Couldn't make it any sooner." Leaning forward, he fondly patted Jefferson on the neck. The crow feather suddenly dangled again, scraped Garth's nose, and he flipped it back into place. When he dismounted, he saw Bird Rutledge standing nearby, thought he detected two large tears streaming down her cheeks. He gulped once. No doubt though about what had passed her lips. He heard it, barely, hoped no one else had.

"You crazy fool, oh, I love you!"

He knew he was home.

Chapter Six

"Colonel Carrington owns a handsome Kentucky jumper," Bird said in affected innocence. "I suppose you've seen the horse, though. Good lines, but I don't think he matches up to Jefferson."

Garth, in bed, was staring at the log ceiling, listening to the small crackling of the fire, and trying to interpret her rambling conversation as well. Fresh from his escapade north, he had begged a free day, had spent most of it sleeping until she unexpectedly came calling. She busied herself like a biddy hen, quickly fed the dying embers and put coffee on for him. She had only ten minutes or so to spare. In one way, selfishly, the brevity of her visit disturbed Garth. But, then again, perhaps not, for it was the middle of the afternoon, a poor time to be conniving, a better time to get caught at it. In a half yawn, he said, "Your mother is going to have a fit one of these days. Just where are you supposed to be?"

Bird swirled around, her eyes rolling. "Oh, but you don't mind me coming, do you . . . ? Playing servant for a real gentleman. Didn't you used to have hired help, one of those little black girls? Did you ride her like you do me? Hmmm, come on now, the truth."

"Nonsense!"

And she went on, teasingly. "Oh, I can just see it all. You, the poor little rich boy all alone on that big plantation. Pappy planted the cotton, and you . . ."

"You're a provocative wench," he cut in. "And I

wasn't alone. I have a brother, you know. We worked like everyone else."

"Provocative? Oh, now, come on, I just thought you'd like some attention after all you've been through."

"In the middle of the day?"

"Mama's busy if you must know. I only have a few minutes. I'm supposed to be down at the corrals. No one saw me, Mistuh Hero, if that's what you're thinking." She giggled and turned back to the coffee. "Oh, my love, you worry too much. Honestly, it's not good to worry. I don't want you to turn into an old man overnight. That's how Papa got all the lines in his face ... worry, worry. It's true."

"Worrying about you, I'll allow."

Reaching over, she tugged impatiently at him. "Besides, it's time to get up." Garth swung his legs from the bunk and she promptly sat in his lap, kissed him several times, and rubbed the bristle on his chin. "You need a shave."

"I need you."

"Tut, tut! I can't stay that long. No time to play now. Later tonight, but not right now. I do have to hurry. Coffee, all right?"

"Ah, sweet, you disappoint me," Garth lamented. "I was so cold up there I thought I was turning to ice. My butt froze in the saddle. I slept in a damned gopher hole. Why, a couple of times, I thought I was never going to see this old bunk again, that the hostiles had my hair, for sure. By jingo, I sure don't get much sympathy from you, bugaboo."

"But I told you, didn't I?" she said in sweet revenge. "It's your own fault. The big volunteer. Anything to show your colors. Oh, you men! Honestly, I do believe!" Bird gave him a final kiss, jumped up and began stirring the grounds.

Grinning, he stretched, his eyes wandering to her posterior, something he knew he would appreciate more than coffee, yet right now that was all he had to complain about, her diminishing generosity. He was back; he was alive; the coffee, why bother? His dark eyes materialized into two sad discs, and he said, "Are you sure . . . ?" Yes, she was sure, and subdued like a mongrel denied, he quietly slipped into his trousers just as she suggested. Some promise on the evening horizon, though. Reluctantly, Garth took the tin cup she had been waving in front of his nose. He thanked her, then asked belatedly, "This horse, the one the colonel owns, yes, I've seen it. So, what about it?"

"Oh, yes," she said. "Yes, the horse, I almost forgot."

"I'll bet you did." He eyed her, the anxious, devious filly, her veil of pretense, no look of innocence about this woman. Bold beauty, yes, of a fetching, primitive sort, like a small, wild animal, one with a bite. "Oh, yes, the horse," he mimicked. "Come on, you're up to something. What the hell is it?"

"But, my love, have you seen him run?"

Watching her pour, he replied, "Yes, I've seen the horse, that's about all. I've seen the old man sitting him a couple of times. Arabian blood, I believe. Why?"

Bird put the pot aside and sat on the bunk, her legs crossed, her chin cupped saucily between her hands. She looked elfin, invitingly so, wisps of hair curled, bent to her huge eyes, eyes that suddenly adored him. She said, "I do love you. You know that, don't you? I dream of you in poetry, not always passion. This means I must love you. How can I say it . . . ?"

"It makes me happy to hear you try."

After another moment, she said, "Do you think you could love me? Or should I ask? You know, I'm a terribly honest dishonest woman. But I mean, really love me? How is it under our control to love or not to love?"

He slowly lowered his cup. "You're a wonderful

woman," he finally said. He quietly studied her, dwelling on her appealing directness. But love? This was the vexing question that he had asked himself when caught in the distressing grip of the cold mountains, when he had wanted to live for love. But what right did he have to love her? "Love?" he finally answered. "Lord, I don't know. Under the circumstances, I don't know if I'm capable of loving you, if I even deserve it. Why should I complicate your life? Look, I thought about you up there. Yessuh, I surely did. You bothered me all the way up and back. I'll allow in one way or another, you kept me going. That's love of a kind."

"I'm glad. I ask for too much, I suppose. That should be enough, but I wish we could do something with our lives, something more than just moments, these fleeting moments."

"The best thing you could do with your life is get me out of it."

"Never, not for now. I'll live each day loving you, however tentative."

Garth gave her a sheepish look. "Do you know, just like you said, I got myself lost, all turned around. I couldn't admit a thing like this to anyone but you. By jingo, I was actually lost out there one whole day. I would have done no worse blindfolded. And you . . . you always came to my mind. That's when I was thinking about you the most. I suppose this means something, missing you so much that way." He sighed and took a sip of his coffee. "Lord a'mighty, I'm no hero, Miss Bird. I'm just a selfish man surviving out here by accident, trial, and error. I'm calamity personified in this frightful country."

Bird's face glowed, his humility professed, another new revealing side to her lover. "It makes me happy that you missed me. It tells me things, nice things."

Garth leaned over and kissed her cheek. "Now, tell me, what did you come sneaking in here for? Your time is about up."

With a long sigh, she finally blurted out in near exasperation, "I don't know how to explain this, but, well, I think I've put my foot in my mouth. Tatum . . ." She stared away, her words dangling.

"Oh, no," groaned Garth. "He's found out . . . ? This?"

"No, no, my love, the horse. Your horse, the colonel's horse," she tired to explain. "Look, that sonofabitch thinks the colonel's horse is better blood than Jefferson. Can you imagine! The things he said, I wanted to give him a boot right in the ass. He makes me furious. I suppose it rubs off, the way you feel about him. Good God, I detest that man!"

Garth started to chuckle. Now, the crux of the matter, now the mask unmasked. "Yes, I can imagine," he replied. "But I wouldn't go letting something like this bother your pretty head. You realize old Tatum just happens to think anything I own is second-rate, my citizenship, my part of the country, even my poor old hat. I declare, that man's mouth is bigger than his . . ."

". . . his big, fat ass," she finished, not to his surprise.

"Precisely, Miss Bird. You're so poetic." Garth tasted his coffee again, then said, "Well, Lord only knows what you've gotten yourself into. And I don't know the full bloodline on Carrington's horse, but I'll share a little secret with you about Mistuh Jefferson. He was worth a thousand dollars before he was foaled, and his papers are pure blue-blood. He's no regular piece of horseflesh, Miss Bird. He's a thoroughbred, both raced and jumped, won five times his price at fairs and two stakes at Camptown."

She rocked back and laughed outright, and then she slapped her hands against her thighs in glee. "Oh, honestly, this is wonderful! Yes, simply wonderful! Can you imagine? Think of it!" Radiating enthusiasm, she said, "Listen, Tatum says he'll be more than happy to

get up stakes to prove which is the better of the two . . .
a race, jumps and all."

Garth was speechless.

She hurried on in a rush, "Oh, Garth, let's do it! Let
me ride Jefferson against him. Honestly, I'll ride his
big butt off. I can do it, I know I can."

"Lord a'mighty, ma'am!" he exclaimed lowly, "why,
what a crazy notion. How could you ever get involved
with that scoundrel? A race! What have you done?
Dammit, I knew you were up to something, the way
you came in here flitting around, all antsylike. Whatever were you doing down at the corral, anyhow?"

Bird quietened and puckered for him. "Only tending
Jefferson this morning. I didn't think you'd mind. I
curried him, and that's when it all started, the argument. The big ass finally upset me, so I challenged
him. Yes, I challenged him to a race. What else could
I do? You never let him get the best of you, do you?
It's almost the same thing."

"I declare," growled Garth, "that fool sergeant
would argue over cold grits and gravy if he had the
chance. But, dammit, you shouldn't have nagged him
on. I can just hear you . . . 'You won't make it over the
first jump, lard bucket, you won't . . .' "

"No, not quite," she interrupted.

"But close."

"Close."

"Yes, I allowed that much. Damned if I've met one
like you in my life!"

"Lucky you."

"Lucky?"

"No one as good." She smiled sweetly.

"Don't try sweet-talking me, either."

"Well, what about old lard bucket?"

A dark thought suddenly hit T. B. Garth and he
openly winced. "Look here, you don't think that corn-
cob thinks there's something going on between us?
You didn't give him any hints?"

"Oh, my God, no!" Bird protested, elevating her small nose. "What do you take me for?" With that, she jerked up a hand, shutting him off. "No, don't answer. One thing that I'm not is a gabbler. But I have been tempted, you know, tempted to tell someone what a man you are, how happy I am. Sometimes I feel like going out and shouting it to the sky."

Garth shuddered at the thought, almost choked on his coffee.

"Of course, you know I won't." She giggled and blew him a kiss.

"You dance with the devil," he moaned. "Yes, ma'am, you're a regular caution." Sighing, he put the cup aside and capitulated. "Well, looks like we have a race on our hands. Dammit, you think that man is ever going to give up trying to gut me? I declare, one way or another, he's out to destroy my reputation, my credibility. Now, it's my horse, by jingo. The persistent cuss, why, I've never seen a flea-bitten hound any worse. You'd think after I got those Cheyenne women off his back, he'd dry up like a stale prune. And after finding the war camp on the Powder ..."

"Oh, but you're too famous to humiliate, now. Your report on the hostiles shocked everyone, I hear. Sergeant Tatum just envies you, my love." She leaned close and whispered, "And if he gets too persnickity, I have a little secret. Ask him what he was doing two nights ago in the laundry with Colored Susan ... just about the time you were curling up in your gopher hole."

"Colored Susan? You mean they were ... they were ..."

"That's right. It wasn't that dark, and I wasn't mistaken, either." And, with a quick kiss, she was gone, almost as suddenly as she had come.

Despite the ominous, detailed scouting report that Garth and John Dominguez had delivered to Colonel

Carrington, there still were officers in his command who continued to orate, contending that the hostiles' massive war camp was nothing more than an exaggerated bluff. They argued that Red Cloud's strategy of hit-and-run established the fact that he was disinclined to meet the army in open combat, superior numbers notwithstanding. The news that other bands under chiefs Dull Knife, High Back Bone, Little Wolf, and Hump had joined with Red Cloud's Oglala did nothing to dissuade their contemptuous attitude of the Indians' ability to wage open warfare. There were also hints that Carrington, his transfer imminent, was too cautious and complacent to undertake a more aggressive campaign. Arguments over battle, or lack of it, persisted, and Garth listened, but he fed little fuel to the smouldering controversy. His warning was already in writing, his statement made—it would be foolhardy, militarily unwise, to move north and engage anywhere under the present circumstances. There were over a thousand warriors in the big war camp and more on the way. The Indians had effectively severed the Bozeman Trail, and it was no longer operational. Garth's lack of enthusiasm to attack was easily justified. It was more than the military impropriety which he considered it to be. Unlike some of the fort's ambitious junior officers, he had nothing to prove, and he failed to share their eagerness to make war. But he understood their attitudes. These were army men of purpose, fighters with promotional desires, and this was a land where brave men could become legendary. Garth, without status, had absolutely nothing to gain, only his life to cherish, and he was no longer a soldier. A lover, he was.

Complexities notwithstanding, some levity penetrated the lowering gloom at Fort Kearny. The horse race was finally on, and that, in itself, however trivial, prompted almost as much controversy among the garrison as the campaign itself. Bets were up, the wagering lively. On the morning of December sixth, a few off-duty soldiers volunteered to set the course, six pole jumps around the main corral, a quarter-mile straight-away into the fort, the finish line in front of headquarters. Sergeant Tatum was there. So were two of Garth's old friends, Corporal Daley and Private Boley, the ex-Confederate. When Garth and Dominguez arrived at the corrals, the two troopers, eager to ascertain Jefferson's chances, quickly encountered them.

"Hey, there, Cap," Boley called, "how does she look?" He came forward, rubbing his hands in anticipation. "You all got old Jeff ready for this t'do?"

Garth warmly greeted the two men, and nodding toward the horse, said, "He's fit and lean for a fine race, gentlemen. We'll take up the stirrups a notch or two for the little lady. That's about all we're planning for this one."

"No strategy, suh?" Boley asked with a worried look. "Nothing special?"

"Not at all. Fair and square, no questions asked, a gentleman's race."

Clarence Daley quickly spoke up, staring over toward Tatum and another group of men. "Well, sure as hell there's been some strategy over there, Reb. Old Tatum's not gonna sit the Arabian. Did you know that? Got himself another rider, one of the old man's best kickers, Jim Hutchins."

"Jim's a good one, Cap," opined Boley. "He's in our outfit. No heavyweight like Tatum, and he knows his horses."

Garth shrugged indifferently. "Never heard any of this. Anyhow, boys, it doesn't matter one way or another." But the thought suddenly struck him that it did matter, and he stopped and whistled lowly. "Well, for a fact, maybe it does matter. I'll allow Miss Bird won't take kindly to it. This is her race, her doing, not mine. She's the one with her hackles up this time, not me. She wants to skin his big butt."

"Ho, ho." Dominguez grinned. "*Señor* Tatum wants

to play games, eh? I think he's afraid of this woman, that she will get the best of him."

Garth began touching up Jefferson's coat with a curry comb. He stared through the corral at Boley and Daley. "You boys know Miss Bird is taking this race personally. I don't suppose she's heard the news about this Hutchins fellow riding or she'd be clouding up like a thunderstorm."

Daley said disgustedly, "Tatum's crawdadding, that's what, going back on his wager, getting another booter to take his mount. That wasn't in the cards, was it? Not the way I was betting. Lookee here, do you think this is gonna make a bean? Do you? You think the girl is good enough to handle old Jefferson, Cap? I ain't one for losing my shirt on this thing, you know. I knew Tatum was up to something, the sneaky bastard."

Smiling, Garth, unperturbed, stopped for a moment and leaned over the top pole. He tipped the brim of his hat and flipped his black feather. "I'd say you boys have your money on this horse here, is that it?"

They nodded, and Boley grinned back, saying, "Shoot fire, Mistuh Garth, you'n me lost the big war, already, didn't we? So, I says to myself, 'Look here, Reb, your luck has to change one of these days.' Besides, me'n the corporal figure it's bad luck betting against you. That's the truth, suh. If old Tatum hasn't got your ass in the bucket by now, well, suh, it jest ain't going to happen. Now, that's the way I figure, anyhow."

"Ah," sighed Garth, "but it's my horse, not me."

"Same thing!" Boley cried back. "Same thing, isn't it? Jefferson's no fool Yankee hoss!"

Then, with a sly wink, Garth suggested, "Well, you gentlemen just simmer down, now, hear? And keep your money right where it is." He hesitated and nodded across the corral at the opposition. "Now, Mistuh Carrington has a fine horse, might even take a bar or two up on this one. Ah, but when it comes to running, well, I'd say there's not another horse west of the Mississippi that can touch Jefferson. Understand, this is my opinion. Now, I can't go putting all the cards on the table for you ... might upset a few of the men around here, and the colonel as well. I sure don't want to do that, not when I'm winning, no, suh."

John Dominguez smiled knowingly at Boley and Daley. "You know what he means? He's telling you in his own way that El Gordo, the fat one, has made a bad bet with the little *pájaro*. I tell you, this horse is too much for the Arabian, better blood. Everyone says that sometimes I make my stories a little too big, eh? Ah, but would I lie to you on something like this?"

Daley whispered closely to T. B. Garth. "You mean you're pulling the wool down on Tatum? Like, maybe, you know something and you ain't telling? Is that it?"

Garth's sad eyes widened. "I declare, Corporal, what a notion! Didn't I tell you this race was fair and square?" He pointed to Jefferson. "There he stands, only waiting for his rider, and all the young lady has to do is hang on when he hits that straight stretch yonder. That's all there is to it. It's going to be what I call a bluegrass waltz, and you can count on it."

"My bet's down," declared Boley emphatically. "I'm not welching one damned bit."

Corporal Daley stared suspiciously across at the men gathering around Tatum. Then, aside to Garth, he said, "I don't trust that bastard, never have. I reckon one of us oughtta stick around here this morning, keep an eye on old Jefferson. You know, that sonofabitch just might take a notion to slip him a bucket of dried apples and water, bloat him all up like a stump toad."

Meantime, Bird Rutledge finally heard about Tatum's change in plans, and as Garth predicted, she was upset, not enough, however, to default on her ride. More determined than ever, she angrily ignored Garth's offer to take over the mount, and with a few choice swear words, stomped away to confront Tatum. T. B. Garth was not around to witness the heated exchange but John Dominguez told him how it ended. After Sergeant Tatum got in his usual last word, Bird pelted him alongside the head with a partially dried horse turd.

About an hour after this brief altercation, the bugle sounded, announcing the race, and under a bleary noonday sun, the garrison residents and troopers, most of them shouting encouragement, began lining up against the log walls. The two riders made a final circuit around the pole corral and trotted their horses back to the starting line. Then, amid great tumult, Bird and Jim Hutchins kicked off together toward the jumps. At this point in time, no one was aware that some of the hostiles' best braves were making a wide circuit to the north, threading their own horses down through the timber a few miles west of the fort.

After the start, Garth ran for a nearby corner, where John Dominguez had perched himself under one of the enfilading blockhouses. The getaway had been even, and the two horses galloped abreast, taking the first three hurdles together. Near the fourth, they were still neck and neck, with General Carrington's big Arabian making a good show of it, certainly much better than T. B. Garth had ever anticipated. He thought perhaps Bird was riding a tight rein, and at this point, he knew that the race was up for grabs. His face went grim. "Dammit," he finally cursed, "she'll have to give Jefferson his head, let him open up. What in tarnation is she doing, holding him back?"

"Ho, ho, I think she uses her head, my friend. Look, if she runs away with it, maybe it doesn't smell so good. Yes, just enough, just a little at a time, that's the way. No one will know. Ah, she's a smart woman, this one." The Spaniard nudged Garth with an elbow. "Hey, I think she's more than smart to you, eh?"

Garth, shading his eyes, watched the horses pound-

ing toward the fifth jump. Jefferson went over with
room to spare, taking the poles cleanly. Garth muttered
aside, "What the hell you talking about, more than
smart to me?"

Grinning, the old scout imparted still another nudge.
"But, my friend, don't you see it? This little one has
something written in her eyes. Yes, I see it, like you
. . . that day on the trail. *'Mano,* when a man starts
talking to himself . . ."

"Dominguez, will you shut up! Watch that horse,
will you, that last pole . . . there he goes! Beautiful!
Yessuh, beautiful." Garth dropped to a crouch and
stared at the far gate. The horses had turned, were
heading home. "Now, let him open up," he coaxed
aloud. "Come on, woman, come on, Lord a'mighty, let
him go!"

And, as though Bird Rutledge had heard this distant
plea, she huddled up over Jefferson's long neck and
gave the horse his head. Responding, the big black
stretched his lead to a length, two lengths, and when he
passed the finish, won handily by more than three
lengths. An elated Dominguez slapped Garth on the
back and cried triumphantly, "Ho, ho, what a horse!
Yes, *muy macho*! And this woman, eh? You better be
careful with this one. I think she wins twice."

Later, in front of the crowded headquarters building,
General Carrington was offering his congratulations to
both Bird Rutledge and Jim Hutchins. Sergeant Ward
Tatum had disappeared, and Boley and Daley, hands
extended, were busy making the rounds, collecting
their winnings. After some talk, the colonel's respects
finally drifted back to Garth, and he moved forward to
shake hands with the post commander. A fine glint
came to Carrington's eyes, a discerning glint. "Mr.
Garth," he said, "I've never seen a horse run like that,
not out in this country. It was a fine match. I enjoyed
it, a lessening of the tension around here, too. Yes,

very interesting, very interesting. You have a great animal, there. I didn't realize how good until today."

"Thank you, suh, and I'll say the same for your
horse."

Carrington stared critically at Jefferson again.
"Good lines, Mr. Garth, exceptional, like a thoroughbred. I've seen horses at Saratoga no better."

Nearby, Dominguez coughed slightly and excused
himself. He went over and put his arm around Bird
Rutledge, who had started to lead the horse away.

"My compliments," Carrington said again, nodding
politely to Garth. "Yes, quite a horse."

"Ah, thank you, Colonel, I'm obliged." And under a
slight flush, T. B. Garth turned away to catch up with
his rider and John Dominguez.

The rest of the crowd slowly drifted back to early afternoon routines, but the ensuing calm lasted only a
half hour. Red Cloud's warriors had come into the valley again for another perimeter harassment. A bugle
sounding assembly suddenly broke the fort's quiet, and
troopers, throwing on coats and shouldering arms, tumbled out of the barracks in double time. A runner came
galloping down from Pilot. Within moments, still another rider pounded through the big gates carrying the
news—a wood train was corralled and under attack up
on Big Piney. Garth, fumbling with his hat, came out
of the Rutledge kitchen, Bird and her mother, directly
behind him. When someone mentioned "wood train"
Bird grasped Garth by the arm and dug in. "Papa . . .
Papa's up that way today," she said fearfully.

Hearing the distant gunfire, Garth cocked his ear,
and with a tug of uneasiness, said, "Sounds like pop-
corn in a hot skillet up there." Then, whatever possessed him, valor, curiosity, or stupidity, he didn't
know, because Bird's frantic shove came simultaneously, and surprisingly he heard himself saying, "I'll
go along and have a look." Crow feather fluttering, he
ran for the main corral to get Jefferson. All he had was

a Colt revolver strapped to his side. Once, outside the
gate, he soon found himself riding beside the trundling
wagons of an infantry detachment, part of the relief
that Colonel Carrington had dispatched. Not too far
ahead, he saw Captain Fetterman and Lieutenant
George Grummond bouncing along, leading a group of
wide-eyed cavalrymen who this time sensed something
more than a routine chase. And they were correct. A
mile up the bend, the screaming Indians were riding
down in frightening waves, charging and circling the
wood train. Fetterman didn't hesitate. He rode directly
into the melee. But if the presence of his oncoming relief column had been designed to thwart the hostiles,
they obviously thought little of it, for instead of fleeing, they split away from the wood train and turned on
Fettermen's men with wild ferocity. The soldiers had to
fight for their lives, and Garth, who had ridden to the
side, where he fired his pistol at will, suddenly found
himself alone. The raw recruits were already breaking
ranks and hitting leather for cover, but luckily, the infantry at the wagons stood fast, continuing to trade
shot for shot with the Indians. When a stray bullet
ripped the cloth of Garth's greatcoat, he dismounted
and ran behind one of the wagons. At long range, his
revolver was ineffective, so he cautiously flattened and
watched. Near the head of the train, Fetterman was
frantically yelling and waving a pistol; urging his men
into the field. However brave or foolish, it was a useless effort. Everyone around the young officer seemed
too occupied with their personal safety to hear an order, much less see one. Worse, some of the troopers
were wildly booting their horses for the nearest trees to
escape the constant barrage of arrows and occasional
bullets whizzing across the clearing.

Garth saw casualties on both sides, hostiles tumbling, soldiers limping away, crawling for shelter,
some trying to snatch bucking horses, including several mounts that had arrows flagging from their rumps.

It was not until almost five minutes later when Carrington and another contingent of cavalry rode into the confusion that Red Cloud's men finally struck a retreat. The colonel drove the Indians up over a small hill where, with a few defiant, parting whoops, they began disappearing, taking their wounded with them. A few isolated shouts and a few moans drifted across the littered ground. Scraping away snow and mud, Garth went down the line looking for Jack Rutledge, finally found him slumped against the great spokes of a wagon wheel, a rifle between his legs, its barrel still oozing black smoke. Bending close, Garth asked, "Are you all right, suh?"

Rutledge, his brow damp despite the cold, nodded and spat between his legs. He pulled out a tobacco twist and offered it to Garth. The scout politely bit into it and crouched beside the woodsman. Rutledge, with a mighty sigh, wiped his forehead and said, "Now, that was a close one."

Chomping away, Garth mumbled in agreement. "Yessuh, I'd say it was, indeed. Appears the hostiles made a fight of it, and I'll allow that surprised some of the buckos around here. Lucky half of you weren't rubbed out, Mistuh Rutledge, damned lucky. Fact is, from the looks of things, I think we may have more casualties than they do."

Rutledge spat again, this time in disgust. "This is it!" he announced flatly. "This is it, for sure, the last straw! I'm heading south at Christmas, pulling stakes. I'm getting my family the hell outta here. No more logs for me." He looked at Garth. "If you know what's good for you, you'll do the same, boy. Tuck tail and run. Can't figger why you took on here, anyways."

Garth's mouth flooded, and he spat away; not with the accuracy of a Jack Rutledge. A brownish stain trickled down his chin. With a gulp, he nodded at the sawyer. "Well, suh, I hadn't thought much about leaving, but I'm sure begging to see a few good reasons."

"Take m'word, boy," Rutledge said, "there's nothing up here for you. You should have never come. Forget that fella you're chasing and get out while you still have two legs under you. Too damned easy to get caught with your britches down."

Garth's big eyes suddenly rolled upward, and he said reflectively, "Yes, you surely do have a point there, Mr. Rutledge."

"What you doing here today, anyways? I told you they'd be after you to fight, didn't I? Just like I said, backing up these raw ones. Scattered like a covey of quail, didn't they? Damned risky business. You don't listen very well, do you?"

Garth coughed and emptied his mouth. "Ah, your daughter, Miss Bird . . . she sort of asked me to come up when the report came in. She said you were . . ."

"Goddammit, are you senseless!" huffed Rutledge. "Don't listen to her. Never listen to her. Worse thing you can do. Why, she can talk a bitch wolf out of a bone. Just hearing that youngster prattle is like seeing a dog walking on its hind feet. It's peculiar, downright hard to take." He pulled himself up and straightened his heavy coat. Then abruptly: "How'd she do . . . ? The race."

"Won going away, Mr. Rutledge, three lengths or more, I'll allow."

Rutledge, his whiskers jutting forward, swelled proudly. "It figgered," he said. "By Gawd, I'll say one thing, she's a winner, m'girl. Let's get the hell outta here."

"Yessuh, she's a winner, all right," agreed Garth. Yes, he certainly knew that, but the sudden thought of her imminent departure caused him to wince. Someone had to be a loser, too.

Chapter Seven

Robert Browning's poetry fascinated Bird. Garth listened, wondering how he himself had come to be fascinated by her, how her complexities continually startled him, the exciting range of her incredible moods. And he barely knew her! Incongruous, he thought, a puzzle, Bird Rutledge, a little savage and strangely not a savage. She read so beautifully, her serenity as fresh as summer's dawn, yet at a turn, she could become a tempest, like a churlish boy with all the brutal frankness and idioms of a stable hand. He knew her anger, he knew her peace, but did he really know her? And for him, was it love or infatuation, or was there that much of a difference? These weren't new questions. He found no answers, either, and that left him still floundering like a crippled crab wondering at the conviction of his own emotional qualities. Bird had freely confessed love, love of a type. "Love is what I feel for you, a kind of love that I have never felt for anyone else."

And then she was saying, "Oh, I like this." Her face glowed in the dim light of the tiny room. "Listen," she said, "listen, my love. This says it so well . . . 'Escape me? Never, beloved! While I am I, and you are you, so long as the world contains us both, me the loving and you the loth, while the one eludes, must the other pursue.' " She stopped and for a moment loved him with her dark eyes. "Ah, you see, you'll never escape me, not as long as the world contains us both. Yes, but who will pursue? Could you? Would you?"

Garth tenderly touched her cheek, his eyes to hers. "You read beautifully," he said. "It seems that you look for all the appropriate lines. If I were poetic, I'd write one for you, something nice. Maybe I'd make you my Pauline, my Elizabeth."

She slowly closed the book, saying, "Life should be like poetry. It would be so simple, so beautiful."

"But it isn't. And other thing, I'm afraid if I pursued you, I might get myself shot, or something worse."

"Castrated?" Bird giggled at her own crudity, suddenly passed over it, mind racing, snatching at reflections. "Do you realize within a month I'll be faced with Bert again? Dear Bert. He'll court me, maybe hold my hand, maybe kiss my cheek, and be so damned proper it might kill me." And clutching Garth's arm, she said desperately, "Oh, shit, how can I? How can I, now?"

He smiled. "Ah, but you said once that he'd never know."

"Oh, it's not that," she returned with a small frown. "Guilt? Not at all! Honestly, you know that. This is too good to feel guilty about. It's ... it's just that no one can change what's happened, us. It's been too wonderful to forget. That's my problem, the remembering. I once read, somewhere, I don't recall, that satisfaction breeds hunger. Do you think so? This is a problem, mine. I'm hungry for you all the time." With a finger, she pressed a kiss on the tip of his nose. "And your problem, too, I do believe."

He laughed gently. "Am I that bare?"

"Your eyes don't lie. Did you know that? They say so much. Yes, they bare you. If you stole a cookie, I'd know. You can't understand this, what's happened, and now you're as confused as I am. What now, my love?"

"Laramie, for you," Garth said pensively. He studied her closely. "You see, for once in my life, I'm trying not to be so damned selfish. I happen to agree with your father. Yes, I do. I think you belong there. It's time to get out of this place. We have to face reality, not poetry, and reality can be a horrible thing, this mess, getting worse by the day. Look here, now, no matter what I feel inside, I have more concern for you than I do myself. And to be honest with you, I can't say this is the way I felt when I first got here. I'm for living, and that's the way I feel about you. This thing about living for the present is all well and good, but there is a tomorrow. That's reality, and you shouldn't be here."

"Reality is one of my slowest faculties. It's taken me years of schooling, two more out here even to accept my heritage. I'm neither nor, one of those, just a breed to most."

"But beautiful."

"Neither nor," she smiled. "My nose is too short and my legs are too long. I know my worth. So do you. You must accept me as I am, what I am. Shall I be red to you, or shall I be white? It's much too difficult to try and be both."

"You're a loving human being, more beautiful than not. Dominguez says the body is nothing without a soul. You have body and soul."

"Do you think Bert would even look at me in Independence . . . Saint Louis?" Her eyes widened skeptically. "Would you?"

"I can't speak for that damned Elbert. I just don't know about that young scamp."

"Would you look at me?" She pinched his arm.

Garth, searching for an appropriate reply, fell back on the flat pillow and stared at the heavy beams above him. "Well, now, Miss Bird," he drawled, "that's not a fair question, it's not . . ."

"Ah, ha, you're hedging! You see!"

"No, ma'am not at all. I daresay, a year back, six months, maybe, why, I would have taken a look. Yes,

I certainly would have. That's natural with me. I like looking at fine women, always have. Why, when I was a boy, I thought my mother was about the loveliest creature I'd ever seen. She smelled like lilacs, sometimes like freshly baked bread, things I remember. She was a walking picture, like most women, to be looked at, to be admired. To me, women are sort of like the lines in this poetry book . . . understood and misunderstood, ah, but so enduring, so appreciated."

"And you appreciate me?"

"Of course, indeed, I do!"

She pinched him again. "But if you saw me in Saint Louis?"

"Bugaboo," Garth smiled, "if I saw you walking the promenade, maybe I wouldn't do anything more than take a look, either. But looking at a woman and knowing a woman are two different things. I know you, at least some of you, all the best parts, anyway."

"You should have never looked at me if you meant that I shouldn't have you. The best parts, indeed! I think you're a rogue, a dirty rogue."

He chuckled. "Yes, I'll allow I've been called that a few times, too." Grabbing her arm, he pulled her down beside him. "Miss Bird, you know what I'd do if I saw you promenading in Saint Louis? Why, I'd sweep you off your pretty feet. Lord a'mighty, I would. I'd hold you tightly like this and kiss you, profess my love in a most gentlemanly way, and then . . . then, I'd probably seduce you."

"You wouldn't dare!"

"The hell I wouldn't!"

Bird Rutledge suddenly giggled in delight, grasped his frontispiece and uttered Browning's immortal words: "Escape me? Never, beloved . . . never!"

There are some men and women to whom things always happen, their lives unavoidably eventful, who either by choice or circumstance seem to be attracted by fate. Had Tyson Bell Garth fled from eminence, it would have found him; had he sought obscurity, it would have clubbed him; and often, when he avoided trouble, it still managed to follow him like a lap dog. Bird Rutledge had been gone only a few minutes. For a moment, he thought she was returning, the quick thumping on the door, and his eyes made a quick scan of the room, saw nothing she could have forgotten, no more than what had been. He opened the door. It was not the love in his fragmented life standing there in the dark; it was the bane, Sergeant Tatum, his broad lips compressed into a self-satisfied and somewhat vindictive smile.

Garth, in a flash, only assumed, but the sergeant's arrival seemed too coincidental, yet unperturbed, the scout made a gracious gesture, his usual, a cavalier sweep of his hand. And with all the fluidity of rich sorghum, he said, "Well, Mistuh Tatum, this is a pleasure. What brings you to my humble step this fine night? I do declare."

"Your pleasure?" Tatum growled. "Your pleasure, all right, yeah, the one who just sneaked out of here. Who in the hell do you think you're fooling, you big fraud? Don't you know that woman is spoken for? Now, it looks like I'm gonna get my turn, huh?"

"Miss Bird?" Garth asked innocently. "Why . . . why, she just stopped by for a chat, that nice young lady."

Tatum, gloating at this new revelation and a rich opportunity for attack, stared at Garth's bare chest and snorted. "You're a goddamned liar, too, stealing another man's woman. It ain't proper for her to be in your quarters, you know that. And what's her ol' man gonna say about this, huh? You tell me that, Reb. I want to see you crawl outta this one, you conniving grayback."

"Oh, law, Tatum, what's the harm of a friendly chat?

Maybe planning another race, give you a second chance."

"Chat, my ass!" Tatum hotly exclaimed. "I've had my eye on you two, damned right I have. This is the third time in two days she's been in here. By God, I'll bet ol' Jack don't know you're consorting with her. Wait till he hears. He might have something real important to say to you."

"Ah, you've been spying, Sergeant," Garth replied, shaking his head sadly. "So, that's it? Finding some amusement for yourself? I should have known what someone like you would make of this."

"Never mind the honey talk. You've cooked your goose this time, and I'm gonna see you sweat for it, too, you bet your ass I am."

Steadying himself in the doorway, Garth nonchalantly twicked at his moustache. Inwardly, he was snatching at straws of redemption, trying to gather himself. "I declare," he finally sighed, "you ought to know better. Now, calm down, Mistuh Tatum, and listen closely. Let's presume you're right in this foolish accusation. Presume, I say. Just who is going to convince Mistuh Rutledge that his daughter has been ... ah, as you say, consorting? You? I'll allow that it will take some proving, won't it? On the other hand, say you're wrong. You see, I happen to be a friend of the family, now, and I'll tell you, that young lady is the apple of her daddy's eye." He gave Tatum a pathetic look. "Now, I'd say that any man who reneges on riding against that woman like you did, sure isn't going to cut much hay talking against her. You know she doesn't hold you in much esteem, anyhow. Take that horse biscuit, for instance, the one she hit you with. Come to think of it, she just might up and tell everyone about how she saw you on top of Colored Susan in the laundry room that ..."

"Colored Susan!" Tatum exploded.

T. B. Garth shrugged. "Happens all the time down in

my country, but out here, troopers, officers, and wives, and all, well . . ."

"Now, wait a minute, just what are you trying to pull on me, you sneaky bastard? Who in the hell is gonna believe that kind of shit, anyways?" He knotted a big fist and waved it menacingly.

"Sergeant, I think we have a standoff, here," Garth said, his eyes nervously searching the dark for onlookers. "So, I suggest you make a retreat before you start attracting attention and make a fool of yourself again."

"Damned your hide," Tatum sputtered. "I'll let the whole post know!"

With his cool front finally crumbling, Tyson Bell Garth succumbed to temptation. "Good night, Mistuh Tatum," he said, and grasping the top of the door frame, he swung his feet out and planted them solidly in the middle of Tatum's bulging midriff. With a bearish whoof, the sergeant staggered backward, finally lost his balance, and landed on his back in the snow. That was enough for T. B. Garth. In one swift defensive blur, he quickly slammed the door, bolted it, and sighing mightily, stretched out against its heavy back, trying to ignore the angry, threatening shouts outside.

Ward Tatum, the spoiler. Garth fought bed, pillow, and frustration. His problems were growing sharper horns. Lord, Lord, one more mistake and he would impale himself. Who knew to what length Tatum in his present state of aggravation would carry this crazy vendetta? Garth sighed. Probably no farther than the barracks wall, hopefully, optimistically. Yet he knew that he had no one to blame but himself. Desire had become his master, yet, it was never meant to be this way. He had never had any aspirations to be Casanova or Don Juan, or Lord'a'mighty, Saint Someone from Somewhere who in a fit of anguish had nipped off his balls to subdue his lustful torment. His was such a simple want, or had been—a wanting woman, no different from himself, who in professing her desire had asked only to "accept me as I am," her modest contentment, his. How uncomplicated, how unselfish. Garth groaned. Ah, the collapse of his short-lived love. Or infatuation? Or, God forbid, lust! Whatever, there had to be salvation in her leaving for Fort Laramie, yet even that had been undermined with a foreboding hint of more to come. Bird herself, with an assist from a poet, had posed a troublesome question: who must pursue? Yes, and she had expressed it with some fond hope, he recalled. Pursue? Pursuit was folly. In his present situation, what did he have to offer, other than the love he had already freely given? Reality battered him. He must also flee, clean camp. He told himself, I shall tip my hat and say *au revoir.* Most certainly, she is better off without me, materially, anyhow. She must be made to understand this. After all, she had told him in a memorable moment of passion that he need not feel obligated. Strange, then, why did he feel obligated? Where did romance begin and convenience end? What kind of a hopeless egg was he trying to hatch?

Reveille. It seemed as though he had merely dozed, sleep fitful, fraught with abstract dreams, Tatum and Bird taking turns chasing him up and down the chinked walls of his tiny room. He hopped about the chilly floor, snatching at clothing. He took a last minute to pen a warning note to Bird, explaining the incident with Tatum, to prepare her, she, the mistress of excuses. That much done, he trudged away to the commissary to meet Gabe Bridger and Dominguez. It was the twenty-first of December, cold, a dusting of gold in the east, a pale moon lowering in the Big Horns. For many, it was a good day to die.

Detailed by Bridger to inspect the north perimeter that morning, Garth and the Spaniard set out toward the headwaters of Peno Creek. They rode at a trot up Big Piney, crossed over, and finally parted to scout opposite sides of their designated area. Garth pointed his horse toward the east fork adjacent to Lodge Trail Ridge. Dominguez was heading northwest toward Rocky Face, a pine-covered knoll with stone outcropping. Once alone, Garth immediately reined into the brush, where, under the safety of cover, he could glass the tumble of slopes and distant flats to the north, the usual area of infiltration by the hostiles. He was cautious, poking along a few minutes at a time, generally moving in a northeasterly route, stopping occasionally to make an observation with his field glasses. Almost every day, the Indians had been near. Within five minutes, he began crossing tracks, mostly old sign already blown in by snow, trails where scouts had come down on missions such as his own. He was becoming more alert with each step, and out of habit, continually checked his rifle. He had learned. Since the near-disastrous encounter on the Powder, he no longer rode with rifle sheathed. Ready for the worst, Garth carried his Henry either under his arm or rested it below the pommel of his saddle.

About a mile from the Virginia City Trail, he stopped again, dismounted, and took time to urinate in the snow. He was near the top of the hill at the edge of a small buckbrush clearing, another ridge flanking him to the north. The snowy ruts of the mining country road were barely visible below him to the left. Garth was just about to remount when a movement across the far hill suddenly caught his eye. He froze, held his breath, and waited. Finally, playing his glasses on the lower part of the ridge, he located tracks, a multitude, at first wondered if they were game signs, perhaps those of migrating elk or deer. He gradually traced the trails upward to a point directly opposite of where they disappeared in the trees. And then, barely discernible, he made out the shadowy forms of mounted riders. They were almost a mile away, motionless, spread out through the cover as far as he could see. No small party, he calculated, probably at least two hundred or more. With quickening heart, he slowly led Jefferson back into the trees, jumped on and bolted for the trail far below. When Garth finally came racing down south of Sullivant, he was surprised to hear shots, a barrage of them, coming from somewhere to his far right. It was not until he passed through the main gate that he discovered what was happening.

John Dominguez was the first man that Garth recognized in the frantic bustle of mustering troops. The Spaniard had beaten him back. Garth jumped off his horse, shouting, "What's going on up there?"

"Wood train, again," Dominguez yelled. He was busy checking the cinch on Antonio. "They have the sawyers tied up below Sullivant this time ... came down Big Piney Gorge."

"Well, Lord a'mighty, then it can't be those scamps I saw!" Garth exclaimed. "They couldn't get down here that fast. They're over the hill on the other side about three miles back."

"Oh, ho, you saw hostiles up there, too?"

"I'll allow I sure did, swarming all over the place! Two or three hundred over the end of the Lodge Trail." Garth hurried away to make his report. "Must be two parties deployed out there," he called back, "One on each side."

By the time Garth had spoken to Colonel Carrington, Captain Fetterman and Lieutenant Grummond, with a host of infantry and cavalry, were charging out the gate, headed for the wood train only a mile away. Their orders were to support the train and repel the attackers. After hearing Garth's report, Carrington ordered Captain Tenedor Ten Eyck to assemble his command on a standby basis. There was a new concern: the threat of an attack on the fort itself.

Meanwhile, several other Indian fighters followed along with Fetterman and Grummond, two civilians, Jim Wheatley and Isaac Fisher, both armed with new Henry repeaters, and Captain Frederick Brown, who despite his reassignment papers, rode off to the action without orders. They all were eager to fight Indians. Garth, along with Dominguez and Portugee Phillips, were sent back to the Lodge Trail hills with orders to make a full reconnaissance, especially to report on the movement of the Indians Garth had seen earlier. Carrington was not discounting the possibility that Red Cloud and Dull Knife might make a direct play on the fort from the northeast side of Sullivant while keeping Fetterman and his men occupied along Big Piney. The truth was, no one knew what to expect in the way of an attack or from what direction, since the hostiles, by now, had been reported on three sides of the fort.

A half hour later, the three scouts were atop the hill, listening to the distant shots being traded back and forth in the sage flat below Sullivant. They strung out twenty yards abreast across the upper edge of Lodge Trail Ridge and slowly moved ahead until Dominguez finally held up his hand. Strangely, the rifle fire over the hill to their left seemed to be getting closer, and by now the scouts were approaching the danger zone of Peno's east fork. A few hundred yards ahead, Garth suddenly pointed. The scouts closed ranks. "Over there," Garth said, nodding with his chin. "That's where I saw them, all strung out through the trees."

Portugee Phil put up his glasses. The spasmodic shots in back of them were growing louder. "Your Injuns are gone," Phillips said. His binoculars moved to the left. "Down lower on the hill, see. The tracks go down below into that scrub pine."

"The shooting," Garth said. "Listen. Sounds like it's coming this way, closer. It doesn't sound right, not this far along the ridge. What the hell's going on down there?"

Meantime, Dominguez, perched on a log, had his glasses trained on the main Peno Creek foothills. He had begun to pick up movement, ever so slight, but his eyes were trained to the keenness of a hawk. He knew what he was looking for. "Yes," he said slowly, fate-fully. "Yes, there are your Indians, my friend, hiding below, waiting for our soldiers, and I think our boys are coming, too, eh? *Sí, amigo,* and coming too far."

Portugee Phil leaped forward, frantically glassing the distant hills below. "Aw, Fetterman's no fool," he said. "What the hell, he can't ride over to this side. There's orders on that. It's routine, ain't it? No one goes through those saddles down into Peno. He's only securing the wood train, probably chasing a few of those redskins up the hill. Or maybe it's old Wheatley wanting to get in a few licks with that new gun of his, see how it handles." He paused and swept the area again. "I hear the ruckus but I can't see a goddamned thing."

Garth had turned back to Dominguez. "How many men do you think are deployed in those hills over there?"

"You say two hundred, maybe three?" Dominguez commented with a following cluck of his tongue. "Ah, so many who can count? I say three times that many, maybe a thousand. Look! Look now! There's your noise, coming up over the hill. Fetterman, I think. Yes, he's chasing them."

Simultaneously, all three men brought their glasses into play, observing the land to the far left. It was a startling, incredible sight, for retreating Indians from the wood train skirmish were scattering in all direc-tions down toward Peno Creek behind a wave of troop-ers in what appeared to be a thorough rout. Fetterman and his troopers had them on the run. Meantime, in the nearby gullies, barely a mile across from the scouts, hundreds of braves sat motionless, only awaiting the signal to kick their ponies out of the sage and scrub pine.

Phillips, now staring in awe, muttered, "What in God's name are those boys doing? It's madness! They ain't supposed to be over on this side. Why,

Fetterman's taking them right down into the stinking flat, running right into a trap!"

"Wikmunke!" John Dominguez cursed in Siouan. "Trap, you fool, trap! Turn back!"

Portugee Phil, jerking away his rifle, fired three rounds into the air, making an attempt at a warning. And on almost any other occasion it would have succeeded, but now it was useless. The sudden din of shots erupting in the bottom obliterated Phillips's warning.

"Go for the fort," Dominguez yelled at him. "Get the word back there, eh, *¡muy pronto!*"

Garth watched silently, helplessly, as the faraway soldiers came riding and running out in full view. The cavalry was galloping boldly ahead, strung out in a long, irregular line, white puffs belching from their weapons like tiny cotton balls. He finally said lowly, "I'm afraid it's too late for help, Dominguez. They're already over the hill, even those boys on foot. The hostiles are taking them right down to the bottom. Fetterman's been tricked, by jingo. He's playing right into their hands."

And shortly later, a horrified Garth and Dominguez saw the first great lines of yelling Indians suddenly begin to spill out from the brushy knolls far below them. The bright colors of tribal war regalia exploded like confetti against the wintry backdrop, and echoes of resounding battle cries and eagle-bone whistles began floating up the ravines, choking the hills with fright. In massive waves, the Indians swept over the ragged lines of the troopers.

John Dominguez put his glasses down and crossed himself. "Let us go," he said. "There is nothing we can do here. We have no time. Back to the fort. Ten Eyck will have to get down there and pick up the pieces."

"Wait!" cried Garth desperately. "We have two rifles. Can't we do something? If there's the slightest chance, anything ... Boley's down there, Daley. That's

Fetterman's whole crew, dammit, we just can't pull stakes and leave them."

Dominguez, reaching for his horse, gave his companion an incredulous yet pitiful stare. "A chance, you say? Yes, my friend, there's a chance ... a chance you'll die with them. For what? A load of wood? A ton of hay? Your pride? *Vámanos, por vida suya, señor,* before it becomes too late for us, too. This is not your war, eh, you remember?"

The cold afternoon had labored away on broken wings, leaving behind a gruesome hatch of death. Despite Captain Ten Eyck's relief effort, called out by Portugee Phil, it was much too late to rescue Fetterman and his men, and the command had been rubbed out, right down to the last man. And that night, a miserable Tyson Bell Garth listened to the clink of picks cracking rock and frozen earth beyond the fort's walls. They were digging a massive grave for the captain's party, forty-nine of them, all of those that the reliefers had been able to recover before darkness. Jack Rutledge was dead, too, a bullet in his brain, and the stiff bodies of thirty-two more officers and troopers were still scattered along the brushy hills and snow-covered coulees below Lodge Trail Ridge. It was a bitter thought: eighty-one officers and men dead, and Fetterman had once boasted all he needed to subdue Red Cloud's warriors was eighty. Clarence Daley and Pete Boley were gone, Sergeant Tatum decapitated, his head carried away, by now probably skewered like a bearded totem on the end of a Sioux or Cheyenne lance. Misery and fright shook hands in the fort. Colonel Carrington was both disconsolate and angry, sorrowed by the loss of courageous men, embittered by the vanity that had caused it. The Indians had won a battle on the field, a stunning victory, and the garrison had been depleted by one-third. John Dominguez went off into the night, scouting the hostiles, following their retreat back to their war village. They had taken their dead with them; they had also taken all the booty from the scattered field of battle, new Henry rifles, Colt revolvers, Springfields, Spencer repeaters, and many rounds of ammunition, but at least for the time being, the Indians were not preparing a direct attack on the fort. They were going back to their villages to celebrate and mourn, and then they would return, better equipped, and with the taste of victory in their mouths, more determined than ever to rid their country of soldiers. This, Dominguez told Carrington, was the way of the Indian. Soon afterward, Portugee Phil, riding Carrington's Kentucky jumper, was on his way to Fort Laramie, carrying the bad news and the colonel's final plea for reinforcements.

Garth, swept up in the disheartening furor, had been unable to see Bird Rutledge until he returned at dark with the last of Ten Eyck's relief wagons. And, after working among the mutilated dead, plucking arrows from butchered bodies, his visit of condolence was brief. Meena Rutledge's wailing grief had sent him reeling back to the small sanctuary of his own room, where he peered out of his solitary pane searching for answers in a black sky. Time was badly out of joint. There were no fast answers. God only knew why, in such situations of perilous extremity, leaders like Fetterman, Grummond, and Brown were so audaciously stubborn, bound so strongly to convictions of honor and valor, only to disobey orders, to sacrifice themselves and drag down their followers with them. Garth knew that patriotism's thin guise was a cover for fools and heroes alike, and heroes often were nothing more than lucky fools. He was terribly disenchanted. In his time, he had seen wanton death, enough to disenchant him, and the ineptitudes and disasters of this day thoroughly dismayed him. Indian fighters! The killers killed. Lord a'mighty he was for living! The vicious brutality of Red Cloud's war certainly was not meant to be a part of his life, although war itself was not anything new. Neither was hypocrisy or recrimination or retaliation. Men fought for their rights, God-given human dignity, and they often died fighting injustice and intolerance. These were just causes. But were they not the causes of the enemy, an enemy whose land had been violated time and again? It was preposterous, he thought, sheer hypocrisy, how the Federals had clamored so long for the causes of equality, freedom, and charity, when at this very moment on the frontier they were doing their utmost to destroy the very virtuous qualities they espoused.

Garth was confused, his mind muddled by complexities, his allegiances bloodied by the Teton-Sioux and Cheyenne, the ferocity of their vengeance; Boley, Daley, even the cantankerous Tatum, all gone in a day; Meena Rutledge, a widow; Mrs. Grummond, a widow, too, and heavy with child; Fetterman, a fool, gallantly brave in death. And Garth brooded on the helplessness of the troopers, many of them his friends, men condemned to endure the unendurable, then doomed to death and oblivion because of the selfish ambitions of others, that inherent greed that makes conflict unavoidable. Those men outside, soon to go down into the earth, they were the real victims of injustice. In the name of humanity, for what? And Garth wondered on the word of John Dominguez: "This isn't your war." His dark eyes, a ghostly reflection in the windowpane, cried out, my God, What am I doing here . . . ? A man without a country.

Chapter Eight

"*Kissin-ey-oo-way'o,*" Bird said. "It blows cold." She came into his room carrying a small tin covered with cloth. She stomped the snow from her boots, pulled off her shawl, and shook her long hair.

"*Kissineyooway'o,*" Garth repeated haltingly. It was the second time that he had heard the word, John Domínguez's dread, black winter, a most dangerous time to be on the prairie or in the mountains. He took the platter and set it aside, then helped Bird remove her coat of coyote furs that hung down just below the tops of her beaded winter Indian boots. Since Jack Rutledge's demise, now three weeks passed, she visited freely, and with her mother's knowledge, Meena, a Cree, whose tribal standards of courtship, happily, were less conventional than the white man's. Meena knew winter was a lonely time, more than ever, now, and if her daughter had taken Garth as a lover, she had taken him as a son. In a cold world, the simplicity of this new relationship, however temporary, was heartwarming to T. B. Garth. Truthfully, it hurt him a little, for he knew that both women would soon be leaving him.

"Cookies," Bird said, lifting the cloth. "Mama sent them, made from wild honey, a cottonwood tree that Papa and the men cut last month."

Garth smiled and humbly thanked her. Why did they make him so rich in feeling, so deserving?—a man with lost directions and muddled intentions. "You're too good to me," he said. And, they were good to him, by love and sentiment. In a small way, Garth himself had been responsible. After the Fetterman disaster, he visited the Rutledge quarters nightly for two weeks, brought what little cheer he could muster. Still another week had passed, and gradually, the proportions of his own small bunk doubled again. His Bird had returned to the nest. As other conditions continued to normalize, decisions came easier, not necessarily for him, but for most of the fort. The arrival of the 1st Battalion of the 18th Infantry from Fort Laramie lifted the spirits of everyone, had made the hostile environment more tenable. Red Cloud's legions had not returned, only because winter had finally come with a vengeance, locking its icy jaws around the land, posing problems for everyone. While the intermittent blizzards had confined the hostiles to their winter lodges, the contrary weather had also made travel to Fort Laramie more hazardous. Most of the civilians, including Bird and her mother, were ready to be evacuated, the trip had been postponed already twice because of bitter north winds and drifting snow. Temperatures fluctuated crazily from one day to the next. Any travel became a risk.

Garth poured black coffee and they sat together on the small bench, straddling it, facing each other like chess players. *"Kissineyooway'o,"* she said again. "You know the term, then, know what it means? Did Mama tell you?"

He shook his head, saying, "No, it was Dominguez, a long time ago. It seems like years ago, long before love or war. We were on the trail. Strange, in a way . . ." And his voice trailed off.

"Strange?"

"It was like there was something out there he couldn't see, couldn't quite put his hands on. But he knew it was there, just waiting for the right time. If the Indian doesn't destroy the white man, the *kissineyooway'o* will. Something like that. I'll allow he believes it, too. The black Demeter, I suppose. Everything white as far as the eye can see, but the connotation of death, a time when the wolves get fat."

"Ah, and you don't believe it?"

"Well, bugaboo, I'm not a superstitious man. Confused at times, I'll admit. I just don't hold to Indian voodoo any more than I do to some of Christianity's contentious beliefs. I'll allow this makes me more of a rebel than I already am, doesn't it?"

A small frown escaped her. "I'm afraid Mama would disagree with you," she said, her dark eyes still and deep. "She knows. The *kissineyooway'o* is real, not superstition. Once, when she was a girl in Saskatchewan it came, only once in her lifetime. Some of her people were caught away from the villages. She says many died. They never made it back ... and they were Indians, too."

"I'm sorry," said Garth. He nodded toward the frosted pane. "If it's this bad, now, then I reckon I don't want any part of your *kissineyooway'o*. You know, Miss Bird, I wasn't meant for this kind of climate ... foreign to my heritage. When I was a boy on the Pearl River, I used to go barefoot in the winter. By jingo, everyone up here sleeps with socks on."

Bird placed a bite of cookie in his mouth. "This is nothing more than winter's bad breath, my love," she said soothingly. "We only say *kissineyooway'o* by habit, when the bitter cold comes from the north. It's the opposite of chinook, the warm wind from the west. The chinook is the enemy of the *kissineyooway'o*. The chinook eats the cold, melts the snow. This is what the Indians pray for in the winter, after the Moon of Ice on the River."

Garth stared away, his mind drifting, and he said directly, "Pete Boley was right, God bless his soul. He said this country wasn't fit for a white man. Semantics. He meant tolerable. Anyhow, he was on the mark. A man has to live by his wits up here. He has to be as clever as a wolf, as mean as a bear, as wise as an Indian, and have the guts of an army mule. That leaves me out. By nature, I'm a peaceful man, Miss Bird. I was never meant to be a warrior in the wilderness."

She said, "Sometimes you remind me of a big, fuzzy wolf. Yes, you have the spirit of a wolf in you, but peaceful, I don't know. You were looking for someone, weren't you . . . ? A man you came up here to kill."

"Sturges," Garth said glumly. "Henry Sturges."

"That's not very peaceful, is it?"

"Ah, but don't you understand, this is only to right a wrong, a terrible injustice." In quiet protest, he held up his hands. "Hell, I don't know what I'll do when I catch up with him, now. I've never picked a fight in my life, but I've sure had my share of them. Lord a'mighty, I'm going on twenty-seven years and I've already been in two wars! By my calculation, that's damn near a fifth of my life just trying to stay alive."

Reaching, holding to him, Bird said thoughtfully, "Do you believe what Boley said? Do you? Don't you know this land is fit for those who love it, those who want it? Do you realize that my mother's people have been fighting all their lives just for the right to exist? The Cree and the Blackfeet have been at war for years. That should be enough, don't you think?" She tossed her head, gesturing around her. "We could do without all of this, the forts, the guns, all of this stupidity. Look what it has done just in the last few weeks. . . . Papa, all of your friends, Frances Grummond, that poor woman. God, if only everyone could really believe this land is unfit for the white man . . . leave these people alone to face their own miseries, not compound them."

"I believe it. I don't belong here."

"Yes, but you didn't come to take anything away, to scalp the land."

Garth quietly probed her, first her boyishness, then the petulant girl behind pouty lips and saucy eyes, and now the woman, mature and thought-provoking, a woman who lived in two worlds, red and white. Good Lord, he thought, the complexity of my lover! He caressed her hand, kissed it, saying, "In every way, you manage to touch my heart. You make my laments so lamentable. When you're gone, I'll sleep worse for it, but I'll breathe a damn sight easier. I want you safe."

"If you hadn't come drifting with a tumbleweed, I would have never known you, how crazy and wonderful you are, how vital and passionate love can be. I'll cry when I go. Maybe I'll die just a little, inside."

"Please don't," he begged. "It only makes it worse to think I've mangled a part of your life."

Smiling tenderly, Bird touched his face, her finger tracing down to his moustache. "No, silly," she said, "you've made my life. You talk like I'm an old woman, already. Honestly, sometimes we only live for moments."

"A supreme moment," Garth put in. "Dominguez's words, not mine."

"Sometimes we spend the rest of our lives with memories of moments. Yes, you're a realist, I know. You want my life in a little white box neatly wrapped and tied with a pretty red ribbon. Security, didn't you say? That sounds like Papa, too. Security, something a woman like me needs, or deserves. Ah, but you know me for what I am. Understand me, my heart with its longings, my body with its desires. Don't condemn yourself for my love of you. Don't kill my lovely thoughts. 'Thou must be ever with me, most in gloom, if such must come.' "

"You're a beautiful idealist." Garth smiled sadly. "Not too practical."

"Not a savage?"

"Never."

"I came bearing gifts," she said.

"You're a gift in yourself."

"I had something else in mind, too."

Garth grinned mischievously. "Let me guess."

"No, not what you're thinking. Ah, my love, I know you too well."

"I don't deny it."

Bird Rutledge picked up the cookie tin and set it on the edge of the little stove. Sliding close, she placed her arms over Garth's shoulders. "I've made up my mind," she said firmly. "I'm going to tell Bert."

"About us! Now, wait a minute. . . ."

"Not us," she went on. "Me."

"But, I thought . . ."

"I've changed my mind," Bird interrupted. "And don't tell me again I'm not practical."

"Or trustworthy? Either of us."

She emitted a long sigh. "Can't you understand? How can I ever go through with a betrothal like this . . . ? Pretending the rest of my life. God, Garth, what a miserable thought! And now that Papa's gone, why? I had to see things through his eyes for too long. He was so good, Garth, so proud of me. And I miss him. But, honestly, this isn't fair to Bert. And besides, you know I don't love the man, nor could I ever."

"Some of my doing."

"Oh, not at all," Bird quickly replied, putting a small pin to him. "Don't flatter yourself, my love. You just happened to come along. Call it fate, accidental. Maybe it brought out the doubt that already was there . . . that the engagement was all wrong, an arrangement. You even knew it, didn't you? Poor Bert." She stopped and stared deeply into his eyes. "My God, how can I blame you for my shortcomings, my stupidity, my mistakes?"

Their foreheads touched, and he asked, "Do you think this has been a mistake?"

"You know better, my darling," she smiled. "I have no regrets, only that I'm leaving you, if only for a while. That kills me. You're very precious to me, in so many ways. Don't you think it would be more of a mistake if I weren't honest with myself . . . ? And Bert? Oh, God, what kind of a marriage . . . ?"

"Maybe a good one," Garth interjected. "Elbert, why, he could make do, provide for you. See here, woman, you're not looking ahead. You don't seem to realize the position you're in, with your father gone, and well, what about you? Your mother? You can't take in washing the rest of your life, be a charwoman around these military outposts forever. Why, I declare!"

"You're not very convincing," she said, kissing him lightly.

"No, I reckon not," he finally muttered. Already too involved, his reasoning did lack conviction. Of course, she was no charwoman, never would be, too intelligent, educated, beautiful. Ha, there were a few men of means out here who would jump through her intriguing hoop given the chance. Puzzling alternatives suddenly pricked him, barbs of apprehension. Knowing Bird, he sensed something in the wind, something beyond lover. Breadwinner? T. B. Garth, a breadwinner? Heaven forbid! Yet, paradoxically, he was heartened by Bird's decision about Elbert Craig. She sensed it, too, and he knew it. Woman was meant to know man, to direct him, to perfect him. He tilted his head, eyed her suspiciously. "Miss Bird, you're not a completely senseless woman. Impractical, yes, but not senseless. I've come to know you too damned well . . . the way your devious little mind operates. Now, what's this all leading up to?"

Laughing, she nuzzled him. "Don't you trust me?"

"From here to the bunk, that far."

She giggled. "Oh, it's really very simple. Mama and I talked about a few things. You needn't worry about me . . . us."

"Elbert? She knows what you're doing about him?"

"Of course she does, and she approves."

Dumbfounded, Garth struck his head. "Oh, law, the whole world is going mad!"

"Don't be silly. She likes you much better than Bert. Mama never made cookies for him. The truth is, she ignored him. She says you remind her of Papa when he was young. She really likes you, she does."

Garth groaned. "It figures. I knew you were up to something, all antsy, moving your little butt around like you're on a hot seat. Go on, what is it . . . ? What have you two planned?"

"Like I said, it's very simple." And Bird held his hands and told him. Meena Rutledge wanted to go up north in the spring to visit her people, relatives that she had not seen since she was a small girl. There were steamers going upriver to Fort Union, and from there, by trail, it was only a few days to the Calling River country in the Queen Mother's land. Garth nodded in approval. Bird went on, excitedly. Papa had left them enough money, and Colonel Carrington had pledged additional government compensation for the sawyer's death. Then, without further elaboration, she stopped and gave him an inquiring look.

Garth commented, "An excellent idea . . . your mother going up there." He cleared his throat, waiting.

"I thought so, too," she said, looking away.

"And you?" he prompted. "You'll go with her?"

She turned back and smiled shyly. Her brows furrowed. "That depends," she answered. "It depends upon you, how much of a gentleman you really are."

"Yes, ma'am, I just had a hunch, I surely did."

"Mama says love is something one feels in the absence of it."

And Garth drawled uneasily, "Absence makes the heart grow fonder. That's the line, Miss Bird. Law, you of all people, should know that one!"

"Why, yes, my love." Then, straight-faced: "Mama says if you don't come to Fort Laramie by spring to claim me, she'll cut off one of her fingers and curse the day you were born. That's what Indians do, you know. In misery, they maim themselves."

A shudder went though him. "I declare, that's crazy, a horrible notion!"

She suddenly broke out laughing at her morbidity, and then Garth guffawed with her. He held out his hands helplessly. "But I don't know what I'm doing next," he finally said. "I have no definite plans. Now, what kind of existence is that? You'd ride away with me into God only knows where?"

"Yes, with you, together, anywhere."

"Well, what happens when I run into Sturges . . . ? If I miss and he doesn't?"

"I'll kill him."

"Nonsense!"

"No, the truth."

"And my home in Mississippi is so damned far off right now, I can't even think about it, getting you down there. And what if I don't show up in the spring? What if the damned *kissineyooway'o* gets me first?"

"You know better. Nothing matters, now. You love me. You need me as much as I need you. We're one and the same, a team. We'd be miserable apart. Admit it."

He said nothing, just pondered, which in itself was an adequate answer. She was ready to meet any challenge. Bird Rutledge kicked off her winter boots to each side of the little bench. She took him by the hand and pulled him toward the bunk. T. B. Garth saw no alternative, either in the present or the future. He succumbed.

No one would have predicted, least of all Garth, that he could make an honorable break from Fort Phil Kearny within another week. Understandably, he had developed a horrible ache to be rid of the place. He was in a bad situation worsening. With Bird Rutledge ready to fly, he saw nothing but sheer desolation on the horizon, had grimly resigned himself to a lonely winter, loveless, a wingless eagle in a hostile land. His relief came inadvertently, surprisingly. Another company of cavalry had arrived from Fort Laramie, and with it, the news: Colonel Carrington, the White Eagle, Red Cloud's bitter enemy, was finally being transferred. His newly assigned post was Fort Caspar, far south on the banks of the North Platte, far from the great war camps of the Lakota and Cheyenne.

Carrington's demise was yet another victory for Red Cloud, who had repeatedly denounced the White Eagle for attempting to take his tribe's land by force; it was a personal defeat for the colonel, a man whose pleas for adequate reinforcements on the frontier road had gone unheeded for months, a man who had never claimed to be a warrior, only a builder of forts. Despite Garth's deep-rooted Confederate attitudes, he could not help but feel sympathy for Carrington. Garth knew something about lost causes and humiliation, and besides, Carrington was about the only officer at Kearny with whom he had found any rapport at all. Because of Garth's military background, the Yankee officers of lesser rank tended to ignore him. True, his own aloofness had matched theirs, but not his brashness. Consequently, Garth took the army's treatment of Carrington quite bitterly, perhaps only an extension of the way he already felt. Disillusioned by the Fetterman debacle, Carrington's transfer, which Garth viewed as a demotion, had clinched it. So, when he expressed his disappointment to the colonel, he received a pleasant surprise—the ousted commander invited him to join the staff at Fort Caspar as chief of scouts. With only a moment of hesitation, that of pondering his own true worth, T. B. Garth accepted.

That same afternoon, Bird received the news, and joyfully, saw her own opportunity. In the midst of winter, elatedly she found an invincible spring filled with hope. She was eager, bubbling over, his Pippa: "You'll love me yet, and I can tarry your love's protracted growing." Indeed, her heartful had been planted. She quickly reminded Garth that the stage was running regularly between Fort Laramie and Fort Caspar along the Overland Trail, only a few days' journey. What was parting but brief, that could not be reconciled? He became the Piper, her man of Hamelin, and she said, "I shall follow you. I have no wish to be left alone against my will, never, now, my love." In time, soon, she hoped, her lover would find suitable quarters at Fort Caspar. It need not be more than a simple room or two, where she could make a home. So little, so grand. And wherever he chose to go, she would joyously follow. Or was it pursue? Whatever, Garth heard her swift outpouring, and he tried to understand. They walked outside, across the snowy parade ground where the winter sun suddenly felt like summer.

In another two days, they were on the trail south. For Garth, farewells had not been too hard to come by, only the one to John Dominguez, the closest friend he had found since the war, a man, who despite Garth's many affectations, had understood and taught him. Dominguez was staying, had elected to hole up and make his pay at Fort Kearny, at least until summer. To Dominguez, it was not goodbye, simply *hasta luego,* for in the West, trails often crossed, sometimes purposefully, sometimes mysteriously. John Dominguez, a man of wilderness superstition as well as knowledge, had lived among the Indians too long to leave. But he was unscarred. In T. B. Garth's book that said a lot for the scout, the only legitimate frontiersman whom he had ever known personally.

So, Garth found himself staring at the white face of winter again, the trail to Fort Laramie, snowy furrows pointing the way. Luckily, the weather had taken a turn for the better, cold but sunny, and the party of troopers and evacuees reached the remnants of Fort Reno on the third night, two days ahead of Colonel Carrington's staff detachment and regimental band coming up behind. At Reno, they whooped it up a bit, with reason. The scouts reported the trail void of Indian sign, a reasonable indication that most of the hostiles were still congregated below on the Powder and Tongue river valleys. The following morning, two deciding factors moved the contingent on south toward Dry Fork: continuing good weather and the obvious absence of hostiles. Little need to wait for Carrington, now. The worst behind them, the troopers filed out in a double column, trailing four wagons, and by late afternoon had passed Pumpkin Buttes and were setting down in a meadow near Antelope Creek to make camp.

Preparations were routine, the unloading of tents, a few supplies for the evening meal, picketing stock and posting guard, a wood and water detail. The entire party pitched into the chores at hand. Garth and several other men set about driving pins for the remuda while a few of the women wandered down the creek searching for privacy and incidental scrap wood along the way. The unexpected alarm came about fifteen minutes after camp was under way. Almost simultaneously, shouts were heard in the thickets where the women had gone and from a distant knoll about a hundred yards to the east. Garth, at the edge of the grazing stock, saw a trooper riding down the small slope. Behind the soldier, facing the evening sun, a few mounted riders were poised in a ragged line. Near the middle of the hill, at the very top, Garth's quick eyes spotted the leader trotting forward, his arm held high. When the arm suddenly came down, war whoops rent the chilly air, and seven or eight Indians moved down at a gallop, making for the remuda. They were heading straight for Garth's position, coming right at him, and alone and without cover, he scrambled to the side and fell, the only place he could, in the middle of the horses. Behind him, the camp was in confusion, yells, scattered shots, and men running for the protection of the wagons.

Armed with only his revolver, Garth was caught in the crossfire. He flattened in the thin skiff of snow. There was no escape, only the horses to protect him. Within seconds, it seemed, one Indian had tumbled from his pony, struck down by rifle fire from the wagons to Garth's rear. But at least six of the riders swept right through the barrage, cutting directly into the remuda. Garth came up to his knees, managed to get off four shots before the first onrushing pony bowled him over. Then, the attackers suddenly swerved to his left, breaking off nine horses from the end of the line. When Garth got back to his knees, his left arm was numb from the crunch of the pony, and as he raised to fire again, a sudden explosion rocked his head. Blackness swept over him. Clubbed from behind, he went sprawling and the last of the raiders thundered over him, yelping and riding away through the cover of cottonwood and willow along Antelope Creek.

When he regained consciousness, the skies above him were black and sprinkled with stars, and he heard familiar voices and the scuffling of buffalo boots. He felt a deep throbbing in his head, the bandage there, its sticky dampness, knew it was blood. Garth discovered that he could not raise himself, not without splitting pain, but his vision was still good. The flames of the night fires were leaping round him, a few figures moving back and forth in the long shadows. Someone finally stared into his face. It was Jim Cutter, the Yankee private, one of his first friends, the companion of Boley and Daley.

"You see me all right?" Cutter asked. "Hey, Captain, you awake?"

Garth nodded and passed a sign with his hand.

Cutter sighed and motioned to one of the men nearby. The two lifted Garth's head and gave him a drink of brandy. Cutter finally said, "We thought we lost you, Captain. You took a right good clout, you know. Bled like a stuck hog. That old hat of yours might have saved you. Wonder you ain't dead, for sure."

"The Indians?" Garth whispered. "What happened?"

"Oh, hell, they're gone. Weren't that many. God-damned thieves, that's what. They left three behind, all dead as doornails. Fellers say you got two of 'em with your hogleg. We lost some horses, though, figure about nine head. Weren't for you, we'd likely lost half of the herd. Your horse is here, though. They didn't get old Jefferson." Cutter grinned and sighed again. "Little rest and you're gonna make it. Yes, sir, Captain Garth, you're gonna make it just fine and dandy."

Garth forced a smile. It had been two years since anyone had called him Captain Garth. It sounded good. Another person bent over him, a woman, and for a moment he thought it was Bird Rutledge. She had a cup of hot soup, and he took a long draft. He stared back at Cutter. "Three dead Indians for nine horses? Nine lousy horses?"

"No fatalities, here, Captain."

"They made a bad bargain of it."

Private Cutter rested back on his haunches. "I don't know, sir. Three of the breed women are missing. Looks like the Injuns got 'em . . . down by the creek."

Garth's breath suddenly hung. Sickness swelled in his stomach and he felt like retching. Without asking, he knew. He had seen Bird go that way earlier, down Antelope Creek. Darkness closed in on him and he heard Cutter's voice, far off, distant, fading like the death of an echo.

". . . Missus Rutledge, that girl, Bird, and the Pawnee widow, Sarah Jennings . . ."

And Garth passed into a black chamber.

The tortuous wagon ride back to the North Platte was unending, the excruciating pain in his head, the ice in his blood, the putrid smell of himself, and for several days Garth rode a fine line, haunted by the dread

of the *kissineyooway'o,* the fear that he was freezing to
death. He lived, but perilously, and in paralysis. His
feet felt shoeless, as though they had never known the
warmth of leather and woolens. In frigid misery, he
welcomed unconsciousness, time and again drifting
into Demeter's black oblivion. Finally, many night-
mares later, he awoke to the reality of the post hospital
at Fort Laramie. He was bathed. A doctor patched his
head, stitched the jagged flesh wound above the forehead. His frostbitten feet moved again and the sharp
pains in his head slowly diminished. On the third day,
the doctor told him that he was lucky to be alive. The
cold had helped preserve him on the trip back. Some
consolation, Garth reckoned bitterly. He was useless.
Equilibrium gone, it would be a month before he could
ride a horse. He was helplessly stranded, out of commission as well as out of a job. Staring over his long
nose at the gray length of covers, he cursed his bedrid-
den plight, his stale world returned. Bird Rutledge was
gone. Once more, disenchantment became his companion.

Fast abed, Garth soon discovered that it was more
than the Sioux war club that had fractured his senses.
The Bird. She was upon him like a ghost, illusionary,
tantalizing. He even smelled her closeness. Her vision
constantly invaded his mind. He was in love, Lord help
him, in love with a memory. He thought of little else,
except the nagging haunt that she was hopelessly lost,
out of his life, and the horrible realization that he could
do absolutely nothing about it. Nor could anyone else,
he soon learned. Visitors came, one of the first, a distraught, embittered bookkeeper named Elbert Craig.
Craig, pleading for action, had been to post headquarters twice, to no avail, and Garth, feeling like Judas,
daring not to show his own deep emotional concern,
listened to yet another lost cause. He had already expected the worst, so the news Craig brought was no
great surprise. Mustering a rescue party was out of the

question, an impossibility, even if the post had troopers available. The recent relief to Fort Phil Kearny already had bled Fort Laramie badly. Additionally, this was midwinter and food supplies were short. No one but an Indian himself could possibly reach the hostile winter encampments safely.

Garth grimaced at that amusing military assessment. Staring away at the frost-covered window, he said disgustedly, "Now, that's some dandy conclusion, Elbert, but what did you expect? You should know by now if the Yankees can't garrison the forts up there properly, much less protect the trail, they're not going to send a company into hostile country looking for three women, breeds at that. Don't you understand? That Fetterman mess sealed it. That's what's stuck in the army's craw, now, fixing the blame for that blunder. Who cares about three breed women? Sure as hell, not the Yankees." He felt a lump in his throat, those lacy patterns on the window, nostalgic, the same ones that he had seen before, night after night, when he had been secure in his little room at Fort Kearny, when Bird had been beside him, when they had warmly contemplated a fuzzy future, and each other. Bird had made living worthwhile, his short-lived love, his long-legged lover. What could he possibly offer Elbert Craig? His own soul on a platter? The Sioux already had eaten his heart. He stared back at the storekeeper. "It's no use, Elbert. Any fool who's been up there this time of the year knows it's no place for a white man. The women are gone. Those Indians aren't playing hide and seek, not anymore. They have the upper hand, now, and they mean business. Everyone knows it, everyone except the Department of the Army."

Ache burdens ache, a guilty T. B. Garth continued to listen to young Craig's lament, all the while wallowing in a helplessness of his own. What irony. He couldn't muster the courage to tell Craig that his lovely breed fiancée had flown the coop long before Antelope

Creek, that either way, Craig would have been a loser, that things weren't as they seemed, that he himself shared Craig's grief because he was in love with Bird Rutledge, too. How regrettable on his part that it had taken something like a Sioux clout to make him realize how much in love he really was. Garth rationalized again, lied to himself. "Maybe the women will be better off, Elbert," he said. "You know, being with people of their own kind. They'll make out. Look at it that way. Sooner or later . . ."

With a low moan, Craig pitifully turned away. "No, never, not a woman like Bird. How can you say such a thing? She's not like them. She's different, Mr. Garth. Surely, you must have talked with her. She's no . . . no savage. She's educated. She has more intelligence than most of the officers' wives."

"No, not a savage at all," Garth admitted, wincing inside. He reached for his pipe, fumbled to light it. "She's a bright one, I'll allow you that, and the Lord willing, and using her wits, she might do more for herself that we can. But you better face up to it, not everyone looks at these breeds the same way you do. Fact is, some of those Yankee women at Kearny didn't rate the breeds any better than a colored. Yes suh, downright snobbish, Elbert."

"Nonsense!" exclaimed Craig. "This isn't Saint Louis. This is the frontier. Everyone liked the Rutledges. They admired Bird."

Garth's pipe flamed and a wisp of smoke rose over his bandaged forehead. Pointing the stem at Craig, he said, "Well, look at it this way, then. Let's assume Frances Grummond or Margaret Carrington had been among those captives, or the colonel's children. Now, let's just assume this. Do you think the Yankees would be taking a second look at this situation . . . ? Maybe mustering up a troop or two of volunteers. Oh, they'd get some takers. Come, now, it makes a man wonder what a life is really worth out here, doesn't it?"

Elbert Craig shook his head and said forcefully, "Army be damned, I shall find a way. I shan't give up on this. A reward, a ransom. I shan't give up. If that's what the Sioux want, money, gifts, they shall have them." Muttering goodbye, he adjusted his glasses and strode away.

But to Garth's dismay, the clerk returned almost daily during Garth's first two weeks in the ward. Worse yet, Craig brought gifts, first a canister of tobacco, then a new pipe, and Garth groaned inside, continuing to wrestle with his guilty conscience while hearing out Craig's lovelorn laments. No escape for T. B. Garth, cooking in his own stew. He tried to masquerade the frayed edges of his mind by assuming his customary air of casualness, his aristocratic elegance, even trimmed his moustache and hid behind a worn copy of *Jane Eyre,* reading without comprehension, in a daze, paragraphs often turning fuzzy, becoming quite meaningless.

Finally, in mid-February, he vacated the post hospital for a rough-hewn room in Brown's Hotel, only to be met with more saddening news. A dispatch had come to the fort from his brother Hugh, telling of the unexpected death of their mother. It would be in the best interests of everyone, Hugh told him, if Garth could return as soon as possible to get matters of the estate settled. Condolences. Garth spent that night writing letters, unburdening his grief and mangled soul to his friend, John Dominguez, advising him of his plans; and regrets to Colonel Henry B. Carrington, the much maligned commander who had entrusted him with the new scouting assignment at Fort Caspar. The great quest was over; he was finished. His hunt for the traitor Henry Sturges had come to a pitiful conclusion, and now, he felt like a deserter twofold, and said as much in the letter to Dominguez, to whom he appealed for assistance in trying to locate Bird and Meena. "Do everything you can," he wrote. "Above all, keep me advised. I badly need your help."

On a blustery day two weeks later, a recuperating T. B. Garth headed back to civilization, riding atop a wagon in an empty supply train bound for Omaha. Lord, Lord, Elbert was there to wave him off. The clerk presented him with one final, parting gift—a discarded Confederate cavalry hat that he had dug out of the rummage in back of the company store. Hiding despair in the depths of his dark eyes, Garth smiled gamely and pointed his nose into the prairie wind. Homeward bound, homeward bound to Dixie. The great black horse Jefferson trotted alongside the wagon.

Garth heard Craig's last words. "You'll be back, Mr. Garth. The future is out here. You'll be back."

With a wave of his new hat, Garth did not look back.

Book Two

Bird Rutledge

Chapter Nine

Bird had never known hatred, the menacing kind of hatred Garth had for Henry Sturges, that haunting obsession to strike back and kill. But she knew it now. She recalled what Garth had told her one night when they had talked about their feelings, the emotions of men and women, and what he believed were the essential ones that most people came to live by: love, hate, and ambition; how the preponderance of any one of the three might diminish, even extinguish the others; that if a man hated or even loved too much, he might lose his soul and all of his ambition as well. In her scheme of life, love was all (or had been), his love, and until the raid at Antelope Creek, she was living with a song in her heart. But after those first days with the Brule Sioux, Bird had quickly learned to hate. Garth was dead, and her world was badly out of balance. When the shock wore off, she became madly incensed, an entirely different feeling than she had had when the hostiles killed her father at Fort Kearny. More than anything, the death of Jack Rutledge saddened her. Garth had been there to console her. At that time, cold hatred and revenge had never entered her mind, but now with Garth gone, she was obsessed, and like him, she found herself wanting to strike back and kill.

First of all, Bird detested the brave, Man Called Cut Nose, the one who had counted coup by crushing Garth's skull with a war club. Worse yet, Man Called Cut Nose had worn Garth's gray cavalry hat all the way back to the small Sioux village along the Little Powder. Like any coup counter, he proudly displayed the torn brim where his ax had made its mark. Bird's eyes blazed with anger every time she saw the forlorn hat, and she secretly vowed that if she ever had the chance, she would kill Cut Nose; she hated this much, and it was the hate that sustained her. And her sorry situation those first days in the Indian camp compounded her belligerent ire. She had never been treated like a slave, confined to a smoky lodge, made to work at the most menial chores while the small council debated her fate and that of her mother and the Pawnee, Sarah Jennings.

A week passed before the three women finally learned they had been captured by a band of horse-raiding Brule instead of hostile Oglala, one of the reasons, Meena opined, that they had not been killed or thrown out in the snow. They were lucky, Meena said, something that Bird found hard to believe. The Brule villages of Spotted Tail had never openly engaged in the battle over the Bozeman Trail. These particular Brule were not on the warpath, either. At the same time, it came to light that Cut Nose's small band of braves had never intended to do anything more than steal a few ponies when they came whooping down on the column at Antelope Creek. Raiding was a game, a challenge, a chance to count coup. It had been subterfuge, too. The Oglala were supposed to have gotten the blame for their game. The Brule had not counted on the fusillade that brought down three of their own men. The killing was unfortunate, bad medicine; it had been a foolish raid, ill-planned, which in the end gave the Indians very little to celebrate. Instead, it had brought about a wailing among the women in the winter village of thirty lodges, a lament for lost sons and a husband. And finally, the Brule had little use for captive women, except for whites who might be traded. Already, there were too many women in the Lakota camps, women without men because of the continuing war.

So, this was the regrettable case when Bird and her mother finally found themselves bound over to the tipis of Plenty Hawk, an older chief who already had a houseful of responsibilities, including a wife, Feather Tail, three children, a mother-in-law, and a younger brother, Long Mane. But he was moderately rich, possessing three tipis, many robes and furs, and a band of thirty ponies. Nothwithstanding, Bird promptly balked at the arrangement when she was led up to the third tipi of her new family. Infuriated, she immediately started a fight with the three taunting women who had brought her. Erupting with a vicious string of curses, she spat on the high, beaded moccasins of one woman, and struck out at another with clinched fists. The third woman, one of greater size, finally wrestled Bird to the frozen ground, and there she sat, still swearing, until she heard the quiet but stern command of a man. The three women immediately backed away, and a few curious children, drawn to the scene by all the commotion, ran into hiding.

When Bird looked up, she saw something more than she expected. She knew in a flash that the man looking down at her was Plenty Hawk. An eagle feather dangled close to his shoulder. About forty years of age, he had a finely chiseled face, a rather sharp, hawklike nose, and small crow feet spangled at the corners of his eyes. He was trying to hide a smile, but the trace of it was too much for Bird to bear.

Angered and humiliated, she cried out, "It's not funny! *Waya-ta-nin makah!*" May you eat dirt! She made a swift flourish: "All of you!"

For a moment, she took in Plenty Hawk's silently amused stare, fully expecting an angry kick. By Lakota's standards, her conduct was atrocious, yet, strangely the kick did not come. Instead, the chief suddenly reached down and swept her up in both of his arms. *"Hopo!"* he said. Let's go! And with that, and Bird kicking furiously, he carried her to the entry of the tipi where he shucked her off like a sack of grain. When she bounded up, he gave her one gentle swat on her backside. That was it. Bird jerked the flap down in his face and screamed in the darkness.

Meena Rutledge, taking up where the women left off, tried to bring her rebellious daughter around by a harangue of her own. It only got her one in return, so Meena finally resorted to rationalizing. Accept fate and bide time, she advised Bird. Bury belligerence; hide it. At least they all had food and shelter, had been given winter clothes, and most of all, they were alive. Bad luck, if this had been Red Cloud's hostiles, for after all, they were fort women, women of the *wasichu*. Bird disagreed. How could anything possibly be worse? She continued to curse freely, and everyone within earshot knew this was a different breed of a woman.

A much more passive Sarah Jennings, a sawyer's widow, who had once lived in a Pawnee village, was given to Black Bull, another subchief. She had the submissive mind of Meena Rutledge. She wanted out, but she was willing to wait, to make the best of their predicament. "I can endure until spring comes," she told the other women. "This isn't new to me. The troopers will come. There are only hunters here, not warriors. Our people will rescue us."

Bird, not easily persuaded, and definitely not in the mood for such reasoning, scoffed back, "You only wish it were so." She whispered bitterly, "Escape! Escape is the only way, don't you understand? I'll tell you this, when the time comes, I'll get out of here, even if I have to get out by myself. I'm no savage. I won't live like one, either."

"No, no," Sarah implored quietly. "I know how these people are. We must stay together. They will hope for a reward, something in exchange, so they won't mistreat us. This is their way. If the soldiers don't come, eventually they'll take us back. You'll see."

"That's hope," countered Bird. "That's only your foolish hope. If you want to know, they're afraid to take us back. They can't now, not after the fight, the killing."

Meena said, "Listen, my girl, there's always hope. We are alive. We have to make do. Do nothing to make things worse."

"Worse?" Bird laughed mockingly. "Mama, look around at this place."

"Yes, that's my hope," Sarah admitted, looking up at Bird. "And fair treatment, if only we can be patient. Don't you see?" She looked away, averted her eyes. "I once had several strange men between my legs. I survived it. I shared. It wasn't unpleasant or pleasant. It didn't kill me."

Bird stared away moodily, incensed by the very thought of such capitulation, that, and becoming just another copulating squaw in a small Sioux village. And for the next several days, hate continued to gnaw at her in a worsening situation. When she was not eaten by hate, she brooded, numbed to the quick by the loss of Garth. Luckily, however, it was not Plenty Hawk who drew her wrath. He was not around that much. It was the camp women, ten or so, who taunted her haughtiness, who berated her around the night fires, the young boys who played pranks on her, some of whom she quickly caught and gave a real head jerking. To make matters worse, most of the men secretly admired the fiery new Woman Called Bird, and by intuition, the women knew it. By the end of the first moon, the women had become an envious lot. With other reason, too. The Woman Called Bird had pitched into working. Her abilities exceeded most of them, not her camp knowledge, but her agility, her strength, and her uncanny way with the ponies she had been tending. And she was a fighter, a free spirit. One of the sullen

women said the breed *wasichu* was worse than a
mountain cat. That was enough to earn Bird Rutledge
another name. In short order, she also became the Cat
Woman, and after that, few trifled with her.

Plenty Hawk, seemingly in no great hurry to tame
his new charge, descreetly kept his distance when he
was about. He was a hunter, had many ponies, and was
away a great deal of the time. In his thirty-ninth winter, he had become a good provider as well as a good
father, and when in winter camp, spent as many hours
as he could with his family. Unlike Bird Rutledge, he
had patience, and unbeknownst to her, much of his patient attitude was by design and tact. He understood the
ways of animals and nature. This was his forte, his
way. For instance, he would never kill the spirit in a
good yearling by complete and total subjugation. By
experience, he knew better; bring the animal along
slowly, win its confidence, but never break it completely, never replace spirit with docility. While he recognized that Bird was unhappy, and played his game
accordingly, he had no way of knowing a man called
Garth was behind her unhappiness.

Plenty Hawk's conversations with Bird were casually brief and usually in the presence of Feather Tail
and Meena, and the old woman Teal Wing, his mother-
in-law, who by custom, only listened, and seldom said
anything to Plenty Hawk. For a time, the language barrier was a small hindrance even to Bird who throughout her time in the forts had learned the basic Lakota
words and phrases. Most of the expressions that Bird
readily knew had come from the stables, many of them
rough words more suitably used during her frequent
outbursts of anger. When she swore, the men laughed.
Plenty Hawk's women talked, pointed, and made signs
and repeated words, and as conditions slowly im-
proved, Bird occasionally forgot some of her inner torment and sometimes even managed a smile. But not
always.

"The night will come," Meena told her daughter one day, "when you will be alone with him in the third tipi. Be a woman. Treat him like the kind man he is. He'll be good to you."

Bird's face clouded into another storm. She was so tired of this same advice, so weary of hearing it. Once again, she turned angrily away. "I'm not Sarah Jennings," she said lowly. "I don't want anything from him, nothing, Mama, nothing. Can't you understand this? I want nothing but my freedom, only to get out of this forsaken place. I do my share of the work. It relieves the boredom. That's enough. Don't tell me how to be a woman."

Exasperated, Meena Rutledge sighed and held up a hand. "Enough, enough," she protested. "Do what you wish. Yes, have it your way. You have the bold manners of Papa, God bless him. Perhaps you're not the vixen I imagined. I only thought . . ."

"You only thought!" Bird exclaimed testily. "Mama, just what do you think? Do you really think I'm a vixen . . . ? That I have to lie on my back to earn my keep around here?"

"No, I only thought you might play the part, play the part of the bitch fox. Listen, my daughter, this man has never met a woman like you. If you play the part, soon Plenty Hawk will hear every word you speak. Convince him. You will find your life better. Your wishes will be his. Soon, he will trust you, give you anything. You will be a total woman, and this village will belong to you. You will not be watched. And then one day . . ."

"Ha, you assume too much," Bird cut in. "Do you take him for a fool? He's a chief, not an idiot. He has a woman and children, friends around him. He must know something about life, enough not to be foxed by a woman. And besides, the thought of playacting makes me ill. When I take a man to bed with me, it's not an act, I assure you that."

Gnawed by apprehension, Bird was both angered and amused, sometimes perplexed, by the varying attitudes of anticipation shown by her mother and others around her. It was a small village, intimate, practically void of privacy, and it was rife with gossip. Everyone seemed to be waiting for Plenty Hawk to make his move, to take this strange new woman. Bird was beside herself. Now, it was not only Meena trying to reinforce her, but Feather Tail, too, the chief's very own wife. At first, Bird had bristled at her mother's advice.

Finally she had come to accept Meena's reasoning—where there is a will, there is a way. That much was past, the reluctant acceptance, not necessarily the will. Even the gabbling women were in on it. They giggled among themselves and watched. Instinctively, Bird knew that she was the brunt of their smutty humor. In a sullen way, it amused her. She was the center of attraction, had been ever since she had been captured. Let them talk. She had already asserted herself, and no one dared confront her, not openly. She tried to ignore the foolish women. But she could not ignore Feather Tail, who was constantly around her. Feather was now the one who really confused her, the way she treated her like a blood sister. The woman did not have a jealous bone in her still youthful body, accepting Bird without a trace of animosity, leading her to believe that this must be the free-living custom among the Sioux; or that perhaps the great disproportion of men to women in the villages had prompted such polygamous arrangements. Whatever, Feather Tail seemed perfectly happy to share her husband freely with Bird. And why not? Bird was now a part of the working family and fully entitled to all benefits. Everyone had a duty, chores to perform, obligations to fulfill, including copulation. Plenty Hawk was master here, provider, father, as well as husband and lover. Feather further surprised Bird by occasionally making gestures, provocative little signs about Plenty Hawk which could only be inter-

preted in one way, his sexual prowess. On the most
recent occasion, when Bird surprisingly came to a full
blush, Feather only laughed and hugged her, saying in
effect, "Don't worry, it will be plenty good."

Totally perplexed by the situation now facing her,
here she was, trapped by Indians in the middle of winter, a hundred miles from nowhere, her lover dead, and
she herself faced with the prospects of taking a new
one, an uneducated savage at that. And she had no way
out. Plenty good? That was a matter of opinion, and
certainly not one she shared with Feather Tail. The
more she thought about her bizarre predicament, the
crazier it became. For one thing, if everything was so
harmonious in the tipis, then why had Plenty Hawk
failed to assert himself, taken up his dutiful rights and
approached her like the stallion Feather hinted he was?
Yes, and with everyone else so concerned, why did he
seem to be so unconcerned, so detached from the issue
at hand? What kind of man was he? A puzzlement.

This day, he was preparing to make another hunt. It
was near the middle of the Hungry Moon, and despite
the chief's ability as a hunter, there had been little
fresh meat in the village for several weeks. Everyone
was subsisting on buffalo jerky, wasna or pemmican,
beans, and dried fruits, the usual winter fare, most of it
prepared months ahead. Flour obtained in the fall trading was now at a premium and used sparingly for flat
cakes. These Sioux were frugal. Spring was still two
moons away. By experience they knew lean winters
and lean bellies went hand in hand, knew what to expect and how to survive. When the buffalo often mysteriously disappeared, when the land became barren,
they had learned to conserve. Free-roaming Indians
never starved. Bird was aware of this. They took the
easiest food at hand, small animals, prairie chickens,
mostly by snares and traps, sometimes by the silent
bow. Occasionally, someone successfully stalked antelope and deer. Shot and powder, and especially the new

bullets, were seldom wasted on small game. The few braves in the Brule band who owned rifles also had learned to conserve as the season of the cold moons drearily wore on. Lead balls had to be saved for bigger game, the red meat of deer, elk, and migrating buffalo, when the village hunters were lucky enough to find the larger beasts.

Plenty Hawk was going after elk, and he was hopeful that his luck would turn for the better. He told the family that the omens were good; the signs told him that he should leave the next day. He said he and Long Mane would ride out at dawn for the higher mountains where in past years hunting had been good. Beside the leaping fire, he held up his rifle and brushed over its long, shiny barrel. This was a time when men cherished their rifles for long shots, and he took extra time to check his weapon, a good carbine he had taken during the fighting against Star Chief Conner's troopers two years back. The Sioux had driven the blue coats home that time.

While Feather and Meena were packing parfleches for the men, Bird left to cut out hunting ponies. It was dusk when she returned with two mounts and a packhorse. And it was getting brisk. She brought the ponies in at a trot, the shaggy beasts snorting and blowing steam into the chilly evening air. After rubbing her hands, she set about picketing the stock in back of the third tipi. The two older children of Plenty Hawk brought hay. When Bird finally secured the ropes, the youngsters scurried away back to the warmth of the main lodge. For a while, Bird stood there, coiling a lariat, watching the horses nose into the hay, and in the dimness, for the first time, she noticed Plenty Hawk. He came close, inspected the picket pins once, and then grunted in satisfaction. Bird thought it rather unusual that he had come out at all. Care of the ponies was her work, not his. She hesitated a moment, wondering at her sudden uneasiness, until it suddenly

struck her. He hadn't moved and she realized this was
the first time she had ever been alone with him. It was
an awkward moment for both of them. The chief said
something, too low to be clearly understood, and when
he touched her shoulder, she froze stiffly, her fingers
tight against the coil of rope in her hand.

"Wan mayak uwe," he said easily. Look at me.

Bird suddenly turned on him, causing his hands to
hike up protectively above his shoulders. The belligerence inside her crouched like a badgered animal preparing to spring. She contained herself, quelled by the
softness of his voice and the broad, reassuring smile on
his face. And his sudden gesture! It actually brought a
smile to her own tight lips. His hands were raised in
front of him, palms outward, as if he were saying,
"Don't strike, I surrender." Bird handed him the rope,
pointing to it. Her hands flashed with her words. "I
will not hit you. It would be bad medicine to hit a man
with his own rope."

Smiling, he took the coil and threw it aside.
"Nunwe," he said. Let it be, no matter. Looking
straight into her widened eyes, Plenty Hawk continued,
saying, "You say I am a man. *Ho,* if I am a man, I am
a good man. Why do you still fear me? All my people
say I am a good man, a great hunter. I go tomorrow to
bring back meat for my people and you. This is good,
but you think I am bad. I see this in your heart. Why
is this?"

Surprised at his frank yet gentle outburst, Bird hesitated, trying to prepare her answer, not intending to
offend, only to dissuade him. She said slowly, "I'm not
afraid of you. See here, around you, your people are
here." She pointed to the south. "My people are there,
across the mountains. I belong there. Nothing has
changed in your village. Who is good that would take
me and my mother away from our people?"

Plenty Hawk rubbed his chin thoughtfully and pondered her words and sign. There was a fine glint of

consideration in his dark eyes. Finally, he nodded. Then, with continuing smile, he replied, "Yes, you are right. Maybe you do not belong here, I ask then, where do you belong? I do not know. Cree Woman says your people are far away by the great Calling River. I know all of this. Whom do you honor? Do you honor the buffalo soldiers who would take our land from us, who build their great war houses where we hunt?"

"I know right from wrong," she said.

He motioned around him toward the night shadows of the hills. "Then tell me, Woman Called Bird, who is bad in this land? You are a Human Being. You should know. Is it we who live here with the bones of our forefathers? Is it the *wasichu* from far across the River Who Scorns All Other Rivers who cover the land like grasshoppers? Hear me, I did not bring you here. I made you welcome in my lodge. You are still welcome."

Bird listened closely, wondering all the while how she could refute anything he was saying. His reasoning was all too true, yet was anything of what he said her fault? After all, she was still being held against her will. Finally, she said with a scowl, "Man Called Cut Nose is bad." For emphasis, she clinched her fist and made a throwing motion to the ground. "It was he who made the trouble, not you. It was he who made your people afraid to take us back. He is a killer."

"*Ho,* so it is Man Called Cut Nose who offends you. Why did you not tell me this before?"

"I was too angry. One day I will kill him."

"I cannot make excuses for the mistakes of Cut Nose," Plenty Hawk stiffly said. "In the excitement of battle a warrior sometimes takes the wrong path. The fight at Antelope Creek was not meant to be. The death of his own brothers has been his punishment. There can be no worse. Leave him be."

Shaking her head angrily, Bird said, "No, Cut Nose

is proud. See how he struts like a prairie chicken! He wears the hat of my friend, the man he killed."

"The white Crow Feather, *Kangi Wiyaka*, was a buffalo soldier who shot Human Beings," motioned Plenty Hawk sternly.

"No, he was not a buffalo soldier. Crow Feather was a gray soldier, an enemy of the long knives. They burned his land and killed his father in the great war of the white men."

Plenty Hawk stared curiously at her and shook his head. "I do not understand."

"This is what you see in my heart," she replied, making a slow motion to her breast. "I hurt here because the man called Crow Feather was a friend. He helped me. He was a good man who did not want any trouble with the Human Beings."

The chief took her by the arm and led her in between the tipis. When he was in front of the third lodge, he stopped and looked down at her again. He said, "Cree Woman says you are brave. I believe this. Hear me. You have many suns ahead of you in this village. If you are not happy here by the Moon of the Greening Grass, then I will take you near the fort on the River of Tongues. From there, you may go. I can do no more. But you must say nothing of this to my family or people. Do nothing to shame me."

Bird, her eyes wide with surprise, stared up at the chief, too startled to answer. She could hardly believe what she was hearing from her mild-mannered master. Just like that, he was prepared to free her!

"Do you understand?" he asked. "If this is your wish, I will give you and Cree Woman ponies when the time comes."

Hesitating, reaching for proper words, she finally said, "You have much honor. What more can I say?"

"It is my way," Plenty Hawk said proudly. But then he frowned, shook his head again, thoroughly perplexed. "But I do not understand. No, this is mysterious like the sky at night. It must be the white blood in you, that you would wish to return to the yellow eyes who burned the land of the gray soldier and killed his father. The Indian in you is not that crazy."

Bird Rutledge tried to smile. How could she answer, possibly explain? It seemed so futile. Actually, she had no plans, really no place to go. What was her future without Garth, the man the Sioux called Crow Feather? With somewhat confused but tender appreciation, she looked up at Plenty Hawk, and in a brief, parting motion, said, "You are a kind man."

Soon afterward, the series of events that transpired convinced Bird that this was not the last she would see of Plenty Hawk before his hunting departure. For one thing, she noticed that the packs for the hunt had been stored in the third tipi instead of the main lodge. Another unusual happening was that old Teal Wing, Feather Tail's mother, who stayed in the third tipi with Bird and Meena, had discreetly moved her belongings into the middle lodge where Long Mane and the children usually slept. If those hints were not clear enough, her mother supplied the clincher near bedtime. After banking the fire and regulating the tipi vent, Meena began rolling up her own robe and blanket. She also was leaving for the night.

That did it. Bird thought she had held her tongue long enough. "Is this another custom?" she asked her mother testily. "No ceremony? Not even a word to me about it? I suppose everyone in this camp but me knows what's going on around here, every nosey woman out there."

"Shhh!" Meena came back. "Don't be silly!"

"Silly?" huffed Bird. "Why, this whole charade is silly!"

"No one but we know. Look, remember, this was decided long ago when he took us into his family. Custom? What do I know about their customs? Everyone works. Everyone shares. Ceremonies are silly when you are already his woman. And what do you care about what a few old women think? Ha, they are jealous!"

"I'm nobody's woman unless I want to be."

"Run away into the night, then. Yes, run!"

Bird's eyes widened in astonishment. "You still have no feeling about your own daughter? This . . . this arrangement, or whatever it is? You're leaving, just like that?"

Clasping her hands to her breast, Meena stared almost tearfully across the small fire. "You know that's not true. I cry inside for you. I love you. I would die for you, yes, just to make you happy. God has chosen this trail for us. I don't know why, no more than why He took Papa. Only He knows, God, the Great Spirit. I only want to make His trail easier for you someway."

Bird gestured helplessly around her. "This . . . this isn't easy, Mama. Ever since Garth . . ."

"I know, I know," soothed Meena. "But if you continue to look back, will you ever be able to see ahead? You're too smart for that. Listen, little one, you are more woman than you know. Your time will come, your day. Yes, I see it. You will soar like an eagle, and not even their great chief, Spotted Tail, will be able to keep you here." Meena kissed her daughter on the forehead. "Patience," she whispered. She nodded toward the fire. "I made tea, chokecherry tea, honey in it." And with that, she tugged on her bundle and left.

This left Bird facing the inevitable, and her fertile young mind began whirling like a dust devil. Thought after thought billowed up before her, giving birth to a myriad of questions, some new, some old, and with a touch of disgust, a touch of anxiety, she scurried about like a frantic squirrel trying to prepare herself. Maybe something unforeseen will happen, she whispered. Maybe he won't come at all. My God, I know so little about this man! First, he sorrows for me, offers me freedom, and now he offers himself. Is this out of pity, too, for my pleasure, for his? My pleasure? God! What manner of lover can he possibly be? Can I believe Feather Tail, these people so prone to boasting of their men's abilities in bed? What do I do, accept him like a corpse or grind off his cock? Accept fate and enjoy myself? Ha, I must pretend, fool him, hurry him away to his hunt, what else? Certainly, as he warned, do nothing to shame him.

And so Bird waited. She folded both hands around an old cup, sipped some of the hot, chokecherry tea, smiled bitterly, suddenly aware of her native posture, squatting, the red maiden waiting. Maybe she was more red than she thought, sitting Indian-like, blanket-draped, naked, toes curled under beaded buckskin, her dark eyes searching the embers for some kind of mysterious sign.

She was still staring at the fire when moments later, Plenty Hawk made his appearance. Her hunched position was unchanged, and without moving, she looked up, trying her best to be casual. Quite the contrary, inwardly, his sudden appearance gave her a small start, possibly a touch of fright which she could never admit, much less care to show. She did greet him; it would have been impolite not to. But her greeting was simple, almost cold, a nod, a touch of the cup to her pouty lips. She watched him put aside his rifle and remove his winter coat. He had a buckskin pouch with him, a bag somewhat larger that the small one he sometimes carried about his neck, the one that held his good medicine, the charms, the conglomeration of signs, bits of bone, feather, and fur that guided his destiny. After he had shed his shirt and leggings, and covered his bare shoulders with a blanket, he squatted across the fire opposite her, the beaded pouch at his feet.

Nervously fumbling at her cup, Bird waited for a word, some opening, anything to break the strain of silence. The small fire sputtered, sending a fresh plume of smoke spiraling toward the vent above. After another moment, she finally dipped the cup back into the steaming bowl of tea and handed it to him. Heavens, this was nothing like she had imagined, neither the situation nor the man! Plenty Hawk, in truth, was handsome in a rugged sort of way, but for a chief, an experienced husband, why so subdued, so docile? Plenty Hawk, his voice gone, his eyes evasive, his hand trembling against the cup, seemed to be faltering worse than she. "Drink," Bird suddenly whispered, almost desperately. And she wondered why she was whispering. She spoke lowly, making a few signs to complement her halting words. "My mother prepared this drink. This is for winter, the time of the cold moons. It will make you warm. See, your hand, you're cold."

Plenty Hawk shook his head. *"Nyah,"* he said. "No, I'm not cold." He began to drink, and Bird watched curiously. Afterward, he took a deep breath and returned the cup. He struck his smooth chest several times and smiled. He felt better. Then, as if to explain his tardiness, he motioned above. "I have made my prayers for the hunt. I ask for good hunting and good weather. I ask to come home safely."

Bird nodded. Good, good.

"I pray to *Wakan Tanka*," he said, passing his hand above him again. He pushed a thumb toward her. "For you, I pray to the Great Spirit, too."

"Thank you. Why me? I'm not a hunter."

"So you will be happy. So you will not be afraid. I understand how you feel. These people will be your people, my family, your family."

Never, Bird said inside, never. These people will never be my people, no more than you can be my man. She tried to arrange her broken thoughts. They were confusing, now mixed with doubts about herself as well as the man sitting across from her. She found herself mildly surprised at his sensitivity, his seemingly genuine concern for her welfare. And once again, he had acknowledged her sorry plight. This time, his simple assurance, almost to the point of being apologetic, tended to lower her guard. "I'm not afraid," she finally replied. "I told you that before." She then noticed the dampness at the edge of his hair and concluded that he had been outside doing more than praying to his God, *Wakan Tanka*. Obviously, he had bathed in the cold river.

Smiling, Plenty Hawk took up the pouch he had brought. He jerked at the rawhide strips holding it and pulled out a brightly beaded necklace. He presented it to her across the fire. *"Ho,"* he then exclaimed, "I have brought this for you. It's for a woman to be happy, a man to make her so. If I were a rich man, I would give you more. Wear it and remember."

Bird fondled the necklace. This unexpected gesture set her back another notch. The necklace was pretty. She had seen similar ones at Fort Laramie among the wives of the Laramie Loafers. She knew the beads' great value, the high esteem placed upon them, and her eyes suddenly sparkled. Even in the dim fireside light, the polished bone, shell, and elk teeth glittered with brilliance. To Lakota women, this was a priceless gift, and his overture had indeed touched her. What else could she do but move her hand to her heart in polite thanks. She then carefully lowered the beads over her head. The necklace fell into place around her neck, and she arranged it, nestling the pendant in between her bare bosom. She looked appreciatively at Plenty Hawk, noticed his newly found concentration, her plump breasts. "This is plenty," she said, nodding respectfully. "You don't have to be a rich man. You are kind and rich in heart. I will cherish this present."

"That is good," he said, making a hasty flourish. "I know you have been an angry woman. You have been here many suns. Even the seasons must change. You are not angry, now?"

"Nyah," she replied, shaking her head. "At first, ev-

erything displeased me. Now, you please me, even though you came as a surprise, without telling me."

Plenty Hawk glowed. "I thought you would understand. I found it too much for me to talk about. I waited for the right signs to tell me you were no longer frightened of me. I'm happy to please you, to come to your tipi."

Please her? Well, only time would tell about this. Bird veiled a smile, and with less reservation, said, "I'm happy to hear you say this." Now, she thought, rapport has been effected, and she knew her position, what was expected of her. Reality. She wanted none of it, but surprisingly, the night was becoming much more tolerable than she had expected. This was a gentle man, and one with manners. He was still sitting on his haunches, much less savage than she had assumed, but quite oddly, she seemed to be more in command of the situation than he. She was beginning to feel sorry for him, this recalcitrant, fumbling man across the way. She had asked herself this question before: what manner of man was he? Was he indeed duty-bound, or was he actually wanting? Certainly, not the latter. Or did he know ways of the fox better than she? If so, his pursuit was cunningly subtle. Bird did notice, however, that his lingering, fixed stare had become less than subtle. The bareness of her middle, she supposed, not the necklace. She laughed, too nervously, she thought, but she knew she had the situation well in hand, and it was her game to play out to the inevitable end. She was the vixen. Directly, she stood and faced him. "What about you?" she asked. "Are you afraid of the woman the Lakota call Cat?"

Plenty Hawk's eyes followed her. He denied the suggestion with a wave of his hand. Then, Bird went directly to the pile of robes, boldly shucked her blanket and sat down. This must not be prolonged, she thought. Now, it must be over and done with, pleasurable or not. The warmth from the small fire enveloped her naked body, and looking straight at him, Bird commanded, "Take off your cloth and come to the robes, it is time."

Yes, she would survive as Sarah Jennings had, a means to an end. And her mother was right—she was more woman than anyone knew, and true, when the Moon of the Green Grass came, she would fly away free like an eagle. But this was the reality of the moment, inescapable. To her great surprise, his love was gentle and caring. And then her worst fear came true—it became pleasurable, exciting, and she fixed her rhythm to his. Helplessly ashamed and groaning, Bird became lost in the passion of the present.

Chapter Ten

On the third morning, Long Mane unexpectedly returned to the village, alone, leading one pack horse, one small antelope draped over its back. Though the women were happy to see the fresh meat, even so little, Long Mane's solitary appearance gave them a scare, their first thought being that Plenty Hawk was in trouble. Long Mane looked troubled, too. He slipped off his pony and stumbled toward the first tipi as the anxious women hovered around, plying him with questions. Obviously, the young brave was sick, his hands numbed by cold. Feather Tail and Woman Called Bird quickly led him inside. As soon as the word spread that Plenty Hawk was safe, Meena and old Teal Wing tugged the antelope carcass away to be butchered. Long Mane, stuttering from cold, tried to explain to Bird and Feather. His older brother was still hunting forty miles to the north, maybe farther, now. Plenty Hawk had set out on the tracks of two elk, one of them badly wounded, and sensing a big kill, had sent Long Mane back to the village to get more ponies for packing. Long Mane's face was drawn. Holding his hands to the fire, he stared at the two women. He felt ashamed, without honor. On the way back, he had become sick, violently ill from eating the warm meat of the antelope before it cooled. He had vomited during the night and again that morning, once became so dizzy that he fell from his pony. He had lost his mittens, too. Now, someone else had to take pack animals back to Plenty Hawk, and quickly. Long Mane was too sick to ride.

The women fully understood the urgency because it was the bad season for a man to be hunting alone so far from the village. In the winter, the Four Winds became too contrary, and if Plenty Hawk had, indeed, made his kills, he would need help. After Feather and Bird made their young brother comfortable, they huddled nearby, trying to decide who would make the return trip. Most of the men were away, still hunting, not that it mattered that much, for preparing the meat was generally a woman's job, anyhow. Feather told Bird that Calf Roper, the oldest son of Cut Nose, was a good worker and knew his way in the hills. Perhaps, he could take the ponies to where Plenty Hawk had his hunting wickiup in the rocks, the Place of the Smoking Water.

"He is only a boy," Bird said contemptuously. "What does he know?"

Feather Tail pursed her lips and thought. This was true, and Calf Roper had never been to the Place of the Smoking Water. Maybe it was too much of a trip for a boy so young to make alone. Finally, she tapped her breast. She was making the decision to go herself. She knew Smoking Water well, had been there several times before she became a mother. But Bird disagreed again. "It may be dangerous," she warned. "What if you get lost in the snow? What if you meet Crow hunters?"

"I haven't forgotten the way," Feather replied. "Calf Roper can help me. There will be tracks from Long Mane's ponies. Winter, now, not the time for Crow, not way down here."

Bird's nose wrinkled. She had devious ideas of her own, and they did not include Calf Roper, son of Man Called Cut Nose, whom she still despised. Winter be damned, she wanted to learn more about the land, directions, the various trails to freedom. Despite Plenty

Hawk's promises, and her amorous night with him, and how much she had enjoyed it, she still had her eyes set on the horizon. Raising a hand in protest, she said, "*Nyah,* I'm the best rider in the village. Everyone knows this. I know how to handle ponies. Let me go with you. Calf Roper is too young and foolish. He's no better than his father."

"You?" Feather quietly exclaimed. "You want to go with me?"

Bird hurriedly went on, explaining, "Look, the old women can take care of the children. I can help you better than any boy. I want to be with you . . . yes, together we can go find Plenty Hawk. I would like this, and it would please him to see us both."

Feather's face lit up, and she replied happily, "Why, I have never heard you speak out like this before. Yes, and with your heart. I did not know . . ."

Relieved, Bird touched two fingers to her lips, kissed them, and touched Feather's lips. "Come," she said, "I cannot explain all of my feelings. They are too confused. But, listen, we are like one, are we not? We now share the same man. Yes, I want to go with you. That should be enough. I want to do my share."

"It will be a long ride, plenty hard work."

Bird only laughed and started pulling out boots and coats. "*Nyah,* together it will be easy. I think it will be fun to ride away for a few days, yes, not to hear the gabble of the other women. I get tired of them. They're like geese. They have big mouths and big butts. They cackle and waddle."

Feather giggled. "You are a crazy woman, the way you talk. Your spirit, it soars like a hawk. What is it? You make me feel like a maiden again, to hear you laugh, to see you smile." Feather shook her head disbelievingly. "Now, you want to make fun out of this work. Yes, I think you are crazy, but I love you. *Hopo,* go fetch us some ponies. Yes, you must come with me. I should have known."

And as Bird Rutledge ran to get the horses, she thought to herself, yes, and she, too, felt like a maiden, again. And she had reason to smile. Indeed she was a crazy woman, a crazy woman in want, a woman whose mind was in horrible disarray after one night in the robes with a man she had badly misjudged. Feather Tail hadn't exaggerated. Plenty Hawk was a caring, experienced lover. And his size! My gracious, such a horrid, devastating thought! But my God, it was true! Horses, she busied herself with the horses, cut out four, and by the time she returned, Feather Tail had finished making the trail packs. One hour later, shortly after noon, they were trailing north, following the tracks of Long Mane. Two of the big camp dogs were loping ahead of the horses. The two women, riding side by side, were laughing like young girls on a picnic. They rode steadily without any delays. Feather knew the trail, probably well enough to have made the journey without following the tracks of her brother-in-law, Long Mane. The young brave's story had been true, although no one had doubted it, because soon, the women passed the place in the snow where he had fallen from his pony. They found his lost mittens. Other signs along the way told of his illness. They also crossed other tracks in the thin blanket of snow, the big pads of wolves crossing the hills in search of food. But these tracks were not fresh, Feather explained, or else the hackles of the two dogs would have been standing.

They headed in the direction of the late afternoon sun, occasionally departing from the trail, taking short-cuts toward a distant, timbered country where Feather said they would have to spend the first night. Bird was taking mental notes, observing each landmark. It was almost dark when they reached the edge of these small mountains. Feather pointed ahead to some tall spruce at the mouth of a dark canyon. This was the place, the campsite. There was water and feed for the ponies, plenty of dead branches for a fire. They quickly built their fire in a grove of trees. Bird's feet were cold from the long ride, and after she had warmed them, she took care of the stock. Forage was plentiful, the hay along the creek deep and free of snow. She picketed the ponies there, only a stone's throw from the grove where the women had rigged their small shelter. By the time they finished their meager meal, darkness had fallen over the valley and a little breeze was sifting down the canyon from the west. Feather Tail said this was a good sign, maybe fresh snow, but much warmer weather, and a better day ahead. But Bird thought that the day just spent had not been a bad one, for they had made a good ride, and they now had shelter and a warm bed of buffalo robes. And the bed felt good. She clasped her arms around her Lakota sister and sighed. She sighed again. Oh, she was comfortably secure, secure but restless. Plenty Hawk. Her mind kept wandering back to the night before he left. Overwhelmed with guilt, she had been too ashamed to tell Feather Tail how fulfilling that night really had been, how she kept reliving it, how passion had swallowed her and all of her inhibitions. Such a bizarre reversal, all of her foxy intentions shattered by her latent desire. She needed to talk, to release her pent-up emotions. Her mind was exploding. But what she was ashamed to confess was that she now was anticipating more. Such obsession, such anxiety. Her control was gone, and she couldn't believe it. She sighed again, and Feather Tail finally whispered, "What is it? What are you thinking about?"

"Nothing. Nothing, my sister. Nothing important." Bird nestled against Feather Tail. "How warm and comfortable this is."

"Yes, and you have other thoughts, too."

"Perhaps."

"Our man, Plenty Hawk."

A man, indeed! Bird stirred and whispered back, "Well, this is why we're here, isn't it?"

"How good it is tossing the blanket with him?"

Bird quickly came up on an elbow. "How do you know these things? How did you know what I was thinking?"

"Because you want to tell me about it. I sensed it. I know how you feel. Joy in a woman is hard to keep secret. Always, she wants to share a secret with another woman, one who is close, one she can trust. You trust me because I love you."

"Yes," Bird admitted, "yes, and I love you, too."

"I know."

"Did he say anything?"

"*Nyah,* but he smiled and nodded to me. I knew. And you, your eyes have been alive. I saw it."

"*Mi-ya!*"

"He pleased you plenty?"

"Yes . . . yes, he did," sighed Bird. "I cannot believe it."

"This is his way. I think he was happy he pleased you. Plenty Hawk knows what a woman wants. He is generous, plenty of man. I am happy you are one of us. You are plenty of woman, too."

"Yes," mumbled Bird. "I know."

When Bird and Feather Tail awoke, several inches of new snow covered the ground. Overhead, the gray clouds were low but moving swiftly east. The snowfall had lessened, only a few big flakes now filtering down between the spreading spruce boughs. And as Feather had predicted, it was much warmer. They rode out in a trot, skirting the base of the hills, keeping close to the forest's edge. Two hours later, Feather turned west into a larger valley heavy with buffalo grass, and shortly before noon, they approached a rocky outcropping. Sage, green grass, and clumps of juniper ringed the entire slope. Beyond this area was a small swamp, still green against the white coat of winter, and this was where Feather Tail stopped and pointed. A film of steam was rising from the distant gush of water. This was Smoking Water, the camp of Plenty Hawk. They heard the whinny of a pony from above, and for a moment, expectantly waited, but there was no sign of their man coming out to greet them. When they came closer, Bird noticed the rear left leg of Plenty Hawk's pony—the horse was lame. The wickiup nearby was vacant and the ashes at the fire site were cold. Bird stared at Feather. "Where is he?" she asked. "He hasn't been here, lately."

Showing no alarm, Feather looked keenly around. "He is out on foot," she said. "He has made a kill."

Bird, examining the leg of the horse found it not to be serious, probably nothing more than a bruise. Turning back to her sister, she asked, "How do you know he's made a kill? How can we be sure?"

The Brule woman pointed to a distant pole suspended between two trees. A small parfleche was hanging from it. The two leaping dogs had already discovered the scent. "He has a liver and heart up there," Feather answered. "He puts it in the bag to keep the birds away." Then, she pointed to the ground. "He came back yesterday, leading this pony. These tracks are cold, see. He has gone back to guard his kill from the wolves and coyotes. This is the way it reads. There are his marks, yonder." And with that, she turned her mount toward the tracks of Plenty Hawk. "*Hopo,* let's go! We will find him soon, and we have work to do before the sun sets."

Plenty Hawk's partially covered tracks were easy enough to follow, especially from the point where he had put on his snowshoes. As the women traced the tracks, the snow became deeper, often plunging the horses in up to their knees. The women crossed several sets of old elk tracks, well drifted in, probably made by the very animals that their man had followed from the open meadows in the basin feeding grounds. They pushed steadily on for another mile, taking their ponies to the top of a wind-blown ridge. About a mile below, a wisp of smoke was coming up from a place deep in the pines. There was no doubt in their minds about the source of the fire. Together, they raised up a long yell, sending echoes reverberating from the snowy canyons around them. They soon got an answering call, and the dogs immediately took off, bounding across the drifts down the sheltered side of the big hill. But no more than a minute later, an outcry of barks and howls erupted in the dark forest. Crying out, "Wolves!" Feather Tail kicked her pony ahead in a run. Bird had no time to panic, because everything seemed to be happening at once. She saw the first of the gray beasts only a moment after Feather had called, a lone wolf escaping through the timber to the side of her. Ahead, the angry snarling told her quite another story. Some of the wolves were fighting with the dogs. She kept waiting to hear a shot from Plenty Hawk's rifle. Suddenly, she feared for his safety. Feather, riding hard, reined sharply to the side, guiding her pony in between the big trees. Shortly, Bird had singled out the pack horses behind, and she, too, went plunging ahead in the same direction her sister had taken. By the time she rode onto the scene, the wolf pack had already broken, long streaks of gray and white leaping in all directions, some fighting a retreat, snapping and slashing at the two attacking dogs. Bird began yelling, kicked her own horse toward the melee, and the trailing wolves finally bolted and disappeared like shadows in the night. In a moment, the forest was silent again.

When Bird looked around, she saw the incredible sight, the partially eaten carcass, the remains of a great *wapiti*, its heavy quarters awash with blood, its stomach viciously ripped open. The packed snow around it was crimson. Her heart sank. Plenty Hawk had lost his meat to the hungry pack. There had been too many to shoot, too many to frighten away. On the other side of the kill, Feather Tail was trying to call back the dogs. When she heard Bird's yell, she motioned, waving her hands that everything was all right. The two women came up to the downed elk, or what was left of it. *"Ma-ya!"* Feather exclaimed softly, shaking her head. "They left little untouched. They have spoiled much of this meat. Only the bottom is left, the flanks, look."

But Bird was not too interested in the gory sight. It sickened her, the loss, the terrible waste. She turned away, asking, "Where is Plenty Hawk? Where is our hunter?"

Feather leaped down from her pony, a knife in her hand. "Don't be alarmed, my sister, he is safe." Tugging at one of the hindquarters, she deftly slit up behind it, jerked, and pulled until great chunks of meat tore away. She cut more from the other side, and then turned to the front quarters. "The dogs will have their share, too," she said. "We will save what we can for ourselves. All is not wasted." She tied the salvaged meat across the backs of the pack ponies. While she was cleaning her hands in the snow, she said, "Our hunter is down that way, not too far. Plenty Hawk must have his meat below us."

Bird curiously stared at her. "But ... but this, the wolves?"

Feather held up two wet fingers. "Two elk, one wounded. The wolves got to it first, but not all. Our man has another elk by his fire. He would never leave one like this unless there is another. *Nyah,* sleep by it, never give it up to the wolves, not without a fight. This is his way. Plenty Hawk is a good hunter. The wolves are hunters. Ah, but no one goes hungry today." She pointed above where ravens were circling and croaking against the leaden sky. "You see?"

And, once again, Feather Tail was right about the hunter, Plenty Hawk. Only a half-mile ahead, the women rode into a smoky clearing, and there beside a leaping fire, stood the hunter chief, his hands proudly akimbo. His rifle was stuck in the snow beside him. On the other side of the fire, the magnificent antlers of a great bull shot up into the air, while nearby in the trees, hanging from rawhide strips, were huge sections of the animal, already quartered and prepared for packing. Plenty Hawk happily stretched out his hands to his women.

Their return to the Smoking Water camp that day was made without delay, and by late afternoon, hundreds of pounds of meat had been strung from the lodge poles. Plenty Hawk, exhausted from his ordeal of guarding and waiting, went to the hot pool and cleansed himself. Bird Rutledge, picketing the horses nearby, could not resist taking a quick look at his nakedness, his sturdy body, yes, and what was hanging down from his crotch. With a sudden blush, she turned quickly away, and shortly joined Feather Tail, and while Plenty Hawk went to the wickiup to sleep, they began preparing for the feast that night. They searched the marshy ground along the creek bottom for dormant tubers and roots. They pulled the greenest watercress from the ponds, and cut elk liver into long strips for roasting. Now, with dusk setting in, the air cooling, the women hurried to the hot pool to wash away the bloodstains from their clothing and bodies.

The bubbling pool at the face of the Smoking Water was a new experience for Bird, and at the same time, a glorious luxury. She had not taken a truly hot bath since Fort Kearny. It was such a wonderful feeling. Oh, she would remember this place! She stretched out in the steaming water, soaking and sighing while Feather pounded their soiled ponchos against a huge rock.

"Plenty Hawk is happy," Feather said, looking over at Bird, deep in the water with only her head showing. "He has taken a big elk. His signs were true. Yes, there was good medicine in his prayers. We have worked hard and pleased him, too. Yes, my sister, you were right, too. He was happy to see us." She began spreading out the ponchos along the bank. Later, she would place them by the night fire to dry. But, now, she quickly eased herself into the water beside Bird. At thirty-four winters and three children, she was still an attractive woman, firm of body, her breasts full with only the barest hint of a sag. She touched Bird's cheek affectionately, and said, "Let me tell you about this secret place. We are lucky to have such a man, one who is so good in so many ways." Bird nodded in agreement, and Feather Tail went on. "Women do not come here much anymore, not like this," and she rippled the water up over her breasts. "In the beginning, Plenty Hawk's father, a big chief called Kicking Horse, brought him to this place. He was only a boy of ten winters. There was no trouble in our land, no bluecoats to fight. Sometimes, there was no game to be found. Other times, Plenty Hawk's family shot buffalo and antelope down along the Smoking Water Creek. Only in the season of the cold moons when the snow is deep in the hills do the big elk live here. I came with Plenty Hawk when I was first married. I came twice, and those were happy days ... and happy nights in the blankets with him." Feather stopped and nodded in back of her. "Over these mountains are the traditional hunting lands, too, but we do not go there much anymore. You know the land where the *wasichu* make long roads and build more soldier houses. Plenty Hawk speaks. He is a hunter. He does not want to go back to war again, but he says one day our great chiefs, Spotted Tail, Standing Elk, and Red Leaf, may ask the braves to join with Red Cloud to make war. If the Brule do not help, the trail of blood may come close to this place, too. This would be bad. This is a peaceful place. I want Plenty Hawk to bring our sons to hunt here. I want the women of our sons to come here, too, like us, to see this place before it is gone forever."

Bird nodded sympathetically. She touched Feather's shoulder tenderly, saying, "You speak with your heart, my sister. I want these things for you, too. Take hope. My friend, the one called Crow Feather, once told me that there are too many Lakota and Cheyenne over the mountains, that one day the buffalo soldiers will get tired of fighting and go home. For you, I pray this is true."

Feather Tail cupped her hands, spilled the water over her head and shoulders. Smiling, she sputtered, "I'm happy your man was not a buffalo soldier."

"My man?" Bird questioned softly.

"*Kangi Wiyaka,* the man you loved. You think I do not know? Cree Woman told me about him. Yes, I have known this for many suns, since you first came. I know the empty heart is much different from the empty belly. Sometimes it can never be filled. I pray for you, too. You see, I was hoping Plenty Hawk could make you happy, bring love to your heart again. You are too young to die inside, my sister."

"Plenty Hawk is generous and kind, and I respect him," Bird replied. "Yes, he pleased me, but it isn't within my heart to love him here," and she touched her breast. Then hesitantly, she asked, "Does he know . . . about *Kangi Wiyaka,* that he was my lover?"

"*Nyah,* only I know," Feather said. "Why does he need to know this? But I tell you, he is a good man, one who would understand. No, it does not matter. The past is over. Plenty Hawk only wants to make you happy. So do I." She laughed and patted her belly. "It is good he is a strong man. Now he has two women to keep happy."

"*Mi-ya,* both of us!"

Feather Tail, with a casual wave of a hand, said, "This is his way. Let me tell you a story. Four winters ago, my younger sister, Blackbird Sings, lost her man. She lived with us before she went to Spotted Tail's big village. After her mourning, she was lonely. She had no man. I asked Plenty Hawk to make her happy. He did. He tossed the blanket with her whenever she wanted. We had two tipis then. This was a happy time. We slept in the first lodge and the children and my mother were in the other one." She stopped and smiled. "Yes, those were happy times."

In a hushed voice, Bird said, "I can't imagine . . . it seems so . . ." and her voice trailed off into a wheeze. But she knew better, was fully aware of such polygamous arrangements among the tribes. She knew about their conjugal habits, had heard many stories from the girls back at school. John Dominguez had lived with these people, too, and had discussed their behavior with Garth.

"Kangi Wiyaka," Feather Tail asked in all innocence, "your man, did he have big medicine like Plenty Hawk?"

"Why . . . why," Bird stuttered. Her voice trailed away again. So did her fractured mind.

"It is good you loved your man," she heard Feather Tail saying. "Yes, it is good to remember these things. I understand."

"My man," Bird said. "I wanted Crow Feather to be my man forever. I don't know if he really was. I loved him. I had such dreams." She added with a tight smile, "Memories are both good and bad. You are right, the past is done, but I can't forget it, ever."

Feather Tail was silent for a moment, letting the hot water eddy around her. Then with a little wink and a twick at one of Bird's nipples, she said, "Maybe for a while tonight you will forget."

Bird gasped, abruptly came up, water cascading down her body. "How do you always read my mind this way?"

"A woman knows a woman," Feather Tail said. Her smile was warm. "We have pleased Plenty Hawk today. Do you think we have come all this way to do nothing but work? *Nyah,* we will stay here for two sleeps. He will please us both."

Chapter Eleven

They called the pony Flame. It was greenbroke and Bird gentled it off. As the weather moderated, she took to riding the new horse, a rather short-legged but spirited roan with two white stockings on the front legs. It was a fine present from her man Plenty Hawk. Eager volunteers always accompanied her when she saddled up, happy to ride along with Woman Called Bird. Her companions usually were children, even the smallest of her own family, Raven, the three-year-old son of Plenty Hawk, who snuggled up in front of her. Next in line, each riding a mount of their own, were Elk Runner, nine, and Little Star Woman, seven. Other children attracted by the high spirit of Woman Called Bird often joined the line. They never rode far, usually a mile or so, always within the perimeters of the camp, along the foothills or down the river bottom. Sometimes they made trips into the neighboring cottonwood groves and scavenged for firewood and buffalo chips. Wherever the ride, it was an event coupled with work and fun. Bird Woman made it that way. She was joy.

The children idolized Bird Rutledge. She knew many legends about faraway, distant lands, stories that had never been told before around the night fires of any of the villages. When they returned from their rides, the children were always smiling. They thought the Woman Called Bird was a different kind of woman. In some ways, she was like the mysterious one who blew on a flute, a strange man from another land far across the great waters, the piper she told them about, the one who had made beautiful music. The children of that land had loved him, too, so much that they had followed him away.

It was after one of these riding forays, near the end of March, when Bird, Elk Runner, and Little Star Woman, returned to discover visitors in the village. The pack string and one freight wagon were drawn up in back of the big talking lodge. Everyone seemed excited. Some of the children were dancing around two of the visiting Brule braves who were guarding the stock and equipment. Inside the lodge, the ranking men in the camp, including Plenty Hawk, were already smoking and talking with the new arrivals. The widow, Sarah Jennings, was the first one to come running to Bird with the news; she was elated; her prayers had been answered; two of the men inside were traders. They were white men! Now, the people back at Fort Laramie would know where they were, where to come and rescue them. She was going to talk with these men before they left. Bird just had to meet them, too.

Sarah's words came rushing out in such a torrent of expectation, Bird barely managed to get a word in. She shooed away the inquisitive children, had them lead the ponies back to the herd. Then, she took Sarah inside. "But who are they?" she asked. "What are they doing here this time of the year?"

"I don't know," Sarah said excitedly. "Does it matter who they are? They're traders. They'll be going back. Is this not good enough? Think of it, they'll get word to our people."

"Our people," Bird said softly. "I wonder just who our people really are, if we even know ourselves, anymore."

"You'll talk with them?" asked Sarah. "Will anyone stop us?"

"Stop us?" Smiling sadly, Bird shook her head. "No, I don't think so. I see no reason." She gestured, made a pass with her hand around the camp. "Look around, Sarah. If those men in there were unwelcome, we would have been hidden already. I don't think it matters one way or another. Obviously, the Brule know them, someone here surely does. They would have never made it this far if they weren't considered friends."

Sarah Jennings pointed. "They came from the Black Hills. One of the Indians spoke a word with your mother. They're going west, on to Virginia City, the two white men."

"The Indians came from the Black Hills?"

"From the villages of Standing Elk and Spotted Tail."

"Brule."

"Yes, the brothers of Man Called Cut Nose and Plenty Hawk, all of these people here."

Bird took Sarah by the shoulder. Certainly, the white men had not come to talk about ransom; no one knew the women had been taken by Brule Sioux. Bird didn't see much opportunity in the visit at all. If these visitors were friends of the Sioux, traveling so freely in hostile country, they were not doing it with the blessings of the whites, not the way their packs were loaded. It looked suspicious. Bird softly cautioned Sarah, saying, "Don't get your hopes up too high, my sister. I'll see what I can find out, then we can talk." And with that, Bird hurried away to her lodge. Almost an hour went by before she learned from Plenty Hawk what the visit was all about. And it was as she suspected, mainly an illicit trading venture on the part of the white men who were making a wide circuit toward the mining camps. But the Indians with them had come for another purpose—they were runners from the village of *Sinte-Galenska*, Spotted Tail, who was trying to gather his people together by the Moon When the Ponies Shed, May. From what Plenty Hawk could learn, the council was going to decide the amount of support the chiefs could give Red Cloud in the coming summer campaign. A few Brule Sioux under Red Leaf already were preparing to fight the bluecoats on the Tongue River, but many of the village leaders were more inclined to take their people back to the traditional lands near the *Paha Sapa* and on down toward the Niobrara in the fall. Plenty Hawk, his arms folded, fell into a troubled silence.

Bird asked, "What will we do?"

"What must be done. If I go back on the warpath, the women and children will be left behind. You will be safe. But it is not my wish to go back and fight. Already in our land we have too many children without fathers, women without husbands."

After another short silence, Bird nodded toward the outside. "The two *wasichu* out there, who are they?"

Plenty Hawk replied contemptuously, "The hangs-around-the-fort chief, Big Ribs, brought them. He has nothing better to do. I don't know their names."

Bird smiled knowingly. She knew about Big Ribs. He was one of the four or five Sioux who made a living as intermediaries, runners between the whites and Indians. Down at the big fort they were known as the Laramie Loafers, and the Sioux who shunned the fort and stayed free of civilization always joked about them and held them in low esteem.

Plenty Hawk spoke again. "Do you want to talk with the *wasichu*?"

Hesitating, Bird shrugged. She wanted his blessing. She finally said, "I have nothing important to say to them. I was only curious. The Pawnee woman wants to speak with them . . . asked me to speak, also."

"Good," the chief said. "*Hechetu welo*, you talk with them. Maybe you will learn something we should know. You know how these people are. Sometimes they speak with two tongues like the treaty makers who always write two papers. Big Ribs is the same color. How can we trust one like him? *Shunka!*"

And later, while some of the Indians were trading and buying ammunition, Bird and Sarah did talk with one of the *wasichu,* the leader one. He was fat, unkempt, fully clothed in dirty buckskins except for his heavy boots, and his name was Jubal McComber. He was astonished to discover two English-speaking Indians in such a remote village. While their plight did not seem to interest him, he did agree to make their whereabouts known when he returned south, for there was a good probability such information might turn a profit. Under the present circumstances, however, that was all he could do. After all, the Sioux were his best customers, and much of his goods just happened to be contraband, some of it stolen from the army. He stared at Bird keenly for a moment and licked his cracked lips.

"Business is business, girl, understand?" he said with a wink. "You know I can't be rilin' up my best customers. If I can work something out, I'll sure be lettin' you know, for sure, I will." He turned back to the packs and went to work.

It wasn't until later that day that Bird found out McComber's business was more than trading bullets, powder, and shot. He peddled whiskey, too. At the same time, she belatedly discovered the identity of his companion, a more suave and mannerly person who seemed to have little in common with his disreputable friend. The traders were preparing to leave, and in passing, stopped in front of Plenty Hawk's first lodge. McComber, with a glance at Bird, addressed Plenty Hawk, speaking in fluent Siouan, but Bird's eyes were on the other man, one that she vaguely recognized but couldn't quite place. Finally, the name she had heard earlier now struck like a bolt. Henry! This had to be Garth's prey, the one he had hunted so long, and she remembered the small picture he had shown her. However, her intense study of this man's bearded features was suddenly shattered by McComber's startling words.

"Hear me, Chief, you have two wives," the trader began. "I have none. I will trade you one of my Henry rifles and plenty of blankets for the breed one standing there. If you want to talk on it, we can talk. I will give you many bullets to go with this rifle, very good for shooting buffalo."

The explosive proposition even took Plenty Hawk by surprise. He stared first at Jubal McComber, then, with a fine glint in his eyes, looked over at Bird. Bird's reaction, however, was instantaneous, pure contempt and fiery anger. She barely heard her man's quiet reply of *"Nyah."* Chin outthrust, she howled out in English, "Why, of all the contemptible bastards I've ever seen, how dare you! You dumb jackass, you think I don't know what you're saying!" Then rapidly: *"Shunka! Waya-ta-in makah!"* Go eat shit, you dog!

"But ... but, ma'am ..." The trader never had a chance, for Woman Called Bird was upon him like a catamount.

"What makes you think I would take you for my man?" she yelled. "I'm no yellow-eyed breed, you filthy panhandler. I'm a Cree woman! A Cree woman, you hear? I wouldn't ride ten steps with a lousy drummer the likes of you, you dirty sonofabitch! Don't you ever wash? This is my man, you hear, and he wouldn't trade me for anything, so go on, get out of my sight before I vomit or put a knife in your fat belly."

McComber leaped back as though struck by a rattler, Bird's angry face right at him. "Well ... well, I'll be damned!" he blurted, dodging one of her kicks.

The violence of the outburst brought several women running to in investigate. They knew the sound of Bird Woman, but had not seen her wrath since those first tumultuous days of her arrival in the small village. The moment was tense, but only briefly. McComber, thoroughly humiliated, was backing away toward the awaiting ponies. The gawking women were now cackling like geese and pointing at him and wagging their fingers. Sarah Jennings had come into the picture, too, running beside McComber, pleading with him. "Take me, take me," she was crying out in tremolo. "I'll pay you back someway . . ."

"Get outta my way," he finally snarled, dodging her flailing arms. "Go on, shoo! Jesus, woman, I see hundreds like you every day! Go on, get, 'fore yer man gets some crazy notion."

Bird, meantime, was shouting at the second trader. "And you there, you, the one who calls himself Henry. I know you! You'll pay one of these days! You hear, you'll pay!"

The man turned, hesitated. He stared curiously at the irate young woman, his brows arched apprehensively. True, he was confused but obviously unwilling to press the matter too far. Jubal McComber already had stirred up a hornet's nest. He had never seen this crazy woman before in his life, and had only known a few in his time with such a vicious tongue.

Bird cried out again, "You're lucky to be alive, Sturges. Sturges, that's your name, isn't it? Henry Sturges, you bastard!"

His nod was ever so slight, mannerly, precise. "Yes," he said quietly. "Yes, my name is Sturges. I don't think I've had the pleasure. I don't know if I want it, Miss . . ."

Down the line, McComber was calling. "Come on, Henry, come on, let's get our butts movin' outta here. Don't be dallyin' with that ornery little bitch. Let's go."

But Bird, fully in motion, kept right after Sturges. She shook a fist violently, shouting, "You're lucky Garth didn't catch up to you. You're damn lucky, you sonofabitch!"

Sturges, ready to mount his horse, stopped dead in his tracks. He suddenly turned, drawn like a turkey vulture to dead meat by the name. "Garth? Captain Garth? You've seen the good captain in this country?"

"You're damn right I have!" she hissed back. And then she lied, not even knowing why. "He's out there somewhere hunting you, don't think he isn't. He's with the hostiles, and one of these nights he's going to sneak in and slit your throat! He's going to cut you like a hog, you traitor!" Furious, she whirled about and stomped back into the first tipi of Plenty Hawk. Her head was throbbing, her heart pounding. Outside, she heard the mumbling of voices, several shouts, and then the pack string and wagon were moving out. Cursing once, she angrily kicked a pile of robes at her feet. Why, she cried, staring up at the open vent, why is it always me? *Shunka* bitch!

Meena hurried in, tutting, and old Teal Wing waddled in, too, but she was grinning and slapping her thigh in glee. Her adopted daughter-in-law's performance had been hilarious. Feather Tail and Plenty Hawk followed. The chief was chuckling. "Son-mum-bitch, son-mum-bitch," he laughed, wagging his head. Bird glared at them all, said nothing. Feather came, clasped her arms around her sister, protectively, tenderly. Plenty Hawk smiled and nodded in approval. Oh, how he loved his women, their spirit, unity, and love for each other. Then, jokingly, he broke the silence. "One rifle, plenty blankets, a good trade," he announced deeply, mockingly, imitating McComber. "What if I had sold you to the *wasichu,* my woman?"

Bird knew it was his idea of humor, but no matter, her rejoinder came quickly and was as sharp as the knife she had sheathed on her hip. Eyes sparking, she looked over Feather's shoulder, retorting, "You would have made a bad trade. You would have sold two instead of one. Do you understand? You would have sold your child, here, in my belly!"

Chapter Twelve

The warpath was not for everyone. Many of the Brule Sioux, shunning the war with the bluecoats, were content to wander that spring and summer, and Bird Woman carried her pregnancy into the Moon of the Red Cherries. The Greening Grass Moon, the time her man once said that she could voluntarily leave, was at an end, and by late June she and her mother were living in the warm canyon country near the Black Hills, far from the Bozeman Trail conflict. Also, in June, she and Meena bade goodbye to the other captive, Sarah Jennings. While a few of the warriors did travel west to join Red Cloud, Sarah's man, Black Bull, along with the evil Man Called Cut Nose, moved south toward the Platte country with Spotted Tail's peaceful band. The departure was sad and Bird almost cried. Sarah's farewell still was filled with plaintive hope, and despite bitter memories of men like Jubal McComber, the Pawnee was certain she could find help and eventually make it back to the settlements bordering Indian lands. It was a sorrowful occasion. Bird, once the dreamer, now a confirmed realist, worried for her, because Sarah was an Indian who wanted to be white, an unlikely transition. Bird was too compassionate to tell Sarah that she could never be white in anything except her name. Yes, and fortunately, Sarah wasn't pregnant, yet. If her hopes came true, going home to rear a breed child would make her life even more difficult.

Likewise, Bird could have clung to her fading

dreams, but circumstances were still firmly controlling her destiny. Without much alternative, she had adopted the Lakotas' way of life. Then, pregnancy, fate's final blow, had come along practically obliterating any chance of her own return to the white man's world. Where was her place in the sun, now? When the initial shock wore off, she experienced a brief period of despondency, but only briefly. Plenty Hawk was spending more time in the village, and consequently, more time in the lodge at night. He knew how to please his two women, and now with all barriers cast aside, Bird became insatiable. When she finally confessed this obsession to her mother, asked how far along in her pregnancy this was safe, Meena simply laughed and told her until her baby dropped low in her belly, until she became uncomfortable. And she reminded Bird. "I once told you it is no sin to enjoy a good man. You own him, now. You own this village, too. You are loved by everyone around you."

Finally, the verdant rush of deep summer came and the Moon of the Red Blooming Lilies was at hand. Bird Rutledge's spirit was continually lifted by the attending love shown her, that wondrous kind of love born of family unity laced with deep affection and understanding. The Brule, as her mother had predicted, were continuing to make her rich in feeling. This was good. In a happy state of expectancy, she began looking forward to the birth of her first child. She found purpose in being, some balm for old scars. Garth's tragic, unforgettable death had almost emptied her soul. The new life squirming inside her belly was slowly but surely beginning to fill some of that fateful void.

Summer lingered and Bird grew bigger. A few runners came, bringing news of the fighting over the mountains along the Powder and Tongue rivers. There were continuing raids and skirmishes, one big fight that had cost Red Cloud many of his warriors. A group of bluecoats equipped with deadly repeating rifles had taken positions behind overturned wagon boxes and had successfully withstood the attacks of Lakota, Cheyenne, and a few Araphao braves. Bird heard of another smaller battle up near Fort Smith where troopers and Indians had fought to a standoff in some hayfields. There were few victories for either side, but one important fact still remained—Red Cloud's army was in control of the Bozeman Trail, and the successors to White Eagle Carrington were doing no better.

Now, the grasses were starting to dry. At times, Bird giggled like a maiden at her comic protrusion, the fat ball of belly that obscured her toes when she looked down. At times, she wilted and groaned at her graceless self. But it was wondrous, this strange new feeling of life. It was ungainly, too. Her hips had widened, her firm butt cheeks had fattened like ripe melon balls. Her walk was somewhere in between a glide and a waddle, and she had the shape of a toad stuck in a wheat straw. Because of her condition, she had deserted the main lodge of Plenty Hawk. He understood. But when he was away, she always returned to be with Feather Tail. Feather Tail loved her, too; Feather thought she was beautiful, which in truth, she was. During the early hours of the long nights, her attentive sister always brought her cool water and cheerful words. They sometimes bathed together in the shady creek where the big trees made a leafy canopy. They lolled in the clear eddies while the children frolicked nearby. They welded the common bond of wives, mothers, and lovers. Happily, Bird never found herself alone or neglected. Meena was always with her in the mornings before leaving for the foothills and meadows to forage. In the daytime, there were always the children. And at night, when Plenty Hawk was absent, Bird slept with her lovely Feather Tail, enjoying her affection and warm embraces. This was good, too, at such an opportune time so far along in her pregnancy. Yes, her sister

Feather Tail was wonderful. Oh, how they had come to love and admire one another.

From Plenty Hawk, when he was about, it was admiration, too, but of another sort. His black eyes were revealing, a fine gleam there. Bird knew he was a proud man, her pregnancy merely an affirmation of his innate pride. He loved his women, too, his growing family, and he worked hard to please them in every way. His only disappointment surfaced when he had to be away too long because of buffalo hunting or scouting. He had played on Bird's emotions in many ways, from those first days of her hostility right down to the affection and respect she now felt for him. Perhaps one of the most touching moments came one sunny afternoon when Plenty Hawk and some of the men returned from a long trip to the Powder River Valley. Woman Called Bird, Feather Tail, and the children hurried to meet the hunter chief; they were always happy to see their man return, their husband, father, their lover, and provider. He and the men were heavily loaded with booty plundered from some broken-down freighter wagons cached in a gully off the river trail, wagons that already had been attacked by their warring brothers. Some of the merchandise left behind was worthless, but luckily, in one of the freighters, they discovered supplies of flour, beans, molasses, tinned foods, and several sacks of coffee beans. Plenty Hawk's braves took all they could carry before the raiders came back to reclaim what they had hidden. Back in the village, the men celebrated and distributed the treasure among the women. Afterward, Plenty Hawk came to the shade of a tree where Bird and her adopted daughter, Little Star Woman, were resting and talking. He was carrying a weathered carpetbag under his arm. He kissed them both, and squatting beside them, he placed the bag at Bird's feet. "*Ho,* I have something else, something I brought only for you," he said proudly.

Bird stared at the bag, curiously wondering at its

worth, the aged piece of cloth, its weathered straps, its color almost faded beyond recognition. Once, it had been beautiful, but now, quite pathetic. Recalling his pranks, Bird hiked her brows at him, not knowing whether to frown or laugh. She had been fooled before by his quaint pranks, but this time he was nodding seriously at the bundle, beckoning her to examine it. Apparently, this was no trick. So, convinced, Bird began pulling at the worn straps, Little Star Woman eagerly trying to help. Bird and the girl dipped their hands into the decrepit bag, but Little Star Woman, significantly, came away without a word. Puzzled, she saw little worth in the contents. Bird, however, exploded joyously in English, "Oh, my God. books!"

Her enthusiasm radiated, bringing a broad smile of satisfaction to the bronzed face of Plenty Hawk, and he grunted, nodded, and said, "The white man's writing." Her happiness was his reward, her swelling beauty, his joy.

There were four books, and one by one, Bird anxiously threw open the covers, her fingers tenderly tracing the titles. In all the lingering months, she had only dreamed of such luxuries. How could anyone know how much she had missed such a simple thing as a book? Now, tumbled in her lap, she saw sheer literary treasure. In her present state, this was more valuable than the white man's treasured pokes of gold, yes, rejuvenation of the mind. Incredible! The startling collection included stories by Dickens, Homer's *Odyssey,* and two worn volumes of Shakespeare. Behind glistening eyes, she tried to speak. Her speech blurred with her eyes.

Plenty Hawk understood, but then, it seemed that he had always understood the slender young creature that fate unexpectedly brought him that cold, wintry day so long ago, the one whose hate and bitterness he had mellowed into love and affection, yes, for him as well as his family. Touching her hand, he said softly, "I need no words. You are happy. This is enough. *Hechetu welo.*"

"Oh, no," she finally whispered. "No, I must tell you. This . . . what you have brought is of great value to me. Yes, I'm happy. You have lifted my heart more than I can say. How did you know. Plenty Hawk must have a strong vision."

He beamed with pleasure. Standing, he placed his hands on his hips, confessing with a shrug, "*Nyah,* no vision, my woman." He tapped his head. "Once, Cree Woman told me how good you are, how many trails you have traveled. She told me how you understand the white man's writing, how you lived in a school across the River That Scorns All Other Rivers. Plenty smart, I remembered. You see, I understand, too. Yes, I knew you would be happy. I will always make you happy. This is my way." He pointed again. "When I go tomorrow, I will try and find you something else. When I return, you must tell me the legends in this writing. Our children speak of these things. Now, you must tell me."

Bird, brushing at her brimming eyes, replied huskily, "Yes, I will try to do this for you." She choked up as he strode away, and smiling down at Little Star Woman, kissing her on the forehead, she finally said, "Plenty Hawk is a kind and generous man."

Bird's first signal came the following day, shortly after noon. Little more than a small cramp, it nevertheless caused her to wince and start thinking. She hadn't experienced this before, so she broke away from the children and went to rest at the entrance of the second tipi, wondering, waiting for another sign. She knew these pains, once begun were supposed to come with increasing regularity. She thought she should tell Feather or her mother, but wanted to be sure this was not imagination. After all of the preparations, she hated the thought of making a false start, embarrassing herself before the women. Bird knew exactly what to do, the place she had chosen, and how long it would take to get there. Only the timing perplexed her, for this warning did seem premature, too early by her calculations. Yet, soon afterward, surprisingly, another twinge hit her, and this prompted her to move. Bird felt her forehead, mopped away the small beads of perspiration, and spoke once to Teal Wing, the only member of the family present at the time. Then, gathering up a small bundle, she left quietly, as though she were simply taking a stroll to escape the afternoon heat. She went down the shady creek trail. No one paid any attention. She was casual enough about leaving, but she did feel remiss in not seeing her mother or Feather Tail before she left, for she knew they would have insisted on helping her. Bracing herself against fear, Bird walked on alone.

The small glade she chose was far below the village at the place Where the Evergreens Meet the Water. It was shady and cool, and green moss covered the ancient rocks around her. In this quiet nook, she made her bed and finally lapsed into heavy labor, only occasionally opening her eyes, wondering at the agony of time, trying to measure its movement in the blurred, leafy patterns above her. The sun seemed to be moving fearfully slow, time almost standing still. But, then at that point when the golden sky blackened, her back painfully arched for the final time. Bird felt the warm sensation of water spilling down her thighs, soon followed by spasms and an oozing of life. In pain, but fascinated, she came up on her widespread knees, peered down, and let the small, wet bundle slide into her cupped and waiting hands. Falling back again, she brought the tiny body up against the flat of her belly, protectively covered it with a cloth. Exhausted, both physically and mentally, she could only trace its movement with her fingers, and in between her own gasps, she soon heard its first faint cries.

Moments later, she opened her eyes. How glorious! Fate was smiling kindly, fear had screamed away, and Bird discovered the sun was still there, framed much lower in the dense foliage, but it was shining, and beyond the trees, the sky was blue. Her eyes suddenly widened, both in surprise and thanksgiving—her mother was here, too, kneeling, attending to the last of it, then cleaning the infant. Bird heard her speaking.

"Are you all right?"

Bird managed a nod. Then: "Yes, and ... and our baby?"

"We have a fine son," Meena said haltingly. "He kicks like a colt, already. And he is a big one, a healthy one."

"A son," sighed Bird. She smiled. "This will make his father happy."

Directly, Meena finished knotting the cord and handed the infant back to her daughter. "Here, take him, let him try to taste you."

Opening her arms, Bird took the baby. She was smiling but she said rather pathetically, "He's not so handsome, Mama, so red, wrinkled like a little old man." She look up at her mother. "I'm glad you came. I never expected ..."

"Let's clean up here," Meena said, eyes averted. "Yes, and then we can talk." She hurried to the creek and came back with wet cloths. For a while, she worked in silence, hurriedly, bathing, rinsing out rags. "Teal Wing told me," Meena finally went on. "I think she suspected. I took your horse and rode the other way, pretending, and came as fast I could."

"Pretending? Pretending what?"

"I was afraid something was wrong ... too soon, I thought, trouble sometimes, not the right moon. I was right. This baby has come too soon, my girl."

Staring curiously, Bird asked, "But what's the matter, this pretending? I don't understand. You look sad. You should be happy, a grandson."

Pressing a wet rag to Bird's forehead, Meena said, "I'm happy, yes, but only you and the baby are fine. Yes, that's good, and in a day or two, he will become handsome. Yes, and he will be more white than he is now. Don't you understand what has happened here? This child isn't Indian. He is white. You have a white baby."

Silently shocked, Bird whispered, "No, it can't be." But in that shattering moment, she knew. Then, slowly, fearfully, she lifted the covering and touched the tiny form huddled at her breast. She traced a fragile ear and ran her finger through the delicate, damp fuzz behind it. Suddenly, she emitted a great sob and burst into tears. "Oh, Garth, Garth," she cried out.

Meena tried to console her, brushed at her daughter's hair. "Here, here, don't fret too much," she soothed. "He's a good baby, strong. God has been good to you. We will think of something, don't worry."

Bird looked back pitifully through the tears in her eyes. "Oh, my God, Mama, but how can I face them . . . explain? Plenty Hawk . . . so good, how can I do this to him, of all people? And Feather, my lovely sister? It's not fair. They've been waiting so long. They've been so good to me. They all think . . ."

"I know what they think," Meena interrupted. "No, we can't do this . . . go back. It's impossible. To shame Plenty Hawk before the others is the worst possible thing. He is a good man." She clutched her breast. "Ah it will hurt him here, yes, too much." She nodded in the direction of the village. "No, we can't go back and destroy everything good that has been done. No one must know." She paused again, staring this time down the creek. "We only have one choice, my girl. We must go while Plenty Hawk and the others are gone. We have waited all this time. Fate gives us no other choice. This is the sign we've waited for. Yes, your child is the sign brought by the Great Spirit. Our time to leave has finally come."

Bird moaned desperately and stared up in fright. "My God, what are you saying? How can we leave, Mama ... the baby?" She winced and wiped at her forehead. "God, I don't even think I can get up."

Meena kissed her. "We shall make it, all of us, I promise you. Listen, I know the way from here, a long ride, but we can make it." She went over to the pony and glanced back at Bird, saying, "Rest for a while, find that gumption your papa gave you. I must hurry back, now, steal some supplies for our bundles ... sneak around like an Indian." She grinned at this.

Bird was numb, her senses fractured into tiny splinters of incomprehension. Her mother's voice was fading away and the sun was sliding behind the great black cloud again. The shadows around her were deepening, yet she was conscious. The tiny bit of humanity nibbling away, trying to coax her swollen breast, told her this. Garth's son, her son. Her love for the man had not been all in vain. Through her misty eyes, she still managed a little smile, tinged with both joy and heartbreak. Her man, really her only man, had left her more than a tragic memory. But what she was now about to part with, oh, this was tragic, too, Plenty Hawk, Feather Tail, the children, lost love, again.

The two women, at least, knew their direction, if not their destination. They did not dwell too long on their chances or fate. To venture southwest was the most dangerous route; the various tribes were scattered all along the fringe of the Sacred Mountains. North would mean crossing into a place they called the Bad Mountains, and water was very scarce there. So, without much discussion, Meena directed Flame northwest toward the Little Missouri River. They had only enough food for three or four days, but with some blessing from Mother Earth, Meena believed they could reach the lower Powder River country in three or four days, a land they both knew because of the Brule. Some had

camped there in the spring and a few had gone on to
the Big Horn Trail to fight the troopers from Fort C. F.
Smith. Both the Teton Sioux and Cheyenne still were
in the vicinity of Fort Smith, a likely sanctuary, if one
could slip by the hostiles at night, a risk that meant
crossing through the Tongue River Valley. Farther
northwest along the Yellowstone lived the river Crow
and although some of them had served as trooper
scouts, neither Bird nor Meena knew much about the
tribe, except that their men had a reputation for being
good horse thieves. Meena's first and immediate concern, however, was the welfare of her new grandson
and her daughter, the problem of good food and water
along the way. Day by day, such demands simply
would have to be met, and for a time that was going to
be her responsibility, at least until Bird had enough
strength to help. Luckily, the birth had not been difficult, and as soon as Bird had rested several hours, she
pleaded to be on the trail. There was no solution to the
problem but to leave, and leave quickly before someone back at the village got worried and came looking
for them. So, she first tried mounting the pony but discovered that she was unable to straddle it without great
pain. She ended up sitting the horse from the side, and
Meena walked ahead, carrying the baby close to her
breast in a blanket.

Only once did they stop, long enough for Meena to
pick a few berries and rose hips, and by nightfall, they
had covered enough ground to separate themselves
from the range of the village. Meena, using the
firesticks she had taken from the first tipi, made a
small fire near a willow thicket and wrapped her
daughter in a blanket. They ate flatcakes and smoked
buffalo strips, while from a lone tin cup they sipped
bitter but hot tea made from the berries and rose hips.
At dawn, Meena first scanned the area behind them,
then stirred the fire and heated the tea. For Bird, it had
not been the best of nights. She was sore through her

middle and her sleep had been fitfully poor, filled with bizarre dreams, most of which she could not remember. Aching from her stomach to her thighs, she elected to walk aways before attempting to ride again, but after a short while all three of them were mounted, following the long coulees down the Little Mississippi, a thin, shimmering sliver far below. By the time they reached the river, Meena's small water bag was almost empty. Finding a sheltered bend where the shallow stream deepened, Meena let the horse drink. She then picketed it in the high grass along the bank, where it could take its fill. There was little conversation between the women. It was almost ritualistic, as if this had been done many times before, the bathing, cleaning the baby, washing rags, warming themselves in the sun, taking rest in the shade of the bankside willows, munching jerky while Bird nursed her new son. Meena then began preparing snares by slicing thin strips from the pony reins and cutting willow forks. An hour later, the women were headed for some hills far across the valley where Meena thought they could make a decent camp for the night and maybe trap some rabbit. Her chores had only just begun.

On the west slopes, they found shelter under an outcrop of a small sandstone cliff. A thick stand of juniper fringed the ridge behind them, and along the bottom of the sandy hill, Meena discovered a multitude of tracks of small and large animals alike, some dissolving into trails leading down through the sage and buffalo grass, others running up the rocky incline toward the Powder River Valley. There was no water about, only what had been—shallow, dusty impressions where pools formed only during the spring rains. So, for this night, they had to make do with what was left in the leather canteen. After placing her snares in the brush, Meena set out to scavenge for wood, but in the immediate vicinity found only enough branches for a night fire. This much of it was disappointing. However, while exploring a small ravine above the camp, she found a worn trail used by buffalo, and its sides were choked with dried dung. Gathering up several armloads, she piled them high under the sandstone shelter. By nightfall, the fire radiated from the nook into their small niche, and in comfort and temporary well-being, the women ate the last of the dried meat and flatcakes. Meena, setting up a small Cree chant, rocked the baby in her arms. She sang about the dangerous trail ahead, asked that the women's fears be overcome by good fortune, by the blessing of the Great Spirit and the cunning help of Old Man Coyote. This was something good to sleep on.

When Bird awoke, the first rays of sunlight were topping the ridges across the wide valley. She felt the baby stirring at her damp breast where it had fed while she slept. A few tiny flames still flickered from the fire and a small mist was dancing above the tin cup beside it. Bird looked around for her mother as she cradled the baby. Finally, she called out and then heard Meena's voice coming back to her from somewhere below in the thickets. The return call sounded happy, had a ring of good news about it, and soon her mother hove into sight carrying a skinned rabbit in one hand, and in the other, another creature of some sort, one that Bird didn't immediately recognize from the distance. She soon discovered it was a butchered porcupine, not snared, but one that Meena had come upon chewing at the snare's leather. Meena had dispatched it with a big rock. Both women were elated and lost little time in heating up the fire. The willow forks from the snares were skewered with strip upon strip of meat deftly cut by Meena, and the cooking and eating went on for more than an hour. Then Meena carefully bagged what was left, enough for several days, she reckoned, and they headed up one of the old buffalo trails toward the next valley, their stomachs full and finally silenced from complaint.

After another impromptu camp on Box Elder Creek, it took them another day to reach the banks of the Powder, familiar country, perhaps only ten miles or so downstream from where some of the Brule had camped in late winter when the buffalo were about, when Bird had first learned of her pregnancy. Luckily, no Indians were about now, nor had any seemed to be following them. They were seeing their first game of the journey, flocks of prairie chickens and small herds of antelope. They dismounted some distance before they reached the river because Flame, his nostrils flared, had smelled water and set himself into a determined trot. Bird finally pulled his bit and gave him his head. When the women came down to the river, the horse was standing at the bank, pacified and content, his thirst thoroughly quenched. After Bird and Meena had drunk and bathed, the stream was easily waded, and leading the pony, they walked downstream toward a shady grove of cottonwood and evergreens. Their good fortune multiplied, for they also found ripe plums, enough to fill their skirts with this new bonanza from Mother Earth.

While Bird rested and tended her child, Meena once again set out along the brushy bottom with her snares, discovering plenty of sign, both tracks and droppings from all sorts of animals. The very smallest of the round pellets, brown in color, were from rabbits; the larger, darker dung belonged to brush deer, but unlike their previous camp areas, here there were no buffalo chips to salvage. As she was setting her last snare, she found other tracks, too, these from unshod ponies. She knew they were made by Indian stock and that they were not fresh. She followed them for a few yards and quickly discovered a multitude of tracks where it appeared horses had bunched or had been picketed. Peering curiously through the long shadows, Meena saw the side of a wagon, one wheel twisted crazily to the side, and debris strewn about. When she edged closer, she found two more wagons, one with torn canvas covers hanging loosely from its skeleton ribs. She didn't take time to investigate. Throwing up her hands in excitement, she wheeled around and rushed back to get Bird.

Upon viewing the sight, Bird was dumbfounded, struck with alarm at such a shattering coincidence—could these be the same wagons Plenty Hawk and the others had found? The hunter chief had said he and his men were returning, that he would try to find her more objects of value. But if so, why hadn't she and Meena found some fresh sign ahead of them? She handed the baby to Meena and quickly followed the ruts of the wagons to see how they had come to rest in such a hidden place. From what she could determine, each one had been pulled from the grassy bench above. Once upon the bench, Bird discovered the freighters had come from the north, because in certain spots she could plainly see where the big wheels had made the depressions in the now drying meadow grass. Bird discussed the various possibilities with her mother as they rummaged through the litter, for certainly there were items of practical use for anyone as destitute as they were. When she noticed the two splintered holes on the side of the second wagon, she came to one quick conclusion—they were bullet holes. One had pierced the board, the other partially penetrating it. She could see a chunk of fractured lead hidden within the hole. Someone had tried to avoid the dangerous fort road in the adjacent valley to the west, perhaps during early summer, only to be ambushed on what they believed was a safer route. Bird assumed that hostiles had pulled the wagons into the brushy bottom to hide them and then return for what had been left behind. Neither Plenty Hawk nor any of the others made any mention of an attack on wagons, for had this been the case, they would have counted coup and celebrated upon their return. At any rate, the women decided it had been a foolish, perhaps fatal, adventure on someone's part. The wagons using the Bozeman Trail always had been escorted by troopers between Fort Smith and Fort Kearny, at least until Red Cloud had frightened off all commercial traffic.

The women's careful search rewarded them with several useful items, including remnants of cloth, a dented milk pail, two empty bottles, two large timber nails, and best of all, a large tin in which they found a sack of dried beans. The broken wooden boxes strewn about, which had contained rifles, were thrown into a pile for the night fire, and Meena, forever resourceful, took her knife and trimmed the best sections of canvas to make into sacks and protective covering. As darkness set in, they brought down hay from the meadow and made their beds under the second wagon. Meena also quickly put the newly found milk pail to use, boiling plums they had picked. Each had a cup of hot nectar before curling up in the hay and canvas under the wagon. Bird sighed thankfully as she positioned her child. This night had been almost like Christmas.

When she stirred at first light, once again she felt her baby rooting at her breast. She could smell smoke from the fire and knew her mother was already up and about, probably checking snares or searching for roots and berries. Bird stared up at the planks under the wagon bed, and while the baby fed she gingerly tested her stomach muscles several times, pulling her knees upward and slowly across her body. She then gently felt her vaginal opening, testing the tenderness there, less each day. How long had it been since the fateful miracle? What, only a week! My gracious! It seemed like ages. Fate had smiled down on her; fate had laughed at her, too. Plenty Hawk, Feather Tail, the children, all gone in a matter of moments, just as Garth had been taken away from her. Oh, how she missed them all! It seemed as though she were forever climbing a mountain, yet never quite reaching the top, never.

Certainly, there had to be a future out there somewhere, one without complications, a happy, never-
ending one. Memories! She sighed and flexed again.
Yes, her recovery was good, each day better, each mile
covered at least one small victory, not only for herself,
but her wonderful baby. Meena wanted a name for the
boy, had mentioned it several times, but for now, Bird
told her, we will simply call him Ty, Little Ty. Among
the Human Beings he can be Son of Crow Feather,
among the *wasichu*, Ty. When he needs a second name,
Bird said, it will be Garth as was his father's. A sad
smile crossed her dark face as her chin pointed down
toward the feeding baby. She remembered how his father had once nibbled there, too, but, my son, she
whispered, he was not as greedy as you. Her eyes came
back to the floor above, and she traced the veins of the
weathered boards. At the front of the wagon, a spider
had built a web, anchored partially to several protruding nails, and as she searched for the spider's hiding
place, she noticed for the first time a plank held in
place by the nails that the spider was using, but it was
unlike the rest of the frame. It was newer wood, pale
yellow in color, entirely different from the gray of the
wagon body itself. A patch, she surmised, but then she
knew about wagons, had been around them all her life.
What an unusual place for a patch, under the frame below the seat. Only from her vantage spot below could
such a repair be seen, if, indeed, it were a repair. And
an extension at this point seemed odd, probably would
add less than eight inches to the wagon body. Anyhow,
just out of curiosity, she thought she would examine it
before they left.

Meena had set the pail of plum juice next to the
small fire, and a small fire it was, made out of the last
of the rifle boxes. Meena was cautious; this was hostile
country, the north-south route of Red Cloud's warriors.
At one time, Bird had asked her mother why she hadn't
stolen the extra rifle from the second tipi of Plenty

Hawk, only to be chastised for such a suggestion. Indignant, Meena told her that she was not a thief, and besides, firing shots might bring more trouble than they already had. Ever since they had fled, her mother had been careful, even to the point of taking the pony on the firmest terrain or to the side of the trails where tracks were more difficult to follow. The fact of it was that in such big country they had left only the barest shred of a sign behind. Had anyone followed, the decision would have been a poor one.

Once up, Bird found a spot of sun at the river's edge. The water was cold in the dawn's air, but she momentarily braved it, splashing her hands and face, sponging her body, before washing the baby. When she returned, her mother was kneeling by the fire, positioning two sticks speared into ribbons of flesh, and along the edge of the hot rocks, still more meat was beginning to cook. Two small sets of thighs and breasts were sizzling from the heat. At a glance, Bird knew the meat was chicken, actually from fool hens, a type of grouse, because this was about the only bird in the hills one could stealthily approach and kill with a stick or rock. Meena looked up from the fire and cursed through a grin. Five of them, she said, but she had been only quick enough for two. The others had flown off into the pine trees. She said her snares were empty, but she had fared well with her digging stick, finding a few old turnips and tiny onions which she promised to cook that night with some of the beans from the tin box. She stood up and peeked at the baby, saying things were not all bad, Little Crow Feather. There would be plenty of food for his mother to make milk and fill his belly.

After they had eaten and stored the leftovers, Bird directed Meena's attention to the strange repair work under the wagon. They crawled under the wheels for a closer look. Initially, Meena thought it might be a small section built to reinforce the front wall, yet on a second examination, she knew it was nothing more than a false front. There had to be a hollow space in between, so she rapped her digging stick against it several times. "It must be a hiding place," she suddenly whispered. "What else can it be?" Shaking her head violently, she added, "No, no, we must not get our hopes up. This may be nothing, nothing at all."

Bird, excitement stirring, immediately climbed out and began searching through the debris for something she could pry with, a tool to wedge in between the boards. Meena followed and quickly pointed to some strap iron on one of the wagon tongues. "Get some rocks," she advised, "big ones to pound with." Bird went to the embankment where the wagons had been pulled down and found two melon-sized boulders.

Hefting the flattest of the two, Meena said, "Good." She then fished out one of the timber nails from her bundle. "Soon I'm going to make a weapon out of this big spike," she said. "I will make a sharp spear for fish, a hunting stick, but now I see what the Great Spirit first meant it to be."

After some labor they separated enough of the iron from the tongue to hammer a strip of it free, and with this piece and the rock they attacked the boards. Ultimately, one piece was splintered and parted from the nails and the women pulled it free, enabling Bird to run her arm down into the hidden space. "There is something!" she exclaimed, pulling back. "Stuffing of some kind." And with that, she began to withdraw wads of cotton and cloth. "It's packed in as far as I can reach, like a mattress."

"Then we must break another board out," Meena told her.

And they forced the second plank away, this time opening enough space to see into the hollow. It was only about eight inches thick but extended the width of the wagon. More of the packing came out, and finally Bird whispered excitedly, "I've got something, a box, I think, a tin box. Out came the box, and it was metal, black, and shiny, long and flat, with one small hasp in its middle. It also was very heavy for its size. "Good God!" Bird exclaimed, staring at her mother. "What do you think?"

"I think this carpenter, whoever he was, went to a lot of trouble. He wanted to protect something very badly, eh? Go ahead, open it."

Bird flipped the hasp and lifted the lid. Inside, packed in between more batting were two smaller boxes made of pasteboard. Wedged along the sides of the boxes were leather pouches, five of them, also four cylinders wrapped with heavy paper. Hands trembling, Bird untied the throngs on one of the bags. "Good God!" she cried out, tumbling a few gold nuggets into her palm. "This is gold, Mama! Why, there's a fortune here!" She quickly put the pouch aside and handed Meena one of the heavy cylinders, saying, "This is money, too, I know it! Feel the weight of it." When Meena, less nervous, had carefully pulled the wrapping apart, she slid ten golden, double-eagles into Bird's cupped hands. "Mama, I can't believe this!" she gasped, tears beginning to well in her eyes. "My God, we're rich!"

Quickly repacking the coins, Meena sighed forlornly. It was as though she had been overwhelmed by a heavy burden. Apprehension seized her, and staring cautiously around, she said, "Yes, this is a fortune. Yes, and I should feel happy to have such riches, but I wonder about the man who owned all of this. Are we his robbers?" She glanced at her daughter, seeking an answer. "What if his spirit is watching? What will his spirit say?"

"I don't know," Bird replied excitedly. "He's probably dead or he wouldn't have left it. I'm not that superstitious. How can he possibly care? What we've found, we've found. Who else is there to claim it? Whoever sacked these wagons missed it, just like they missed that bag of beans." She held up one of the pouches to the sky. "Look at all the beans we can buy with this! No, Mama, this is ours!"

Inside the first of the smaller boxes, the women found two gold rings and a watch; in the other was a grooming set, including razor, a small mirror, and soap. Bird snapped the watch cover open, revealing a shiny, ivory face with black roman numerals. The back was decorated with flowery scrollwork and a set of initials. She handed the watch to her mother and went back to the box containing the small bar of soap, saying, "I have little need for a timepiece, but this . . . this is real treasure, Mama. Soap!" And she smelled its fragrance.

"I wonder if he was a married man?"

"Why? What difference does it make?"

Meena was staring thoughtfully at the rings. "These rings, you know. See, look how small they are. Too small, I think, for a man."

"A small man, maybe," Bird said, taking one and fitting it onto a finger. "Here," she said, proffering the other one to her mother. "You can wear this one."

Shaking her head, Meena pushed Bird's hand away. "No, I think it's for his wife, a dead man's wife. You keep it. This isn't for me."

"Mama, I don't think he cares about the rings or the money, not now. Why, if he saw us standing here looking the way we do, so damn poorly . . . if he saw our baby, I really don't think he would mind a bit. He would look at us and say, 'Help yourselves, ladies, it's all yours, and God knows you need it.' "

Meena, unimpressed, managed a weak smile. "You know he wouldn't call us ladies." She began replacing the treasure back into the metal box, reverently touching each item as she packed. When she had finished, she gave Bird a concerned look. "If this is ours, then we must find a way to hide it, piece by piece, until the time come when God gives us the right to use it.

Someone would kill for this, kill us and leave us to the animals and birds."

Bird, fitting the gold rings on her fingers, said, "Someone already killed for it." She hurried away to inspect the underpinning of the other wagons to see if they had been altered in any way, but found nothing unusual.

Bird and Meena had successfully crossed the Powder River Valley by late afternoon, and by the time the shadows were long had found a good campsite near a small spring with many game signs around it, mostly made by elk and deer. Around the spring, there was grama grass for the pony, not much wood for a fire, but the camp location was excellent. The women could see several miles in three directions, the exception being to the west, where many of the game trails eventually led to the Tongue River Valley. A half circle of aspen fronted the spring and in this grove they stretched their newly acquired canvas between two trees, making an adequate shelter. In the pine woods above, Meena gathered a few dead limbs, enough for the night fire. She elected to wait until dark to cook because they had crossed a profusion of pony tracks on this side of the river, tracks that went both north and south. Whether these were made by war or hunting parties didn't make any difference, since at this point, with their items of great value, isolation was paramount. They had hidden the gold coins, one by one, inside the leather binding of the saddle, and after emptying the pouches, placed the nuggets and watch at the bottom of the bean sack. Bird, elated at the discovery of the soap, put it in her bundle, and slid the fine razor behind her knife in its sheath; the small mirror went into Meena's bundle. Filling the black metal box with rocks, they dumped it in the deepest part of the river. Meena concluded that only a most thorough search of their belongings would reveal anything, but this was a chance they had to take.

For the present, food ceased to be a serious problem. Meena would have preferred to have some good red meat for her daughter to make better strength to pass on to the baby, but she was thankful for what they had. She had soaked beans and turnips in the pail during the day's ride, packing canvas into the top of the container to keep the water from splashing out. There were only a few fat strips of the porcupine meat left, just enough to give her potluck some flavor. So, another night passed without incident, and the women were up at dawn, taking water and eating leftovers. When the sun was on their backs they pointed Flame up the small rocky trail and let him pick his way through the meandering draws that led into a few timbered slopes on top. By midday, they were far enough where they could see gaps in the small mountains, and they caught the first glimpse of the distant Tongue River Valley. This was to be the first day of encounter with other humans and it came quite suddenly, after they had made one stop to rest in a shady saddle interspersed with pine, juniper, and scrub fir. Both of the women were back on the pony, Bird in front, and Meena, holding the baby, behind her. They had just come into the foothills when Flame abruptly stopped and tossed up his head, throwing Bird up against his neck. Instinctively, she pulled up the slack on the reins, and even before looking below, instantly was off the pony, grasping at his muzzle, for the horse's keen nose had been better than their eyes. In a distant swell of burnished knolls, they saw dark forms moving about, and upon closer examination, determined they were riders, a few of them trailing heavily packed ponies and travois. Bird immediately turned Flame around and backtracked into the nearest cover, a heavy patch of juniper and sage. From this place they were hidden well enough but no longer could see the activity. Meena, transferring the baby back to Bird, crept down the hill, and within a few minutes returned, panting, her forehead beaded with sweat. She had gone close enough to determine the people below were either Sioux or Cheyenne, mostly women, and were hauling meat, probably buffalo. Somewhere down the valley, and not too far, their men had made some kills and now the butchers and women were returning to their village across the valley. She thought the camp must be far away because she had been unable to see the river, not even a sign of the big trees that grew along the banks in the lush valley bottom.

Bird motioned to the north. "Then we better go that way before we even think about cutting down. If we can find some water, we can hole up and cross over to the river farther north in the morning." She glanced back at Meena. "How far do you think it is to the river?"

"I can only guess. Half a day, maybe a little more."

Bird was pensive. "Maybe we can make it over there tonight, that way," and she pointed to the northwest. "Cross over when it's dark."

Meena gave her a questioning stare. "How do you feel? And what about him?" she asked, nodding at the sleeping infant.

"I'm fine, and so is he," returned Bird. "Then, let's go along this hill for a while and stay out of sight. We'll see how it goes, see if we can find a creek somewhere. We can't stay here."

Meena agreed and took the baby, placing the canvas sling across her stomach. Her eyes momentarily brightened and she said, "You know what I think we should do? I think we should see where those people came from. Not too far away, I bet. Yes, we should find out where they got those buffalo, maybe sneak down there and see if we can find us some meat they left behind."

"Meat!" Bird huffed with a grim smile. "I don't remember anyone ever leaving meat behind."

"You only went once. You know nothing about making meat."

"Once was enough. I got sick, and good reason."

"Sometimes, they discard a head or two. Too much to pack and not much meat."

"Good God, Mama, they broke the heads and ate the brains!"

"Good food," Meena said. "Papa liked calf brains scrambled with eggs and he was a *wasichu*."

"I forgive him for that." Bird smiled. Jerking the reins, she added bitterly, "But I don't forgive the Tetons who killed him, those people down there." She pointed her small nose toward the valley below and viciously spat. "Piss on them!"

It was late in the afternoon when Bird and Meena finally came down off the hillside about two miles from where they had watched the Indians. They were on one of the plateaus of the valley and, here, the prairie grass was beginning to brown on top. Nearer the ground, the lower shafts still had a healthy deep green to them, good forage for buffalo. The women kept their eyes ahead, searching for sign, either where the animals had been killed or any strip of greenery indicating the presence of water, but almost as far as they could see, there was nothing but the late summer hues of grama and sedge. Sometime later, several dark specks in the sky gave them their first clue. Watching closely as the birds came lower and lower to the ground, Bird finally reined Flame in that direction, where they soon came upon the tracks of the Indian's ponies. It was about a ten-minute ride before they discovered the first offal. Three big ravens flew up, crying in alarm, setting off another flight a short distance away. Bird kept moving the pony ahead through the trampled grass until her mother told her to stop. Sliding off, Mena handed the baby back up to Bird. She had spotted the head of a young cow, its tiny horns still intact but quite useless to the hunters because of their size. Within seconds, her knife was out. Bird threw down a piece of canvas and moved on ahead, searching out another kill site where a head or anything may have been left behind. Finally, in luck, she dismounted, only about twenty-five paces from her mother, and went to work trimming away hide from the lower skull of another cow until she could carve into the scant meat that had been left on the upper neck. It was tedious work for Bird, but her mother was adept with a knife and soon had gone on ahead searching for more scraps. Between them, they finally filled two pieces of canvas with the trimmings, not the choicest of meat but an adequate supply, perhaps four pounds, enough to last them a few days. As usual, the skulls of the animals had been smashed open and the brains scooped out, and huge slits up under the jawbone at the throat revealed where the tongue had been severed and pulled away. No matter, for even without these choice parts, Meena was happy; she had red meat, now, good for her daughter's blood, good for making healthy milk for her grandson.

After cleaning their hands in the grass, they rode off, Bird nursing the baby and Meena scanning the horizon. Finally, Meena let Flame have his head, and within fifteen minutes the pony led them north to a small outcropping of rock below which lay a muddy pool, its edges pocked with buffalo tracks. A small marshy plot below had been turned into a wallow of brownish muck, and the evening air reeked of urine; small, black gnats were hovering in dense clouds over the tepid water. Cautiously avoiding these biting insects, Meena dismounted and quickly climbed into the rocky area above, searching for the water's source. She soon found a small trickle coming from a crevice, and above this, she found another small marsh where the water was clear but clogged with willow and fallen aspen. The remnants of an aged beaver dome stood like a stark sentinel in the middle of the little pond, indicating that at one time the water here had been plentiful.

The women went further up the draw, following the tiny stream to the trees, where in a shady glen they came upon an unusual and mysterious sight. Standing in a semicircle around a sunken firepit rimmed with big rocks, were five small wickiups, or what had been wickiups. Only the frames and some scattered brush that had once supported the coverings remained. Meena curiously fingered the ashes in the pit and looked up at Bird. "Not used for many years," she said. "Maybe hunters came here long ago and waited for the blackhorns to come and drink down below, you know, the old ones who had no horses. Maybe they made medicine and talked here with the spirits. I don't know." With a deep frown, she pointed around at the silent surroundings. "No sign, here, nothing. I think this is a sacred place not meant for women."

Bird, choosing practicality over superstition, gave her mother a curious stare. She was tired, dirty, and wanted to rest, holy place or not. "But is it safe?" she asked.

Meena shrugged once. "Those buffalo hunters won't come here, if that's what you mean. They will be home tonight feasting on roast hump and ribs, good liver. About the spirits, I can't tell you."

"Ghosts, be damned," Bird cursed, dismounting, "we don't have much of a choice. It's getting dark and we both stink like buffalo. This is it, Mama, we stay and get some rest."

So, in the fading light and purple shadows, they unpacked their small but precious belongings. Bird picketed the pony near the edge of the clearing where it could crop grass. Then, they selected the best wickiup, made a few repairs, and covered it with their scraps of canvas. The remaining bough shelters were torn down, dead limbs broken into smaller pieces and stacked by the rock firepit for the night fire. After washing with the luxury of soap, Bird began roasting some of the fresh meat while Meena cut willows and began thatching a grid for smoking the rest of it. Much later, when Bird and the baby retired, Meena banked the fire with green willow and placed the grid of meat over the smoldering embers.

The next morning when they awoke, a fine mist was in the air and low clouds were sweeping across the valley as far as they could see. Rain was near, so because of the infant and the thought of a discomforting ride, they elected to remain in their hidden camp. Even the pony would benefit, Bird said. For a while Meena busied herself carefully packing the smoked meat into one of the pouches she had made from the salvaged canvas. Once this was done, she set out to see what she could forage before it began to rain. Meanwhile, Bird secured the wickiup by extending a flap at the opening and fashioning it into a small awning. She took rocks from the old pit and arranged them in front of the little lodge, then fished out embers and rekindled a fire that radiated heat toward the shelter. It was a good camp, out of the wind, better yet, out of sight from the long rolling plains below, and on such a bleak, overcast day, there was little chance of smoke being seen.

A light drizzle had set in by the time Meena returned. Crouching under the awning, she spread her hands to the fire, then pulled her blanket away, and opened the bundle to show the fruits of her foraging. In a meadow across from the draw, she had found a few more turnips, old and tough, but edible, and from near the little stream, she had picked a handful of leafy horsemint. She pressed one of the shoots up behind Bird's ear. She said it was sometimes a good aroma for a man to smell, but really better for tea, if only they had some wild honey to go with it. She also had more rose hips and a few buffalo berries. Her search for chokecherry bushes had been unsuccessful. No matter. Once they reached the river bottom, she thought they would be able to find a plentiful supply.

It was on this misty afternoon that Bird first saw the wolf. While she was eating she had noticed the pony, how suddenly alert it had become, its ears pricked and head thrust forward in a steady stare. Slightly turning, Bird squinted through the light drizzle and finally made out the head and shoulders of an animal, shaggy and wet, at the edge of the clearing facing toward the campsite. At first, she took it to be a coyote, but, no, its head was too big and its coloration not quite right. She realized then it was a wolf. More surprised than alarmed, Bird slowly stood, expecting it to bolt at her slightest move. Strangely, the animal only shifted its head to the side, somewhat like a snake, as if to get a better view of her. Now, by closer inspection, she readily saw that it was a young wolf, the color of bleached elkskin, and probably no bigger than an adult coyote. She thought to herself, this youngster is watching a human for the first time, curious, hungry, probably drawn to the camp by the odor of cooking. Then, inexplicably, she gave the piece of meat in her hand a flip. By the time it hit the ground, the young wolf was gone. Bird, drawing a deep breath and wondering at her own unusual behavior, sat down again and whispered back into the wickiup, "Mama, I've just seen a wolf!"

Meena came out quickly on hands and knees, rubbing her eyes. "A wolf! Where?"

"Right over there by the trees." Bird pointed across the glade. "I frightened the poor thing. He wasn't much more than a pup, all silver and white."

"Good riddance," muttered Meena sleepily. "He should go back where he came from, back to his den with his mama." She crawled back into the wickiup.

Bird said nothing, just sat there pondering her strange affinity for the wolf and the way she had foolishly tossed away their hard-earned food. She rearranged her blanket, took another piece of meat off the hot rocks, and had taken no more than several bites when she noticed the small wolf was back, standing in the same spot, once again intently staring at her. "Wolf," she called lowly. "Wolf, what are you doing

here? Mama says you should go home. Go, get out of
this rain. Why have you come here, anyway?"

And once more the wolf shifted its shaggy head, snake-
like, back to one side, then the other. Finally, his nose
came forward testing the air, and he cautiously edged out.
Stretching his full length, he snatched up the piece of
meat and leaped back into the scrub pine. How magnificent! Bird sighed happily. What a crazy, beautiful animal,
she thought, a shiver of excitement running through her.
What a lively, bold little creature! Once again, she caught
her breath, hardly believing what had happened. Then,
without any hesitation, she tossed out the last bite in her
hand, hunched up her knees, and waited to see if he
would reappear. Time passed and the woods were quiet,
the only noise coming from the patter of rain on the awning, and Flame, down below, cropping grass. Just about
when she was ready to give up, she caught a movement
from the side of her eye. From this angle, the animal appeared more gray than white, but when it returned to its
original place by the trees she saw the white silvery tuft
of its neck and shoulders. "Wolf," she spoke again,
slowly getting to her feet. She moved out from the awning and took several steps. "How can you be so hungry?
There is one more bite for you, that's all. See, on the
ground, there. Wolf." Moments went by as they returned
inquisitive stares. Finally, Bird eased back toward the
wickiup and called his name again. "Wolf, come and eat."
Only when she settled down on her haunches at eye level,
did the young wolf come forward, sniffing the ground in
front of him. He soon found the small morsel, but instead
of bounding away as he had in the first encounter, he momentarily stood there, blinking, swaying his head in that
peculiar manner. Bird could see that his eyes were a
bright, greenish yellow, and his slick nose was as black as
a new stove pipe. Then, he turned and trotted away without so much as a wag of his bushy tail. Trembling inside,
Bird crawled back out of the drizzle. She heard Meena
speaking inside the wickiup.

"What are you saying? Who are you talking to, the spirits of the dead?"

"I was talking to the wolf, Mama, wishing him light snow and good hunting this fall with the pack."

"Yes, yes," returned Meena mockingly. "And what did he say to that?"

"Why, he thanked me, of course. He said thank you, and he hoped the Great Spirit would answer all of my prayers."

"Mi-ya!" Meena exclaimed with a little laugh. "I think you should come out of the rain before you get a fever."

Off and on throughout the day, Bird kept her eyes on the fringe of the camp. Her friend, however, did not return, or if he did, he kept well hidden.

The next morning, a small breeze was blowing from the southwest, a good omen, since this wind was always warm, making for a pleasant ride down to the river. By the time the women were away, the sun had broken through, and except for some lingering patchy fog, they could see a far distance ahead. Bird did not mention it, but she had caught a glimpse of the wolf that morning. She and her mother had differing opinions about wolves, even such a small, curious one. Despite this little disagreement, Bird secretly deposited a piece of jerky at the edge of the glade after they broke camp, a parting gesture of kindness, she thought. She had struck a strange kinship with the wild creature, the incident at the ancient camp exciting her almost as much as discovering the cache of gold in the abandoned wagon.

Early afternoon they came upon a small sandy creek, barely a trickle in places, but at each bend there were rocky eddies leading into shallow pools. Bottlenose dragonflies were everywhere, slender, azure bodies flitting, then suddenly hovering in midair, their tiny wings a blur of silver. To Meena, this was a good sign—the river where these insects were born had to be close by. Dismounting, the women took their cup and drank fresh water. After a short rest, they planned to follow the little stream down to the river, riding along in the cover of its brushy banks, for even though they had seen no fresh tracks, they knew hostiles were about. By Meena's calculation, Fort Smith, the nearest white refuge, was somewhere to the west, two or three days away. Most of the Sioux and Cheyenne were between them and the fort, presenting the same barrier that they would have encountered south had they elected to try and reach Fort Kearny. Meena sighed, lamenting that by the measure of safety, they were not much better off than when they had started. Bird demurred, reminding her mother how unexpectedly well they were faring, now possessing not only food, but money, money they could use if they reached an outpost somewhere. For the present, they had been blessed with good fortune. Beyond this, however, she was reluctant to discuss what might be ahead of them, for even thinking about the future often distressed her. There were the good memories, though, and these heartened her, gave her some consolation, recalling the best of times, particularly those wondrous hours with Garth, and now the fine son that he had given her. Strange, she mused, staring off into the golden fields, strange how something or someone always came along to fill the void.

Bird, her mind in the mists, heard Meena talking behind her, muffled words, as though coming from behind one of the hills. It must be time to ride again. So, she asked herself, what day was this, anyhow? How many days had they been on the trail? It seemed like forever. Now, she found herself counting campsites because who knew or particularly cared what day it was? Camp of the Willows, Camp of the Rocky Ledge, Camp of the Wagons, and so until she knew that it was more than a week, eight days. Or was it nine? Was all of this really relevant? Perhaps, not to her, but there was only a touch of Indian in Little Ty. He was more *wasichu* than Indian; he could never know his father, true, but at least, a *wasichu* should know his birthday, certainly, yes, September near the end. Rousting herself from the grass, she said aloud, "The twentieth of September. September twenty, eighteen-sixty-seven."

Leading up the pony, Meena paused with a questioning look. She pointed her new hunting spear to the sky. "What is this you are saying? What is it, now? Does someone up there answer you like the talking wolf? Are you touched by the sun as well as the spirits?" She stared away, cupping an ear. "I hear nothing, except maybe a crow off yonder in the bushes."

"I was talking about a birthday, Mama. Yes, a birthday for your beautiful grandson, the one who makes my tits so sore."

"You should be thankful you have big tits and plenty of milk for his little belly," returned Meena. She gave Bird a boost up. "So, what about a birthday? He's only a baby."

"The day he was born, the date, don't you see?"

"Some days ago, now. Is this so important? What day, I don't know. A sunny day in the afternoon, August ... maybe September." Clucking the horse ahead, she added, "The Moon of Dying Grass, that is the month, for sure."

"No," Bird replied. "No, I've decided on the date, the exact date. It's September twenty. His name will be Tyson Rutledge Garth. That sounds rather impressive, don't you think? Yes, Tyson Rutledge Garth. It has a nice ring to it."

"Yes," Meena said, suddenly feeling misty. "Yes, I think that's a very good name. Papa would like it. It would make him proud." Taking a quick peek back, she asked, "Is this what you were telling God?"

"I think God already knew, a long time ago."

As Meena predicted, when they reached the Tongue

River bottom, the vegetation flourished; groves of large trees and clumps of bushes were everywhere; the meadows were still thick with green grass, and elated at the prospect of finding berries for their larder, the women eagerly dismounted and began walking along the river's edge. Their enthusiasm, however, soon waned when Bird, walking in front, suddenly stopped and pointed ahead. A worn trail, almost the width of a wagon, came to the bank and disappeared into the water, only to reappear on the far shore. It was an ancient crossing, yet when they inspected it more closely, they discovered fresh pony tracks, most of them headed upriver. The trail on their side curled off like a snake through the woods toward the northeast, the direction of the lower Powder and the Yellowstone country, and was probably first made by migrating buffalo. Now, obviously, it was a route shared by humans. This ominous sign thwarted any plans the women had of making a quick camp and searching for berries. Instead, they went downriver almost two miles, avoiding the open meadows, keeping inside the dense thickets, until they found a secluded place not too far from the water. It lacked the space and mysterious charm of the wickiup camp, but luckily, they were surrounded by thick berry bushes, some undermined with animal runs where Meena optimistically had thoughts of catching rabbits.

It was late in the afternoon, but their chores were finished before dusk closed in. Meena had set her snares and built a small shelter, and picking together, the women managed to fill their pail with plums, chokecherries, and another small fruit that Meena called redcap, a fragile and seedy berry somewhat akin to a raspberry. With hostiles about, building a fire to stew the berries was a worrisome task, particularly with the well-trodden crossing only a few miles above, so it was only when the sky had turned black did they finally strike their fire. That night, their ears tuned to every little rustle and sound in the forest, they had what Plenty Hawk called the "one-eyed sleep."

If it had not been the best of nights, the day started out little better. Something had disturbed the pony and Bird found it in an open meadow in full view of the river, grazing and trailing its picket pin. When she returned with the horse, she found Meena holding out a dead snowshoe hare, yet cursing because another set had been torn apart and the rabbit eaten by a coyote or wolf. She didn't know which, but the tracks were there, mixed in with a few tufts of hair. When she mentioned wolf, Bird gave her a startled look. Bird immediately recalled the previous afternoon when glancing back over the pony, she had seen a flight of prairie chickens exploding into the sky, and then moments later, caught a fleeting glimpse of a gray animal bounding through the tall grass. Obviously, after her unique experience with the wickiup wolf, that had been her first thought, wolf! Ultimately, she had decided this was only coincidental, really a crazy notion, completely irrational on her part, that such a wild creature actually would follow her across the valley. How bizarre! Her mind had been playing tricks on her, so she dismissed the incident, believing that most likely the gray object was a coyote, an animal with enough cunning and quickness to catch a chicken. That was where she left the matter, until now, until Meena's theory on what had pilfered her snare. Then, Bird wondered what had spooked Flame, a pony that never wandered. Her fertile imagination once again was swelling like a puffball, but because of the missing hare and Meena's ire, she was reluctant to get a second opinion about her own thoughts. No, this wasn't the time to talk about the spirit wolf, the remote possibility that it and the night killer could be one and the same.

Meena, hunting stick over her shoulder, left for the river to clean the snowshoe, and Bird, still pondering the possibility of the young wolf's return, busied herself arranging their meager supplies and gear for packing. A flight of magpies came flitting through the trees,

crying and dipping in between the branches, and
Flame, standing nearby, let out a small whinny. Bird
came alert, turned around, and found herself starting at
a slender young man standing beside a pony across the
small clearing. Her breath quickened. He wore a red
blanket poncho that hung down below his thighs, and
holding back his hair was a beaded red-and-blue headband. As he approached, Bird immediately recognized
the Sioux beadwork on the headband, the small con-
necting, elongated pyramids, the red-and-white trim so
evenly spaced in tiny squares. And he was carrying a
rifle that she knew was a Henry repeater, and she wondered from what dead trooper he had taken it.

He said in Siouan, "We saw the pony from over
there," and he nodded toward the river. "*Ho,* I thought
I had found myself a lost pony but instead I find a
woman." He looked cautiously around the sparse camp
once before returning her silent stare. He asked,
"Where is your man who is so poor he has only one
horse and no tipi?"

Bird, preparing herself for the worst, understood
most of what he had said, and there was no mistake in
the ridiculing tone of his voice. With some hesitation,
and rather brokenly, she said, "I have no man. What
you see is what you see."

"I see Lakota moccasins," he returned, pointing his
rifle at her legs, where the high-tips curled down in a
fringed flap below her knees. "But you do not speak
like a Lakota. Where do you come from . . . ? Where is
your village?"

Motioning behind her, Bird said, "My home is beyond the Yellowstone by the Calling River. I am going
back to my people." The young Indian looked surprised. And Bird added, "I am a Cree woman."

He carefully edged around her and squinted into the
shelter at the baby lying curled up in a blanket. Turning back to her, he said scornfully, "*Wasichu.* You are
wasichu, a live-in-the-fort woman, and you are lying to

me. You say you are Cree. You try to speak like a Lakota. You wear rings on your fingers like the bluecoats. What are you hiding?"

Bird's fright began to turn to contentious anger. "I told you," she retorted, "I am going home. I have nothing to hide. Are your ears as bad as your manners? Go, go see for yourself, if you will, but do not touch my son, because in the time it takes two dogs to smell each other, I will kill you." Defiantly, she placed her hands on her hips, yet letting one drop down to her knife and razor.

Unaccustomed to such words from a woman, especially one so young, the brave's face flushed, and shaking his rifle menacingly, he said, "Your tongue is too sharp, she-dog woman. *Ho,* stand aside. Yes, I will see what you have besides this fine pony."

What happened next was so fearfully fast and unexpected that Bird collapsed, literally. Meena suddenly came up behind the young brave, and with a powerful, leaping surge, embedded her timber-nail spear in between his shoulder blades. The strike was solid, devastatingly heavy, a crunch of bone, yet not a spurt of blood as the long point pierced the brave's heart. With one gasping outcry, he fell forward into Bird's arms, causing her to go down with him. In his death throes, he was flapping over her like a beheaded chicken. Trying to shake loose, Bird cried out, "Good God, Mama, you've killed him! Get him off! Get the sonofabitch off of me!"

"Quick," Meena hissed, pulling at the stricken man, "another one is coming! He saw me at the river. You know how to shoot. Go, do what you have to," and she shoved the fallen rifle into Bird's hands. "Hurry, and remember Papa, all he taught you."

Ducking madly through the brush, Bird bounded like a deer toward the sheltered bank where earlier they had washed and taken their water. Approaching the river, she fell into a running crouch, and oh, God, it was true, another rider was coming, already halfway across, his horse belly-deep, and he was heading directly toward her. She hid. She had no time to find a log to support the heavy barrel, so she bellied up prone, and rested her elbow on the ground. Edging the chamber lever back, she nervously checked to see if a round were in place. It was there, but was she shaking too much to make a good shot? Yes, remember what Papa had taught her. Cocking the hammer, Bird took a deep breath, a careful aim at the man's chest, and pulled the trigger. A blasting jolt hit her as the rifle recoiled sharply against her shoulder, but when she looked through the small, hazy pall of gun smoke, all she saw was a riderless pony splashing away back to the opposite bank. Except for the sound of rippling water, everything was suddenly quiet. She got to her knees and warily scanned the other side, quiet there, too, only the pony trotting away, no other riders in the distant meadows. But out near the middle of the river below her, Bird noticed something drifting in the slow current. All she could make out was a head and one outstretched arm. "Good God," she muttered, "I've killed a man . . . a man I didn't even know!"

By the time she returned, her mother was already tightening the cinch on Flame. Only one shot, one shot and no outcry, and Meena knew. "He's dead," Bird confirmed, and still trembling inside, she scurried about snatching up their belongings, shoving everything she could get her hands on into the bundle and two canvas bags Meena had made. At this point, it was not a matter of how they packed, but how fast. They were aware of how far the echo of a rifle shot sometimes carried along a river bottom or in the foothills. Hardly a word was spoken until minutes later when it was time to go. Bird asked about the body of the young Teton. She was trying not to stare at it. Meena quickly removed a knife and cartridge case from the man's belt and put them into her bundle, then grabbed sticks from the shelter, along with every other scrap of brush she could find, and covered the body, all done with dispatch. When she finished, she went over to the brave's mare, brown-and-white in color, picked up the reins and handed them to Bird. A buckskin sheath was attached to the side of the Indian saddle. "Here, take the rifle, there's a place for it," Meena said. Bird secured it, and after her mother hoisted up the baby in its canvas sling, they headed downriver in a fast trot.

Lean and spirited, the Teton pony had been broken to neck rein, and Bird soon discovered that a mere touch to either side brought immediate response. Even with her anxiety (she found herself continually looking over her shoulder), she did enjoy riding this fine young mare, and when they stopped to rest miles downstream from the site of the killing, Bird led her to water and affectionately rubbed her nose. At this point, the women finally had a chance to eat a meager breakfast and discuss the horror of what had happened. However protective and spontaneous their action had been, Meena was sorrowful. When she had made her hunting stick, she had no thought of using it to kill a man, only to finish off a rabbit, maybe another porcupine, or to spear a fish in the river, yet when she saw the Sioux warrior threatening her daughter, there was no time to talk or plead or dwell on consequences. She knew the Tetons were either going to rob or kill them, maybe both. And besides, if they had been spared, what would have been their fate at a hostile village, especially with the baby? These Indians weren't friendly Brule. Who wanted that questionable outcome? Bird didn't rationalize on it. She tossed her head negatively, no, she would rather die than go through the uncertainties of another Indian camp, particularly a hostile one.

Because of the way the two Sioux had been equipped, (Bird found only a blanket and a pouch of dried elk meat tied on behind the mare's saddle) the women agreed that these men were probably scouts returning to their village up the valley after searching for game or signs of troopers. Regardless of what their mission had been, the fatal ending would certainly bring out other villagers seeking the missing. Sooner or later, the gray horse that bolted back across the river was going to return home or be discovered. Bird surmised that locating the two bodies might be more of a chore, but if ever the Teton caught up with the killers they would have no trouble identifying the mare she was now riding, or the precious rifle attached to it. This unpleasant thought put a small knot in her stomach, for to warring people, the gender of hair on a scalp stick made no difference whatsoever.

Fearful of another unexpected encounter, the women decided to cross the river and head for the distant grassy foothills on the west side where tracks would be more difficult to follow. Ultimately, they came to an area above the hills where small slopes of juniper and pine stretched across the landscape. Riding in this cover for another mile, they came upon a brushy creek meandering northward. (Bird was to learn later that this was the Rosebud, a small stream that coursed through the middle of the Northern Cheyenne nation.) Bird and Meena stopped only long enough in this bottom to water the horses, wash their own faces, and clean the baby. By dusk, they found a dry camp farther west in a stand of ponderosa. For this night, it would have to do, so they curled up under the spreading boughs of a big tree, using its deep layer of pine needles for their beds. And this night, too, Bird heard the mournful but melodious cry of a wolf.

The next morning, long before first light, Meena had a small fire going and was warming berry mash and cooking the rabbit she had snared at the Tongue River camp. By dawn, she wanted no sign of smoke that might point out their location. Even though she and Bird knew it was too early to be followed by the Sioux, if indeed, they could be tracked at all, their fear was in the unknown, the danger all around them, for they were now crossing an area between the prairie and the Backbone of the World, the great Rocky Mountains, and this passage was used by many tribes. Bird knew something of the country, but only from descriptions of it and the colorful and sometimes frightening tales that she and Garth had heard from either John Dominguez or Gabe Bridger when they had often talked long into the night around a crackling fire back at Fort Kearny. A sacred land to many, it was a land to be both respected and feared, and as Bridger had said, one's life in it most often depended upon skill, a friendly pact with nature, and a good horse, all of which the Indians possessed and many white men did not.

They were huddled in their blankets under the tree, eating and watching the sun rise over the great expanse of hills to the east. West of them, the faint bluish teethlike peaks of mountain wilderness were beginning to pop up, barely discernible in the morning light, but the women knew this was their way, the upper part of the Bozeman Trail, the great Yellowstone Valley, and civilization, what precious little there was of it, and once there, another time of decision.

The two horses were picketed down below in a shallow depression where there was ample grass, and as Meena was preparing to retrieve them, Bird noticed her suddenly stop and lean forward. Bending low, the butt end of her hunting stick firmly planted in the ground, Meena was peering into the shadows of the trees. Finally, she turned back toward Bird and pointed her stick at the woods. She said that she saw a wolf, a strange sight, because before it ran away, it was sitting on its haunches like a dog watching her. Was this some kind of an omen? she asked. Why would a wolf do such a thing? Shaking her head doubtfully, she shouldered her stick and went on down the hill toward the horses. Bird immediately put the baby in the blanket and quickly scraped up the carcass of the rabbit, a piece of neck and back, and the bones from the legs.

Excitement stirring, she hurried over to the trees where Meena had pointed, thinking that now it was a certainty, that this just had to be the wickiup wolf, that this was something more than her imagination, the gray streak in the grass, the missing rabbit, the lonesome cry in the dark last night. No, this was reality, her wolf! For a moment, she stood there expectantly, probing the shadowy boughs and trunks, hoping she could, likewise, catch a glimpse of him, her curious follower. And once again, as she had done before, she called, "Wolf! Wolf, where are you? Why are you pursuing me? Come, Wolf, come!" She sensed he was there somewhere in the tumble of bushes and trees, listening, watching, anticipating her next move. She threw out the carcass and bones. "Wolf, come, now! Come and get your breakfast." Another moment elapsed, and after what seemed like an eternity, Bird saw a slight movement between two scrub junipers. Indeed, it was her young friend, his black nose glistening, and the unkempt, silvery shoulder hair standing out like a halo in the dimness of the forest. Another tinge of excitement ran through her; her arms tingled as if pricked with tiny quills, and she wondered if the hair on them was also standing, perhaps an extension of the strange bond between two creatures, one human, one animal, yes, animal but spiritually human. Soon, Bird found herself witnessing one of the strangest and most fascinating things she had ever seen. Slowly advancing from his hiding place in the junipers, the wolf crept close to where she had tossed the remains of the rabbit, and here, he briefly paused, lowered himself into a crouch, and walked slowly around in a figure eight. He stopped, momentarily stared at her with his green eyes, then, snatching up the carcass portion, he trotted away. Bird was trembling all over. She absolutely could not comprehend what she had just seen. Extending her arms from her robe, she stared at them. As she had surmised, the hair on them was standing straight out.

Shortly, she heard Meena calling, returning with the ponies, and when she finally came back to their resting place by the big trees, her mother was asking, "What were you doing up there, looking for that wolf? I scared it away."

"I saw it," Bird said. "Yes, I saw it, too. You didn't chase it away at all. It was there waiting for me."

"Mi-ya!" exclaimed Meena, bringing the horses close to the tree. "Waiting for you! And I suppose you talked to it, eh? You talked to it like the last time, that day in the rain?" Wagging her head, she lamented, "We must end this trip soon before it's too late for you, one day talking to the sky, the next day to a wolf." She clucked her tongue and started saddling the Teton mare.

Bird only smiled, saying, "Mama, you would be surprised about this little wolf. I think he's rather special."

"Ah, then you did talk to it?" Meena returned skeptically. "So, what makes him so special, as you say?"

Bird, hoisting her saddle onto Flame, continued. "Well, because he's the same one I saw when we stayed in the spirit camp back on the Powder. He's been with us all the way, probably ate one of your rabbits the other night, too." And thinking about this, she laughed. "You see, he's not so dumb."

"What! You really think this is the same one, the one who stole my snowshoe? Why, that's crazy, Bird! Wolves don't follow people around like dogs. What a notion! What are you trying to tell me, one of Papa's fairy tales?"

"No, he's the same one, all right. I've seen him three times, and I know you won't believe this, but just a little while ago, he did a dance for me . . . like this." Bending over, Bird mimicked the wolf, mincing around in a series of tiny steps.

With an incredulous look, Meena said, "I don't understand. Why would he do something like that. Are you fooling me, making up such a story? I think this is crazy . . . you're crazy."

Bird laughed again, almost nervously, because it was now inevitable; she would have to confess she had been feeding the wolf. "Well," she hesitantly began, "I suppose in his own peculiar way he was trying to thank me. He knows my voice, and . . . well, I fed him several times, left some food for him . . . just a scrap or two."

Meena winced, and stomping angrily in the dust, she cried, "You left him our food, the very food our lives depend upon! Now, look what you have done. No wonder he sits like a dog! You see, he follows us. He will steal us blind . . . my traps. Where is your mind, daughter? You can't do this anymore. No, we have too many other things to think about, the hair on our heads, for one thing. Enough is enough. You must forget this animal, leave him alone."

Bird paused thoughtfully, holding the pony's bit, playing on her own imagination and her mother's superstitions. Then, in a whisper, she said, "Don't you think this is rather unusual, the way he appeared that day, out of the mists like a . . . a ghost? Think about it. And that camp, like you said, maybe a sacred place where the ancient ones prayed to the spirits. Maybe you're right . . . this wolf is some sort of an omen. What is he trying to tell me? Think how strange it is."

Meena, contemplating her daughter's words suspiciously, thought deeply for a few moments before answering. Yes, this did seem mysterious. "I don't know," she finally said. "I have heard stories from the old people about ghosts, about the Owl Maker, a witch, up in the Place of Many Tipis who sometimes throws spirits back to Mother Earth when they have come to the sky unprepared. Sometimes they become ghosts in disguise, this is true, the way it's told. Yes, both good ghosts and evil ones, too, following old friends about, doing crazy things, just as if they had never left them in the first place. But on the other hand, I don't find your wolf so crazy eating our food. Why can't he find his own like the others out there?"

"We don't have to worry about food," Bird said confidently, resting a hand on the scabbard holding the Henry repeater. "Look, Mama, you can forget about the wolf and your snares, too. From now on, this will keep us in meat, more than we can ever eat."

"It makes too much noise. People will hear."

"In the right place, the right time." And Bird nuzzled her head against her mother's shoulder affectionately, telling her that there was something about the small wolf that strangely compelled her to befriend it, a compassion, an empathy that she found difficult to understand, let alone, explain. At length, Meena reluctantly relented, with allowances that the spirit wolf's companionship would depend upon its behavior. If it compromised the journey in any way, it would have to go. Let nature take its course, Meena said, knowing that eventually, at the proper time, the wolf, like all ghosts, would leave in response to the calls of its own kind. On this conciliatory note, the women rode out to the northwest, the morning sun at their backs, with each knoll becoming a lookout as they carefully scanned ahead for signs of other riders. After several hours, they came to a small depression where at the upper end they saw some rust-colored bluffs. Below the bluffs was a meadow of green grass surrounded by broken stands of golden willows. Without prompting, the ponies, already alerted to the presence of water, turned on their own and headed in this direction. Sometime later, the women found the water's source, a clear, cold spring, its banks lined with watercress and pond weed. Bird pointed to a grassy bend where the water disappeared at the lower end of the meadow. The wickiup wolf was there, bending low in the shallows, taking his fill, too.

The short stop at the spring was productive. Refreshed, with a new supply of water, and edible watercress packed away in a wet bundle, they rode west back around the bluffs into the rolling hills again. In this area, buffalo sign was all around but both the tracks and droppings were old, indicating that herds had fed here in early summer when the grass was young and tender. A few antelope were about, small bands often in the distance and well out of shooting range, so Bird, now ever hopeful of bagging fresh meat, had to bide her time. The women, although still wary of this unfamiliar land, concluded they were now far north of Sioux and Cheyenne villages on the Tongue and Big Horn rivers, where most of the hostiles were concentrated, this, at least, one less worry. Also, the scarcity of buffalo made it unlikely that they would encounter hunting parties, or even a camp for that matter, because the terrain, lacking trees and plentiful water, did not lend itself to a village site. Even though their chances of getting through undetected were improving, the fact was that neither Bird nor Meena knew exactly where they were, only that the Big Horn River was somewhere west and the Yellowstone north. They were now reasoning that anyone traveling these barren hills would have a similar purpose, that of only trying to get out of them.

A higher range of hills, their tops sprinkled with pine, finally appeared in the distance. This was a more likely area to find a water hole for the ponies, as well as another campsite for the night. By now, they were riding into the sun, the air warm and dry, and the women, their sense of urgency and fear slowly diminishing, were ready to stop and make camp. Closer to the foothills, Bird could see a few bushy draws and eroded gulches, and it was in one of these long coulees where they found the last trickle of the summer's water. Scooping out a depression in the sandy creek bottom, they made a small pool, capturing enough water to bathe themselves and the baby.

One of the first things Bird noticed here was a profusion of small sharply pointed tracks beside the dying creekbed, and more important, they were fresh, most of them leading up toward the pine-covered hillside. She knew deer were in the area, probably feeding and bedding on the sheltered slopes by day and coming down to drink at night, so soon after camp was made, she shouldered her rifle, and within ten minutes had walked to the fringe of the forest, following a freshly used game trail all the way. Eventually, she came to another trail that broke off in two directions, one leading to the top, the other a smaller path turning off below her into another ravine. Choosing the lower trail, Bird slowly sneaked along for about a hundred yards before coming to a clearing where she could see the little valley below. On a small, sage-covered bench, not more than fifty paces, were five deer, four of them bedded down, another standing, nostrils flared, staring directly at her. She realized there was precious little time to pick and choose. By the time she had cocked the rifle, all five were up and moving. Taking aim at the closest, Bird pulled the trigger, once again feeling the slamming jolt against her shoulder. However, this time, unlike the incident on the river, she saw the target fall, a tumbling mass, skinny legs kicking, cartwheeling off the bench, sliding halfway down the grassy slope. It was a small buck, a fork-horn, and dead by the time she reached it. Grasping one of the small antlers, she skidded the deer to the bottom. She was only a quarter of a mile from the camp, and she saw Meena standing near the creek waving. Soon afterward, her mother arrived with Flame. After cleaning and halving the animal, it was packed back to their camp, and in the darkness this night, the women feasted on strips of roasted liver, had boiled watercress that tasted like spinach, and finished the last of the berry mash. For the young wolf, Bird left the deer's neck and a side of ribs at the edge of the clearing. When she called him, he came, lowered himself, and ate.

Chapter Thirteen

Bird and her mother first saw the big, winding river from a distance, shimmering like a band of silver ribbon, coursing its way down through a valley of green meadows and huge, towering trees, and they knew in a moment they had reached the Yellowstone. After following a well-worn trail several miles, they unexpectedly came upon several cabins and the remains of an old stockade overlooking the river. This, as lonely as it appeared, was the first sign of civilization they had seen in over a year. Smoke was drifting up from one of the cabins, and in a nearby field enclosed by a jack-pole fence, were horses, mules, and several cows grazing in the warm valley breeze, while in an adjacent enclosure were two big stacks of fresh hay and another log shed with a corral around it. A great surge of relief and expectancy swept through each of the women as they stopped and stared almost unbelievingly at such a peaceful setting, for this had to be a holy place, a revered sanctuary untouched by the wilderness war. Bird quickly slipped off her pony and handed the baby up to Meena. Running down to a large gateway, she cupped her hands and called out a hello. A boy soon appeared at the door of the biggest cabin, followed by a bearded man with a rifle. They stood there in silent appraisement, looking first at Bird, then Meena, who was coming up behind with the ponies. The man, after some hesitation, finally beckoned them up to the big cabin, and by the time they reached the porch, a woman also appeared by the doorway. Seeing Meena carrying an infant, she came hurrying down the stoop, exclaiming, "They have a baby! Here, come in, come in. You bring that child right inside and rest."

As the woman rushed by, Bird held out her hand to the bearded man, a tall strapping fellow, his woolen trousers held up by faded, red suspenders. "My name is Bird Rutledge," she said. She nodded as her mother passed by into the cabin. "That's my mother, and, dear God, we've come a terribly long way."

"John Goodhart," the man replied, returning a lusty shake. His blond brows were arched over his blue eyes. In apparent awe, he stared at Bird, first at her bronzed face, then down to her moccasins, and back to her face again.

Bird asked wearily, "What is this place? Where are we?"

"Manuel's old fort," Goodhart answered. "My homestead, now." Handing the rifle to the boy, he gazed down at Bird again in wonderment. "Used to be a post for the fur trade." Scratching his beard, he said, "Being Indian, I take it, how is it you speak such good English? Where did you folks come from, anyway?"

Wiping her forehead, Bird emitted another weary sigh. "Indian, yes, part, anyhow. Oh, it's a very long story, Mr. Goodhart, one you may find hard to believe. We've been riding for days all the way from the Little Missouri." She paused and looked back again at the perplexed expression on his hardy face. "May I come in? I'm so tired and thankful to be here, but, really, I'm about ready to drop."

"Why, certainly!" he exclaimed, extending his hands in apology. "What am I thinking about, anyways, dammit. Just taken aback, I reckon. Yes, get on in there and sit yourself down." He turned to the boy. "Take care of those horses, James, and bring the packs over here on the porch."

James, somewhat darker than his father, and about

fourteen years old, pointed to the pole gate. "There's a wolf down there, Dad. What about that? Never seen anything like it. He's sitting there looking."

Bird whirled about, saying, "He's mine. It's all right, don't worry, he'll stay down there until I call him." John Goodhart leaned forward, peering curiously at the strange sight, a wolf on its haunches acting like a dog. Bird put a hand on his shoulder. "No, it's really all right," she said reassuringly. "He's only a young one. I'll tell you about him, later."

Once inside, there was momentary confusion. Bird and Meena were asking directions and distances while the Goodharts, slack-jawed, staring back and forth, were both listening and questioning as the women's bizarre story of their perilous trek began coming out in bits and pieces. As it turned out, Goodhart knew John Dominguez. And Gabe Bridger, he said, had actually holed up at Manuel's Fort several times, but long before the Goodharts arrived on the scene. The fact that Meena was a widow and that Bird's man had been killed shortly afterward so distressed Molly Goodhart that tears welled in her eyes. She herself was half Indian, Absaroke, or Crow as they were commonly called, and this seemed to make her sympathy for the women even more profound. She was an attractive woman with typically high cheekbones and the straight nose of a Crow. Part white, true, but she knew what it was like to live in a red world that was becoming more blanched every day. As for Goodhart, he had been trading with Indians, mostly Crow, for furs, hides, horses, and anything else of value, but since the boats were now coming up the river as far as a new landing at the mouth of the Powder River, he was making more money by taking people and supplies west to the upper portion of the Virginia City road and on to a settlement called Bozeman City. Goodhart, however, had made one freight trip down to Fort Smith with the soldiers but soon gave up on this route when the Teton-Oglala and Cheyenne began harassing the wagons. The trail along the upper Yellowstone was much safer, at least for him, because of Molly's relationship with the Absaroke. Also, he rarely encountered any Blackfeet from the north, and never met Sioux or Cheyenne on the Yellowstone. This disclosure brought a sigh of relief from Bird Rutledge.

When Bird asked what day and month it was, offhand, Goodhart thought it was October, but no one knew the date until after he checked a calendar behind his trading counter. He marked off days from his last trip up the river and decided it must be October seventh. That would be just about two months since all of the fighting down around Fort Smith. If anything more had happened in the meantime, news had not come down the Big Horn River, at least not yet. He said wagons chancing the Bozeman Trail south were now military and heavily guarded. Private freighters like himself had been frightened off, and with good reason, since several had been ambushed and their loads looted by hostiles. Bird and Meena exchanged anxious glances, however neither mentioned the wagons they had accidentally found.

During this long and frequently animated discussion, Bird told the Goodharts that she and Meena wanted to get to one of the forts, eventually back to Laramie, where they had friends, people who could help them get started again. John Goodhart's face soured at this notion. Presently, it was almost impossible to get to Fort Laramie the less arduous way, down the Bozeman Trail. The only other routes, he said, were out of the question because of the great distances involved, the advent of cold weather, and of course, more important, the infant they were packing. If the women wanted to go to Bozeman City, he could help, but both he and his wife believed it would be best for the two women to rest a week or two before they made any decisions. Ultimately, everyone agreed to this, so Molly and James helped prepare the second cabin for occupancy. The women stowed their gear and made beds, and James brought a load of wood for the rock fireplace and a large kettle for hot water. When this was done, they all sat down in the Goodhart cabin for a potluck supper. To Bird and her mother, it was more like Thanksgiving. The bean and cabbage soup was laced with large chunks of bacon; the steaming corn bread was topped with molasses; there was fresh milk and a berry pie. The cabbage, it turned out, was from Molly's garden, where Bird and Meena later were astonished to find a bountiful supply of carrots, onions, corn, and squash.

At dusk, Bird finally took Goodhart and James to the front of the old stockade to see her wolf, the wild creature she had befriended on the trail. She had with her large pieces of venison cut from one of the front quarters left over from her kill at the gulch camp. Standing silently in back of Bird, the Goodharts waited as she called. Within seconds, the wolf appeared and lowered itself in front of her. Reaching out slowly, she affectionately rubbed its head several times and then placed the meat in front of him. He picked it up, retreated several yards and began eating. Bird turned back to the awestruck couple. She said regretfully, "He's growing every day, it seems, and I'm afraid one of these nights when I call, he won't come. I'll probably feel worse about it than he will."

"Oh, shucks, Miss Bird," James put in, "he'll find new friends just like you will."

She smiled at the boy. "Yes, I'm sure of that, but I'll miss him, his inquisitive stare, the way he looks at me, sometimes. He tries to read my mind, and I get the strangest feeling, like he wants to tell me something, like he wants to talk."

"Perhaps he does," Goodhart mused. "The Indians tell of a time when all the four-legged talked with each other, the Universal Tongue, they call it. The Great

Spirit never blessed the two-leggeds with this ability. We have only to assume."

"Oh, I suppose it's my imagination. I just can't explain it."

They walked back toward the cabin, the older Goodhart shaking his head. "Who knows? Maybe in time you'll find an explanation, but I tell you, that's the darnedest thing I've ever seen."

On the third day after her arrival, John Goodhart told Bird that he was going on a trip down the Yellowstone to trade with the River Crow, and if trail conditions were safe, attempt to reach the outpost at Fort Union. If she wished, he would be obliged to purchase some woolens and cloth so she and Meena could outfit themselves and the baby. The nights were becoming more chilly, he explained, and soon they would need more than blankets and buckskins to keep warm. This was a matter that already concerned Bird, so she immediately agreed to Goodhart's offer, and shortly thereafter, she returned, and to his astonishment, placed two hundred dollars in gold coins on the table in front of him. She told him she would gladly accept his offer, but not his charity, not when she was able to pay. Quietly stunned, Goodhart stood aside as she wrote out a list of supplies that she thought would benefit all of them, including, not only staples, but a new pair of boots for James (she had observed that he needed them) and something for Molly and Goodhart himself. When Bird finished, Goodhart finally asked how she had come by so much money, received a wink in reply, and a comment that she was a pretty good horse trader herself. Perplexed and somewhat amused at her vague wit, Goodhart, nevertheless, did not pursue the matter. He already had formed his opinion about Bird Rutledge, that she was unquestionably intelligent and undeniably courageous and compassionate. He put her money in his pouch, telling her that he and James were taking the freight wagon and a team of mules, and probably would be on the trail shortly after dawn. At the same time, he suggested that the women strongly consider wintering at his post, at least postpone any thoughts of lengthy travel until spring. Their company during the winter would be appreciated, and it certainly would make Molly happy. Discussing Goodhart's friendly proposal that night, Bird and Meena concluded that under the present circumstances and lack of reasonable alternatives, staying at the old outpost was the best decision they could make, for after all, the Goodharts had given them a good little home and a warm welcome to go with it. And as Molly Goodhart kept insisting, the welfare of the infant should be considered above all else. Already preparing to be a second grandmother, Molly was delighted the next day when Bird told her that she and her mother had made up their minds—they were going to stay in the cabin for the winter. Who knew? By spring, hostilities along the Bozeman Trail south might be at an end and the route safe to travel again. If not, they had an alternative, one suggested by Goodhart—they could join up with army-escorted freighters from the gold country and travel to Fort Benton and from there, take one of the steamboats down the Missouri to Omaha. In celebration of this decision, Molly prepared a large pot of venison stew, and long after supper, the three women were still laughing and talking on the little porch. Down near the pole gate, the young wolf was dozing, its silvery head resting in between two great paws.

During the absence of John and James, Bird took over the outside chores, tending stock, bringing in wood, and milking the two cows. It was the first physical work she had done in months, and besides strengthening her muscles, it also helped freshen her mind, relieving it from some of the haunting burdens of the past, the death of her father, the loss of Garth,

and the grievous but necessary flight from her Brule
Sioux family. Bird also began working with her wolf,
shouldering her rifle and taking jaunts up into the high
meadows, coaxing him to follow more closely and to
stop on her command. With some old boards and a few
short logs, she made him a small den behind the big
shed, filled it with hay, and within two nights, he had
made it his home. Bird could only hope that her friend
was going to stay with her, at least until he was full
grown, until he could join others of his kind and compete on his own.

But Bird soon discovered that in her newly found
freedom from what had been, memories of the past
sometimes materialize themselves into reality in
strange ways. Early one morning near the end of October, a few days after John and James returned from the
trading trip, two wagons showed up near the gate. A
large man sitting at the reins in the front wagon
shouted several times and waved. Bird saw Goodhart
and young James walking down to greet the travelers.
In the back wagon was another man, smaller, who
jumped down and stretched several times, while to the
back, two riders, both Indian, sat stoically on their ponies, arms folded under their blankets. Curious about
the white men's sudden appearance, Bird lagged behind the Goodharts, yet within earshot. The men exchanged greetings, and she heard the first man asking
about the route downriver toward Fort Union. Molly
came down, too, and began making sign with the Indians, who, Bird found out later were Bannock from a
land over near the gold diggings. The laughter and
crude mannerisms of the group's leader suddenly
struck home, bringing Bird closer to get a better look
at him. Indeed, as she suspected, it was the same trader
who had once appeared in the Brule village of Plenty
Hawk seven months ago! McComber, she remembered,
that was his name, the vile creature who had offered
Plenty Hawk a rifle and blankets in exchange for her.

Bird suddenly felt a rush of anger, a flush at her cheek-bones upon seeing this fat rascal of a man again. At this same moment, McComber caught her hardened stare, and his tobacco-stained mouth gaped in amazement. Bird said with a small bitter smile, "So, you remember me."

Face aglow, McComber forced a stubby laugh laced with both surprise and scorn. "Remember you! Who in the hell could forget you? How'd you get way up here, anyways? That chief finally get rid of you, trade you off?" Stroking his beard, he muttered, "Be damned, if this don't beat all!"

John Goodhart, somewhat surprised himself, said, "Well, I take it, you people know each other from somewhere down the trail."

"Oh, I know him," Bird answered. "Yes, I certainly do. He had the nerve to try and buy me once, as if I were some kind of horseflesh at auction. My God, can you believe it, for a rifle and some lousy blankets!"

"Bit off more than I could chew, I reckon," returned McComber, grinning and spitting to the side. "Yassir, sure did." He looked down at her again, then up at the sky as if he were trying to recollect something. Suddenly, he slapped his palms together. "Now, I remember. There was this feller askin' 'bout you and your maw, feller called Domino. I reckon you know him, runs with the troopers a bit now and then, scoutin' and such. Wanted to know if I'd seen or heard of you, so I told him, for a fact, I sure had seen you, all right."

"John Dominguez?" Bird asked, feeling a sudden lump in her throat. "How long ago?"

"That's the one, Dominguez." He paused and clucked his tongue. "Hell's bells, woman, I ups and tells him you're hangin' out at one of Red Leaf's camps. Why, that's be, let's see, maybe four months ago or so. Didn't know you'd skeedaddled all the way up here." Leaning down, he winked at her. "Run away, did you?"

Bird, pulling her blanket close, turned away and said over her shoulder, "What I do is none of your damned business." Suddenly, in afterthought, she looked back and asked, "Where's that other one, the educated man who was with you, the one called Sturges?"

"Henry? Why, he's dead and gone, I reckon. Split with me, he did. He was bushwhacked, I hear, him and a couple others from the diggin' down on the Powder, a couple months back." Jubal McComber stopped and chuckled. "Yassir, figgered he could make it through dealin' with the Cheyenne, but he figgered wrong. Troopers found 'em and put 'em under right proper, I hear. Yassir, ol' Henry took himself a ride up the Great Hanging Road. He's a dead, gone man, he is."

Bird hurried away, McComber's chilling, irreverent revelation gnawing inside her like a pack of hungry mice. She heard him saying, "She's a spitfire, that one, yassir, she sure is."

Once back in her cabin, Bird quickly rummaged through Meena's bundle, anxiously scratching her nails to the bottom. Seizing the gold watch, she flipped open its lid, and the sharply engraved letters in the middle of the fancy scrollwork leaped out at her: H. B. S. Henry B. Sturges! Oh, my God, how ironic! How ironic in so many ways. Sturges, ambushed! Poetic justice! Sturges, the traitor who brought Garth west in such a suffering, futile search, Henry Sturges. And only because of him had she met and lost her lover, the father of her son. Garth dead, Sturges dead. Pondering the series of fateful events again, she walked outside to the nearby rail fence and stared across at the grazing horses and cows. They seemed so content in the peaceful meadow.

Chapter Fourteen

Autumn was in the air, the days becoming shorter, a browning of the grasses, tinges of yellow and orange gilding the trees along the Yellowstone bottom. John Goodhart told Bird that when the blowflies disappear from the corrals, this was one of the best signs of cold weather ahead, but Molly, his half Crow wife, pointed to the livestock, a better sign, she thought; the animals were beginning to get shaggy, taking on their winters coats. Meena, too, had an opinion, looking daily to the northern skies where the great flights of snow geese were beginning to come down from the Queen Mother's Land, the surest sign of winter's approach. Whatever, activity around the small outpost suddenly centered on preparing for the cold months, the Moons of Ice on the River, and before the first hard frost came, Molly and Meena had harvested the garden, canning some of the vegetables, and sacking the rest for storage in the deep earthen cellar behind the large cabin.

James was joining his father every day with a team of mules, helping skid up dry logs from the river bottom to saw and split into firewood. When free of this chore, he worked with Bird, tending the stock and two cows who were now supplying Little Ty with a different taste of milk, along with an occasional dab of mashed food that his two grandmothers were continually trying out on him. Some afternoons, James went with Bird on short hunts along the bottom, and by mid-

November the two of them had filled one corner of the big horse shed with cloth-covered quarters from five deer they had killed.

One sunny afternoon when John and his son came in with a load of logs, they told the women about a huge dead tree they had felled, one swarming with bees, John promptly displayed one of his wrists to verify it, the two angry welts on it standing out red against his tanned skin. Meena immediately set about procuring honey-gathering materials, a large pot, several jars, rags for smudges, and protective shawls and a hat, and within a half hour, she was riding away with James down to find the treasure, for in her mind, a windfall of honey was much better than a pound of sugar. James was yelling back to Bird to join them, and after some encouragement from Molly, she handed the baby to Goodhart's wife and followed, accompanied by Wolf, who now most often loped along some distance behind her. They soon found the downed cottonwood not too far off the trail, an angry cloud of bees swarming about the partially splintered trunk. Bird, totally unprepared for such a threatening task, quickly elected to lead the ponies back toward the trail to less hazardous ground. Meantime, Meena, scurrying around like a bee herself, was directing James in firing up the smudges. Soon, the air was filled with the acrid smell of smoldering rags, and Meena, covered with her shawls, gloves on her hands, and only the narrow slits of her eyes showing, took James's ax and swiftly widened the hole, exposing the comb. With a large wooden ladle she began scooping out huge sections of the comb, pouring the dripping honey into the large kettle, then into the jars, filling all of them to their brims. James, leaping back and forth, laughing and cursing, swatting at bees, was taking the containers back to where Bird stood by with the horses. Even though it was all over in a half hour, the smoke filtering up along the bottom had attracted unexpected visitors, four of them,

mounted and silently watching from near the trail.
Wolf's deep, throaty growl alerted Bird, and she immediately went for her rifle. The moment was tense, but
at the same time, James turned and saw the Indians. He
quickly called out to Bird that the Indians were Crow,
brothers from upriver. Bird then held up her hand to
the growling wolf, who obediently went to his
haunches with his head thrust forward, his green eyes
warily on the intruders. With James at her side, Bird
approached the four men who because of the wolf
seemed to have little interest in dismounting. However,
they were smiling broadly, the two in front holding out
their hands in a friendly greeting. Obviously, they had
been observing long enough to witness some of
Meena's frantic performance at the hive and still were
finding great humor in it. Because of James's mother
and his own frequent contact with the Crow, he knew
the Absaroke tongue, but one of the men had already
recognized him, and his first question was about the
shaggy wolf sitting like a dog, watching them, occasionally shifting his head back and forth. Was it safe to
slip out of their saddles? James, in turn, asked Bird.
With a smile, she nodded back at the Indians. Then the
men dismounted and began their conversations partially in tongue, partially with sign. These four riders,
it turned out, were from Man Called Tree's village, or
Ben Tree as he was known to white people, and they
had been two days east, where they had located some
buffalo, not too far from the river. They were returning
to arrange a hunt to make more meat before Cold
Maker came.
   The name Tree suddenly aroused Bird's curiosity,
for she had heard many tales of this mysterious frontier
man, both at Fort Laramie when she was a youngster,
and later at Fort Kearny when Gabe Bridger, a longtime friend of Tree, talked about him. Yes, one of the
Crow told her, their chief went by many names and
Ben Tree was one of them, Like herself, Tree was a

breed, part Osage, she recalled, and in the settlements
he was both feared and respected but was almost unknown personally by white men. A renegade, he had
become one of the great leaders of the Absaroke, had
lived with them for ten years, was legendary, rarely
seen, and only discussed, mostly in tales of his wilderness exploits. It was told that a white man who could
boast that he had met and talked with Ben Tree was
considered either a braggart or very fortunate, since
few ever lived to tell of such an encounter.

The older Crow brave who was doing most of the
talking was called Little Bear Man, and because he had
counted coup, he wore an eagle feather hung from his
long, dark hair. He also possessed a white man's saddle
and a new Spencer rifle, and Bird thought that either
he was an Indian of moderate wealth or else he was a
very good thief, most probably, the latter. He was
happy to hear that Bird and her mother were Cree.
Even though the Absaroke had little contact with this
tribe, the Cree were longtime enemies of the Blackfeet,
who in turn, were detested by the Crow. Because of the
wolf, Little Bear Man thought Bird must have big
medicine, since this animal figured prominently in
many of their legends as a source of great power in
battle and hunting. However, he was not impressed by
Meena's honey gathering.

"Why," he asked of James, "does this woman take
honey when the sun shows its face? Is it not better to
come when the sun hides its face and the bees are cold
and do not fly?"

When this was translated to Meena, she grinned and
licked at one of the sticky gloves she was removing.
"Tell him that he has good vision, but I am a woman
two times his age and I have more wisdom than he has
vision, for I know if I wait until the sun hides its face
this brave's namesake, little bear, will come and eat the
honey before I do. Tell him I am much smarter than a
bear."

When they heard this, the Crow scouts all smiled and nodded their heads. Indeed, this Cree woman had wisdom. And then Little Bear Man said with a sly smile, "I would like to have a taste of this fine honey. Ask the Cree woman if she has the wisdom of the Owl Maker, who has the power and kindness to grant me this wish."

Listening intently to the translation, Meena let out a howl, and nodded knowingly. "This young brave speaks well," she said, placing a hand on his shoulder. "Tell him I do not have the wisdom of the Owl Maker, but that he has the cunning of Old Man Coyote, who has the great power to steal my honey before I can eat it."

Hearing this, Little Bear Man slapped his thigh and laughed, and with this much said, Meena motioned to Bird who picked up one of the big jars and presented it to the young Crow. Bird passed sign to him, saying, "Our hearts are big as you are cunning. It pleases me to give you this gift. May your trail back home be a safe one."

"*Eyah,*" Little Bear man said, taking the honey and proudly showing it around to all of the others. After packing the jar behind his saddle, he turned back to Bird, and moving his hands swiftly, said, "I saw you kill a deer and you did not see me. It was many suns ago. You did not see me from so far away, but your wolf has good eyes and he saw me through a mountain." Little Bear Man pointed toward the far hills to the southeast.

And Bird's eyes widened in surprise. Could it be? The only deer she had slain in that direction was at the gulch camp several days before they had arrived at the outpost. But if he had seen her, and he was a friendly, why hadn't he stopped, at least ridden over to investigate? As if reading her mind, Little Bear Man said, "My brothers and I had six ponies we couped from the Lakota in the Greasy Grass. At the time, I thought you might be a Lakota. We were in a big hurry to get across the Big Horns that day." He smiled at her. "It pleases me to know such a woman who has big medicine and rides with a wolf. I will tell my people about you and they will be your people." Little Bear Man leaped back into his saddle, and with another wave, said, "Our paths will cross again." The four men turned their ponies and rode away.

This was Bird's first meeting with the Absaroke but it was not her last. The word about her spread quickly, and during the next several days she met others, usually along the trail or at the post, and while these friendly people did not know her personally, they knew who she was, and they called her by many names, Bird Woman, Honey Woman, and Woman Who Rides with Wolf. It was late November when she finally met the man who intrigued her so much, the head chief of the mountain Crow, Ben Tree, the invisible one. She and James were coming back to the post late one afternoon after retrieving two mules that had strayed several miles from the upper pasture when, from far off, they saw lodge poles shooting up against the backdrop of trees near the stockade. With the two mules trotting ahead toward the corral, they stopped momentarily to take a closer look, and James, peering under the shade of his hand, told Bird that they probably were tipis of the Crow hunters who were returning from a hunt down the Yellowstone. As they approached the post, he pointed out the great packs stacked up along the stockade wall, some black in color, hides from the buffalo the Indians had killed, and there was a nearby remuda of thirty or more ponies. Perhaps, Little Bear Man, the one they had met in the bottom a short time ago was with them, he told Bird. After the honey incident, by custom, the Crow were bound to reciprocate in some way. This was a habit with them. And as they rode down, he explained that it worked both ways. If someone stole their ponies, they would steal them back, and if someone killed their people and there was terrible grief in the village, a council would be held and avenging the deed carefully planned and carried out.

By the time Bird and James sent the strays running into the corral and stowed their saddles, several of the tipis had gone up, and one in particular caught Bird's eye, a large beautifully bleached white one with huge red sunbursts spreading out from its sides, and below, at the bottom alternating red, blue, and yellow bands. "How beautiful!" Bird exclaimed, shouldering her rifle. "What an attractive lodge!"

"Yes, that's a real looker, Miss Bird," James agreed. "And I'll bet we're in for a real time tonight, a big feast, maybe even some dancing. Mother knows that tipi mark. She was in the village a couple of times. I don't remember it, but that tipi is one of Chief Tree's. That's his mark. His wife is called Rainbow, and that's what it is, a regular, darned rainbow, for sure."

When they arrived at the first cabin, the door was open, people inside seated around the big table, laughing and talking, and Molly was busy with her coffeepot, Meena to the side, bouncing the baby on a knee. Two men dressed in leggings and long elk-skin jackets were seated next to John Goodhart, and they both stood when James and Bird entered the room, then shook hands across the table with young James. One man was older, truly Absaroke, firm of jaw, his alert, dark eyes wrinkled at the corners, but he was strong and straight as an arrow. Goodhart told Bird that his name was Big Cloud Who Rides Over the Mountain, Big Cloud for short, and that with his special medicine, he was the one who directed the buffalo hunts. The other man, dressed almost identically but with a silver-trimmed bear claw necklace and a holstered pistol at his side, was Indian, too, but then again, not quite Indian. His tanned face was much younger, and except for a scar, free of wrinkles, and his long, straw-colored hair was neatly swept back and tied in back with a thong of leather. What struck Bird most of all about him, was his steel blue eyes that seemed to penetrate her very depths as she shook hands with him. His name was Man Called Tree, and he was impressively awesome with his bronzed, hawklike features, the trace of that scar running across his cheekbone, probably from some ancient battle in the wilderness, Bird imagined. From the stories she had heard, this was a totally different sort of man than she had expected. Killer, renegade, a surly breed who would just as soon shoot a person as look at him? Tall tales, she guessed, and this was startlingly compounded when he addressed her in a rather subdued and sympathetic voice.

"This is a pleasure, Miss Rutledge," he said, smiling. "My people have been telling me about you, how you came here, and some of your troubles. I talked to your mother, too, and it seems to me you two have been having a difficult time of it. I know what it's like. I've been along that trail myself. Sometimes, life out here can be hard as a rock, but at least you're in good hands here with these fine people. I'm certainly obliged to meet you."

"Thank you," Bird replied, rather shakily, she thought. Actually, his kind words had swept her back to other times and places, strangely coincidental, one of them, that time when she had first spoken to Garth, when he had been flabbergasted by her use of the English language. Yes, and her mind flashed back to the last chief she had met, Plenty Hawk, who, laughingly, and with a pat on her behind, had tossed her into his tipi. And here, standing before her was the much maligned, reputed killer, Ben Tree, who had all the charm and grace of a Sunday preacher, and, God, such a handsome man! Collecting herself, she finally said, "I've heard about you, too, a little, that is, from one of our mutual friends, Mr. Bridger. He never called you Ben Tree, though, not even your tribal name."

Man Called Tree chuckled. "I have many names,

some good and some in rather bad taste, but I reckon I know what Gabe was calling me. Benji. Ever since I was knee high to a grasshopper, it was always Benji. God bless him, how is my old companion? His eyes were going bad the last time I saw him, maybe five years back. Told me he was going to give it all up and go back to Independence, just sit in his rocker and reflect. I told him it wouldn't work out, not for him."

"It didn't," answered Bird. "He's fine, though. He still rides well, his hair is quite gray, and sometimes he wears these little spectacles, but he's always telling good stories, funny, not crude, and some that make your hair stand on end. Garth, my dearest love, my son's father, was a scout for him. We talked many nights. Another man, John Dominguez, was with us, too. Do you know him, Domino?"

The chief nodded. "Yes, your mother mentioned him, and I do know Dominguez. Met him years ago when I was maybe sixteen, I don't exactly recollect, at my father's mule ranch outside Independence. I was home on vacation from school, and as I recall, he was leading a wagon train west. I ran into him again on the trail some years later, just after my father and brother were ambushed. He had a bad case of the nerves. Told me some hostile Cheyenne had jumped him and he almost lost his hair."

"Times haven't changed that much, then, have they?"

"Not at all. In fact, the whites seem to making it worse down below here, poor treaties, misinterpreted, some purposely. Our people don't trust the whites, anymore. It's that simple." A wry smile crossed his rugged face. "Fact is, the whites don't even respect their own people. Over at the diggings they're always quarreling, shooting each other over a few pieces of gold. If it's not gold, it's bad whiskey. A damned greedy lot, I'll tell you."

"You're not a conformist, I can see that."

"No, and with good reason." He placed his hand on Goodhart's arm, saying, "There are exceptions. John here didn't come up here to tear out Mother Earth's hair, maybe just curl it a bit." Goodhart laughed at this. "No," Man Called Tree went on, "for me, it's much easier this way. I've found my direction, and I enjoy my family, my adopted brothers, and that's the size of it."

Bird sighed. "This seems to be my big problem, direction. And we do have a few things in common, don't we ... ? Breeds, lost loved ones, injustice. I haven't tempered my feelings of hate, though, and if the bastard who killed Garth walked through that door, I'd probably put a bullet through his head."

Man Called Tree smiled wanly at her, the complexities of her emotions, a woman not at peace with herself. He spoke again, saying, "Miss Rutledge, may I tell you something? One can't be bitter forever. It destroys the soul. It takes strong will, patience, and the blessing of the Great Spirit to put something like this behind one, and sometimes it takes a very long time. Enjoy the best of the present, your son, your mother, forget the past, and never dwell too long on the future. Better yet, come and visit my village next spring. You might be surprised at what some of our wise ones can tell you about the renewal of life. Considering the source, I'm not the best person to be giving advice. Let's just say I'm speaking to you as a new brother, one who makes you welcome."

"I'm sorry," Bird returned quietly, "I don't want to burden you with my troubles, not when you're here to celebrate such a fine hunt. And I do thank you for your kind words and invitation. Mr. Bridger said you were an extraordinary person. It was quite difficult to believe, I must confess, particularly after hearing all of the other stories about you down at Laramie." She laughed. "And for some reason, I envisioned you as an older man, a grizzled old outlaw."

Everyone laughed at this. Man Called Tree, grinning, said, "There are two sides to every story, and people have the tendency to enjoy the worst. Isn't this true? By the time a story is retold a dozen times, it's usually never anywhere close to the original version. Age? Oh, I was idealistically young when I first visited this country with Gabe, but by measure of experience, I suppose I'm very old. But, then again, not quite as old as Big Cloud, here." He patted his Crow brother on the arm. "Now, Miss Rutledge, this is old! But let me tell you, his mind is as keen as a razor."

Big Cloud smiled proudly as if he knew every word his chief was saying, even to the point of nodding in agreement. Although he had not understood any of this brief conversation, Big Cloud knew that it was the truth because Man Called Tree spoke for a thousand people in his village.

Bird, staring incredulously at the buffalo priest, said, "Does he understand English? ... understand what you're saying?"

"No, not a word, but he trusts me, and what's what this is all about, isn't it? Trust?"

Curious, Bird then asked, "Wherever did he get such a terribly long name. It's not a name, it's a whole sentence!"

Laughing, the chief turned to the older man and spoke to him in Absaroke, and in turn, Big Cloud grinned and nodded his head again. He enjoyed telling tales, and he began slowly in a voice that counted almost sixty winters. Everyone at the table and in the kitchen leaned forward to listen as Man Called Tree translated. "In the beginning, when I was a small seed floating about with no place to go and with no name, my mother took me into her body. She said she would make me a big Human Being and give me a powerful name. This was good, for at that time I had been nothing but a speck in the Great Milky Way. She put me in hiding for many moons until I grew into a very small

Human Being. I was very small. I complained in her belly about this. She told me this was nothing to worry about, that she would give me a big name. When I came out of the great darkness, she saw a big cloud. It was a cloud full of water and it crashed into a mountain and fell like rain under the mountain bringing much water down into the village. It was flood. She told me I would be called Big Cloud Who Rides Under the Mountain. And this is the way it was for many winters. But my luck was bad and even the sun hid his face when I walked by. One day, another man said to me, 'I think it must be your name. You have a crazy name. Some witch must have hit your mother with a scalp stick to give you such a name like this. A big cloud *under* the mountain must be bad medicine because big clouds do not go *under* mountains. They must go up and *over*.' I thought about this a long time. So, one day, I went to the council and told the chiefs they must change my name. I was a poor man and my luck was bad. I had only one horse and he was lame, and I had no wife. They thought this was pretty bad, all right, and told me to go away and they would decide what to do. When I came back they said they had decided. From that day on, I was to be called Big Cloud Who Rides *Over* the Mountain. Just as my friend had said, they told me over was better than under. And this was true. I took a maiden for my wife and I had five children in ten winters. Other maidens looked at me and I pretended I did not see them. I was already too busy with one woman. I soon became a great hunter chief as I am to this very day."

All of the people around the table were smiling; there were a few sighs; in the back, Molly gleefully clapped her hands. All of this pleased Big Cloud greatly, that everyone had appreciated his story, and he stood up and graciously bowed.

* * *

Later, the Crow hunting party built a huge fire down near the gate and began roasting buffalo hump and ribs, and Molly and Meena took down two large pots of beans, freshly baked bread, and two jars of the river bottom honey. The celebration lasted until almost dark. There were several chants and some dancing by the Crow, and Big Cloud ceremoniously recited the story of the hunt. At its conclusion, Chief Tree asked about Bird's wolf, the one some of his people thought was a spirit, the one that could see through a mountain. He spoke seriously without skepticism about her wolf, and she said she would be happy to show him the animal. Cutting off a section of ribs, Bird took Man Called Tree up behind the second cabin far away from the Crow tipis where she called out his name, only once. Soon, they heard the soft pads of the wolf coming down from the big shed. He came close enough to see, lowered himself in his customary manner, and let Bird affectionately rub the thick fur on his head. After accepting his food, the spirit wolf turned and trotted back into the night.

"Well, well," mused Man Called Tree. "Now, that was some little performance, wasn't it? Unusual, to say the least. I think you love this wolf, don't you?"

"Yes, I do, and he loves me. He trusts me. Isn't this what you said this afternoon, the little lecture you gave me? Trust?"

"Yes, I reckon I did say something like that." But then as they slowly walked back toward the tipis, he said politely but advisedly, "I realize you've become attached to this wolf, but you better understand he's a wild critter. You may be building yourself up for another big letdown."

"I know," Bird agreed forlornly. "That's what I told John. I only hope when he decides to leave he breaks it to me gently. I've had enough of these disastrous, godforsaken departures in my life. They keep nagging at me."

"Yes, I understand. The Lord gives and takes, and as

we both know, He seems to do more taking out in the wilderness. But life goes on, and let me tell you, it's not too wise to quarrel with your Maker when you realize He was the one who put you here in the first place. We live and we die. This is the fateful pattern. It can't be broken. The problem is that few of us have the wisdom to accept it. Everyone wants to live forever."

"Are you a fatalist?" she asked. "Do you have wisdom?"

He shrugged, saying, "Fatalist, perhaps so. Wisdom? I doubt it, but what is written is written, this much I believe. Yes, in some mysterious way, destiny is preordained." He paused, as they neared the warmth of the fire. "Let me tell you a story," he said, "not with the subtle humor of my brother, Big Cloud, but nevertheless, a true story."

"Told first to you by an old white man, I suppose." She smiled.

"No, told to you by an Indian," he said. "Once, long ago, an old holy man by the name of Buffalo Horn pulled an arrow out of a young man's thigh. This man thought he was going to die of blood poisoning, but the shaman told him, no this wasn't true, because the signs read otherwise. It was so written. And it was true—the man suffered greatly but he did recover. Later, Buffalo Horn had a vision. He told this same young man he was going to be cold in the earth eight winters. The young man had no idea what the wise one was talking about. Cold in the earth eight winters? What a crazy notion! It was just too mysterious for him to comprehend. Well, shortly after this, the young man's father and brother were killed, his Crow bride, too, and he became bitter and angry with life, and he felt that, indeed, he had been forsaken by God and buried in the cold ground. He deserted the white world, and in a deep trance, he wandered the mountains for eight years, exactly eight, until these deaths were avenged.

Yes, and he had been cold in the ground eight winters. He came back to life in sunshine but discovered somewhere during his long journey he had lost his soul. He was no longer a man but a shell." Holding his hands to the fire, he looked at Bird from the side. "Now, what do you make of something like this?"

"Coincidental, perhaps?" she inquired. "I don't know."

"No, not coincidental. It was foretold, all of it, step by step, almost to the day. It all happened."

"This man in your story, it was Ben Tree?"

"Yes, Ben Tree was his name," he answered. "Ben Tree died by his own hand."

Bird, watching the flames cast leaping shadows, said, "And this new Ben Tree, what about him?"

"Man Called Tree," he corrected.

"Oh, yes. And did he find his soul?"

"The point of my story, Miss Rutledge," he said, touching her shoulder. "Spiritual renewal is for anyone who has the faith to seek it. Faith. If you've lost faith in the Great Spirit and faith in yourself, you have nothing."

It was almost five months before Bird saw her new friend again. When winter set in, understandably, activity along the Yellowstone came to a standstill, and Bird seldom met any of her Absaroke friends. They were more inclined to stay along the sheltered bottoms of the Clarks Fork where they could hunt deer and elk that were migrating down from the higher Rocky Mountains to the west. Although white travelers shunned the river trail because of the contrary weather from the north, Bird soon discovered that many days at Manuel's old post were sunny and pleasant despite the chilly winter air, and snowfall at the lower elevation was minimal, thus enabling her to continue her long hikes up the meadows with James and Wolf. Often, the two men and Bird went hunting down in the river bottom, seeking out deer and grouse, sometimes riding their ponies, who seemed to enjoy the nippy outings as much as their riders. When they returned to the post, Meena and Molly usually had a big pot of steaming soup on the iron stove, and all of them would eat in front of the rock fireplace, their feet extending out to its radiating warmth. Nights were spent playing cards around the table, and Bird, who had a willing student in young James, always found time to tutor him in elementary arithmetic, simple spelling, and reading. She thought that by spring his progress would be sufficient enough for him to work on his own, perhaps find the enjoyment in books that she herself had discovered when she was young.

The spirit wolf, as everyone expected, began wandering off by himself by late winter, sometimes disappearing for several days at a time. He was becoming a good hunter, too, for Bird often found the remains of animals near his den, and once, even saw him digging out field mice from their winter burrows in the meadow. There was little doubt that he had found company in the hills; the evidence was clearly there, other tracks like his own tracing the slopes and river bottom, and urine sign on logs and bushes, marking out territorial boundaries. The day finally came in early spring when Wolf was gone for six nights, and Bird, in tears, realized that her time with him was nearing its end. He came to her call on the seventh day, leaping about in a frenzy of joy, rolling at her feet, and then, with that strange, fathomless look in his eyes, the one she had always tried to understand, he finally turned and loped away up the meadow toward the higher hills. A few days later when Man Called Tree and six other Crow came by for a short visit, Bird told the chief about Wolf's departure, that once again, she sincerely believed her spiritual friend was trying to tell her something. Man Called Tree embraced her consolingly as she softly wept.

Chapter Fifteen

William Coonrad owned a cabin at the mouth of a small canyon six miles from the frenzied activity and turmoil of fledgling Bozeman City. He told Bird and Meena Rutledge it was his wintering quarters, that during most of the year he worked his claims down in Alder Gulch near Virginia City. He was more than happy to let them have it until fall just to have someone in the place, to maintain it and keep out the pack rats and look after a few of his cows pastured in the bottom. Also, he had a shed and corral, good fertile land along the creek, an ideal place for Bird to work her ponies, all eighteen of them that she had acquired from the Crow. And if she and her mother decided their venture was profitable, Coonrad pointed out some land on the other side of the creek, and a grass bench above which they could stake out and homestead themselves under Jack Rutledge's name. Moreover, if William Coonrad stuck rich pay dirt within a season or two, he was going to return to his parents' home in Kentucky, fix up the old farm, breed thoroughbreds, and live like a king the rest of his life. To Bird, all of this sounded too good to be true. Prior to meeting Coonrad at the smithy shed, she had searched two days for something suitable to meet her immediate needs, adequate shelter for Meena and the baby, privacy, and what had been in the back of her mind, ultimately, a place where she could raise cattle.

The women moved into the little house the same

June day that Coonrad left. He planned to return in early November, and he assumed by then, Bird, if successful, would have her own cabin built across the canyon. There was now a sawmill in the valley, and a few carpenters had come in because of the new construction in Bozeman City. Nearby hillsides were covered with lodgepole pine, an excellent source of cabin logs, and labor was cheap, herders and roustabouts always around looking to make a few extra dollars for a grubstake. So, looking to the future, Bird began working with all the fervor she could muster, from daybreak until dusk. Donald Blodgett, the smithy, became one of her best sources of business, sending miners and drovers her way, both to buy and trade horses and mules. And Bird reciprocated, riding into Blodgett's shop every week to have her stock shod. Each horse she sold was well groomed, healthy, and fit for the long trails, either south to Virginia City or north to Last Chance Gulch and Fort Benton beyond. Chief Man Called Tree had been wise—there was money to be made in the Gallatin Valley. By early September, her accounting showed a profit of nearly a thousand dollars, more than enough to start planning for her own new cabin. In addition, the women still had the sacks of gold nuggets and four hundred dollars in double-eagles from the plundered wagons of Henry Sturges. By frontier standards, the women were moderately rich.

By the middle of September when Bird turned her attention to building, she only had two horses left in the corral, not including the two Indian ponies the women originally rode from the Big Horn foothills. Flame and the Sioux pinto mare were considered family, now, and Bird was disinclined to part with either. All told, she made forty transactions during the summer, either buying, trading, or selling. The remaining stock had ample grass on the bench and in the upper canyon for winter. When spring came, Bird planned to rebuild the herd with another purchase from the Crow.

Continually on her mind, though, was the matter of
selling beef because it was so much in demand, particularly down at Bannack and Virginia City, and nearby
Bozeman and Fort Ellis, the new western post for patrol of the Bozeman Trail. So, one afternoon near the
end of the month she saddled up and rode above the
bench out to the open range about five miles from
the cabin. She came upon several hundred cattle grazing at will in random groups. A few had strayed down
to the grassy hummocks of a distant coulee where the
grass still had a good head of green. It was here, in the
shade of a lone cottonwood, Bird finally came upon a
drover, resting back against the tree with his legs outstretched, a young man, barely twenty years old, and
he had a rifle resting against the tree trunk.

Bird gave him a hello. He slowly got to his feet,
smiling at her all the while. "Thought you might be a
relief man, but should have known it was too early for
anything that good," he said. "Sun's too high." He
grinned again. "Didn't expect to see a woman, neither."

"I'm out for a little ride, looking over the country,"
Bird said, making a willowy stretch of her lean body.
"You have the only shady spot in the place."

Reaching down, he picked up a canvas-covered canteen, very similar to army issue. "Care for a drink?
Just plain old water, though."

Bird politely took the canteen and drank a few
mouthfuls. "Thanks," she said, wiping a trickle from
her chin. "My name is Rutledge, Bird Rutledge. I've
been working horses this summer over by Six Mile
Creek. I saw all these cows and I thought I'd take a
look."

"Robert Peete's the name," and he extended his
hand. "Glad to meet you. You must be the woman I
heard about, then, over yonder by the hills. I sorta' pic-
tured you being different, you know, wrangling horses

and all." His continual smile was infectious and Bird had to laugh.

"Really?"

Peete hastened to explain, saying, "Well, you know what I mean. You ain't much bigger than a grasshopper, and you ain't old and ugly, not what I'd expect, anyways."

"And just what have you been hearing about me?"

"Oh, shucks, I don't rightly know, ma'am, I suppose like you being able to make horses talk, do most anything you want with the critters, saying you have a knack with them that's downright unreal, something like that." Nodding toward his horse, Peete said, "This one's all right, but let me tell you, I never do trust one of these nags. Seems like they spend most of their lives eating and crapping, just waiting for the right time to haul off and kick you one, or bite you in the ass when you're all bent over looking around for the damn cinch."

"Contrary." Bird grinned. "They're contrary, just like a lot of people who will do the same thing to you if you stand around in the same spot too long."

"Yes, ma'am, that's about it, I'd say."

Motioning toward the cattle, Bird asked, "Who owns all of these?"

Peete told her the owner was a man named Adam Stuart, that he had twice as many on another range over toward the three forks of the Missouri River. There were six drovers working for him, frequently day and night because of thieves. Some of the original cattle came from a herd that Nelson Story brought up from Texas before hostilities broke out along the Bozeman Trail. But most of Stuart's stock had been born and raised on the Gallatin Range. "Yeah," Peete went on, "there's always someone looking to come in and steal one or two of the old man's critters to fatten up their larder, mostly whites, too, if you can believe it." He glanced away quickly, hastening to add, "Not meaning any offense to you, though."

·She ·smiled at him in his embarrassment. "No offense taken, Mr. Peete."

"You don't talk much like an Injun, neither." He grinned. "They say you have schooling, and that's a fact. Right pretty, too."

Bird laughed and thanked him for the compliment. She remounted, saying, "Look, do me a favor. Tell Mr. Stuart if he ever gets over my way to stop in. Tell him I'd like to buy some heifers and a few cows next spring, say, thirty or so. Oh, yes, and tell him I'll need a good bull, too."

"Is that a fact!" he said again.

"That's a fact, two of them. You tell him it's a cash deal straight across the board if he can deliver what I want." Bird reined around, and for a moment, studied the young man, barely a man, a very polite and decent sort, cute, too, and not to her surprise, he had touched a little spark within her, one long dormant and badly in need of rekindling. "It was a pleasure meeting you, Mr. Peete." She smiled down at him. "When you're over in the Six Mile, drop in for a cup of joe . . . yes, and who knows what else?" And with this boldly said, she kicked away.

Robert Peete, still grinning broadly, tipped his faded hat and yelled, "You're some woman, you sure are!"

"Yes, I am," Bird called back.

By the time Bird arrived back at the cabin, it was almost dark. She saw a man sitting on a horse in the clearing, another horse close by but riderless, a visitor inside, she thought, probably someone who had come to buy or trade a horse. So, instead of riding to the corral, she pulled up in front of the cabin. The door was open but before she could get off her pony, she heard her mother inside, shouting excitedly, then caught a glimpse of her moving about, frantically waving her hands. Seated at the table by the lantern was a large man, partially turned toward her, and in an instant Bird recognized him, his unkempt clothing, his fat backside. It was Jubal McComber! My God, this was the last man in the world to whom she would sell a horse! Why had her mother even let him in the house? Meena knew how much she detested the man, and to be sitting there at their very table as though he owned the place! A swift flush of anger hit her cheeks, and she slipped out her rifle as she dismounted. McComber turned slightly when she came through the doorway. "Well, here she is, now, the little Bird Woman," he said, a bright glow on his fat cheeks. "Been expectin' you, I sure have."

Bird looked over at Meena, who suddenly and protectively plucked the baby out of the high chair. Her face radiated more fear than anger as she clasped Ty to her breast. "That man," she said, "he says bad things about us. I told him to go, get out, but he wants to talk more. There is nothing to say but get out!"

Bird, her dark eyes ablaze, stared at McComber. "Will you tell me what the hell this is all about? What's she talking about, this 'bad things' business . . . ? And make it damn quick, McComber, because you sure as hell are not welcome here."

The trader held up his hands in protest, his eyes wide in innocence. "Wait a minute, now, hold on, little woman! Why, is this the way to greet an old friend of the trail? Now, calm down, both of you. Hell's fire, I didn't mean to get everybody all riled up, I sure didn't."

Bird spit back, "You're no friend, so cut out the bullshit and speak up."

"He says we're robbers," Meena cried out. "He says . . ."

McComber, turning on Meena, once again held up a hand. "No, now I didn't say it exactly that way, no . . ."

Bird stuck her face out at him like an angry hen. "Come on, what's your dirty game, speak up?" Then, glancing over at Meena, she said, "Please be quiet, Mama, for God's sake, and let him speak his piece and get out of here."

McComber shifted uncomfortably in the chair and began scratching up behind an ear. "It's like I told yer maw, y'see, I'm comin' down by Manuel's two weeks past, and like always, I stops to see Goodhart, jest for a little chat. Well, after one thing and another, John ups and shows me this gold watch of his. Yassir, says you gave it to him, and I says, that's a right pretty watch, John, it sure is. But I thinks to myself, I've sure seen that watch before. Y'see, I recognizes the fob. Hell, I've seen it over a hundert times, I reckon, and when I looks inside, sure enough, there's ol' Henry's mark. So, I says to myself, when I get back over to the Gallatin, I'll see if I can find Miss Bird and ask her about this little ol' watch, y'know, how you came by it." He winked once and arched his brow questioningly.

Bird, her anger suddenly fused with fearful apprehension, in agony over what she knew McComber was intimating, tried to collect herself. Finally: "So, I had Sturges's watch! What business is this of yours? Certainly, I did, and I gave it to John. How I came by it is none of your damn business. You come in here like you own the place, scaring the hell out of my mother. What kind of a man are you? Now, get out, go find some deep hole to crawl in, you lousy, intimidating bastard!"

"Well, if that's the way you want it," McComber said, shrugging indifferently. "I reckon you're right, ain't none of my business. It's sorta strange, though, how you'd come by all those ponies I heard about, where you'd get that kinda money to buy a herd that size. Why, feller at the livery stable told me you had a string nigh onto twenty. Yassir, Miss Bird, it's none of my business. Oh, I 'spect the people up at Fort Ellis might be interested, though, knowin' hows Henry and those other fellers got all shot up and robbed, mebbe that you was right through there at the same time." He pointed to the little washstand. "And that pretty little mirror over there I saw when I came in, well, I'll bet I saw it a hundert times, too, ol' Henry standin' there, hummin' a tune, jest shavin' away, trimmin' that fancy beard of his. Y'know, I was thinkin' if I could look around a bit, mebbe I'd find a few more things. Aw, but no, ain't much use in that. Hell, that's law business for the sheriff down in Bannack, 'less you had somethin' else we could sorta share, say, like John's gold. Hell, woman, we could fergit this whole thing, like it never even happened. Yassir, we sure could."

"All right, you've had your say," Bird returned .sharply. Raising the rifle, she pointed it at McComber's fat belly. "Get up!" she hissed. "Get up, I said!"

McComber, rising slowly, holding out a hand and protectively, sputtered, "Now . . . now, don't be pointin' that thing, woman, hear me? Jesus, it jest might go off. I'll be gettin' along, jest like you say, jest put that thing down a'mite, don't go . . ."

"You bet your fat ass you're going," Bird said vehemently. She pulled the trigger, the shot resounding like the blast of an artillery shell in the small room. Meena screamed and little Ty let out a howl. McComber, hit squarely in the chest, pitched over backward and collapsed. When Bird turned back to the door, she heard the gallop of a horse. The other man was fleeing.

Book Three

The Pursuit

Chapter Sixteen

Friend Garth:

I received your last letter at Laramie. There have been many changes. The forts in the Powder country will be closed soon. I think Red Cloud and his people have won the war. Another peace council is being planned. I write to tell you that I met a trader about a year ago. His name is McComber and he told me he saw some Cree women in a Brule hunting camp near the Black Hills. Late in the year, when I could I rode over to that country. I found nothing. I met some Santee. They said these Brule went north to hunt buffalo. The women McComber saw were Bird and the others. He said one cussed like a trooper. I say this must be Bird. The Bozeman is closed. I know the way to this land if you decide to come. I am out of work. I need a job. I am willing to help you if you can come before winter. I will be up at Fort Fetterman the first week in September. The telegraph is in. If I do not hear from you, I go to Julesburg. *Adiós*. Your friend, J. Dominguez.

After receipt of John Dominguez's letter, Tyson Bell Garth once again made arrangements with brother Hugh to supervise the work at Garth House. The big farm was operational. Most of the rebuilding had been completed by midsummer, but there were a few fields of corn and cane to harvest. The cotton already had been baled and shipped. Allowing travel time to the

frontier and a six-week journey down the valleys,
Garth told his brother that he expected to be gone no
longer than three months. Hopefully, he would be
home for Thanksgiving. He had no desire to spend
winter at Fort Laramie.

T. B. Garth stepped from the train in Cheyenne City
with high hopes. His old scouting companion finally
had sent him some heartening news. Bird and Meena
had been seen alive and well. Domino had failed in his
search for them but was ready to help him. This was a
new quest, not to kill a traitor to the cause, but a search
for a woman he dearly loved and her mother. Lord,
Lord, how ironic and fickle could fate be? He was
back again in a country he detested, one that had almost destroyed him, and he had come willingly, desperately on another search.

Cheyenne City. Garth quickly realized this was not
the same outpost of 1866 when he had ridden in on
Jefferson trying to catch up with the elusive Henry
Sturges. Change was all around him. Like most of the
other stops on the new Union Pacific tracks, Cheyenne
had mushroomed into a thriving boomer town. Board-
walks fronted the busy stores and saloons along the
dusty thoroughfare; horses and wagons of every description, even a few ponderous Conestogas with their
long-eared mules at rest, were tied up alongside hitch-
ing racks. Dress among the people was another conglomeration, anything from derbies and vested suits to
leathers and dirty denims. The few women Garth saw
were decked out in brimmed bonnets and summery
long hooped dresses. As a sign of the changing times,
he did not see one Indian.

After settling in at a dingy hotel room above the
Elkhorn Saloon, he went to the telegraph office to send
an arrival message to John Dominguez at Fort
Fetterman. Fetterman? What a distressing note, that
someone would dare name a fort after an officer who

had disobeyed orders and led eighty-one men to their doom. To Garth, this was as ridiculous as changing the name of Jackson, Mississippi to Lincoln.

Next, Garth strapped on his revolver, and bought a new Winchester rifle, plus two boxes of ammunition, allowing that where he was headed it was a good investment. The following morning, he was riding the stage to Fort Laramie. When he arrived at the famous old post, he saw troopers, entire companies bivouacked around the walls, all recently evacuated from Fort Kearny and C. F. Smith. He heard the news. Indeed, the army had abandoned the forts, and the jubilant braves of Red Cloud and Dull Knife had moved in and burned them to the ground. The war was over.

Garth spent the night in Brown's Hotel. He was up and about at dawn. He bought two fine Indian ponies, both sturdy three-year-olds, fat and healthy from a good summer on green grass. Shortly after nine o'clock, he addressed himself to the rest of it— outfitting, and greeting at least one familiar face, that of Elbert Craig.

The musty old store was just as Garth remembered it, shelves still heavily stocked, the lone aisle cluttered with equipment of all kinds, stacks of colorful woolen blankets cherished by the Indians, dried and tinned food, trinkets, an assortment of frontier clothing, and racks of saddles and other tack, almost anything one needed for a trip into the interior. Garth saw no sign of either Elbert or his crotchety father. Another man, a pudgy fellow with muttonchop whiskers and a soiled apron, met him near the long counter. They passed greetings and Garth handed him a long list of the supplies he needed. Carefully checking off each item, the man stared up at Garth in surprise. Anyone placing an order this large had to be planning a long trip either across the prairie or into the mountains, for all of this camping equipment, the accoutrements for horses, not to mention the lengthy list of food supplies, was a very sizeable and costly purchase. Garth simply agreed but declined to offer any information as to his direction or mission, only that he had more than adequate funds to take care of the transaction. This much said, the man went to work, hurrying back and forth, pulling out boxes and rummaging through the shelves, and stacking each item to the side as he found it. Meantime, Garth kept looking about for some sign of Elbert Craig, and finally, as the clerk was pulling down a saddle, asked, "Where's the Craig boy, Elbert?"

Pausing to admire the saddle's rich leathery shine, the man looked up curiously at Garth, saying, "I don't suppose you've been around here for awhile. Old man Craig sold out, about a year ago. You a friend of Bert?"

"An acquaintance, yes, I know him from a while back."

The clerk gave him a dark look, one of consternation and foreboding. Leaning close, he said, "I don't know about Bert, no one does. That's why the old man moved back to Saint Louis. Fool boy of his took off a year back, up country, he and two others. Never did come back. Probably dead, if you want my opinion." Hoisting the saddle to the counter, he asked, "How does this suit you? Good leather, double cinch, real quality in this one, the best." Garth, his mind temporarily muddled, simply nodded, his stomach suddenly feeling quite empty.

"Dead?" Garth said in a hushed tone. "What do you figure . . . ?"

The clerk shrugged once and shook his head. "Indians got 'em, that's my notion," he answered lowly. "Fool stunt anyway, riding off like that looking for some half-breeds, women, I hear tell. And those two with him, they were fort Indians, probably left the boy high and dry when the going got tough. Hostiles got no more love for their kin down here than they have whites." He passed the edge of a hand across his throat

once. "That's the size of it, mister." The storekeeper
shoved the saddle aside and stepped around a stunned
T. B. Garth. "Now, you'll want a good blanket to go
under this thing, and I've got some good ones . . ."

Lost in troubled musing, Garth barely heard him.

When they worked, Will Scruggs and Charles
Muleen were muleskinners. When they loafed, they
were Platte Valley drifters, and this was most of the
time. They drank, gambled, thieved, and shot buffalo.
In the spring, they were usually tending freight wagons
on the Overland up the North Platte, running the route
between Fort Laramie and Fort Caspar. When September came and their usually empty pockets jingled, they
thought it was time to quit because it always took them
a long time to prepare for winter. Just the mention of
the word "work" usually made their hair stand on end.
They always returned to a camp on Whitetail Creek
and took up their off-season activities, grudgingly, and
with a considerable amount of profanity. They disliked
making firewood for the winter. One day, about seven
miles east of the La Bonte stage station, they found
two stray horses grazing in a meadow off the trail.
They were on their way back to the cabin on Whitetail
Creek, and having nothing better to do, moved out the
two horses ahead of them. It was open range and the
strays carried no brands, and both of the men considered their act a pure cut-and-dried business enterprise,
a lucky one, at that. They could always sell horseflesh.
In their short gallop across the flat, neither man spotted
the file of tracks heading north toward the river from
the Medicine Bow Mountains. Had they, they would
have been considerably less enthusiastic about their
small roundup. Only an hour earlier, a returning Cheyenne hunting party had crossed ahead of them, and
these two strays belonged to the Indians.

The following afternoon, it was raining, and Will
and Charlie were snaking in two huge logs for fire-

wood. They were already in a bad mood. Soaked to the skin, they were eager to get back to the cabin and warm themselves with a little red-eye. Cutting and laying in wood was not their favorite pastime, but freezing to death was worse, and in their ten years on the frontier, they had been through some bad times, Charlie, in fact, losing the tips off both of his ears to frostbite. The Indians who hung around the forts had taken to calling him Rotten Ears, and after this, he had little respect for redskins, probably because some of the white folk thought the nickname was humorous and also had picked up on the handle. Near the outskirts of camp where they were pulling in their wood, Will suddenly stopped in his tracks and let out a yell. Someone was stealing horses from the corral. He dropped the reins of the team and started running toward the pole fence, brandishing his revolver, calling his partner, Charlie, to mount an attack, and Charlie, who relished rolling in the mud, quickly responded, tackling the intruder near a pile of manure. Within seconds, it was all over, and Charlie found himself straddling an Indian boy. Will came running up and promptly had the barrel of his pistol poked against the young man's forehead. Charlie, meantime, quickly plucked away the skinning knife at the Indian's side, saying, "You ain't gonna be needing this." He looked back up at Will. "He's Cheyenne, this one. Ain't no telling where he's come from." He hunched over and peered through the damp woods. "Wonder if there's any more of the buggers out there? By God, if there is, we got some fancy talking to do."

The boy sat up and raised a hand, pointing below to the two pinto ponies, and made a quick sign. Charlie said, "He says those ponies belong to his family."

Will growled back, "Ain't no excuse for trespassin' our property. You tell him we got those critters fair and square. They's ours by law. Ask him where his folks are?"

Charlie promptly turned back and made sign again.

Unafraid, the Cheyenne shook his head and made a somber reply. Then, back to Will, Charlie said, "He says if he don't bring back these ponies, his pa'll come lookin' for him, and there'll be plenty big trouble. They's over across the river apiece."

"His paw!" Will glowered at the Indian. "He's lying, that's what! Ain't no Injuns round here nowhere or we'd smelled 'em, wouldn't we? We'd crossed their tracks. He's just out trying to count coup, make himself look good, that's all."

Charlie sighed, and wiping at the mud on his face, said, "Well, what if he ain't lying, Will? And what are we gonna do with the bastard? I sure as hell don't want him bringing his kin back here all screaming mad. He ain't no fort Injun, that's for sure."

"Hang him!" Will barked outright. "That's the only thing to do with a hoss thief, you hang him. Get him off our place, and string him up. Case he does have kin, they won't be nosin' round and findin' him here. Hell, if we let him go, no tellin' who'll be comin' back. I ain't one to be givin' up on those horses. There's money in 'em, for sure." He grinned and winked at Charlie. "We can spook off his pony, throw him in the river, and who's gonna know. We got two horses and one less Injun."

Perhaps no one would have known had it not been for T. B. Garth, who just happened to be trailing west this same rainy afternoon; or had it not been for the young Cheyenne, Bear Paw, singing out his death chant down in the damp cottonwood grove. When Garth rode quietly off the trail to investigate, he came directly up in back of the mounted trio, not even expecting it, but it took him only a glance to see what was happening. Never looking for trouble, he seemed always to find it, and here, by jingo, were two white men trying to fit a rope around a young Indian's neck, a singing one at that. Much too occupied to notice Garth, one man was throwing a coil of rope over one of the tree's outthrust limbs while the other was attempting to steady the horses. But Garth noticed them. Law, law, they were his old friends from way back, the two Chugwater drifters who had once objected to his fine old Confederate hat, Charlie and Will. And Charlie, the scamp, had pulled a pistol on him. At this moment, Garth's horse let out a snort, bringing the two men whirling about face-to-face with their rebel nemesis, the very same one who had thrown their pistols down the hole in the outhouse at Chugwater.

Charlie blurted, "Jesus H. Christ, Will, look what the wind's blown in! It's him, the Reb! Where in the hell did you come from, boy?"

Flabbergasted, Will just sat there on his horse, fumbling at the hanging rope. The young Indian's singing voice trailed off in the mists like a broken chord.

And Garth said easily, "Good afternoon, gentlemen. What seems to be the problem here?"

"What the hell does it look like?" replied Will, finally finding his voice. "This man's a horse thief."

Garth, hunching forward under his poncho, pretending to get a better view, carefully slipped his Colt revolver from its holster, and rested it hidden from sight across the pommel of his saddle. He said, "Why, it looks to me like you have a boy here instead of a real hanging man. Now, the next thing I know, I suppose you boys will be asking me to take off my hat in respect to this poor fellow, is that it?" Staring across at Charlie, he asked, "Is this one of those jokes like you tried to pull on me? Why, I think you must be joshing, preparing to string up a boy."

Charlie's face flushed. He started to reach for his revolver. "Man, we done had enough of you once. Get outta here, you . . ."

"No, no," warned Garth, waving his own pistol under the rain slicker, "I sure wouldn't do that, not when this is pointed at your flea-bitten ears. Why, I just might take a notion to trim them up a tad more."

Flipping back the covering, he then pointed the Colt directly at Will. "Now, let's stop this nonsense and untie the boy and see what it's all about." Then, he motioned back to Charlie. "Throw your pistol over here, nice and easy."

Cursing, Charlie tossed his weapon aside. Meanwhile, Will, tearing away the ropes from the Cheyenne, was telling Garth that none of the affair was any of his business, that he was taking sides with a horse thief who had been caught red-handed trying to sneak two ponies out of their corral. The young Indian, finally aware that someone was befriending him, was frantically making sign, trying to make his benefactor understand his side of the story. Ultimately, Garth got the drift of it, and eased off his saddle. Removing the pistol from Will's holster, he tucked it inside his own belt, and said, "I think this boy is saying these ponies belong to him, either him or his people. This is what I make of it, Mistuh . . . Mistuh?"

"Scruggs," was the angry retort.

"Yes, that's the boy's story, Mistuh Scruggs."

"You damn well better remember my name, Reb, 'cuz the next time we meet, I'm gonna pull yer shades for good."

"That's tellin' him!" interjected Charlie.

"Oh, law," scoffed Garth, sadly shaking his head. "What do you boys take me for, some kind of a country bumpkin? You never learn, do you?" Irked, he suddenly lashed out with the toe of his boot, catching Will a hard one in the leg. Will let out a yowl and the horse shied. "Now, get down and sit for a spell," Garth ordered. "Why, I declare, if I gave you a fair chance straight on, I'll wager you couldn't possibly come close to pulling my shades, no more than your partner did back at Chugwater." Will dismounted, and holding his leg, started jumping around like a one-legged turkey, bringing a broad smile to the young Cheyenne's face. Garth ordered the two men to sit up against the

trunk of the tree, then motioned back to the boy to
bring the rope and tie them. The men groaned,
growled, and bickered among themselves as Bear Paw
swiftly wound the rope around the tree, binding the
men's arms down to their stomachs. After he had finished, he defiantly spat at their boots, lifted back his
head, and triumphantly screamed at the rainy heavens.
"Wagh!" he finally cried, beating at his small chest.
Retrieving Charlie's pistol, he shoved it inside his belt
and spat one final time. Then he stared up at Garth
with a questioning look in his dark eyes, wondering if
this had met with his new friend's approval.

Garth smiled at the boy, made several signs, awkwardly, he thought, but well enough to make him understand. He now wanted to see the disputed horses in
the corral. Talking to himself, Garth said, "This stock
better be Indian blood, boy, because I sure hate the
thought of coming back down here and apologizing to
this white trash."

Charlie desperately shouted, "Y'can't leave us here
like this. What if no one comes along? Damn yer ornery hide, Reb, have a heart. We'll take a chill tonight.
There's griz about, too."

T. B. Garth snorted at this. "You fellows may attract
a bear," he shouted back, "but he sure won't be interested in eating you."

A long string of curses followed.

The following morning, Garth rode out of the La
Bonte stage station, where he had holed up during the
rainy night, his thoughts dwelling on how Will and
Charlie had fared in the wet river bottom. Truthfully,
the welfare of the two scoundrels wasn't too much of
a concern. In fact, he felt quite noble about the humorous incident, albeit one that could have had tragic consequences, for after looking over the contested ponies
with Bear Paw, there had been no doubt in his mind
about ownership—they definitely were not the prop-

erty of the two Chugwater ruffians. Garth thought that had he not intervened, sooner or later the Cheyenne would have, and one thing he had learned on his first adventure in this land was that these Indians weren't stupid in any sense of the word. Will and Charlie, he decided, were lucky; they were miserable but alive; the Cheyenne would have killed them.

So, after whistling up a Dixie tune, Garth hit the trail anew, and later this same day finally spotted the blockhouses poking up through the river mists along the North Platte—Fort Fetterman, the new gateway to the Powder River country, the army's posthumous tribute to the vain but gallant man who had lost the war's biggest battle. Black memories for T. B. Garth, the reluctant warrior recalling the foolish bravado of Colonel Carrington's quarrelsome junior officers. Now he was riding into another fort, not too much concerned about his reception this time, in fact, as he noticed, the few troopers he did see, paid no attention to him or his hat. Indeed, times were changing. He remembered another time, not too distant, when his Confederate presence had posed more of a threat than an angry Indian, when everyone knew him by sight or by reputation, when his contest with the cantankerous Tatum prompted as much conversation as the slippery Lakota and Cheyenne. Two years of futile fighting had changed the Yankee perspective—Indians were the only topic, now, mostly the hostiles who had proved to be something more than hit-and-run savages. No accolades for T. B. Garth this day, not like that long-ago return from the great war village when everyone stormed out to greet him, even his sweet little Bird, who later learned the truth, that he actually had been lost. True, and as she had told him, he was a damned fool, always letting pride get the best of him. But now there was one man at Fort Fetterman who was paying some attention to his arrival, the lean, weathered Spaniard, Juan José Dominguez, and the meeting that took place by the parade grounds was one of mutual respect and admiration, and on the part of the more expressive Dominguez, fondness, the traditional *abrazos,* his hands soundly patting Garth's back as he embraced him.

Pulling Garth's saddle and slipping the pack from his second horse, the two men talked briefly about Garth's trip, then about Dominguez's recent journey with several friendly Lakota to the village of Red Cloud. His party had delivered and brought back messages about another forthcoming peace council. In his own good time, Red Cloud was coming down to Fort Laramie in the fall. It wasn't until they were touching their mugs of brandy together that Garth seriously broached the news that had brought him back to the frontier—just how good was Dominguez's information about Bird and her mother, and how cold was the trail? The veteran scout quietly enlightened him. There was a trader whom he had met by the name of Jubal McComber. McComber seemed to have free passage through the hostile country, and during the spring of sixty-seven he had run into three breed women at a Brule camp somewhere in the Powder River Valley. The women were all captives and spoke English.

"No names, nothing more?" Garth hesitantly asked.

"This particular one, he says, spoke good English," answered Dominguez. His dark face broke into a wide grin. "She spoke bad English, too, worse than any muleskinner he's ever heard. This is what he tells me, eh? A bad argument, and she gives him a lashing with her tongue. I say to myself, this can be no one but our little *pájaro.*"

Elated, Garth smiled under his mustache. "I wonder what ever possessed her to take on this McComber? If these Brule were friendly, why he could have gotten those women out of there, saved everyone a lot of trouble."

"Ho, ho," the Spaniard laughed. "This fellow is a bad one, I'll tell you, trading whiskey and ammunition to the Indians. He's also a smart one, eh? You want to know? He tried to buy this woman from the chief. He wants her for his woman, and she raises hell. I think this is what you say 'possessed her' to fight. This is not a good trade. You see, my friend, this fellow is *muy gordo. ¡Qué feo!* He's been hit by the ugly stick many times."

Garth said with a scowl, "Well, this chief must be some kind of a rare bird. Did he turn down the deal . . . ? Or didn't she want to get out of that place? It seems to me . . ."

Dominguez held up a hand, interrupting Garth. "Wait, wait, *un momento,*" he said. "My friend, you haven't seen this man, McComber. He is so ugly even his pony looks the other way. I tell you, Garth, some white men are more savage than the Indians, and who would want to ride away with this fellow, eh? Maybe she likes this chief better. Maybe he's not so ugly, eh? What she has is not so bad. This is my opinion, what I must think."

"Dominguez, sometimes your opinions frighten the hell out of me. I just can't picture her living with some chief. Why, that woman would more and likely chew his ear off."

"You forget, she is Indian, too."

"Half Indian," corrected Garth, disgruntled.

Dominguez shrugged and gave Garth a sad but understanding smile. "This is true," he agreed, "but let me tell you this, she will stay Indian and live Indian until the troopers come, or someone like you, who wants to buy her and take her away." He held up two fingers. "Two years, '*mano,* two years she's been gone, and nothing but McComber's word, eh? These Brule are free Indians, one day here, one day there. They don't go near the forts too much. What chance does she have? McComber? I say go to hell, first. No, this isn't easy, my friend. I tell you, we must think about what we plan to do, maybe some bargaining, eh?"

"You get me up there," Garth said. "If there's bargaining to be done, I'll do it. I brought enough money to buy a whole damn tribe if I have to."

"You brought enough to pay me?"

"You're busted?"

Dominguez shrugged indifferently. "Maybe it will be a long winter for me. I always need money."

Laying a hand on his friend's shoulder, Garth grinned and said, "Well, *amigo,* starting as of now, you're on the payroll. We'll strike a fee, something comparable to Yankee pay, if this is agreeable."

"How much?"

Garth pursed his lips, stared at Dominguez thoughtfully, and replied, "Well, I'd say you're worth about two hundred dollars, one hundred down and another hundred when we get back."

"Yankee or Confederate?"

"Damn your hide, Yankee, of course. That other currency went to hell four years ago and you know it."

"I'll take it," Dominguez said with a smile. "And how did you get so rich, eh? I see all these fine things you bring, ponies, plenty of food, and your new rifle. I think to myself, what did my friend do, rob a bank, swoosh, swoosh! And to pay for such a little ride, like a vacation!"

"I didn't rob any damn bank, by jingo! Let's say I inherited some bank funds. Now, where do we go from here? I'll allow there's Indians scattered all over those hills now with the war over, and probably most of them out of sorts with white folk."

Pointing his chin to the north, Dominguez said, "We go that way in the morning, down the Powder, start from the beginning, try to find some friendlies, eh?"

"The last time I rode the Powder with you, you damn near got me shot," Garth growled. Then in afterthought, he said, "And why didn't you tell me about the Craig boy, Elbert? There wasn't even a mention of him in your letters. From what I hear, the hostiles got him. That sutler down at Laramie said he went running off with some of those fort Indians. They probably deserted the poor chap."

"Ah, the Craig fellow!" exclaimed Dominguez. He struck his forehead. "Yes, I do remember that."

"Well, why didn't you tell me?"

"But, my friend, that was long ago! I didn't think it was so important. Was he such a good friend?"

"Dammit, he gave me this very hat!" Garth replied, pointing to his Confederate headpiece on the table. "He went to a lot of trouble to find one that suited my style. He was the only one there to see me off."

"I didn't know this."

"He looked after me when I was in the infirmary. After that Fetterman mess, he was about the only friend I had left down there, and I just don't like the thought of some Indian decorating his scalp pole with Elbert."

For a moment, John Dominguez fell silent, his eyes narrowing into a thoughtful squint. Finally: "You don't like something else, too, eh? Ah, yes, I see, you never told him about little Bird and yourself, and he goes hunting, and swoosh! And now you say, 'Maybe it's my fault.' You steal his woman, and you feel guilty, eh? Ah, how can you blame yourself? This is fate, nothing but fate."

"Fate, hell! If he had only known . . . if I had told him, he may not have gone chasing away, the crazy fool."

"Yes, fools and lovers. He was a fool and you, the lover."

"It wasn't just a case of stealing his woman," Garth said defensively.

"Ah, then, she seduced you?" countered the Spaniard with a sly grin.

A troubled look came over Garth's face. He had come to truly love Bird Rutledge, something at the time he thought was impossible, and now he was blab-

bering away like a guilt-ridden idiot, confessing his in-
nermost feelings to John Dominguez, of all people, a
man who enjoyed sticking little thorns of provocation
into him at every chance. "Seduced? I don't know,
damned if I do. That's something I never did quite figure out, who did what to whom. All I know, is that it
worked."

"Yes, I know."

"You know? Now, how would you know something
like that?"

Dominguez gestured helplessly with empty hands.
"But, what else? You didn't come one thousand miles
just to see me, or to try and find that Sturges man you
had such an itch to kill." He slapped a hand on Garth's
back. "I feel hungry, my friend. Let's go over to the
mess and get some of that Yankee grub you like so
much. Tomorrow's another day, much talk later, something to do besides dodge arrows, eh?" He grinned but
Garth did not grin back.

Even with hostilities temporarily halted because of the
absence of soldiers to shoot, the land along the Powder
and Tongue rivers was no less dangerous. Garth and
Dominquez faced a paradoxical problem—on the one
hand, they wanted to avoid Indians, on the other, to
search them out, those scattered few who might give
them a clue to the whereabouts of the missing women, no
easy task, this. The bloody land, now healing, had broad-
ened considerably for the Indians; war parties were dis-
persing; the Indians now had no reason to confine
themselves to that narrow corridor along the Bozeman
Trail; they wanted to roam again. Without buffalo soldiers
to fight, villages might be anywhere from the lofty Big
Horn Mountains to the sacred Black Hills, or as far south
as the murky Niobrara and Fort Randall. For Garth and
Dominguez, this meant only one thing—a long trail
ahead.

Though Garth knew the task was formidable, he was

hopeful. He had one of the best guides on the frontier with him, a man who understood Indians and one who could parley with them. Dominguez did not want to dash Garth's hopes, but he wanted to prepare him for the worst. He tried to explain. In his time, he had known of men disappearing in less than a week, never to be heard of again. Bird's trail was cold. The land they were now facing was measured in the hundreds of miles in all directions, and all of it belonged to the Sioux, Cheyenne, and Arapaho, or for that matter, any other tribe that wanted to use it. Garth listened but wasn't dissuaded or depressed. Instead, he remained ever resolute and hopeful, which earned him the continuing admiration of his companion.

So, with a prayer in their hearts, and fully aware of the hazards they faced, they rode northwest on the morning of September ninth, Garth with his great expectations, Dominguez with a touch of guarded apprehension. A compassionate man under his tough hide, Dominguez hated to see his friend hurt and wondered if Garth had prepared himself emotionally for another disheartening possibility, the sometimes disastrous effects of human bondage and what it could do to the soul of a woman.

It was that time of year, warm days, the nights beginning to feel the first touch of early autumn frost. Some Indians called it the Moon of the Drying Grass, prelude to the falling leaves, the red man's summer. Taking advantage of the ideal weather, the men made long tracks for two consecutive days, staying well to the right of the main trail, their eyes always on the distant rims, searching for feathers. In all this riding, they saw none. On the third day, however, shortly after noon, they crossed the first sign of Indians, a multitude of pony tracks, reasonably fresh. The absence of travois grooves along the ground was the first thing Dominguez noticed, no moving village here, he de-

duced. Dismounting, he inspected more closely, and after a probe or two at some pony droppings, he believed
the sign to be only a few hours old. He pointed northwest toward the Tongue River country—the Indians
were probably headed for the Tongue or the Big Horns,
to a village, or a hunting grounds, whatever, they were
not too far, and this led him to break off any more riding for the day. Dominguez reasoned contact with the
Sioux was now possible at any time.

Not that John Dominguez, the man of discretion,
was particularly worried about the natives, no, it was
more a matter of conditions—he wanted a confrontation on his terms, spot the Indians first, hopefully only
a few, and get a good look at them before making any
decisions on a meeting. He wanted the element of surprise on his side, quite a trick for a white man. He still
believed smoking and talking was the best tact, yet he
did not consider this entirely foolproof. Dominguez
had another hope, too. When he and Garth did meet Indians, he wanted them to be preferably Oglala, which
for the moment threw Garth into a fearful quandary, recalling that one of them had put a ball through his
sleeve during one of the wagon train skirmishes at Fort
Kearny. But his companion explained—although, indeed, they were fierce warriors, many of them, even
Chief Red Cloud, had known the Spaniard for years. A
frequent visitor, they respected his abilities. He had
been on past peace missions as an interpreter, and had
eaten and smoked with the Teton-Oglala many times.
Despite his scouting activities for the army, Dominguez allowed his record was mostly a plus, and Teton-
Oglala, he reasoned, were apt to be more receptive to
this trip into their lands than Cheyenne or Arapho, not
to mention Crow or Blackfeet who frequented the great
Yellowstone Basin to the north. Truthfully, they were
all good horse thieves, and Dominguez did not trust
any of them too far.

With yet unidentified Indians about, the two men

chose discretion, electing to move down Crazy Woman Creek to its confluence with the Powder by riding at night. Once safely camped in some remote niche, they could range out and try to make contact that was halfway dependable. They never quite made it to the creek junction, but they did make the contact. It was near sunrise when Dominguez suggested they stop and bed down for a few hours of sleep. He also wanted to rest the horses and let them graze. Garth promptly agreed, though, unlike his partner, he wasn't thinking too much about the horses—he was thinking about himself, that he was tired and hungry and had been a little nipped by the cool night air. Dominguez was pointing to a small willow-lined gully to the right of the creek bottom when they both detected the faint odor of wood smoke. Simultaneously, they traded looks. Garth impulsively reached over and was about to muzzle his horse, when after another anxious moment, Dominguez shook his head. No, he said, the smoke was drifting up the creek from a considerable distance, probably a half mile below them. Dismounting, he withdrew his rifle and motioned to Garth, who quickly followed suit. After securing the horses, they took off to investigate, slowly threading their way along the creek until, several bends below, they came within view of a camp, surprisingly, a very small one. In the faint light of dawn, they saw a lone woman bending over the fire, two men huddled beside it, both of them covered with blankets. There were three horses picketed in the flat nearby. This seemed to be the extent of it, bringing a quiet nod of approval from Dominguez. He whispered to Garth, "They're eating. Do you want some breakfast?"

Garth's nose wrinkled distastefully. "No, thank you, suh," he whispered back. "I'm not that hungry, not when we have bacon and beans back in my packs."

"Then we will walk down and talk with them, eh? But I tell you this, if they are friendly, they will offer us some breakfast. Remember, these people are very hospitable. Sometime, they get offended, you know. It's not good to offend them. They will tell us nothing. Maybe you just pretend you're hungry, eh?"

Garth nudged his companion ahead. "Dammit, John, get on with it. Breakfast, indeed! You keep your eyes open they don't go shooting us instead of feeding us."

The men moved quietly ahead, but not too far, for just about the time Dominguez was preparing to make his friendly greeting a great, growling mongrel leaped out seemingly from nowhere, his fangs bared, the hackles on his back standing straight up. The two Indians at fireside whirled around, one reaching for his rifle. At the same time, Garth, his eyes two great balls of white in the dim morning light, was thrusting his rifle barrel far in front of him, trying to ward off the snarling dog. Unpertured by all the commotion, John Dominguez stood coolly motionless, his right hand raised, his palm outthrust. Surprisingly, this seemed enough, because one of the men promptly called the dog off, and relieved, Garth let out a deep wheeze and shouldered his rifle. "Lord a'mighty," he sighed, "let's hope these people have better dispositions than this crazy hound. Why, I was about ready to whack the ornery scamp."

But in his usual casual demeanor, Dominguez said, "Ah, but it's nothing, my friend. Look, you see, everything is fine, the fellow over there is holding up his arm. Good, eh? He wants us to come in. We go, and remember to smile. It's better this way."

And Garth, feeling nervous in his already empty stomach, attempted to smile, rather weakly, he thought. He, doubted very much if the Indians even noticed. His own eyes were on the big dog sitting to the side, resting on its haunches like a mangy monarch, a deep rumbling still coming from its throat. From the side, Garth saw Dominguez making a few beginning flourishes with his hand, and then, abruptly, he started speaking Siouan with the youngest man. The second Indian was a much older man, wrinkled, bowlegged, and partially covered by a deep red Hudson Bay blanket, and once the preliminary talk was finished, he sat down and continued eating. The young woman was dressed in a buckskin dress which was split partway up the middle for riding. The typical blue tattoo on her forehead, indicating she was Lakota, glistened against the glow of the fire, and she wore a beautiful, multicolored necklace. She smiled shyly at Garth, obviously aware of his uneasiness over the growling dog, and to allay his fear, she reached over and slapped the dog across the muzzle. With one last growl, it stretched out lazily in front of her.

After another few minutes of conversation which seemed like an eternity to Garth, Dominguez finally turned and translated—these were Hunkpapa, the two men, from the village of Tantanka Yotanka, Sitting Bull, and in turn, Dominguez pointed, making introductions—father, son, and daughter-in-law, the woman, an Oglala. They were headed for Red Cloud's camp by the mountains to visit her relatives. Dominguez looked at Garth again. "He says they are celebrating over on Little Goose Creek, a big powwow, dancing, feasting."

Garth nodded. "I can understand that, all right." Glancing at the handsome young brave, he asked, "Did you tell him about us, our business?"

"Yes, my friend. That's the first thing he wanted to know, what we're doing up here." And the Spaniard went on, smiling all around and continually nodding with approval at the Sioux, all of whom were visibly impressed. "I told them we're looking for a young woman living with some Brule. I also said we came at the invitation of Red Cloud."

"Oh, law," Garth groaned, "that's stretching it a bit. Now, they'll probably want us to go along over to Goose Creek. That's a long ride over there."

"Stretching it? Are you forgetting I smoked with

Red Cloud? It's good to boast with these people. Listen, *amigo,* I'm only thinking ahead for our safety. Talk a little, smoke a little, eat a little, don't you see? Pretty soon, they'll tell others about us, and then those people tell someone else, and so on. It's the Indian telegraph, like the singing wires, only our friends here, they do the singing."

The younger man was busy talking to his wife, and the wrinkled old man, squatting nearby, was mumbling in between his bites of food and staring and pointing his spoon at Garth. Garth looked helplessly at Dominguez. "This one, what's he saying about me?"

"Well, first, he said he liked your hat," Dominguez replied. "Now, let's see . . . yes, now he's saying you're just like him. He knows all about the gray soldiers, how they ran from the bluecoats. Yes, he says the bluecoats chased him once, too, and he ran plenty fast. He's laughing about it."

"He thinks that's funny?"

"Yes, and you should, too. Smile, show him you like his little story. The old man will feel better. It's the polite thing to do."

"Ha, ha." Garth grimaced.

"Ah, but wait!" Dominguez went on. He gestured excitedly to the side. "This one, he thinks Red Leaf's village is somewhere north . . . yes, up on the Greasy Grass. This is what he heard. *Sí, hombre,* they went up there about one moon ago!"

"Oh, Lord!" exclaimed Garth, his eyes to the heavens. He gave his hands a resounding clap, bringing the big dog to its feet, and the startled eyes of the Sioux upon his upturned face. "Now, we're getting somewhere!" John Dominguez hastily explained, telling the Indians that this woman they were trying to find belonged to the gray soldier, and he was plenty happy to hear this news about Red Leaf's village because it was believed the woman was living with the Brule. Amid their nods and smiles, Garth then asked, "How far to this place, how many days to this Greasy Grass?"

The Spaniard thoughtfully tugged at his small goatee for a moment. He wasn't sure, he said. It all depended upon what was ahead of them in the valleys to the northwest, the Tongue and the Big Horn. Riding by daylight, maybe four days, perhaps five; night riding, avoiding hostiles, a few days longer, these were his estimates.

"Well," Garth concluded, "the sooner the better. Fact is, I didn't much like that pussyfooting around last night. Now that we're into these buggers we might as well take our chances and keep on going. At least, we know where we're headed now, this Greasy Grass country."

John Dominguez asked, "You aren't tired . . . ? Hungry?" He pointed to the tin kettles by the fire. "This woman says we're welcome to flatcakes and mush."

Garth nodded and smiled. "Yes, John, I'm tired and I'm hungry, but not that hungry, not when we have coffee, beans, and bacon back in my packs."

"This is just like grits, my friend," Dominguez said. "It would be polite to . . ."

Aware of Dominguez's advice not to offend these people, Garth said with a continuing smile, "I hate grits. I've always hated grits, dammit!" He turned to leave.

"But what shall I do . . . ?"

"What you've always been telling me," replied Garth, his smile turning devilish. "Parley with them, eat with them, and tell them I'm going to get some tobacco. I'll do the smoking with them."

Chapter Seventeen

Late one afternoon in the vicinity of the eastern Rose-bud mountains, John Dominguez took out his field glasses and played them along the fringe of slender aspen ahead. What he made out was a file of mounted Indians, at least ten or twelve, silently waiting in the shade of the yellowing trees. Next to him, Garth was staring intently, focusing in with his own glasses. Only moments before, he had first seen the shadowy movements of what he thought were horses. "What do you make of it?" he said. "Can you tell anything from here?"

Dominguez quickly cased his binoculars. "Too far to say, but they see us, too, and they're waiting for us to make a move."

"Well, suh, what do we do? This is the direction where that Sioux said the Brule were hanging out. Maybe they're Red Leaf's riders. Maybe your Indian telegraph got through."

John Dominguez squinted at the sun, then studied the neighboring hills. Strategically their position was poor. They were caught in the middle of a grassy meadow, and protective cover was scarce, something the Spaniard had made an effort to avoid ever since they had been riding in the daylight. But now he had made a tactical error. "My friend," he finally said, "I think we are another day's ride away from the Greasy Grass, and I don't know who these people are. We have only two choices. We ride over there and meet them, or find a place in back of us, wait, see if they'll come to us. Smoke or fight, Garth. I tell you this . . . from here we can't outride them, not with our packs." He surveyed the grassy knolls again and smiled. "Ah, but from over there on the hill, we can outshoot them, eh?"

Garth, giving him a dark, negative look, said, "I didn't come up here to fight these rascals so I don't see any choice. Besides, if they're Sioux, maybe you can talk us out of here. And, if they're Brule, we've hit the right trail."

Dominguez put on a big smile and moved his hand forward. "*Vámanos,* we take our chances, ride in bravely, show them we're friends." He winked. "And remember, always a little smile, eh?"

Setting his gray hat firmly in place, and giving his horse a nudge, Garth growled back, "Let's go, but damned if I feel like smiling. If I took your advise and went around grinning all the time, well, by jingo, everyone would think I was the village idiot. Damned if you don't take the cake, John. You remember the last time we were together? I recollect we were running for our lives. Yes suh, and south of here I froze my ass off under a rock." He scowled across at Dominguez. "Not only are you a trustful soul, but you have a short memory. Some of these fellows have long ones."

"But that was two years ago!" Holding his hand up in peace, he said, "This is different. Remember, *amigo,* these Brule aren't on the warpath."

"They weren't supposed to be the last time, either," retaliated Garth, "and look what they did to my head. And, dammit, they stole my woman, too."

"Everyone makes a mistake, sometimes, eh? And look, we have no troopers along. I tell you, this is different." Trotting along, he stared ahead and suddenly pointed. "You see, here they come to greet us."

Garth tried to collect himself. Sure enough, the Indians were coming, most of them, anyhow, all except two who were riding the opposite way, back down toward what appeared to be a distant river bottom. About midway across the meadow, one of the approaching braves moved to the front, and the riders in back of him swung out wide, forming two lines, one to each side of Garth and Dominguez. "Well, now," Garth said uneasily, "what do you make of this? I'd say they're flanking us, and I damn well don't like it."

"Easy, my friend, easy," warned the Spaniard. "They aren't yelling. This is a good sign. We wait, but don't make any play for your rifle."

Suddenly, the lead rider raised his hand and shouted out several commands, and after staring at the two men, he abruptly wheeled his pony about, motioning to the two white men to follow.

"Cheyenne," Dominguez yelled to Garth as their horses came close together. "He wants us to follow, probably a village in the valley somewhere down there where those other two went."

"Cheyenne!" Garth exclaimed. And, then for the first time, he noticed that his friend was no longer smiling. "Why in the hell didn't that Sioux boy say something about this?"

"Because I am Domino. I should know these things, eh? Arapaho, Cheyenne, a few Crow ... all up here, Indians all over the place."

"And you didn't?"

"I tell you this, I didn't expect to run into them this way." He waved and forced a smile, but it was a tight, small one, yet he said optimistically, "Don't worry. When we get to their village, we'll talk. I know some of these people, the old ones."

Garth rode, not easily, but troubled, his big eyes warily on the solemn braves to each side, trying to anticipate what was in store for Dominguez and him around the next bend, what manner of reception they would receive from these Indians who for so long had been harassed by the army. These were alien Cheyenne. Admittedly, Dominguez had not struck the rapport with them that he had with the Sioux; they hadn't even given him a chance. Either his easy going friend was not truly worried, Garth thought, or he must be one remarkable actor. What little Garth knew about the Cheyenne had come from Dominguez, the Sand Creek massacre of Black Kettle's people, a gory tale in itself. Nor had he forgotten the stories about General Patrick Conner's invasion of the northern valleys in sixty-five and his infamous order to kill every male Cheyenne over twelve years of age. Garth doubted any Cheyenne had forgotten these events, either, including their most recent battles in the Big Horns where Dull Knife's warriors sustained heavy loses in the so-called Hayfield fight over near Fort Smith, the now, nonexistent Fort Smith. Somewhere, sometime, Garth mused, the piper had to be paid, and he allowed that a small token of that payment might just be forthcoming, that someone in the village up ahead was going to be both judge and jury. This was the worst side of it. At the uncomfortable present, all hope was hinging upon the veteran riding beside him, just how well he could parley with these people.

The ride with the escorts ended about an hour before sunset on the banks of what Dominguez believed was a fork of the Big Horn River. A large, vibrant village loomed in front of them. To Garth, it was suddenly apparent that their arrival had been fully expected. Two huge animated lines of villagers had already formed, but unlike the braves who silently greeted them in the meadow miles back, these awaiting people were already setting up a shrill tremolo, and many of the women, much to Garth's horror, were angrily shouting and shaking sticks. It was worse than he had expected, and to his astonishment, a few were even wagging their bottoms at them, not a friendly reception by any means. He shouted to John Dominguez, "When we make it to the big man, you better do some fancy talking. For some reason, these people are ready to skin us alive."

But to Garth's amazement, Dominguez was smiling again, even nodding at the people, holding up his hand as though he were the prodigal son returned. "Dominguez!" Garth cried desperately. "Did you hear me?"

In reply, Garth received a casual nod, another smile, another wave. "Don't worry, my friend. This is customary with these people. When they learn . . ."

"What the hell are you telling me! They're about to tan our hides and you're sitting there waving at the scoundrels!"

"Yes, it's true, but I tell you, it will be all right. Look at it this way . . . what do these Indians want with men like us? We aren't bluecoats or pilgrims. We're outcasts, two men without a country, *los vagabundos*. This is the difference, you see, and when they find out why we have come . . . well?"

"Why look at their faces! I don't think these devils care much about bloodlines or politics, and those hairy things they're waving at us . . . are they what I think they are?"

"Scalp sticks." Dominguez grinned. "Look, I'm what you call a greaser, eh? My country left this land long ago. The Iron Hats couldn't hold it. Who wants me? I have no claim to make here. I want nothing from these people but friendship. And look at you! Why, you're no bluecoat, eh? Ah, but you are beautiful, the gray soldier, your fine sombrero. They know what that hat means, my friend, they know this."

Garth, astounded by his partner's nonchalance, stared up imploringly at the fading golden sky. Shaking his head, he whispered to himself what Dominguez had told him to do, trust in God. "Lord, deliver us," he mumbled.

Directly, the mounted leader ahead reined in, parting the band of hecklers, and Garth saw a huge tipi in front of them with four braves standing by the opening.

They were carrying long lances decorated with feathers and wrapped with animal skins, and through all the commotion, Dominguez said these men were Dog Soldiers. As soon as he and the Spaniard dismounted, one of the braves stepped forward and quickly relieved them of their sidearms. Alarmed, but without recourse, Garth watched the Indian tuck both revolvers in his belt. He glanced over at Dominguez, who, true to form, was already carrying on a conversation with one of the other Dog Society members, smiling and chatting, making sign, as if he were a long-lost friend. Dominguez turned to Garth and said, "This is our lodge. We will wait here until this little misunderstanding is cleared up."

"The village jail, you mean," drawled Garth. "What happens now? What were you saying to that scamp?"

"I tell him to take care of our pistols and packs. No misplacing them, eh, or there's all hell to pay."

Garth merely grunted. "I'd say that's the least of our worries."

"No, I think it's going to be all right. They think we're spies, maybe bad *hombres*."

And Garth blurted, "Spies! Well, Lord a'mighty, where in the hell did they ever get an idea like that! Spies for whom? And we come riding into this valley in broad daylight! Why, you ought to be able to shoot that nonsense full of holes."

"Ah, you see, but they are suspicious. We have no shovels, no picks, no merchandise to sell, no whiskey, and we bring no messages. To these people, this is crazy business, yes, very suspicious."

"Well, dammit, you tell them our business," Garth growled, finding his way into the darkness of the tipi.

"This fellow outside tells me where we are, too," Dominguez went on. "We're in Morning Star's village. This means we're in big company, my friend. You know Morning Star? That's what his people call him. The Sioux call him a different name, Dull Knife. That one you know, eh? *Tahmelapashme,* a mean fighter, Red Cloud's partner, swoosh, swoosh."

"Oh, law, law," lamented Garth. He sat down wearily on a large buffalo robe and held his aching head. "I knew things were going from bad to worse. Mistuh Bridger told me this old boy hates whites with a passion."

"Yes, that's Dull Knife, and before too long we'll have to talk with him or one of the lesser chiefs, explain what we're doing up here on their land. This is what you want, eh? Maybe this chief listens as well as he fights." Squinting in the darkness, Dominguez examined the quarters, found several piles of robes and some wood for a fire. "Ah, this isn't so bad, Garth. We have a good roof over our heads tonight, a place for a warm fire in the morning."

Garth stared gloomily through the dimness at Dominguez. He asked, "What are our chances? What if he doesn't listen . . . ? Doesn't believe our story?"

Resting back, Dominguez sighed. "Friend Garth, sometimes I think you worry too much. Don't worry, the chief will listen. He's a wise man. Besides, I have this feeling, it's not our time, not yet. Time to rest, that's all, rest and wait."

But Garth found rest impossible, and just could not comprehend his partner's blind faith and intuitive "good feeling." He felt like a horde of pack rats was invading the lodge, carrying away the remaining shreds of his battered life. And outside, the many strange noises were alarming, too, and his attending thoughts, too horrible to dwell on, that the angry populace out there was making preparations for some barbaric ritual in which he and Dominguez were to play leading roles. Certainly, if the mood of Dull Knife, were no better than that of his people, then he and Dominguez were in for a great deal of misery. Garth stewed in fearful insecurity for what seemed like an eternity. Beside him, hat tipped across the peak of his nose, his old friend of the trail actually appeared to be dozing. But, in reality, the wait in the darkened lodge was only a half hour. The two men quickly came to attention when the tipi flap suddenly widened, and in came the same brave who had escorted them into the angry village. After a few words, they were led away, followed by a curious but somewhat less belligerent crowd, including several large, growling dogs similar to the one that had stopped Garth dead in his tracks on Crazy Woman Creek. This led him to the swift conclusion that the Indians were even training their beasts to hate the white man.

Unlike the dim quarters they had just vacated, the big council lodge in which they were now standing was fully open at the front and around the sides. Many people were gathered in the sunset around the outside to witness the proceedings, and a crier was there, too, to call out what was being said. The overhead vent illuminated the scene, a semicircle of solemn, dignified chiefs, some of them in feathers, obviously the judge and jury of the Cheyenne camp, including *Tahmelapashme* himself, who was seated in the middle. However, it was not Morning Star who spoke first. It was a younger chief, Little Wolf, who opened the questioning. After a few moments, Dominguez raised his hand in a gesture of peace and began talking back, motioning to himself and Garth in explanation. Occasionally, one of the chiefs along the row interrupted him, and at one point, one of Dominguez's answers brought a smile to their somber faces, one chief laughing outright. After another lengthy exchange, Morning Star spoke briefly, then quietly passed a hand in front of himself. In return, Dominguez made a sign of peace again, and the council was suddenly over. Surprisingly, to Garth, not a harsh word had been exchanged, yet even so he came away uneasy. While the session had been peaceful and businesslike, the fact that they were once again being led back to confinement sorely dis-

tressed him, and he had the dread impression not all
had gone well, or at least not as well as his companion
had expected. Dominguez partially confirmed it. With
a tired smile, he said, "It's not too bad, but they know
who we are. They know we were down at Kearny with
Bridger at the Battle of the Hundred Slain. That's what
they're calling that Fetterman fiasco. These are smart
Indians, my friend, and like you say, they have long
memories."

Garth disgustedly kicked up a small cloud of dust
with the toe of his boot. "But scouting and fighting
are two different occupations. Didn't you explain
this ...? Why we came? Lord a'mighty, they know
damn well we aren't Yankees. They certainly know
who you are."

"This is true, that's what they called me, 'Dough-
me-no.' "

Garth said angrily, "Dammit, suh, this smacks of
guilt by association. And how did they know we were
at Kearny in all that confusion? You didn't let the cat
out of the bag, did you?"

"Listen, friend, these people have good eyes, too.
They have field glasses just like we do." The scout's
dark eyes twinkled. "One of those chiefs, the one
called Little Wolf, was a brave, then. He and that
young Oglala, Crazy Horse, and another Cheyenne,
Little Horse, were all over the place. Little Wolf says
he and Little Horse fought four times around the fort.
You know what he asked me in there? He says, 'Why
does not the gray hat wear the crow feather anymore?'
Gray Hat, my friend, that's you. *Sí*, they call you Gray
Hat."

Garth blanched and fell back on his robe.

"So, I tell him, because a Sioux couped it,"
Dominguez continued. "That made them smile a little,
eh? And when they heard this redskin stole your
woman, too, well ..."

"Oh, for God's sake, John!"

"But did I lie?"

"You made me look like a damn fool!"

"Ah, but they think this already," replied Dominguez with a grin. "The one chief, he says anyone who comes up here looking for a woman two years after she's gone, must be chased by the Horned Hairy Water Spirit, the *minio* ... that's a bogeyman creature who sometimes does crazy things. He says smart white men don't do things like this unless they're touched. No, they go out and trade for another woman. That's what he said, and everyone laughs."

"Some more of their weird humor, I suspect," Garth grumbled. "They don't even know the woman."

And much to Garth's surprise, Dominguez answered, "Oh, yes they do. Little Horse says she's the one they called Bird Woman who used to ride so fast down to the Horseshoe station many moons ago. One time some friends of his tried to ride with her and she ran away from them."

"Well I'll be damned," Garth cursed lowly. "By jingo, I wonder just who doesn't know that woman!"

"Maybe she's more famous than we know, eh?" and Dominguez went to the front of the tipi and looked outside. The four guards were still there, and he made a few signs and comments with one of them again. Turning back to Garth, he said, "Things are looking better, I think. He says we can sit out here, take some fresh air, and no one will bother us."

Garth joined his companion at the opening, and they both sat cross-legged, watching the people going back and forth in the fading light, and strangely, hardly anyone was paying any attention to them, now. Dominguez said that someone would bring them something to eat, maybe not too much, but enough to keep their stomachs from growling all night. And, this time, he advised Garth, it would be smart to eat the food. Garth glumly agreed. Shortly afterward, Dominguez noticed a woman standing some distance from them, intently staring at their small group. Her long hair was in a wild tumble about her shoulders, her widened eyes set in a fixed stare. He immediately recognized her as a white woman, and with a quick nudge, said to Garth, "Look at that one, the tall woman over there. What do you make of it?"

Garth squinted in the dusk and was startled by the unexpected sight. "Why, she's white . . . a white woman!" He started to speak out, but Dominguez quickly took his arm.

"No, not yet, I think she's touched."

"Touched?"

The mysterious woman suddenly turned, and gathering up her long buckskin skirt, she laughed over her shoulder and hurried away, leaving Garth and Dominguez sitting there staring curiously at each other. John Dominguez spoke to one of the Dog soldiers, and after a moment, explained to Garth. "He says she's been in this village for four years. Some of the women found her up north on the river stumbling around eating raw fish." He silently crossed himself.

"Poor damned woman," lamented Garth. "Lord, Lord, four years! When we get out of this mess, we should talk with her, find out who she is . . . what happened, how the Cheyenne got hold of her."

"Who can help her?" asked Dominguez. "He says she doesn't talk. These people think she has some kind of a taboo, and this keeps the *mistai,* the ghosts, away from the village. She has strong medicine, a healer, perhaps."

Garth scoffed. "Sounds like nonsense to me, witchcraft."

"Who knows?" was the quiet reply. "I tell you, this is a strange land if you don't understand it, and these people are no different. Yes, and they know this country, what it can do to a man, or a woman. Ghosts make these Indians uneasy, this I know, and who am I to quarrel with their beliefs? Sometimes, I see these strange things myself, the medicines they make. Look, my friend, these people, they hold hands with nature. The white man? He only knows how to fight it."

Daybreak, noise, but not drums. Relieved, Garth listened, but then realized it was much too early for the foreboding sound of doomsday drums. But the village, by all accounts, was stirring, whatever the consequences to himself and Dominguez. Outside, he heard the sounds of women shuffling about, calling greetings back and forth; a camp crier, shouting news and events forthcoming; the ubiquitous dogs, their incessant barking out there, sniffing for scraps and pissing on tipis; and the sleepy cries of children, only a few, but close by. Rolling to the side, he pulled on his boots. After a stretch or two, Garth poked his head out between the hide flaps. People clad in blankets were moving about. He saw a few of the women he already had heard, the dogs, too, but the guards, the Dog Society soldiers who had been stationed at the tipi entrance, were gone. This surprised him, and without dwelling on it too long (and because of necessity) he hurried away to relieve himself in the nearest clump of willows. Strangely, no one followed him. At the river nearby, he found a small channel and splashed cold water into his sore eyes, for his sleep had been fitful and fleeting, filled with bizarre dreams, including ones of the Horned Hairy Water Spirit who had chased him up and down the walls of the tipi most of the night. After washing, he looked around cautiously. Still no one had approached, probably, because like the crazy woman, he, too, was taboo, but when he was returning to the tipi, he suddenly came face-to-face with the first of the women. Garth braced himself, expecting the usual harangue, and he protectively pulled up his collar and started to make big strides. Only a few giggles followed him. Other women appeared on the scene, and they were covering their mouths in mirth. This left him so perplexed and speechless he did the only mannerly thing he could do—he tipped his hat. The women, by now, were all around him, and one began speaking and making sign. When he helplessly shrugged, a pretty young maiden stepped up and took over, motioning to both her mouth and stomach. Did he want to eat? Thunderstruck by this startling turnabout, one day ugly sticks, the next an invitation to breakfast, Garth nodded approvingly and pointed to the distant guardhouse. Quickly making a sign or two of his own, he dashed back to the tipi, rushed inside, and started kicking the mound of robes where John Dominguez had buried himself. "John," he shouted, "get your ass out here! Dammit, suh, I need help, reinforcements. Something incredible has happened. You won't believe this, but the guards are gone and there's no one around but these giggling females outside. I can't make out a word they're saying, but damned if I don't think they want to feed us. Do you hear me, man? Something's happening!"

"*¿Qué pasa?*" Dominguez mumbled, pulling himself up. He blinked several times and looked around. "The guards, you say, gone? Impossible!"

Garth hurried back to the entrance of the tipi and threw aside the flap. "Look! And out there, all those people, grinning and carrying on. Why, I declare, if this doesn't beat all! I roamed around ten minutes, all the way down to the river, and not a soul followed me. Then, this one little lady comes up and asks me if I want to eat."

Moments later, both men were outside, Dominguez calmly stretching the kinks out of his back, silently surveying the awakening scene. Two curious boys ran up, looked at them briefly, then ran away. Dominguez saw the women nearby, staring at them, and true to Garth's word, they were smiling, obviously in approval. Checking the eastern horizon, the scout figured it was not much later than seven o'clock, and he turned to Garth. This, he said, explained the absence of men;

they were still in bed waiting for the tipis to warm up. Down at the river while Dominguez washed, Garth was continuing to look around in disbelief. "I can't believe this," he said. "Yesterday, they were ready to peel our hides."

But Dominguez, as usual, seemed unperturbed— time would tell, he said. Their present state of freedom, he opined, might be for any of several reasons, simple or complex. Perhaps the Cheyenne believed their story, even to the point of having some sympathy with Garth's plight. Or perhaps a great medicine chief had been suddenly struck by some mysterious caprice, or had scratched out a disturbing omen in the ashes of his night fire. Whatever, it was a good sign, and ultimately, Dominguez gave Garth a friendly pat on the shoulder. "You know what all of this means? I think maybe today we'll ride out, go find those Sioux somewhere around here, not too far." Wiping his face on the sleeve of his jacket, he nodded back toward the rising smoke. "Maybe you'll eat breakfast this time, eh? Smile a little, and take care not to upset these people by telling them you'd rather have beans and bacon."

"John, you devil, you're my guiding light." Garth beamed. "The ways things are looking right now, I could sit down and feast on Yankee polecat and not mind it."

They were soon eating beside the little fire in their tipi, women hovering about, serving, but offering very little in the way of conversation, or even amends for their angry tirades of the preceding day. Dominguez did not ply them with questions, explaining aside to Garth that any interrogation on his part would be highly improper and contrary to custom, first, because these were women, and second, because he and Garth were now considered to be guests, welcome ones. Once, he grinned at Garth and spoke lowly. "But from what I do understand, it's not me they're interested in, it's you."

Garth's dark eyes rolled. "Me?" He scowled back. "Dammit, are you joshing me again. Why me?"

"I can't say. You aren't that handsome, eh? But for some reason, they think you're special. Yes, you're right, my friend, something has happened." And he shrugged, adding, *"¿Quién sabe?"*

Garth, glancing around self-consciously, went about trying to eat his breakfast, a mush of some sort, flavored with berries, he suspected, and flatcakes, crusty, but palatable, and coffee, Cheyenne version, bitter and black, but no grits, thank the Lord. Taking a cue from John Dominguez, he occasionally offered up a smile to the women, who, indeed, for some unknown reason, were still continuing to observe him. But it was almost two hours later before Garth and Dominguez found out why—first, a brave came to the front of the tipi, returning the men's revolvers and rifles; two women followed with more firewood, and shortly thereafter, four more men showed up, shouldering all the goods from the packhorses. After several words with Dominguez, they deposited the gear inside the lodge and left.

"What's going on?" Garth asked suspiciously.

Dominguez thoughtfully scratched at his little goatee. "I get this funny feeling we're going to be staying about for a while. They say Morning Star and these two others, Little Wolf and Two Moons, are coming to pay their respects, something about a celebration or initiation. I can't figure this out, my friend, maybe later, eh?"

Their wait was only momentary, for not too long afterward, Morning Star, or the man the Sioux called Dull Knife, and his followers, did appear on the scene, preceded by a few leaping, excited children and several of the large camp dogs. Both Garth and Dominguez stood, the Spaniard with his hand elevated in greeting. But even before the chiefs reached the tipi, Garth saw a small face among the children that suddenly explained everything, and it hit him like a cannonball.

"Well, I declare!" he exclaimed aside to Dominguez. "I know what this is all about! I know, now! There's that boy I told you about, the one those two scoundrels down on the North Platte were trying to string up! Look at him over there, he's grinning like a possum in a sugar pot."

"A Cheyenne boy?" inquired Dominguez. Emitting a long, forlorn sigh, he said, "Mother of Mary, why didn't you tell me this! Look at all the trouble it would have saved! *Hombre,* Garth, how can you do this to such an old friend?"

"Dammit, John, how'd you expect me to know?" Garth replied, giving the boy a wave. "I barely understood him. I knew those horses were his. He was Indian, Sioux, Cheyenne, something or another, hell, I didn't know what he was."

But it no longer mattered. The big chief and several other leaders were facing them, and after the ensuing conversation, and Dominguez's rapid translations, everyone ended up smiling, including T. B. Garth, once again, hero by accident, for it now turned out that the boy, Bear Paw, was the first son of the young chief, Little Wolf, the same Little Wolf who had signaled for the beginning of the ambush on Fetterman and his troopers, who had led a thousand screaming Sioux and Cheyenne down the Peno Creek hillsides. Garth remembered this frightening scene all too well, how John Dominguez had pulled him away from a hopeless situation. But, now, it was a different story, the two scouts invited to be guests in the village, to be feted at a celebration, and Garth, by the word of Little Wolf, to become an adopted brother in the tribe. As elated as Garth was about his redemption, the adoption part of the Cheyenne directive was another matter, and somewhat frightening, at that. This was the initiation that one of the braves earlier had mentioned to Dominguez, and the thought of his participation in some barbaric ritual dampened Garth's newly found elation like a soggy bedroll. Skin piercing, branding, and tattooing went far beyond the realms of what he considered honor and brotherhood. And later that day, sunning themselves in front of their tipi, Garth made this known to John Dominguez. "I'm not up to this sort of thing," he mumbled. "Why can't they just point us toward Red Leaf's people like they promised and be done with it? I didn't come up here to be adopted by a bunch of contrary rascals who damn near made crow bait out of me once before."

Dominguez, reclining comfortably, blew a stream of smoke into the late summer air. He pointed his pipe stem at a group of nearby children who were watching them. "Life is hard, friend," he said, philosophically. "Life is precious, eh, for these little ones, too easily taken away. You saved this boy's life. More important, you turned against your own people to do it. This is big medicine, eh?"

"Oh, law, those old boys were mountain valley trash, no better than road agents, and you know it. I could have blown them away and no one would have cared one whit."

"Does it matter? You saved him from a terrible disgrace. To these people, hanging is the worst kind of death, yes, terrible dishonor and humiliation. You see, if he dies in such a bad way, his *tasoom*, his shadow or soul, is lost, maybe it goes wandering around forever like one of these *mistai*, eh? His soul never gets up what they call The Great Hanging Road, the long trail from here to up there, the *ekutsihimmiyo*. This is the great Milky Way, what we call heaven. So, you see, Little Wolf has a good reason to honor you. Yes, it would be a bad thing to refuse this show of friendship." Dominguez drew contentedly on his pipe again and rationalized. "Besides, once you become a brother of Little Wolf that makes you a father of Bear Paw, and this gives great honor to the boy. Yes, and then we have free passage through this country, too. We don't

have to hide from anyone." Reaching over, he gave
Garth a couple of pats on the arm. "This initiation is
nothing, my friend. They probably will only give you
a little mark, nothing of great pain, nothing to worry
about."

Garth suddenly sagged inside. "Mark me? Now, you
look here, suh, putting some kind of a brand on me
may be nothing to you, but it's my skin, and I'm already ass deep in sorghum with this brotherhood business, getting all bottled up in this village for a few
days just so everyone around here can find another excuse to celebrate. I've already been marked once by
these scamps. How about this ... you tell them it's
against my religion. Maybe this will discourage them."

"Discourage them?" Dominguez groaned back.
"You want me to make these people angry all over
again? Tradition, Garth, tradition. You're lucky Little
Wolf has no eligible daughters or sisters, or you would
be leaving here with a wife. No, we celebrate, accept
the honor they give to you, visit a few days ..."

"I don't want to visit a few days," moaned Garth,
trying hard to avoid finality. "We're losing precious
time. Can't you explain?"

Dominguez shrugged and replied fatefully, "When
they're ready to go, we go. A few more days, they'll
take us right to these Brule. Look, maybe they don't
cut you at all, eh? Just pretend it's a joke. But, I ask
you, what is better than this?" He pointed his pipe
around the peaceful camp.

Garth stared gloomily across the grounds, thinking
only of his beloved Bird Rutledge. For one thing, that
was better, or could be, just riding away to civilization
with her instead of John Dominguez, his relaxed, indif-
ferent companion, the great fabricator, his trustworthy
friend. Yes, riding off to some warm rendezvous far
below the North Platte, far from the Indian nation. Any
number of things could be better, but as matters now
stood, all of them were nothing more than misty

dreams clouding his mind. Looking over at Dominguez, he smiled, a learned smile, he thought, and gestured helplessly. "Oh, law, John, what's the use. There's no honorable way out of this. We're just going to have to let the chips fall and make the best of it." Fateful acceptance, submission, pain, all for the price of honor and brotherhood. Shit! Garth died inside.

The white woman and her mocking laughter had been a fleeting but disturbing thought in Garth's mind, and granted, his own problems that first night in the village had been too pressing to concern himself with her pitiful plight. As John Dominguez had pointed out, to what avail? Obviously, she was crazy, beyond the help of either of them. Even though Dominguez thought it was best to forget her, to Garth, the unexpected sight of this poor, deranged woman had been a curiously disturbing experience, one not easily dismissed. The Cheyenne, he learned, called her Lost Woman, and he met her a second time, face to face, while returning from the pony herd where he had gone to look over his horses. The boy, Bear Paw, his new son-to-be, and several smaller boys were with him. The encounter with Lost Woman was momentary, yet significant in several ways. Garth looked up and there she was, directly in his path, observing him in her usual wild-eyed manner. Offering a quiet greeting, he paused long enough to examine her features. She was a woman of some strength, high-boned in the cheeks, blue eyes, and except for a few pox marks, had a ruddy, healthy-looking complexion. Had her hair been clean, it would have been blond. A Germanic woman, Garth deduced, and perhaps in her late thirties, and once quite attractive, too. She neither spoke nor smiled, nor did she laugh as she had the first time. She simply stared intently with those wide eyes of hers, then brushed past him and hurried on her way. Garth searched Bear Paw's face for some revealing expression, but he was somber, his face unrevealing, as were the faces of the other boys. Garth made the motion of speaking and pointed at the disappearing woman. Bear Paw nodded toward the brightly painted lodge in the distance and then gestured, playing his hands out wide. "Big," he motioned. Spiraling a finger from his forehead toward the sky, "medicine." His fingers came from his mouth, and he shook his head. This woman did not speak, but, indeed, she was some kind of big medicine. Garth watched Bear Paw trace patterns into the dust, little figures reclining. Closing his eyes, the boy moaned, then there were more gestures, digging, preparing. Bear Paw slowly erased the figures and drew them again, this time standing, and Garth understood. Lost Woman was a healer, a useful person. She helped the Cheyenne get well when they were sick. Incredible, Garth thought, a crazy white woman, yet with the presence of mind to tend sick Indians, red people, who for all he knew, may very well have rubbed out her family, maybe not these Cheyenne, but Indians of some tribe not too far to the north. What a turn of fate! He stared at the tipi where Lost Woman had disappeared, wondering if he should pursue the matter, make at least one more effort to talk to her, or if he should forget it, as Dominguez had advised. Not now, one of the boys let him know. One of them was tugging on his buckskin and pointing up ahead where Garth could see a crowd forming near the lodge of the Dog soldiers, the *Hotamitanio,* as Dominguez had called it, a powerful warrior group in the tribe. He pressed on with his young charges until he made out the feathered dress and painted faces of the braves. Bear Paw proudly touched Garth on the chest, danced around in a step, and smiled broadly. This celebration was for Garth, men making preparations for the ceremony that evening, for his adoption into the tribe. The line of women and maidens standing to the side saw him coming and immediately set up a tremolo. Some were laughing, others shuffling their moccasins, raising up small clouds of dust around their decorated feet. Once again, Garth reflected on his earlier arrival in the village, how they had jeered him and spat at the hooves of his horse. He lifted his chin, stood erect. He was not an Indian, not by any stretch of the imagination, yet this greeting, however primitive, was strangely exhilarating, thoroughly rewarding. It brought a blush to his tanned face. These women loved him! He tipped his cavalry hat to the entire line, and after a gracious, sweeping bow, he stepped lively along past the confusion, picking up a few more children in his wake.

There was no doubt who the man of the moment was. Men were waiting for him at his tipi, sitting in the sunshine with Dominguez, talking and smoking. With a smile, Dominguez quickly told Garth that these braves had come to help prepare him for the first part of the initiation, a sweat bath to cleanse him and rid his body of impurities, a simple ritual that a holy man would perform. A simple ritual? To Garth, this should have been assurance enough, but before he could even pose a question, the three escorts were leading him away by the arm. He glanced back, trying to get at least one reassuring word from his wily companion, but this proved useless, for Dominguez, ever smiling, was waving goodbye with the stem of his pipe. *Adiós, mi amigo.*

The cleansing, much to Garth's relief, was nothing more than a vigil in a steamy wickiup facing the east with the medicine chief occasionally mumbling a few incoherent words, waving a long-stemmed pipe, and throwing bits of dried grass into the fire and hot rocks. For the greater part of an hour, Garth, stripped of his clothing, sat cross-legged, longing for a breath of fresh air, his burning eyes watching every move the holy man made. Shortly after the first sound of some drums outside, two men, heavily painted, entered the sweat lodge and put a loincloth around his crotch. They took him outside, and without a word, started daubing streaks of vermillion the length of his face, taking special care to lift each side of his drooping moustache. Surprisingly, this caused one of the men to chuckle, and, at the same time, enabled Garth to expel a little of his apprehension. Soon, another medicine chief came along and began shaking a hoof rattle. Leading a long line of men, he moved away, chanting, Garth directly in the middle of it all, his white skin glistening like a dew melon in the later afternoon sun. He had never felt more foolish in his whole life.

At the great council lodge, there were several hundred people on hand, and the lodge itself was opened again at the front and around the bottom so the ceremony could be witnessed by all. Inside, all of the village men were fanned out in front of three chiefs. The sound of drums and an occasional whistle were deafening to Garth, but had the noise suddenly ceased, Garth was certain everyone could have heard the beat of his own heart, for by now, he was entertaining thoughts of pain. He sighed when he finally saw Dominguez standing near the front of the open-faced lodge, and directly, the Spaniard eased up next to him and followed the medicine chief up to the front of the gathering. Presently Garth caught the silently amused look of Dominguez from the side of his eye. His whispered lowly at the scout, "I'll take this out of your pay, dammit!"

Dominguez quietly replied in a dignified way, "Ah, but you look fine. A little pale from the neck down, but think nothing of it. Yes, I think everyone thinks you look fine."

"That's a damn lie, and I smell like a smoked sausage!"

Dominguez smiled and pressed a finger to his lips. Moments later, they were standing before three men, all chiefs, Little Wolf, Morning Star, and a third man who Dominguez, in a hushed voice, identified as Sleeping Rabbit. Behind these chiefs, seated in three rows, were the remaining chiefs and high-ranking braves. After a few ceremonial words from the medicine chief, a pipe was passed and smoked among the leaders, then presented to Garth, who took several puffs before handing it back to the lead chief. At this point, Little Wolf turned and began talking, slowly at first, then with building emphasis and dramatic gestures. Garth could hear the crier out in front repeating everything Little Wolf was saying. And as Dominguez was whispering in translation, Garth himself began to get a hint of what was being said. Obviously, Little Wolf was telling Bear Paw's version of the incident on Whitetail Creek, telling it with great animation, often reaching over and placing his hand on Garth's shoulder, indicating that he was now speaking the commanding words of Gray Hat. Mumbles of approval frequently rose up from the gathering inside, followed by grunts of anger when Little Wolf took up the words of Will Scruggs and Charlie Mullen. The medicine chief came back another time and spoke, making various signs and motions. Finally, taking Garth's right hand, he turned it palm up, cut a small gash at the base of the thumb upward across to the forefinger, and Garth, watching the blood trickle down to his wrist, winced and ground his teeth but uttered not a sound. Likewise, Little Wolf's right palm was sliced, and the medicine chief took the bleeding hands of the two men, clasped them together, and let their blood intermingle. There were quickening drums, shouts from the crowd, and the piercing sound of eagle-bone whistles, smiles, too, from all the chiefs, hands on shoulders, nods of approval. The end came swiftly and dramatically, with Dominguez whispering in Garth's ear, "We are very fortunate, my brother. The men who brought us here thought we were the ones who tried to hang the boy! Had Bear Paw been away from the village, we would be dead by now."

Garth, feeling weak in the knees, muttered, "Lord a'mighty."

Little Wolf was speaking again, stringing beads around Garth's neck, next a leather and beaded band around his head, a headpiece decorated with a single black-and-white feather.

"An eagle feather, Señor Garth," explained Dominguez, "not the plumage of a crow."

Little Wolf placed both his hands on Garth's shoulders and spoke again, addressing himself to everyone in the lodge. He talked proudly.

"And you have a new name," Dominguez added with his perpetual grin. "He says from now on, the Cheyenne will know you by these beads, the signs on the leather, Man Who Hides His Gun, he says. Gun Hider, I think. He says you are a warrior of great cunning, yes, from hiding your pistol under your poncho that day." Dominguez nudged Garth. "Now, you show him you're pleased. Place your hands on his shoulders, and don't forget to smile."

Tyson Bell Garth, alias Gun Hider, did as he was told. Outside, many drums began beating, and, once again, the women were in tremolo. The celebration was beginning, and Gun Hider, with nothing more than a three-inch cut in his hand, was free of pain.

It turned out to be a night of revelry for the two white men, and the feast was astonishing, generous portions of roasted buffalo and elk meat, toasted cakes and great bowls of broth. Soon, everyone was eating, and those not eating, were dancing; first, women alone, in long lines, then circles; then, the men; and finally, both sexes together, singing and dancing, making symbolic gestures, none of which Garth could understand, but the primitive vitality of it all was fascinating, and several times, he found himself unconsciously moving his feet, clapping his hands in unison with the beat of the drums. Once, during the festivities, he was surprised to notice Lost Woman in a file of stomping women, a faint smile playing across her plain features. Dominguez saw her, too, and commented aside to Garth. "Ah, *amigo,* like I told you, this is a strange land for us. These people like to be happy, to sing and dance, celebrate any occasion, eh, the gift of life, the gift of the land, the blessings of the Great Mystery. There you see a woman who is now all Indian. She lives here, and she will die here. She doesn't even remember she was once white. Maybe this is best, eh?"

"But, why?" Garth asked, watching the white woman who seemed to be thoroughly enjoying herself, twisting, turning, throwing her head back in wild abandon. "The humanity of it! What could have happened to her?"

"Does it matter, now?" Dominguez shrugged and took a puff on his pipe. "*Así se va.* Before we leave this great land again, you'll know these people better. Humanity, you say? I tell you, Garth, for you and me, sometimes I think it's best we don't have a country, you the rebel, and Domino, the greaser. You see, then we don't have anything to be ashamed of, eh?"

Later, under the bright early autumn moon, Garth washed away his ceremony paint in the cold waters of the Little Big Horn and nursed the cut on his palm. It had been a long night for the man they now called Gun Hider, but surprisingly, a good one, much less of a ritualistic ordeal than he had anticipated. He had concluded his own amenities by paying his respects to the chiefs involved, gifting them with tobacco and small clay pipes that he had carefully buried in his packs down at Fort Laramie. And, luckily, he found a special gift for his chief sponsor, Little Wolf—the revolver he had confiscated from Will Scruggs that rainy afternoon along the North Platte River. His own two Cheyenne gifts were impressively unique. Slipping back into his long underwear, Garth decided he would keep the ceremonial beads handy, maybe even wear them over his buckskin shirt. The eagle feather and beaded headband had already been fitted onto his gray hat earlier that night, much to the delight and admiration of young Bear Paw, his adopted son. Possession of a new feather, and one of such high esteem and significance, brought a reflective smile to his face. Once again, a feathered rogue, yet perhaps this time not so humorously controversial. Pausing at the river's edge, he stared up at the purple sky, thinking about another time, another feather, old friends, old enemies, most of them buried under the black ashes of what had been Fort Kearny, memories of torn allegiances, forlorn causes. And, now, fatefully ironic, he had just taken a blessing and a brotherly pledge from the very people who had helped destroy all of that old comraderie. Refreshed in body but weary in mind, he took one last look at the star-spangled sky, and at a trot, started back for his tipi. He passed the remains of the bonfires where a few old women were now cleaning up, where in the shadows the big dogs were vying for rib bones and other scraps. A few women paused to nod and giggle as he jogged by waving his hand. The dogs, thankfully, chose to ignore him.

Man Who Hides His Gun and John Dominguez extended their stay in Morning Star's village two more days, which the Spaniard believed was the appropriate length of time for such an honored visit, for after all, since Gun Hider was now a member of the tribe, by custom, he was obliged to accept all of the friendly hospitality the Cheyenne offered. Garth willingly agreed. In fact, since he was so happy to be alive, he allowed that even a visit of three or four days would not have been out of the question. While Dominguez idled and told big stories, Garth spent some of his own time hunting antelope with Bear Paw and a few braves, and contesting other Cheyenne in riding games.

So, shortly after the middle of September, T. B. Garth, the Gun Hider, had fulfilled his obligations with his brothers and once again prepared to take up the quest for Bird Rutledge and her mother. Little Wolf appointed two of his tribesmen, Big Dog and Swift Runner, to go along with Garth and Dominguez and help them locate the Brule village somewhere to the northwest. Neither of these young braves had participated in the fighting around Fort Kearny, but they both had distinguished themselves in the Hayfield battle near Fort Smith. Garth passed a few friendly signs with Bear Paw at the departure, and in a brotherly gesture, placed his hands on the shoulders of Little Wolf, telling him that one day, God willing, their paths could cross again. In turn, the chief spoke a few words to John Dominguez and nodded toward Garth. The Spaniard, translating, said, "Your brother here says he has asked *Heammawhio,* the Wise One Above, to help you find the Bird Woman. He also says he has a warm place in his heart for you because, through his son, you gave honor to him."

Dominguez, for once, didn't have to remind T. B. Garth to smile. Waving, the riders turned toward the Little Big Horn River, the shouts and shrill cries of the women resounding behind them, and when a rejuvenated Garth looked back with a final salute, he saw Lost Woman, laughing and holding her hand high in the air.

Chapter Eighteen

"What do you make of it?" Dominguez said, folding away his binoculars. "The Indians say it's a place of the dead, a burial grounds. They don't go up there, too many *mistai* around."

Glassing the grove of trees, Garth finally said, "Looks like the ribs of an old covered wagon. That's about all I can make out from here. Ask the boys what a wagon is doing way up there off the trail. Rather peculiar, I'll allow."

Pointing downriver, the Cheyenne called Swift Runner, was already talking to Dominguez. The other young guide called Big Dog was sitting silently on his pony, his dark eyes apprehensively on the far-off trees. After a moment, Dominguez turned back to Garth. "My friend, I think this explains some of it." Nodding toward the banks of the Little Big Horn, he said, "Swift Runner says not too far away from here is the place where the Cheyenne women found the crazy one, Lost Woman. We're about thirty miles from the village, maybe another day's ride down to the Big Horn. He says up there in those trees is probably where Lost Woman came from, where her people camped, maybe to hide."

Staring back at the clump of trees, Garth said, "She probably wandered away, ended up down here, and was floundering around in the river when the women found her." He shook his head, adding, "But this doesn't explain

all of it, John. What's the reason . . . ? Why was she all
alone? Her family? Her people?"

"I'm afraid the answer is up there on that little hill,"
Dominguez answered. "For some reason, the place was
abandoned, eh?"

"Sickness," Garth said. "If they were attacked by Indians, it seems unreasonable she alone would have survived." He stared at the lone wagon again. "I want to
go up, have a look," he finally said.

Dominguez said a few words to the two Cheyenne.
They frowned and pointed down the river. They would
go find a place to camp for the night. They had no desire to accompany Gun Hider and Domino up to a
place of spirits.

It took the men only several minutes to reach the
site, a site well chosen for a camp. Well protected in
the cottonwoods, it afforded a view in all four directions. The wagon was badly weathered, the canvas top
in shreds and rotted. Remnants of a charred fire pit
stood in front of it. Garth walked around the wagon
and stopped abruptly. In front of him were four rock-
covered mounds, graves.

In a low voice, he said, "John, come over here. You
were right. Here's some of the answer."

"*Sí, amigo,*" Dominguez said. He crossed himself,
bent low, and inspected the rocks.

"What do you think?"

The scout stood, backed off, and leaned up against
the trunk of a cottonwood. It was a quiet place, not
even the sound of a bird could be heard. Patches of
maturing grama nodded in the faint breeze, but the
turning leaves of the cottonwoods barely fluttered.
Dominguez, his brow thoughtfully raised pulled one of
the long stems and began munching on it. Sorting out
the evidence in his mind, he stared first at the graves,
then at the nearby wagon. The burial mounds were
without markers, but a second inspection told him part
of the story—one of the graves was larger, the rocks

well arranged, the slabs of stone, ponderous and heavy, while the other three graves were much smaller and varied in size. On these, the rocks seemed to be randomly placed, and most of them were round and smooth. Weeds, dead and withered between the stones, were spreading out like dried tentacles in all directions.

The desolation overwhelmed Garth. He said in a quiet voice, "John, this is one of the loneliest spots I've ever seen in my whole life. What the hell could have happened here?"

"This, *amigo,* must have been God's will," he answered fatefully. "It's not the work of Indians, this I can tell you." He went up to one of the wagons and started explaining how he read the sign. He said he could only believe one thing—smallpox struck the family, and one by one, they died, the father, probably first, children next; ultimately, it struck the mother, but she managed to survive. These pilgrims came to this site, he believed, because originally they were part of one of the early wagon trains on the northern trail, and they were shunned and forced to leave when the pox broke out. They wandered and ended up sick on the Little Big Horn, camped up away from the river for security. The father's grave had been a family effort, the large, heavy rocks indicating that everyone had participated, but the smaller, rounded stones, came from the river bottom down below, most likely brought up by Lost Woman, the mother.

Pointing to the small graves, Dominguez said, "She sees them go, one at a time, eh? She digs out a little grave, covers it with these little rocks, yes, and pretty soon, she is left alone, crazy in the head, sick, but not sick enough to die." He suddenly crossed himself. "*Sangre de Christo, mi familia,* rubbed out!"

"So, you noticed those pox marks on her face, too."

"Yes, and maybe that's another reason our two friends don't come up here, eh? Bad medicine, the white man's bad medicine."

They began rummaging through several of the rotting boxes, found nothing of consequence, only remnants of what had been, shredded clothing and linen, and a few rusted tools. In the second wagon, Garth uncovered a small metal box. Forcing open its lid, he discovered a Bible and several letters. He opened the cover of the Bible and read the family name. Schmidt. He had been right about Lost Woman, indeed, she was German. "I wonder," he said, "if she should have this . . . ? Have the boys take it back with them." He handed the aged book to Dominguez.

John Dominguez thumbed its fragile pages once and replied, *"¿Por que?"*

"Faith," queried Garth. "Peace of mind? Something spiritual?"

With a disturbed look, Dominguez returned the Bible. "No, this is not for me to decide. Peace of mind, you say? Maybe something like this will cause her to remember all she has forgotten. When they found this woman, she had no one. At least, with Morning Star's people, she has someone, and maybe, my friend, this isn't bad. In our eyes, we think this is a poor life for Lost Woman. Who knows, eh? I think sometimes what a hopeless thing it would be if the spiritual life could only be lived under ideal conditions."

Silent for a moment, Garth finally nodded, but he took the letters and slipped them inside his buckskin shirt. "Relatives, perhaps," he explained, looking sadly at Dominguez. However, he placed the Bible back in the box and gently closed the lid. "One of these days when I get back home, I'll look into these letters, see what turns up."

"Bueno." Dominguez smiled. "You feel better, now?"

Garth, sick at heart, shook his head. "No, not really." He stared down at the graves. "No, not at all, but I suppose you're right about their mother. The Cheyenne will take care of her."

"Or, maybe the other way around, eh? Maybe this is what God left her, charity." He crossed himself again, remounted, and followed his partner back down the hill. Neither of them looked back at the lonely site.

The next morning, after a meager breakfast of hard biscuits, molasses, bacon, and coffee, the four men crossed a few small foothills on the east side of the Big Horn Valley. Swift Runner, who had been this way many times with Cheyenne war parties, said he knew where the Brule village would most likely be, not too far from where many buffalo had been seen earlier in the month. And his word was true, for by late in the day, after coming to the top of a long, rolling ridge, he stopped and pointed to faraway smoke. Dominguez and Garth quickly dismounted and glassed the area. The distant smoke they saw was heavy, but through the filtering haze, they made out a few grazing ponies and the faint outlines of lodges. Swift Runner said a few words to Dominguez, who then told Garth that this was Red Leaf's big hunting camp. Another village, led by Spotted Tail, was farther up the river near where Fort Smith had once stood. In another two weeks, the Sioux would be gone, moving south to the Tongue and Powder River country to prepare for winter.

"Well, my friend," Dominguez said, "this is what we've been looking for these many days. We've come a long way together, and who knows, maybe this is only the beginning of the trail. Then, again, maybe we'll get lucky. We cross our fingers, eh, hope for the best."

Garth, making a feeble attempt at lightheartedness, responded with a gallant smile, realizing that John Dominguez's sympathetic concern was genuine, that the wily scout all along had been trying to prepare him for the haunting possibility of shattering disappointment, that their long search might prove fruitless. Yes, he did agree with Dominguez—"hope for the best."

With a small, fearful lump in his throat, Garth called out gamely, "I assume our boys here will get us safely past the women and dogs this time?"

Remounting, Dominguez laughed and shouted, *"Adelante, muchachos!"* With a wave of his hat, he kicked his horse into a trot toward the village. "Yi, yi, yi, yi," he began screaming. Both Swift Runner and Big Dog broke into wide grins when the Spaniard finally reined up at the Sioux camp perimeter. Far out in front of them, coming from all directions, was a scattering of women, children, and dogs. Garth straightened his hat and stared directly ahead, this time determined not to be intimidated by any adverse, welcoming furor. But the heckling and jeering was not forthcoming, and the greeting oddly minimal, for only a few old men were joining the gathering, and of the people present, most were simply staring up in curiosity, not outrage. Curious himself, Garth shouted, "Where is everyone? The place looks half deserted."

Dominguez, waving and smiling as usual, pointed toward some trees. "Making meat," he yelled. And Garth saw large piles of buffalo hides, some stretched for drying, others in bundles. Women with fleshing knives in their hands were standing near, shielding their eyes, staring at the new arrivals. Smoke was everywhere, and slabs of meat were being cured on top of the large racks of willow. "Yes," Dominguez went on, "most of the men are out hunting the curly cow. I think tonight we'll see plenty of people here, and some more celebration, too, if the hunting is good."

Big Dog was shouting and making signs at a man standing off to the side, and after this brief exchange the Cheyenne scout motioned to Dominguez, directing him to a nearby red-and-white lodge. In front were two blanket-covered men, one with a feathered lance propped alongside him. Obviously, he had been out hunting, for the front of his leggings were stained with dried blood. His companion, smaller in stature but impressive with an outthrust jaw and a heavily beaded jacket, stood like a statue, motionless, his arms folded, his red blanket dropping away from his shoulders. Neither man spoke until Dominguez raised his hand in greeting and introduced himself and Garth. The two Cheyenne had already leaped from their ponies and were off to the side, talking to several other older men who had joined the small group. After a brief exchange with the two solemn men in front of the tipi, Dominguez turned and told Garth to dismount and get out some of his tobacco. The man with the crooked medicine stick, he said, was none other than Red Leaf himself. His statuesque companion was Short Bull, another chief. Since Red Leaf had welcomed them, it was now proper to smoke and talk. Wasting no time, Garth, anxious for information, quickly dug out tobacco and two of the small clay pipes. Amenities first, but he wanted to get directly to the point—where was his woman and her mother?

Garth got his answer in short order, even before everyone was seated on the robes in front of the lodge. Two of the men quietly talking with Swift Runner and Big Dog at the side were frowning and shaking their heads negatively, and it was obvious to him the women were not in Red Leaf's village. Dominguez, however, went right on with his probe, the chiefs listening, occasionally staring across at Garth, who sat glumly nearby, his legs crossed and his feathered hat in front of him. The hat itself was a curiosity piece, nothing new in Garth's life, but Dominguez had to explain to the Sioux why his friend was wearing an eagle feather and carrying a Cheyenne charm around his neck. Garth looked from face to face as the conversation continued, and, finally, after a lengthy exchange between Short Bull and Dominguez, the scout leaned across and explained. "These fellows remember two Cree women who were at the big council a year ago last summer over in the Black Hills, but that's all. This man, Short

Bull, says there's a man from one of those villages hunting with them, now. Maybe he knows something, eh? They say when he comes in tonight, we can talk with him." One of the Sioux spoke again and pointed across the grounds. After a moment, Dominguez turned to Garth again. "The young woman of this hunter is here if you want to see her. This fellow says she will know about the women." Garth nodded affirmatively but impassively, for some of the hope he had entertained was, by now, slowly diminishing. A young boy listening to the proceedings was dispatched to find the woman.

And shortly, she came back with the messenger and spoke with an attentive Dominguez. Her name was Yellow Bird. A Hunkpapa, she had recently married a young man from one of the wandering Brule Sioux bands of Spotted Tail, the chief who had a camp somewhere farther south on the main river. Although she had never seen the two Cree women, her husband, Long Mane, had spoken of them many times because they were members of his family at one time. Long Mane, she said, was once a brother-in-law to Woman Called Bird. Dominguez asked her, "Do you know where these Cree women are now?"

Yellow Bird shook her head. She pointed north. "No one knows where they are. My man says they disappeared many moons ago, during the Moon of the Drying Grass. They went toward the Land of the Big River Who Scorns All Other Rivers, Cree country. I know nothing more."

John Dominguez thanked her, and with a curious stare back over her shoulder at Garth, she left. Rubbing his chin thoughtfully, Dominguez made a helpless gesture, saying, "The little *pájaro* and her mother left the Brule a year ago, maybe headed for the Yellowstone or Missouri River. This means they're probably north of us somewhere in the land of the Cree, Meena's people." He tapped out his pipe and studied Garth's worried face. "That's wilderness, my friend, the land of the *kissineyooway'o,* the Queen Mother's Land. A bad time for us to be riding so far, maybe getting caught by winter before we get home."

Crestfallen, Garth stared away, his eyes glazing. "We've come so far, John. What's the plan? Where do we go from here?"

"Talk to this girl's husband," the Spaniard suggested. "He was part of Bird's family."

Garth's shoulders sagged, and he looked away bewildered. Bird was free, good enough, but he had come a year too late. The trail was so cold, the land so remote. He felt numb all over. But, why, he wondered, in all this time had not some word come down the big river, the Missouri? Bird was a literate, intelligent woman, had friends back at Fort Laramie. Unable to accept fate, Garth said, "It doesn't make sense. It's not like Bird, not the woman I know."

"Ah, my friend, you mean the woman you knew."

"Look here, doesn't it seem strange to you no one down below here has heard anything about the woman? There are posts all along the rivers, now. Something should fit here, but it doesn't."

"Yes, a puzzle," returned Dominguez. He was silent for a moment, trying to find a ray of hope, something to enlighten his confused friend. Finally: "Tonight, we'll meet this boy, Long Mane. Yes, and maybe tomorrow we'll find a new idea of our own, another place to visit." Turning back to the two chiefs, he said a few polite words. In turn, Red Leaf had another boy take them to a lodge where they could spend the night.

But the proposed meeting with the young hunter Long Mane never materialized. The hunting party did return that same evening, two dozen ponies and travois loaded with fresh meat. And there was a short, impromptu celebration and feast, during which Garth kept his eye out for Yellow Bird in hopes of meeting her husband. He saw neither one of them until he and

Dominguez returned to their tipi, where the two Cheyenne had built a small fire, and sitting to the side of the young braves was Yellow Bird. But she was alone. John Dominguez politely addressed her. However, the young woman's eyes mysteriously were on Garth, and she kept them fixed on him even though she was talking to Dominguez all the while. Soon, Dominguez began a translation. "She says she is sorry for you, now that she knows about you and the Cree woman, but her man doesn't want to come here because you must be a ghost, eh, maybe bad medicine for his family."

Garth, his eyes rolling to the heavens, grimaced and sputtered back, "Oh, law, John, what kind of nonsense is this? Do I look like some kind of a spook?" He glanced over at Yellow Bird. "Ask her . . ."

Dominguez interrupted, holding up his hand. Yellow Bird was speaking again. The Spaniard's eyes suddenly lit up and he emitted a long sigh of understanding. "Ah, but you see, a man in Long Mane's village killed you. You were called *Kangi Wiyaka,* she says. That's Crow Feather. That's what these Brule people call you. Hey, you have many names!"

"Killed me!" Displaying his scar, Garth smiled, "You tell her that the lying scoundrel never killed me, you hear? Just tell her he came damn close, that's all."

Addressing Yellow Bird again, Dominguez pointed to the scar on Garth's head. Her reply took some time, and as soon as she had finished, she backed away into the shadows, her eyes still on the man the Brule called *Kangi Wiyaka.* Exasperated, Garth said, "Well, I assume she believes the same nonsense, that I'm nothing but some kind of white bogeyman, is that it? Dammit, is everyone crazy around here?"

"No, no," implored Dominguez. "Listen, to these people this isn't so crazy. You see, this Long Mane has a big storm in his head tonight. He thinks you have returned from the land beyond, that maybe Owl Maker, a witch, has sent you back, and because you're a great warrior, she touched you with the spirit of a white wolf. Yes, you went away with a crow feather, and now you come back with an eagle feather, big medicine, a sign of battle."

"Good Lord!" exclaimed Garth. "I can't believe what I'm hearing." He looked around to make a few signs of his own to Yellow Bird but she had disappeared into the night.

"Yes, this is true," Dominguez continued. "This brave, Long Mane, says he heard the cry of a wolf for three nights, and when you came here, he knew what the sign meant. You see, some of these people believe when the wolf sings at night, he's calling for his lost brothers."

"And now this boy is hiding in his tipi with a headache!"

"My friend, I don't think you understand what has happened, here," Dominguez said somberly. "If these people think you're a wolf spirit, that this Sioux brave couped you, so does your woman, eh? To her, you're a dead man. For two years, you have only existed in her mind. Bird thinks you're dead."

Garth suddenly reeled inside. Kneeling beside the fire, he clasped the sides of his head and stared into the tiny flames. It was as though a Yankee ball had ripped a hole through his brain. He was beyond thinking anymore.

Chapter Nineteen

Counting the days, even the time he considered squandered in Morning Star's village while they were being honored, Garth figured it was now near the end of September, perhaps the twenty-fifth or twenty-sixth day. The two men had decided that since they had exhausted their search in the Big Horns, they might as well scout around the Yellowstone Valley. Once there, they planned to follow the river back to its confluence with the Powder, where they could ride south and eventually get back to Fort Laramie sometime in mid-October during Indian summer. John Dominguez, attempting to relieve Garth's depression, told him that in all probability someone along the Yellowstone would know of the women's whereabouts, since the Sioux woman, Yellow Bird, had said their direction was north. He pointed out that if Bird and Meena escaped this way, their most likely first signs of civilization would be some trading post along the Yellowstone or Missouri rivers. With a newly found optimism, the Spaniard believed that someone at one of these isolated outposts was more than likely to have some conclusive news for them. His prediction was right, for about mid-afternoon they rode down into the weathered stockade of an ancient trapping post on the Yellowstone called Manuel's Fort.

Dominguez knew the outpost and its people, had last visited it five years back when most of the area hostilities directed at interlopers came from Blackfeet and

Absaroke, or Crow. Several new forts to the north, plus government compensation, had pacified a few of the Blackfeet. There were exceptions. John Bozeman, the so-called trailblazer of the short route through the Big Horns had been killed several years past by angry Blackfeet. But as for the Crow, they weren't too alarmed anymore since people crossing their traditional lands at this time were travelers, not settlers, and they had no quarrelsome forts in their vicinity, primarily because of a contentious breed chief by the name of Man Called Tree who had prohibited them, and church missions, too.

John Goodhart, who lived in the biggest of two cabins at the post, heartily greeted Garth and Dominguez, and in short time they were all seated around the table drinking coffee. At this point, the Goodharts were unaware of Garth's proper name, because when the two men arrived at the gate, Dominguez jokingly introduced him simply as Gun Hider, a name that suited his appearance, his regalia of feathered hat, beaded necklace, and buckskins, a proper name for a man who had just brought them unscathed through a hostile land. But when he revealed that they were searching for a woman called Bird Rutledge and her mother, Meena, a startling silence fell over the room. John Dominguez said that this man with him, Tyson Garth, had returned all the way from Mississippi to try and find these missing women.

Molly Goodhart's sharp and alarming outcry broke the quiet. "But everyone thinks you are dead! Your woman, Mr. Garth, she said you were killed by Lakota!" Suddenly, everyone in the room was aghast, including T. B. Garth, who felt the cup in his hand trembling. Yet, this was certainly no new disclosure to him; Indians already had fled from the sight of him, a ghost from the past, the spirit returned, a wolf, no less; but Molly's revelation, the mention of "his woman," brought him upright in the chair, his nerves jangling like a bell-mare mule. "You've seen her? You've seen Bird and her mother?"

"Why, yes, right here!" Molly exclaimed. "Many nights Bird sat right there in that very chair! Yes, she and her child, Meena over there, all of us in here together. Good heavens, we were a family!"

Garth felt weak all over. "Lord, Lord!" he wheezed, then with a curious look at Molly Goodhart, he asked, "Child? What child?"

John Goodhart laughed loudly, and slapped Garth on the shoulder. Molly, hands cupped to her mouth, was suddenly rocking back and forth in joy and merriment. And young James started laughing, too. Goodhart said, "Yes, a baby, your son. You're a father, Mr. Garth, but I reckon there's no way you would know this, now, is there?"

"No," Dominguez intervened, smiling, "not when he's supposed to be six feet under." Giving Garth a friendly pat, Dominguez said, "My friend, you have a son. I must congratulate you."

"His name is Tyson," chimed in Molly, "just like your own." She clasped her hands together in thanksgiving, tears in her eyes. "And to know his father is alive, oh, my gracious, the Great Spirit has blessed us!"

Visibly shaken, Garth shot Dominguez a quick glance, then stared back at John Goodhart questioningly. "How ... how long have they been gone?"

Goodhart held up his hands and everyone looked at him expectantly. A long story, he said, and he told Garth and Dominguez to sit back and enjoy their coffee because the tale he was about to tell was rather incredible. And as Molly began refilling the mugs, her husband started recalling how it all had come about; the bedraggled appearance of the women at the gate late in the summer a year ago, arriving with only a few meager possessions; the baby, bundled in a canvas sling; and a young wolf following along at their heels.

Goodhart went on, relating some of the women's experiences, how they had survived along the trail, and he told of their incident with the Sioux braves on the Tongue River. But it so happened, Goodhart related, that Bird and her mother were not as destitute as they appeared, that they had a considerable sum of money and insisted on helping pay for the winter supplies, and had even bought gifts for everyone. Yes, the women's presence turned out to be a blessing instead of a burden.

Molly interrupted, saying it was one of the best winters they had ever had at the post. Even the Absaroke chief, Ben Tree, upon hearing about Bird Rutledge and her spirit wolf, had come over from his camp on the Clarks Fork to visit several times. Once, they had talked long into the night, especially about Gabe Bridger, their mutual friend, and Man Called Tree had also mentioned Dominguez as a friend of his father.

A remarkable young woman, Bird Rutledge, opined John Goodhart, to be so capable, so compassionate, to understand so much for so few years in life. When spring came, he said that Bird became restless. The women had weaned little Ty, for this 'is what they called the boy, and then her wolf started roaming, sometimes disappearing for two and three days at a stretch. Then one day the wolf left for good. Goodhart stopped talking and stared sadly at his coffee mug—that was the first time anyone had seen Bird cry, he said. Goodhart's eyes suddenly brightened, and he told how the wolf had reappeared about the first of September, sitting by itself on a grassy knoll far above the post. And as he and James silently watched, another wolf, smaller and much lighter in color, came down and joined Bird's big friend. In a series of leaping, joyous turns, they finally disappeared back over the hill. This, Goodhart said, would have pleased Bird, to know her wolf had found a lady friend, and he believed this was the sole purpose of the wolf's return visit, to show off his mate. Finally, he said, Bird and Meena left for the Clarks Fork early in June, where they were going to buy a herd of horses from the Crow. Man Called Tree, the Crow chief, had told Bird she could make good money over in the Gallatin Valley selling and trading horses to people traveling back and forth between the gold fields, especially good ponies gentled to pack and ride. And she knew how to handle horses. If the truth were known, Goodhart said, Chief Tree probably sold her the ponies for a pittance, since, it was told, that he himself owned a herd of over a hundred. So that was it, sighed John Goodhart, that was the last they had seen of Bird and Meena. Molly, wiping at her eyes with her apron, got up and went to the stove. She said she would cook up a little something for the men's supper.

When Garth, heartened by these new developments, asked Dominguez how far it was to the Gallatin Valley, his friend only shrugged. It had been so long since he had traveled that way he could only guess, but Goodhart spoke up, telling him that with a wagon, the trip usually took nine or ten days. On a good horse, a man could trim it to six or seven days. The knowledge that Bird and her mother planned on herding ponies that distance gave Garth another troubled moment, until Goodhart reasoned it was unlikely the women had ridden alone. Bird Rutledge was admired too much by the Crow, and in all probability, a number of Indians had helped her, riding at least as far as the pass leading into the valley. Down below the pass in Bozeman City and around Fort Ellis, was where the "crazies" lived, and the Crow seldom ventured this far, anymore. They disliked the bad smell and the way the "crazies" stared at them. Dominguez laughed and commented that this probably was some of Ben Tree's influence on the tribe, his dislike of too much civilization.

Garth, contemplating, trying to package this startling new turn of events, finally asked, "About those horses,

did she give you any indication what she planned to do
after she sold them? You know, what plans she had,
anything like that?"

Goodhart thought for a moment. "No, nothing for
certain, but I sort of had the idea she was going to look
the country over a spell, and if it suited her, she was
going to put her roots down; make a fresh start. Lots of
open range over that way, good grass, plenty of water."

Molly, listening from the kitchen, called out, "She
said if they did not like that place, she was going to get
on one of those big boats and go back to Fort Laramie.
That's what she said to me. If those people over there
were no-accounts, they were going right back home to
their friends."

"Fort Benton," interjected Dominguez. "They would
ride up to Fort Benton, that's where she means. They
can catch a steamer up there and go on down the Missouri, get off at Omaha, and backtrack to Laramie,
eh?"

"Yes," Molly said. "Bird says they have plenty of
friends at that place, know the people in the big store,
too."

The "big store," Craig's store? Garth asked himself.
He sighed, thinking about poor Elbert. But, of course,
Bird would know nothing about this unfortunate matter, that Elbert had gone off chasing after her, only to
be swallowed up himself somewhere in Indian country,
that the old man, heartbroken, had sold out and moved
back to civilization.

John Dominguez set his mug aside and looked
knowingly across the table. He had come to a quick
but plausible conclusion. "Look, if they went down the
river, it would only be when the boats are able to go,
when the water is high enough up here to ride over the
sandbars, eh? And you see, if they left this summer,
well, Omaha to Laramie is not that far . . ."

"And," Garth interjected, picking up on the scout's
point, "I rode through there a month ago. Hell, I spent

the night there. Someone would have known about those women being back after two years in the hills, even that clerk at the store. Why, he's the bird who told me about Elbert running off."

"So, maybe, just maybe," continued Dominguez, "they are still up here. Ah, and if this is so, we have only one choice, eh? We go up the trail and take one last look, eh?"

"Yes suh," agreed Garth with a clap of his hands. "And the sooner the better."

"Well, if it's decided," put in John Goodhart, "but you're certainly welcome to stay around a few days and get some rest. Oh, I know your feelings, I sure do, to get on with it, and I have a feeling myself, yes, I think you're going to get some good news over there. I just hope you catch up with them before they hit the trail again. When Bird sets her mind to something, she's like a stubborn mule. She gets what she's after." He laughed heartily, saying, "Well, she doesn't look like a mule, but she sure works like one." He suddenly dug into a pocket, pulling out a gold watch, dangling it from its fob. "Look at this, what she gave me," he said proudly. "After all the work she put in around this place, I should have been giving her something. No, I didn't, and she ups and gives me this the day she left."

Admiringly, Garth said, "By jingo, that's a right pretty watch, all right, yes suh, it is. Law, law, I wonder where she picked it up?"

Goodhart stuffed the watch back in his pocket. "Never said, and I didn't ask," he replied. "Wouldn't have been too mannerly on my part, but I reckon, maybe, it must have come from the same place she got that new Henry repeater, off one of the bucks they killed on the Tongue."

After a good night's rest in the second cabin and a hearty breakfast of sourdough pancakes and bacon, Garth and Dominguez were away early the next day,

headed up the Yellowstone Trail toward the faraway
Gallatin Valley, a trip the Spaniard figured would take
the better part of a week. The first three days, including one of fog and light rain, proved uneventful, almost to the point of monotony. They were riding
upstream in comparative isolation, usually a mile or so
away from the wide river, along the barren, grassy flat-
lands where occasionally they saw a few buffalo in the
distance. Though in no great need of meat, Dominguez
did shoot one antelope and dressed it out for future use
farther up the trail. It wasn't until the fourth day of
their journey, near the Stillwater River, when they first
encountered people and they were quick to ascertain
these were Indians. A small group was approaching
from the west, the riders slowly walking their ponies
five abreast. Dominguez, edging up nervously in his
saddle, told Garth to put his Cheyenne necklace inside
his shirt out of sight because he believed the Indians
must be either Crow or Gros Ventre, neither of which
tribe had much use for Cheyenne. As it turned out, the
men were Crow, heading back to their village near the
Clarks Fork. Dominguez cordially greeted them and
passed sign for a few minutes while Garth sat nearby
closely watching to see if their serious faces would
eventually brighten. Ultimately, the Indians did begin
to smile and nod, sharing their glances between
Dominguez's swift-moving hands and Garth, whose
own smile of relief was clearly visible under his moustache. Finally, the Spaniard told Garth that these men
knew all about the Bird Woman. Indeed, she and some
other Crow had gone through here about four months
ago with a band of horses. One of the braves was
called Little Bear Man and he knew Bird personally,
and said she owned a spirit wolf who could see
through mountains. "I think your *pájaro* impressed
them," Dominguez said, dismounting. He looked up at
Garth and smiled. "These fellows are curious about
you, eh?"

Garth grimanced. Well, this was nothing new; every Indian he had met thus far seemed curious about him for one reason or another. He glanced around at the five Crow. They were all smiling, not broadly, but their faces reflected no animosity, and this for a change was much less unnerving to him. "Well, at least they don't think I'm a ghost, John. What's on their minds?"

"They just want to know why you're chasing a woman . . . why you have come so far just for a woman?"

"And I suppose you told them one of your damned cock-and-bull stories," Garth replied sarcastically. He watched Dominguez go back to the packs. "So, what did you tell them this time?"

"I told them a coyote pissed on your tipi, a bad sign, eh? Yes, and that the Bird Woman ran away, and a Sioux chief got her. She ran away from him, too, and now you're plenty mad. That's the truth, more or less, eh?"

"A damn sight less, I'd say."

Dominguez came back and hoisted up a quarter of the antelope to one of the Crow as a gift. The Indian called Little Bear Man nodded and placed the meat in front of his saddle. Making another series of signs, he pointed questioningly at Garth. Dominguez said, "He says your woman once gave him a jar of honey, and he asks one more thing. Why are you wearing that eagle feather? You want to answer this time, or shall I tell him another bullshitter?"

"Oh, law," muttered Garth, shifting uneasily in his saddle. Finally: "Just tell him I made coup on a Sioux brave, whacked him alongside of the head, and stole his feather."

With an incredulous stare, and then in mock alarm, Dominguez said, "But, it was a crow feather that time! And it happened the other way around. The Sioux made coup on you!" Shaking his head, he pleaded,

"Are you asking me to tell a lie, such a big one like this?" He crossed himself and remounted.

"Tell him, dammit!" was the sharp reply. "Our horses are already ankle deep in your shit."

Shrugging, Dominguez made sign. The Indians were all nodding, and finally Little Bear Man emitted a long "ah," and held up an open palm to Garth. With his chin thrust forward, Garth readily returned the acknowledgement and gave the Crow brave a crisp salute.

"Mother of Mary!" Dominguez softly declared, moving his pony ahead. "And you call me a liar!"

One day later, the two men spread out a small map that Goodhart had drawn for them, and carefully traced the distance they had ridden. Placing a gnarled finger on a spot where a small river came down from the south, Dominguez said that he believed this was their present location, for only a few marks farther on the map, the Yellowstone River made a large bend away from the trail, turning south toward its headwaters in the big mountains, those mountains known to the Indians as the Backbone of the World. By this place on the map, Dominguez reasoned they were only two days from the Gallatin Valley. Both men were in good spirits, their progress excellent, without incident, and, unlike the Big Horns, running into hostiles here had ceased to be a worry. Dominguez folded the map and placed it back in his saddlebag. Fording the small river, they rode down through a few brushy draws to a long piece of benchland lined with giant cottonwood trees. When they were about halfway down the bench, Garth noticed his partner taking quick glances to his left up toward the wooded hillside. Barely turning, Garth made a brief scan of his own. Then, he heard Dominguez's casual voice.

"Did you see something, my friend?" Unconcerned, the scout kept moving his pony slowly ahead.

"A movement, that's all," returned Garth. "Game of some kind?"

"No, I don't think so. No, I think someone is watching us, maybe following, waiting to jump us at the right place. What I saw was red, and I know of no red animals, eh?"

"That's quite a distance up there," Garth said, tilting his hat against the sunlight.

"Creo que sí," agreed Dominguez. "Yes, I think so, but if you see a flash, this means we hit the dust, get under the horses." He pointed ahead with his chin. "You see that clump of trees off to the left? If we can reach those shadows, we slide off, take the ponies into the trees, and you get up to the top of that hill, work back through the rocks. Your old friend will sneak through the middle. Yes, and we find out what this is all about."

Garth found himself foolishly whispering. "Yes suh, understood." Once in the trees, he fell into a crouch, slowly working his way up through the brush until he reached the trees about ten minutes later. He was edging his way around the rocks that Dominguez had pointed out when he suddenly came upon a small grassy depression entirely hidden from the trail below. Four horses, their ears pricked, stood there staring at him, two with saddles, and the other two fully packed. Just as he was preparing to investigate, he heard a voice from the rocks somewhere behind him. The words were meaningful, very sharp, and very clear.

"Drop the rifle, mister, or I'll blow a hole in your back big enough to drive a wagon through!" At the same instant that he was lowering his rifle, he heard a woman's shrill scream from somewhere below him. But, by then, the frightful chunk of ice stuck in his throat, mercifully, was melting away. He knew the voice behind him, had heard it many times, both day and night, and for two years now, in his dreams. The woman at his back cried out, "Mama, are you all right? Do you hear me?"

Garth, a tremendous swell in his heart, swallowed once, and then said hoarsely, "Oh, law, woman, you wouldn't shoot a poor man in the back, would you? Not one who's pursued you all across this godforsaken land?"

There was dead silence behind him. But he heard a tremolo voice quavering up from below, saying, "Yes, I'm all right."

Then, from behind again: "Garth . . . ? Garth? Garth, you sonofabitch, is that really you? It can't be . . ."

Lowering his hands, he slowly turned and looked toward the rocks. "Yes, ma'am," he said, grinning broadly and spreading his arms wide, "it's me. It's not some damn bogeyman you're looking at. Come on down here, you little bugaboo."

Leaping like a mountain goat through the tumble of rocks, Bird Rutledge flew into his welcoming arms, wailing and crying, and in between her great sobs, she was moaning repeatedly, "Oh, God . . . oh, God, dear God." Finally, she broke away, tears streaming down her cheeks. "I thought you were dead . . . out of my life . . . forever. Oh, dear God."

Garth tenderly stroked her head as she fell back against him again, trembling uncontrollably. "Seems like everyone in this infernal country thinks I'm dead," he said, "like I'm some kind of a spirit returning from the great beyond, one of the Owl Maker's boys, something crazy like that."

From below, Dominguez's voice rang out up through the draw. "Ho, up there, come down and help me. Your mama has fainted away. Bring your water."

Bird Rutledge whirled around. "That's John Dominguez . . . that's John down there!" she said, giving Garth a surprised look. She cried back, "Yes, just a moment, I'm coming." Wiping at her eyes, she slowly backed away, still half sobbing. "Oh, let me look at you, just for a minute, you crazy Crow Feather, let me see you."

Garth reached up and flipped the eagle feather. "This is eagle, dammit, and hard-earned, little woman, I'll have you know." Bird, taking a waterbag from the pommel of one of the saddles, started away, but she stopped abruptly and pointed to the trees. "Over there, go over there. There's a surprise under that big fir. He belongs to you." She jumped away, shouting, "Oh, God, oh, God, how merciful!"

When Garth, carrying his year-old son, picked his way down to the others, he saw Meena propped up against a tree trunk, waving a hand in front of her face, her breast heaving under her red jacket. She was speechless, sighing and moaning. Dominguez glanced up at Garth and said, "When I told her you were up there, she just went down, swoosh, swoosh."

"Yessuh, my usual intrepid self, up there with a gun in my back." Garth grinned happily. "And, look here, John, look what I found up in the trees, this little bug juice. Yessuh, this is my son." He was rocking the baby up against his shoulder, packboard and all. "Ty," he said, addressing the baby, "this is John Dominguez, an old friend of mine, and he tells the wildest stories you've ever heard."

Bird was helping her mother to her feet, and Meena, still trying to catch her breath, reached out to touch Garth. "Yes . . . yes, it is true, like Dominguez says, it is really you." Lowering her head shamefully, she said, "Never have I done this before, fainted like this. To do such a thing, ah, me, I don't know, but to know a man like you is still alive, again. Oh, you dear soul."

"I was never dead, Mama," Garth said. With his free hand, he tilted back his hat, exposing the deep scar at his hairline. "I'd say the scamp came pretty close, though, wouldn't you?"

Meena sadly shook her head, saying, "*Ma-ya,* what they did to you!"

Bird, suddenly inflamed, traced Garth's scar with a finger. She cursed, "That bastard, Cut Nose, this is what he did, and he went around the village for a week wearing your old hat, bragging about how he couped a buffalo soldier. The stupid ass didn't even know the difference between a bluecoat and a scout!"

Garth tried to soothe her, her sudden outburst, so reminiscent of days gone by, his fiery, beautiful lost love reclaimed. "It's all over and done with, bugaboo, and the war is over, too." he said. "We're survivors, a little wear and tear, but we're survivors."

"I'll never forget that horrible day the rest of my life," she said bitterly. "It ended every dream I had. It scarred me, too, not up here," she said, touching her head, "but, in here, my very heart and soul."

Dominguez put an arm around Bird and said consolingly, "Ah, but you see, he has returned, and now everything will be good again, maybe better than before, eh, this fine son you have. Come, I think we should go down below, get our horses from up the trail, go someplace, camp, smoke, and talk. Yes, time to celebrate a little."

An uneasy silence momentarily fell over Bird and Meena, each one glancing at the other, until Garth finally spoke. "I agree. This is one helluva place to be riding horses, up on this hillside."

Meena said, "We don't like it down there . . ."

And Bird said evasively, "Mama and I thought you were someone else. We have to stay off the trail. It's not safe." Pausing, she added, "We have a problem, and I fear it's a big one."

"She killed a man," Meena said suddenly. "We must hide at Goodhart's or go live with the Crow for a while. No one will dare come where Man Called Tree lives."

Garth stopped short. "She what?"

"Killed a man," Bird replied flatly. She took the baby from the crook of his arm and placed the packboard on her shoulders. Wiping her eyes, she went on. "Yes, three nights ago back at our place, I shot this man, so we packed and got out. We didn't have any choice, and would have had absolutely no chance if we stayed. They would have hanged me. That's why we're up here, side-hilling. It's safer. They know who we are. Someone's bound to follow, come along looking for us."

"Oh, law." Garth sighed. "Not a posse!"

Bird shook her head. "I doubt it. The nearest law over there is in Bannack, miles away. No, probably soldiers from the fort."

"You killed a trooper?"

"No, not a trooper, A filthy lout who worked for them off and on, a contractor. He hauled freight, wagons, that kind of work. Jubal McComber."

Dominguez, eyes widening, said to his astonished friend, "McComber, *amigo,* remember? Ho, ho, he's the one who tells me where he saw Bird and her mother, up with those Brule . . ."

"The man who tried to buy you from some chief?" Garth asked Bird. "That fellow?"

"Yes, the same," she said, her brow arching. "You know about it . . . ? Plenty Hawk?" And her heart suddenly felt like molten lead.

"We heard."

John Dominguez clucked his tongue several times. "Ah, but this one is a no-account, *'mano,* a bad one. Why, I ask, should the troopers bother? He works both sides of the fence. Yes, he trades guns to the hostiles. I know this man. Why, he's the one that fellow you came looking for was with, the one called Sturges, eh? I remember, you had this terrible itch to kill the fellow."

Garth frowned at Dominguez, more of a hopeless frown. He said, "You never mentioned Sturges was with this McComber. Dammit, John . . ."

"It doesn't matter," Bird said. "Sturges is dead.

That's what started this whole mess. That fat pig of a McComber was going to blame Mama and me, tell the people at the fort we had a hand in it, oh, all sort of foul things. God, how was that going to look? We had everything except Sturges' clothes. Well, I came home and there was McComber, pushing Mama around, threatening her. We had words, so I shot the bastard. There was another man with him, outside, but he made tracks on his horse."

"Henry Sturges, dead?" Garth asked, absorbing yet another shock. He gave Bird an incredulous stare. "Good Lord, how? When?"

Bird's smile was grim, ironically grim. "The same way your old troop got it in the war. He was ambushed, ambushed over on the Powder, he and a couple of his drivers. Mama and I stumbled on the wagons, oh, maybe a month later. It was sheer luck. We found a few things hidden away the Indians missed, some money, pouches of gold, and that watch. We had it all, but it was that damn watch that caused the roof to cave in."

"Ah, yes, I remember," Dominguez said, "the watch you gave to Goodhart. Yes, a fine watch, one to be greatly admired. He showed it to us, a very proud man."

"Well, McComber saw it, too," said Bird with a sigh. "John was so delighted when I gave it to him, the only watch he's ever owned. He showed it to McComber the last time he went through, didn't have the faintest idea of the connection, what conclusions McComber would make. That bastard knew we had money, but we found it and that gold. We didn't kill those men to get it. We found it."

"Law, law," moaned Garth, nervously stroking his moustache. "Yessuh, the weevils are in the cotton for sure on this one." With widened eyes, he glanced over at Dominguez. "Miss Bird is right. This is one big mess."

Dominguez tapped the side of his head, saying, "We must think on it, eh? You go get their horses. I'll go fetch our outfit, and we'll find a place up that creek to bed down out of sight, talk there. If someone is following, this is best, find a good place away from the trail, make some coffee, talk over some plans how to get out of here."

Later, after they had strung out the horses, Dominguez took the lead, making directly for the creek bottom that he and Garth had crossed earlier. He turned up and followed the stream for a mile until he found good shelter under the pine and aspen. There, the men stretched tarps between the trees and arranged all of their bedrolls underneath, and when it was dark, they struck a fire, ate supper, and Garth helped Bird with the feeding of little Ty.

Over their coffee, Garth and Dominguez took turns relating the events of their journey up through the Big Horns, each humorous embellishment of certain incidents bringing smiles, and sometimes even laughter from the two worried women. But the story of Lost Woman caused Meena to moan in despair, and she recalled how many Indians, stricken by the pox, had died in the upper plains, stories that she had heard from the old people when she was just a little girl.

After Dominguez, Meena, and the baby were in their bedrolls, Garth and Bird continued to talk quietly beside the fire. Garth finally remembered Goodhart's story about Bird's wolf, his late summer return with a mate. After he had retold the story, Bird was silent for a long time. Believing he may have struck a discordant note unknowingly, he finally said, "John told me he thought you would be happy to know this. He made a point of it, saying to be sure and let you know about your wolf when we caught up with you."

Staring into the fire, and leaning against his shoulder, she answered quietly, "Yes, I am happy. I fell in love with that little fellow the very first time I saw him. It's hard to talk about. I don't think anyone can understand what went on between us."

"The Crow boy we met on the trail said your wolf was a spirit of some kind, that he could see through a mountain. By jingo, that's some crazy notion. Do you believe it?"

"Oh, yes, I do now," she answered. "After all this time, I think I know what my wolf was trying to tell me. He knew you were alive. He knew you were on the trail. The red in me believes this. Don't you understand, somehow, he was sharing your spirit. In some way, don't ask me how, he seemed to know."

Garth momentarily reflected, remembering the fear he had instilled in Long Mane back in the hunting village of Red Leaf, the young man who had refused to come out of his lodge to meet the shadow of the gray warrior, Crow Feather. Garth finally said, "Your brother-in-law, the one called Long Mane, was in Red Leaf's village ..."

"Long Mane!" Bird whispered. "You saw him? Were the others there ... ? Plenty Hawk, his wife ... ? The children?"

Garth shook his head. "No, not his family, only Long Mane's wife, some girl from another tribe. She visited with us. The boy, he wouldn't meet with us, wouldn't tell us a damn thing. He had this same notion about wolves, thought I was some kind of a ghost or wolf spirit returned from the dead. I was wearing this eagle feather instead of my old crow feather. Symbolic, Dominguez said. Even the young woman kept her distance, thought I was some kind of a spook."

"You were killed," Bird said. "My people believed this. What else could she think?"

Garth paused, reflecting on her words, "my people." "They treated you well, these people, this family? Knowing your temperament, and from the stories John was always telling me about captives, I feared the worst. By jingo, I labored over it every damn mile, couldn't get it out of my mind. Yes, and after seeing Lost Woman ..."

Bird took his hand and kissed the little red scar across his palm, one of his Cheyenne mementos as he now called it, another wilderness scar. Now, it had come to the Brule, her foster family, Plenty Hawk and Feather Tail, the children. She remembered what Feather had once said, "The past is over," and now she wanted to forget it. What could she say? "I labored, too," she finally said. "I thought you were dead, out of my life forever. I learned something about hate, how destructive it can be. Oh, in time, things changed. Yes, of course, they treated us well, better than most, I suppose. They have their ways. They took us in as part of the family. We learned to share. What else? It would have been miserable otherwise. Do you understand?"

Garth nodded. "I think so. This fellow, Plenty Hawk ..."

"Kind, understanding," Bird immediately replied. "He was going to take us to the nearest fort in the spring that year, give us horses, let us go. He knew how I felt. He had nothing to do with the incident at Antelope Creek. In fact, felt bad about it." She hesitated, and gave him a wan smile. "Then, I found myself pregnant. It shattered my hopes, my dreams, changed my perspective. Everyone thought it was Plenty Hawk's child, everyone except Mother. I think she suspected. And I should have known. When Ty was born, we left ... left in a hurry. Now, do you understand?"

"Law, law," muttered Garth.

She sighed. "Well, it's passed. I had to kill two men along the way, too, and now I'd just as soon forget the whole crazy thing. It's like a bad dream! It's over."

"I'm sorry."

"You don't have to be," Bird said, kissing him. "Mama always said things turn out for the best. Don't you remember?"

"Long ago."

"But don't you remember?"

"I remember." He smiled. "And you always knew what was best."

"Yes, I still do. This much, I haven't forgotten." She stood, peered cautiously at the nearby shelter, pressed a finger to her lips, and then whispered, "You're reading my mind, again, aren't you?"

"Our minds were always one."

"I want you," she said in a hushed voice. "I want you to bathe me, make love to me. I'll get some things, a couple of blankets, and we'll find a place down in the trees by the creek."

Garth sputtered, "Bathe? Look, bugaboo, that water's cold at night."

"Yes, but I'm not."

T. B. Garth nodded knowingly. Ah, sweet wilderness and two peas in a pod, he felt like he was home again.

The next morning, they were back on the trail, riding east toward John Goodhart's post. From there, Dominguez agreed with Garth that it was probably better to cross over to the Powder River and follow it up to old Fort Reno, a route very similar to the one Bird and Meena had taken when they fled from the Brule Sioux. The most immediate concern, however, was the present—the women were still horrified at the thought of getting caught on the Bozeman Trail and being returned to the Gallatin for killing a white man. John Dominguez tried to allay their fear, his belief being that if anyone was following, they would have had ample time by now to apprehend the women, troopers in particular, for they most often rode at a brisk trot when they were on such pressing business. Nevertheless, he elected to ride a half mile to the rear on this morning to cover the backside. He reasoned that if someone did appear, he would have time to gallop up and guide the women into hiding. That pacified Bird and her mother.

None of the group gave the slightest consideration about being approached from the east, where the closest fort was hundreds of miles away.

But it suddenly happened, and only a short distance from the creek crossing. They were rounding a small bend in the trail when Garth abruptly reined up. Directly ahead, only a stone's throw, were riders, ten of them, and they were all dressed in dark blue, two abreast, coming right into their position. Garth whirled about, frantically looking back for Dominguez. Meena, upon sighting the troopers, emitted a small shriek of alarm, and Garth turned back, trying to steady his horse. "Just sit easy, dammit, and don't panic," he quietly commanded. "Act natural, and we'll see what they're up to, where they're going. Might just be some of the boys riding home with nothing more on their minds than the commissary."

Bird, ever observant, quickly shot down this assumption, saying, "They have no packs, great scout. All they're carrying is bedrolls and rations. It's a patrol, heading back to Fort Ellis, all right. Somehow, they got around us, so you better start thinking fast or we're all going back with them."

Garth found himself reaching for elusive straws in the wind. He glanced back again over his shoulder, searching the back trail for his companion. Then, he sighed deeply, for Dominguez, his savior, had finally come into view. "No ideas, my lady, not yet," he said, "but the great storyteller is coming up the trail, and he sure as hell will have an idea or two. He always does."

Garth, his mind in a muddle, rode out a few yards to meet the first trooper, a young lieutenant, moustached, wearing a rakish hat, sabre, and a sidearm. The officer, holding his gloved hand high, called out to Garth, "Good morning, sir, where are you coming from?"

Motioning with a nod of his head, Garth replied innocently, "Back there, up the creek aways. Set up camp there last night, took a bit of a rest."

The young officer nodded, shifting his eyes warily back and forth. "We must have ridden by you late yesterday, then missed you on the trail." He leaned toward Garth's horse and extended his hand. "Lieutenant Martin Harris, here, H Company, Fort Ellis."

Garth moved close and gave his hand a firm shake. "Ty Garth, suh, at your service." John Dominguez arrived at this moment and eased his horse to the side of them. He had a wide, unconcerned grin on his wrinkled face, and his eyes were narrowed into two black slits. Garth had seen that look many times on the trail—his old friend was thinking. "Juan José Domínguez," he heartily spoke out. "Sometimes, my friends call me Domino." Looking beyond the officer, he asked, "How is the trail down that way. No hostiles, I hope."

"We only rode five miles that direction," was the crisp reply. "Bedded down for the night." he fixed his eyes on Bird Rutledge, then asked pointedly, "Who is the woman with the child?"

"Why, damned my manners!" Garth exclaimed. "I plumb forgot these ladies. This one is my wife, Mrs. Garth, and that one over there is Mrs. Dominguez." He then glanced at the Spaniard, who was sitting impassively, hands draped over his pommel. "Yes suh, that's Domino's wife."

"Well, where are you coming from?" the trooper asked again, but this time rather curtly.

"Like I told you, suh, from our camp. We're going on down to the Missouri."

Lieutenant Harris, obviously annoyed, said, "No, no, no, before this camp, where was your point of origin?"

Garth glanced aside at Dominguez for help, and the Spaniard quickly responded by pointing to the wilderness to the north. "We came from back up there, my woman's country, Blackfeet. We came down the Musselshell, yes, hunting for the big bull elk." He slowly brought his hands up to his head and forked them out like antlers. "As you can see, our luck was not so good, eh? No big horns this time. Maybe next time, we do better."

During this bit of conversation, Garth finally noticed the smiling face of a sergeant sitting a big black horse directly behind Harris. The trooper slyly winked at Garth, and then it suddenly struck home. Lord, Lord, it was Jim Cutter! Young Jim Cutter, the Yankee recruit from Fort Kearny, the same trooper who had tended him on the trail after he had been felled by the Brule war club! He heard Lieutenant Harris saying, "We're looking for an Indian woman, one Bird Rutledge by name, a breed." He nodded toward Bird. "She certainly fits the description. Your wife, you say? Does she speak English?"

Turning back, Garth said, "Is that so, a breed, you say? This is sure a coincidence, isn't it? A lot of these women look alike, you know, and as for speaking English, well, my wife never has been able to get the hang of it. Lord knows I've tried. Just as well she can't. Talk your leg off, sometimes. But, what's this woman done that brings you all the way out here, this Bird person?"

"Killed a wagoneer," Harris said. "Shot him several nights ago over by the fort. We thought she may have ridden this way." He stared keenly back at Bird again. So did Garth, and his eyes rolled. She had transferred the baby to Meena and her rifle was unsheathed and resting across the front of her saddle! Lieutenant Harris spoke again to Garth, saying with a note of regret, "I realize this may inconvenience you people, but we've followed some confusing tracks up and down this trail. I think it would be wise if we all went back to the fort to sort out this thing."

At this point, Jim Cutter's voice interrupted the exchange. "Begging your pardon, Lieutenant, sir, but I don't think this would be too wise, at all. Fact is, sir, it might prove downright embarrassing."

Lieutenant Harris jerked his head back. "Explain, Sergeant, and be brief about it."

And then T. B. Garth intervened. Peering around the young officer's shoulder, he gave a little salute to Jim Cutter, and said, "Well, how are you, Jim? By jingo, it's been a long time, two years, I'll allow. Nice to see you again."

"I'm doing fine, sir." Cutter grinned back. "Good to see you back in the saddle."

Harris, with a flick of his hand, motioned Jim Cutter forward. "Sergeant, do you know this man?"

"Why, yes, sir, I sure do, way back from when I was a greenhorn. I know all of these people, Domino over there, the captain ... their wives."

"Captain?"

"Yessir," Cutter answered. "Captain Garth."

Garth sighed forlornly. "Confederacy."

"We were all together down at Laramie and Kearny, sir," Cutter went on. "These men were our scouts down at Kearny, and darned good ones, too. Begging your pardon, sir, but if some of the officers had listened a little more to old Domino and the captain, there'd be a few more of 'em around talking about it, that ruckus up Peno Creek."

Garth gave Harris a weak smile. "I think maybe Jim's exaggerating a bit, there, sir."

"No, sir," Cutter replied emphatically, "not at all. I sure don't forget things like that. They told 'em not to go out there that day. They knew exactly how many hostiles were in those hills, right where they were, too. And look what the captain has to show for it, right there under his hat. If you think I don't know him, look under his hat."

"I think Jim means this," Garth said, tilting his gray hat back with a forefinger. The ugly scar glared under the bright, morning sun. "One of the two most unfortunate events in my life."

"I see," Lieutenant Harris said, nodding. "And what was the other unfortunate event, may I inquire?"

Garth grinned. "Losing the big one against the Yankees."

"That . . . that was before my time," the young officer returned with a disapproving stare. Motioning Cutter back, he said, "That will be all, Sergeant."

"Good to see you, Jim," Garth called. "If we ever get over Fort Ellis way, I'll be sure to look you up. Never know where General Crook is going to send me next. I just follow the trouble, you know."

"All right, men, let's move out," Lieutenant Harris shouted. "Good day to you, Mr. Garth, Mr. Dominguez, ladies, and my apologies. I wish you a safe journey. Sorry, we can't tarry longer, but we have some ground to cover." He touched his hat as Dominguez and Garth parted to let the troop file by.

As Jim Cutter passed, he called to Garth, "Sure was some horse race she rode that day, wasn't it? Hot damn!"

For a while, the little group sat silently on their horses and watched the troopers disappear around the bend. Then, Garth, with a mighty sigh, turned and chuckled at John Dominguez, who responded by fanning out his hands across his forehead like the antlers of the great bull elk. "Yes." Garth smiled. "And thank the Lord for Jim Cutter, too."

When Garth looked over at the two women, Meena was still holding the baby, but her closed eyes turned skyward to the Great Spirit, her lips moving in silent prayer. Bird Rutledge, fighting back tears, managed to purse her lips in a kiss to each of the men. "I love you both," she said chokingly, "you gallant sonsofbitches."

"All right," Garth cried out, imitating the recently departed Lieutenant Harris, "let's move out. We have some ground to cover. On to Laramie!"

John Dominguez waved his weathered black hat in the air, threw back his head, and howled like a wolf calling the pack together. The echo reverberated eerily back and forth penetrating the stillness of the Yellowstone bottom, and reached up to the highest spires of the timbered hills. And from somewhere in this great expanse of majestic wilderness, high in a mountain meadow, the echo became reality, hauntingly melodious, and it rode the warm currents of the morning winds back to them.

Epilogue

After brief stops at John Goodhart's and the Cheyenne village of Morning Star, T. B. Garth and party arrived back in Fort Laramie in mid-October. Garth, Bird, and Ty continued on south, arriving at Garth House, south of Jackson, Mississippi, late November, 1868. In the fall of 1869, Bird Rutledge Garth gave birth to a son, John Dominguez Garth.

The Spaniard, John Dominguez, was employed by the U. S. Army, serving as an interpreter. He worked between the posts of Fort Laramie and Fort Caspar. He and Meena Rutledge shared a two-room cabin overlooking the Laramie River.

Elbert Craig, after an unsuccessful search for Bird Rutledge, joined the army at Fort Buford in 1867. He was later transferred to the quartermaster's office at Fort Ellis, Montana Territory, arriving there three weeks after the murder of Jubal McComber.

The widow, Sarah Jennings, was returned to Fort Laramie in the winter of 1868. She later went to Fort Leavenworth, Kansas, to live with a sister and brother-in-law.

Bear Paw, the young Cheyenne saved by T. B. Garth, distinguished himself in battle at the Little Big Horn River in 1876. He was twenty-one years old.

The Vision of
Benjamin One Feather

His father was Man Called Tree, yellow-haired chief of the Absaroke Crow in their quest to survive in the Wind River Range of the Montana Territory. Now it was Benjamin One Feather's time to take up the struggle . . . to seek the meaning of the vision come to him with manhood . . . and to find the path of his people's salvation in the shifting tides of battle from Little Big Horn and the Rosebud to the grim vengeance sweeping north on U.S. Cavalry hooves.

Here is the story of a brave people's fight against a foe who defied defeat. Here is the story of a noble youth coming of age amid the mighty clash of two civilizations—to become all that a great hero can mean and be.

White Moon Tree

White Moon Tree was the proud son of a proud father, Ben Tree. But he was far different than the brother he loved, Benjamin One Feather. He was not a seeker in the world of the Great Spirit; he was a rancher in the unfenced Montana cattle country. Even more, he was a gambler, ready to stake all on the draw of a card or a gun. And when a band of savage killers ravaged the range, and a beautiful orphaned girl asked that her father's murder be avenged, White Moon Tree took on odds few men would dare in a game of guts and glory that only a man made in the mold of heroes could win.

The Shooter

They called him "the ultimate shooter." His gun fit in his hand as naturally as a bullet in a firing chamber, his courage was hair-trigger, his draw lightning fast, his aim true as death. He went by many names, but his real name was Hardy Gibbs, grandson to Amos Gibbs, the greatest gunsmith of them all. His childhood ended when his parents were slain by Quantrill's Raiders. His young manhood was shattered by an even more savage act that drove him over the line between the law and lawlessness—and sent him on a trail of violence through the West at its wildest for vengeance at its fullest. He is the hero of an epic novel by a riveting storyteller who brings the American past alive in all its true-grit reality and undying glory.

The Seekers

Kidnapped by Indians when she was little more than a girl, Katherine Coltrane became the wife of a warrior. Rescued by bluecoats years later, she was forced to leave her infant daughter behind. She became a woman alone in a violent world of men. Surviving by her iron will and silken flesh, she carved out a vast cattle kingdom and defended it in range wars that swept the Wyoming territory like wildfire. She found men who matched her strength and passion—frontiersmen, soldiers, outlaws, men who loved her or feared her, but could never tame her pride and independence. Yet Kate never stopped the relentless search for her lost child—in an epic quest that had to bridge the gap between Indians and whites on a frontier split by savage struggle.

Tolliver

Army doctor James Tolliver cared not for the color of a man's skin. He only wanted to heal the wounded. He knew when he "borrowed" a general's horse to save a dying Lakota Sioux brave that the army would likely brand him a traitor. But he didn't reckon that his grateful patient would kill a guard to spring him from prison. And he never imagined there would be a huge price on his head, with every officer, bounty hunter, and two-bit drifter on the unforgiving frontier gunning for him—a fugitive, wanted for treason and murder.

Thus begins an adventure of epic scope—an unforgettable saga of a soldier who breaks rank to become "Big Black Bear"—a full-blooded member of the fearless Lakota tribe.